COMPLICITY

COMPLICITY

Iain Banks

LONDON NEW YORK SYDNEY TORONTO

A *Little, Brown* Book

This edition published 1993
by BCA by arrangement
with Little, Brown Publishers.

CN 6072

Typeset by Hewer Text Composition Services, Edinburgh
Printed and bound by Clays Ltd, St. Ives plc

CONTENTS

For Ellis Sharp

CHAPTER

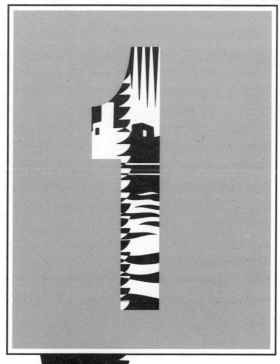

INDEPENDENT DETERRENT

Y ou hear the car after an hour and a half. During that time you've been here in the darkness, sitting on the small telephone seat near the front door, waiting. You only moved once, after half an hour, when you went back through to the kitchen to check on the maid. She was still there, eyes white in the half-darkness. There was a strange, sharp smell in the air and you thought of cats, though you know he doesn't have cats. Then you realised the maid had pissed herself. You felt a moment of disgust, and then a little guilt.

She whimpered behind the black masking-tape when you approached. You tested the tape securing her to the little kitchen chair, and the rope holding it against the still-warm Aga. The tape looked just as you'd left it; either she hadn't been struggling or she had but it had had no effect. The rope was good and taut. You glanced at the shaded windows, then shone your torch at her hands, taped to the rear legs of the chair. Her fingers looked all right; it was a little difficult to tell because of her dark olive Filipino skin, but you didn't think you'd cut off her circulation. You looked at her feet, tiny in the low-heeled black slippers; they appeared healthy too. A drop of urine fell and joined a pool on the tiled floor beneath the chair.

She was quivering with fear when you looked into her face. You knew you looked terrifying in the dark balaclava, but there was nothing you could do about that. You patted her shoulder as reassuringly as you could. Then you went back to the telephone seat by the front door. There were three phone calls; you listened to the answer-machine intercept them.

'You know what to do,' his scratchily recorded voice said to each caller. His voice is quick, clipped and vaguely upper-class. 'Do it after the beep.'

'Tobias, old chap. How the devil are you? Geoff. Wondering how you're fixed next Saturday. Fancy a foursome out at sunny Sunningdale? Give me a tinkle. Bye.'

(beep)

'Ah . . . yes, ahh, Sir Toby. Mark Bain again. Ah, I rang earlier, and the last couple of days. Umm . . . well, I'd still very much like to interview you, as I've said, Sir Toby, but, well, I know you don't usually give interviews, but I do assure you I've no axe to grind, and I do very much appreciate, as a fellow professional, what you've achieved, and would genuinely like to find out more about your views. Anyway. Clearly it is up to you, of course, and I do respect that. I'll . . . ah, I'll try your office in the morning. Thank you. Thank you very much. Good evening.'

(beep)

'You abrupt old bastard, Tobes. Give me a ring about that diary story; I'm still not happy. And get that bloody car phone repaired.'

You smiled at that one. That rough, colonial voice, its commanding tone contrasting with the Harrovian chumminess of the first message and the whining, working-class Midland entreaties of the middle one. The proprietor. Now there was a man you'd like to meet. You glanced up into the darkness towards the wall at the foot of the stairs, where there are various framed photographs.

4

There is one of Sir Toby Bissett with Mrs Thatcher, both smiling. You smiled, too.

Then you just sat there, breathing carefully, thinking, keeping calm. You took the gun out once, reaching round under your thin canvas jacket to the small of your back and easing it from between shirt and jeans. The Browning felt warm through your thin leather gloves. You snicked the magazine out and back in again a couple of times and ran your thumb over the safety catch, making sure it was on. You put the gun back again.

Then you reached down, pulled up the right leg of your jeans and slipped the Marttini out of its lightly oiled sheath. The knife's slim blade refused to glint, until you tipped it just so and it reflected the little, flashing red light on the answer-machine. There was a small greasy smudge on the steel blade. You blew on it and rubbed it with one gloved finger, then inspected it again. Satisfied, you slid the knife back into its leather sheath and rolled the denim back down. And waited until the Jaguar drew up outside, engine idling in the quiet square, bringing you back to the present.

You stand up and look through the spyhole in the broad wooden door. You see the dark square outside, distorted by the lens. You can see the steps down to the pavement, the railings on either side of the steps, the parked cars sitting at the kerb and the dark masses of the trees in the centre of the square. The Jag is right outside, beyond the cars at the kerb. Street lights reflect orange on the car's door as it swings open. A man and a woman get out.

He's not alone. You watch the woman straighten the skirt of her suit as the man says something to the driver and then closes the Jaguar's door.

'Shit,' you whisper. Your heart is pounding.

The man and the woman walk towards the steps. The man is holding a briefcase. It's him: Sir Toby Bissett, the man with the quick, clipped voice on the answer-machine. As he and the woman reach the pavement and make for the steps, he takes the woman's right elbow in his hand, shepherding her towards the door you're looking through.

'Shit!' you whisper again, and glance back down the side of the stairs towards the hall and the kitchen, where the maid is and where the window through which you entered is still half open. You hear their footsteps on the pavement. The skin on your forehead prickles beneath the balaclava. He lets go of the woman's elbow, switches the briefcase to his other hand and reaches into a trouser pocket. They are halfway up the steps. You start to panic, and stare at the heavy chain hanging at the side of the door by the bulky Chubb. Then you hear the sound of his key in the lock, startlingly close, and hear him say something, and hear the woman's nervous laugh and you know that it's too late and you become calm, standing away from the door until your back is against the coats on the coat-stand, and you slide your hand into the pocket of the canvas jacket and it closes round the thick weight of the shot-filled leather cosh.

The door opens, towards you. You hear the Jag's engine purring away. The hall light comes on. He says, 'Here we are.'

Then the door closes and they are there in front of you and in that instant you see him turned slightly away, putting his briefcase down on the table beside the answer-machine. The girl – blonde, tan, mid-twenties, holding a slim briefcase – glances at you. She does a double-take. You are smiling behind the mask, putting one finger up to your lips. She hesitates. You hear the answer-machine spin back, squeaking. As the girl starts to open her mouth, you step forward, behind him.

You swing the cosh and hit him very hard across the back of the head, a hand's width above his jacket collar. He collapses instantly, falling against the wall and down over the table, dislodging the answer-machine as you turn to the girl.

She opens her mouth, watching the man crumple to the carpet. She looks at you and you think she's going to scream and you tense, ready to punch her. Then she drops the slim briefcase and holds her shaking hands out in front of her, glancing down once at the man lying still on the floor. Her jaw is trembling.

'Look,' she says, 'just don't do anything to me.' Her voice is steadier than her hands or her jaw. She glances down at the man on the carpet. 'I don't know who – ' she gulps, eyelids fluttering nervously. You watch her trying to speak through a dry mouth. '– who you are, but I don't want anything . . . Just don't do anything to me. I've got money; you can have it. But this isn't anything to do with me, right? Just don't do anything to me. Okay? Please.'

She has a refined voice, a Sloane voice, a Roedean voice. You half-despise her attitude, half-admire it. You glance down at the man; he looks very still. The answer-machine lying on the carpet clicks to a stop at the end of the tape. You look back to her and nod slowly. You move your head to indicate the kitchen. She looks that way, hesitating. You point towards the kitchen with the cosh.

'Okay,' she says. 'Okay.' She walks backwards down the hall, hands still in front of her. She backs into the kitchen door, swinging it fully open. You follow her through and turn on the light. She keeps walking backwards and you hold up one hand to make her stop. She sees the maid in the chair tied to the stove. You motion her to another of the red kitchen chairs. She glances at the wide-eyed maid again and then seems to come to a decision, and sits.

You move away from her towards the working surface where the roll of black masking-tape sits. You cover her with the gun as you push the balaclava away from your mouth and pull out a length of tape with your teeth. She looks calmly, steadily at the gun, some of the colour gone from her face. You keep the gun pressed into her waist as you loop the tape round her slim, gold-braceleted wrists. You keep glancing through the doorway, down the length of the hall to the dark shape crumpled at the front door, knowing you are taking an extra, unnecessary risk. Then you put the gun away and secure her dark-stockinged ankles. She smells of *Paris*.

7

You put a ten-centimetre strip across her mouth and leave the kitchen, putting the light out and closing the door.

You go back to Sir Toby. He hasn't moved. You remove the balaclava and stuff it in a jacket pocket, lift your crash helmet from behind the coat-stand and put it on, then take him under the armpits and haul him upstairs, past the framed photographs. His heels bump on each step. Your breath sounds loud inside the helmet; he's heavier than you expected. He smells of something expensive you can't identify; a strand of his long grey hair falls to one side, onto his shoulder.

You drag him into the sitting room on the first floor, shouldering the door to the hall closed as you enter. The room is lit only by the street lights outside, and in the semi-darkness you stumble and almost fall over a coffee table; something falls and breaks.

'Shit,' you whisper, but keep pulling him towards the tall french windows looking out over a small balcony onto the square. You prop him against the wall by the side of the windows and look outside. A couple pass on the street; you give them two minutes to leave the square and wait for a couple of cars to pass, then you open the windows and step outside, into the warm Belgravia night. The square seems quiet; the city is a faint background roar in the orange darkness beyond. You look down at the marble steps leading to the front door and the tall, black spiked railings on either side of them, then you go back in, take him under the armpits again, lift him through the windows and prop him against the stone parapet of the waist-high balcony.

A last glance around: a car passes across the top of the square. You hoist him up so that he's sitting on the parapet; his head tips back and he moans. Sweat dribbles into your eyes. You feel him move weakly in your arms as you manoeuvre him into the right position, glancing down at the railings, three or four metres below. Then you tip him backwards over the edge.

He falls onto the railings, hitting with his head, hip and leg; there is a surprisingly dry cracking, crunching noise; his head twists to one side and one of the railing spikes appears through the socket of his right eye.

His body sags, arms hanging to each side of the railings, over the marble steps and the stairwell leading to the basement flat beneath; his right leg hangs over the steps. There is another faint crunching noise as the body spasms once and then goes limp. Blood spreads blackly from his mouth over the collar of his white shirt and starts to drip onto the pale marble of the steps. You back away from the parapet, glancing from side to side. Some people walk into the far end of the square, maybe forty metres away, approaching.

You turn and go back into the sitting room, locking the windows and avoiding the coffee table and the broken vase lying on the carpet. You go downstairs and walk through the kitchen, where the two women sit tied to their chairs; you leave via the same window you entered by, walking calmly through the small back garden into the mews where the motorbike is parked.

You hear the first faint, distant screams just as you take the bike's key from your pocket. You feel suddenly elated.

You're glad you didn't have to hurt the women.

*

It's a clear cold October day, fresh and bright with a few puffy little clouds scudding above the mountains on the chilly breeze. I look through the binoculars towards the shallow slant of Helensburgh's grid-pattern streets, then move the view up to the slopes and woods behind, then track left, across the hills on the far side of the loch and the mountains beyond. Further round still, towards the head of the loch, I can make out the gantries, jetties and buildings of the naval base. There are some distant shouts and the noise of hooters over the buzz of boat and helicopter engines; I look down to the little spit of shingle straight across from me, where a few hundred demonstrators and locals are gathered, stamping their feet and waving banners. A chopper clatters overhead. I look out into the firth, where another three helicopters are circling above the black mass of the submarine. The tug, escorting police launches and circling inflatables move slowly into the mass of CND boats. A Jet Ski cuts across the view on a wall of spray.

I put the glasses down and let them hang from my neck while I light another Silk Cut.

I'm standing on the roof of an empty freight container on a bit of waste ground near the shore in a village called Roseneath, looking out over the Gare Loch, watching the Vanguard arrive. I lift the binoculars again and look out at the submarine. It fills the view now, black and almost featureless, though I can just make out the different textures of the hull's sloped and upper surfaces.

The protesters' inflatables buzz round the perimeter of the sub's satellite system of escorting boats, trying to find a way through; the MOD inflatables are larger than the CND boats and they have bigger engines; the servicemen wear black berets and dark overalls while the CND people wear bright jackets and wave big yellow flags. The huge submarine in the centre moves forward in their midst, ploughing sedately towards the narrows. The RN tug is leading the submarine in, though not towing it. A grey fisheries patrol boat follows the flotilla. The big helicopters bark overhead.

'Hi you; give us a hand up, ya bastart.'

I look over to the edge of the container and see the head and arms of Iain Garnet. He waves.

'Following our lead as usual, eh, Iain?' I ask him, hauling him up from the top of the same oil-drum I'd used.

'Fuck off, Colley,' Garnet says amiably, bending to dust off the knees of his trousers. Iain works for our Glaswegian competitor, the *Dispatch*. He's late thirties, getting heavy round the waist and thin on top. He's wearing what looks like a late-'seventies skiing jacket over his crumpled grey suit. He nods at the cigarette in my mouth. 'Can I take a fag?'

I offer him one. His face wrinkles with disdain when he sees the packet but he takes one anyway. 'Jeez, Cameron, really; Silk Cut?

The cigarette for people who like to think they're giving up? I had you down as one of the last of the serious lung abusers. What happened to the Marlboros?'

'They're for cowboys like you,' I tell him, lighting his cigarette. 'What happened to *your* fags?'

'Left them in the car,' he says. We both turn and stand there, looking out across the blue-glittering waves at the small armada surrounding the giant submarine. The Vanguard is even bigger than I'd expected; huge, fat and black, like the biggest, blackest slug in all the world, with a few thin fins stuck here and there as an afterthought. It looks too big to fit through the narrows in front of us.

'Some fuckin beast, eh?' Iain says.

'Half a billion quid's worth, sixteen thousand tonnes – '

'Aye, aye,' Iain says wearily. 'And long as two football pitches. You got anything *original* though but?'

I shrug. 'Not telling you; read the article.'

'Big wean.' He looks around. 'Where's your man with the Instamatic and the dodgy model-release forms?'

I nod towards a small speedboat waiting near the entrance to the narrows. 'Getting a fish-eye view. What about yours?'

'Two,' Iain says. 'One here somewhere, the other one sharing a chopper with the Beeb.'

We both look into the sky. I count four Navy Sea Kings. Iain and I look at each other.

'Cutting it a bit fine with the helicopter, aren't they?' I ask.

He shrugs. 'Probably arguing about who tips the pilot.'

We both stare out at the sub again. The protesters' boats are constantly charging in towards the Vanguard, only to be headed off each time by the MOD boats, bulging rubber hulls bumping off each other and then bouncing over the chopping waves. Preceded by the tug, the Trident sub's bulbous nose moves smoothly towards the narrows. Ratings wearing yellow life-jackets stand at ease on the deck of the huge ship, some in front of the tall conning tower, some

11

behind. The people on the spit of land across from us are shouting and jeering. A few might be cheering.

'Give us a shot of your binocs,' Iain says.

I hand him the glasses and he squints through them as the Navy tug leading the sub moves slowly through the narrows. *Roisterer*, says its nameplate.

'How's things at the *Caley* these days, anyway?' Iain asks.

'Oh, same as usual.'

'Wow!' he says, taking his eyes away from the glasses and looking shocked. 'Steady now; sure you want to say that? We're still on the record, you know.'

'You'll be on the fucking *Record*, you hack.'

'You east-coast boys are just jealous of our computer system because ours works.'

'Oh, sure.'

We watch the long, grossly phallic shape slide into the narrows, its tall hull obscuring the crowd of people on the spit of land across from us. Little capped heads sticking out of the top of the conning tower look over and down at us. I wave. One of them waves back. I feel a strange, guilty happiness. The helicopters are noisy overhead; the swirling pattern of CND and MOD boats is compressed by the narrows; the inflatables dance and bob around each other, bumping together. It looks a bit like spastics trying to dance an Eightsome Reel, but that isn't an image I'd use in the article.

'Some demo down in London yesterday, eh?' Iain says, handing me back the binoculars.

I nod. Last night I watched television pictures of the drenched crowds as they wound slowly through the London streets, protesting against the mine closures.

'Yeah,' I say. I grind the cigarette out on the container's rusting roof. 'Six years too late to do any good, people realise Scargill was right.'

'Aye, he's still a bumptious cunt, though but.'

'Doesn't matter; he was right.'

'That's what I said; a right bumptious cunt.' Garnet grins at me.

I shake my head and nod at the fisheries boat tailing the small fleet squeezing its way through the narrows. 'What do you think; would you say that boat's bringing up the rear, or bringing up the stern? I mean, we are talking nautical here.'

Iain squints at the ship as the huge bulk of the submarine continues to slide past us. I can see him trying to think of a remark, thinking there must be something on the lines of, No, it's bringing up its dinner, or something equally strained about a nautical remark, but they're both poor-quality leads and he obviously realises this because he just shrugs and takes out his notebook and says, 'Search me, pal.'

He starts scribbling squiggles. Garnet must be one of the last of the shorthanders; few people of our generation trust in Pitman any more, preferring to rely on Olympus Pearlcorders.

'You still off-diary this weather then, Cameron?'

'Yeah, a roving news-hound without portfolio, that's me.'

'Uh-huh. Hear you've got a tame blemish on the face of the body public feeding you morsels these days, that right, Cameron?' Garnet says quietly, not looking up from his shorthand notation.

I look at him. '*What?*'

'A massive harbour breakwater,' he says, grinning toothily at me.

I stare at him.

'A facial blemish,' he says. 'A breakwater; a small insectivorous subterranean furry animal. No get it?' He shakes his head at the grossness of my ignorance. 'A *mole*,' he says patiently.

'Oh?' I say, hoping I appear suitably mystified.

He looks hurt. 'So, is it true?'

'What?'

'That you've got some mole in the security services or something equally hush-hush feeding you tasty stuff about some big story in the offing.'

I shake my head. 'No,' I tell him.

He looks disappointed.

13

'Who *told* you this, anyway?' I ask him. 'Was it Frank?'

His brows go up, his mouth makes an O and he draws in a breath. 'Sorry, Cameron; can't reveal my sources.'

I give him a pained look, then we both turn to watch the submarine.

There is a faint, distant cheer as one of the CND inflatables finally manages to break through the encircling military boats, evades the police launches and speeds in to bump into the sloping black stern of the Trident submarine, sliding briefly up onto its rump like a gnat trying to mount an elephant, before being chased away again. A TV crew capture the moment. I grin, feeling vicariously pleased for the protesters. After a while the tall grey shape of the patrol boat *Orkney* hums past, following the huge submarine.

'Orkney,' Garnet says thoughtfully. 'Orkney . . .'

I can almost hear his brain working, trying to make a connection with tomorrow's big Home News event, when the report into the Orkney child-abuse fiasco will be published. Knowing Garnet, a comment involving seamen is far from out of the question.

I keep quiet, trying not to encourage him.

He throws his cigarette butt away. Perhaps misinterpreting the gesture, somebody at the stern of the *Orkney* waves at us. Iain waves cheerily back. 'Aye, get yer cox'n, lads!' he calls, not loud enough for anyone on the boat to hear. He sounds pleased with himself.

'How amusing, Iain,' I say, stepping to the edge of the container. 'Fancy a pint later?' I jump down via the oil-drum.

'Going already, are you?' Iain says. Then, 'Na. Got to interview the Faslane Commander and get back to the office.'

'Yeah, I'm heading for the base too,' I tell him. 'See you there.' I turn and walk across the waste ground towards the car.

'Don't give us a hand down then, ya snobby Edinburgh bastart!' he calls.

I hold up one hand as I walk away. 'Okay!'

*

14

I pass the submarine a minute later as I drive out of the village and towards the head of the loch and the naval base on the far side. The submarine looks oddly, menacingly beautiful in the bright sunshine, a blackly gleaming hole in the scape of land and water. I shake my head. Twelve billion quid to take out some probably already empty silos and incinerate a few tens of millions of Russian men, women and children . . . except they aren't our enemies any more, so what was always obscene – and definitively, deliberately useless – becomes pointless; even more of a waste.

I park the car for a while on an elevated stretch of the road past Garelochhead, looking down the loch and watching the submarine approach the dock. There are a few other cars parked and groups of people watching; come to try and get some of their tax-money's worth.

I light a cigarette, winding the window down so I can blow all that unhealthy smoke away. My eyes are smarting with tiredness; I was up most of last night, working on a story and playing *Despot* on the computer. I look around to make sure nobody's watching, feel inside my North Cape jacket and take out the little bag of speed. I dip a moistened finger in the white powder in one corner and then suck the finger, smiling and sighing as the tip of my tongue goes numb. I put the bag away again and continue smoking.

. . . Unless, of course, you counted the Trident system's use in geopolitical economic terms, as part of the West's vast arms build-up; the build-up that broke the communist bank, finally devastating a Soviet system no longer able to compete (it bankrupted the US, too, turning the world's greatest creditor nation into the world's grossest debtor in two easy presidential terms, but a lot of dividends had been paid out in the meantime, and the debt was something for the next few generations to worry about, so fuck 'em).

So as communism disappeared and the threat of total, global holocaust evaporated and just left us with everything else to worry about, and as those enticing Eastern markets opened juicily up and

15

the old ethnic hatreds pressured into solution under the Comrades bubbled and frothed themselves up to full bursting pressure ... maybe this giant black slug, this potentially city-fucking, country-fucking, planet-fucking prick sliding up between the thighs of the loch could take some of the credit.

Hell, yes.

I start the car, feeling charged and alert and justified again, fully firing on all cylinders and just fizzing with the good great god-damn Gonzo juice of the determination to get down to that there nuclear submarine missile base and *cover the story*, as the blessed St Hunter would say.

*

At the base – past the peace camp where protesters wave placards, past the dense-meshed fences topped with rolls of razor-wire and through the tank-stopping gates, after showing my press accreditation and being directed to the relevant building for the press briefing and typing part of the story into the lap-top while waiting for everybody else to arrive – the naval officers answering the questions look fresh and fit and seem decent and polite and somehow regretfully but steadfastly sure that they are doing something that's still important and relevant.

Later, the protesters in the peace camp outside – most wearing layers of droopily grubby cardigans and ancient combat jackets and sporting dreadlocks or side-shaves – seem just the same.

I drive back to Edinburgh listening to *Gold Mother* with the speed wearing off fast, tailing away like an engine losing revs all the way along the M8.

*

The news room of the *Caledonian* is busy as usual, crowded with desks and shelves, partitions, bookcases, terminals, plants, piles of papers, print-outs, photographs and files. I thread my way through the maze, nodding and saying hello to my accomplice hacks.

'Cameron,' Frank Soare says, looking up from his terminal. Frank is fifty, with bouffant white hair and a complexion that succeeds in being moderately ruddy and childishly smooth at the same time. He talks with a sing-song voice and, after lunch usually, a slight lisp. He likes to remind me what my name is whenever he sees me. Some mornings, this helps.

'Frank,' I say, sitting at my desk and squinting at the little yellow notes decorating the side of the terminal screen.

Frank sticks his head and shoulders round the other side of the screen, providing an unambiguous visual cue to the fact that he still thinks coloured shirts with white collars are neat. 'So how's the latest component of Britain's vital and totally independent deterrent, then?' he asks.

'Seems to work; it floats,' I tell him, logging onto the system.

Frank's Biro taps delicately at the topmost of the little yellow notes. 'Your mole rang again,' he says. 'Another wild-goose chase?'

I glance at the note. Mr Archer will phone me again in an hour. I look at my watch; about now.

'Probably,' I agree. I check my Olympus Pearlcorder has a blank tape in it; the recorder lives beside the phone and gets to listen in on any potentially exciting calls.

'You're not moonlighting, are you, Cameron?' Frank says, bushy white brows furrowing at me.

'What?' I say, putting my jacket over the back of the chair.

'You haven't got two jobs and this mole is your excuse for getting out of the office, have you? Is it?' Frank asks, trying to look innocent. His Biro continues to tap against the side of the terminal screen.

I take hold of the end of the Biro and gently push it away, directing Frank back towards his own seat. 'Frank,' I tell him, 'with the imagination you've got, you should work for the *Sun*.'

He sniffs and sits down. I scroll through the e-mail and the wires for a bit then frown and stand up, looking over the terminal at Frank, who's sitting with his slim fingers poised over the keyboard, chuckling at something on the screen.

'What did you tell Iain Garnet about this so-called mole?'

'Did you know,' Frank says, sounding mischievous, 'that Yetts o' Muckart becomes Yetis o' Muscat under the spell-check?' He grins up at me, then his expression becomes serious. 'Pardon?'

'You heard.'

'What about Iain?' he asks. 'Did you see him there today? How is he?'

'What did you tell him about this "mole"?' I peel the note off the screen and wave it at Frank.

He looks innocent. 'Amn't I supposed to say *anything*? Well, *I* didn't know,' he protests. 'I was talking to him on the phone the other day; must just have come up in conversation. Terribly sorry.'

I'm about to say something when the phone rings with an outside call.

Frank smiles and makes a lobbing, pointing motion with his Biro. 'That might be your Mr Archer now,' he says.

I sit down, lift the receiver. The line is terrible.

'Mr Colley?' The voice is machine-like, synthesised-sounding. I don't doubt it's Mr Archer but I could believe I'm talking to Stephen Hawking. I switch the Pearlcorder on, stick its earpiece in my ear and put the microphone attachment over the telephone earpiece.

'Speaking,' I say. 'Mr Archer?'

'Yes. Listen; I have something new on this thing.'

'Well, I hope so, Mr Archer,' I tell him. 'I'm getting – '

'I can't speak for long, not on your phone,' the mechanical-sounding voice continues. 'Go to the following location.'

I grab a pencil and a pad. 'Mr Archer, this had better not be another – '

'Langholm, Bruntshiel Road. Phone box. Usual time.'

'Mr Archer, that's – '

18

'Langholm, Bruntshiel Road. Phone box. Usual time,' the voice repeats.

'Mr Arch – '

'I have another name for you this time, Mr Colley,' says the voice.

'What –?'

The line goes dead. I look at the phone, then peel off the microphone attachment as Frank's smiling face appears round the side of the screen. He taps his Biro absently on my keyboard. 'Our friend?' he inquires.

I tear the sheet off the pad and stick it in my shirt pocket. 'Yep,' I say. I log off the system, gather up the Pearlcorder and pull my jacket on again.

Frank smiles radiantly when he sees me doing this and clicks something on his watch. 'Off so soon? Well done, Cameron,' he says. 'I think that's a new record!'

'Tell Eddie I'll phone in the story.'

'On your head, my boy.'

'No doubt.' I head for the door.

*

I do a very little medicinal powder in the gents, then, having so girded my septum, bloodstream and hemispheres in the magic powder, I take the 205 down to Langholm, deep in the western Borders. I compose the rest of the Vanguard article in my head as I drive; it's a Sunday so getting out of the city is easy, but the roads in the countryside beyond are full of crap drivers, mainly little old guys wearing bunnets and staring intently through the steering wheel; I can remember when they all drove Marinas and Allegros but nowadays they seem to be issued with Escort Orions, Rover 413s or Volvo 340s, all apparently fitted with governors limiting their speed to thirty-nine and a half miles per hour.

I get stuck in a line of traffic and, after a couple of hairy overtakes which result in various people flashing their headlights at me and which are purely the result of the speed, I decide to slow down, stop shouting at people, accept my lot and enjoy the scenery.

The trees and hills look sharp and vivid in the slanting late-afternoon light, slopes and trunks coated yellow-orange or standing in their own shadows. Crowded House provide the sound track. The sky fades to deep violet before five and the headlights of oncoming cars start to hurt my eyes; obviously I was too conservative with that last medicinal blast. I stop in a lay-by just past Hawick for a booster shot.

Langholm is a quiet little town near the border. I don't have a map of the place but finding Bruntshiel Road takes only five minutes of driving around. I check out the phone box at one end of the street and park the car alongside.

There's a hotel two minutes' walk away; time for a drink.

The lounge bar is dustily ramshackle and has yet to suffer the atmosphere-bypass operation brewers call remodelling. It's moderately busy with a mixture of people.

A double whisky doesn't take too long to knock back, and keeps the system in equilibrium, what with the speed aboard. I've been economising ever since I got my new PC so it's a Grouse instead of a single malt but it does the job. My mobile goes while I'm finishing the whisky. It's the paper, reminding me it's nearly deadline time. I turn away from the inquisitive stares of the locals and mutter into the cellphone, saying I'll be phoning in real soon now, honest. I buy some cigarettes, have a pee and return to the car. I mate the Tosh to the cigarette lighter in the dash and type out the rest of the Vanguard piece by the light of the street lamp above the phone box. I'm yawning but I resist the pull of the little plastic bag.

I finish the story then take out the modem and call the story into the paper. Back in the car, there's still ten minutes until Mr Archer calls. He's usually prompt. I nip back to the hotel for a quick single whisky.

The phone in the box is ringing when I get back. I run in, grab it,

20

and fiddle with the Olympus, clicking it on and untangling the wires, cursing under my breath.

'Hello?' I shout.

'Who is that?' says the calm, mechanical voice. I get the recorder working and take a deep breath.

'Cameron Colley, Mr Archer.'

'Mr Colley. I will have to ring you back later, but the first name I have for you is Ares.'

'What? Who?'

'The name I have for you is Ares: A-R-E-S. You will remember the other names I have already given you.'

'Yes: Wood, Ben – '

'Ares is the name of the project they were working on when they died. I have to go now but I will call back in an hour or so. I will have some more information then. Goodbye.'

'Mr Archer – '

Dead.

*

Dead is also what the people Mr Archer has been calling me about are. They were all men; their names were Wood, Harrison, Bennet, Aramphahal and Isaacs. Mr Archer gave me the names the first time he brought me on one of these tour-of-Scotland telephonic rendezvous. (Mr Archer does not trust mobiles – can't say I blame him.) The names sounded vaguely familiar at the time and seemed to have a weird implicit seriality about them, plus, as soon as he mentioned them, I suddenly thought of the Lake District, without knowing why. Mr Archer gave me the names and rang off before I could ask him anything else about them.

I still have this tetchy pride about remembering things myself, but in the office the following morning I logged into Profile and let it do the hard work. Profile is just a staggeringly gigantic database that probably knows your maternal great-grandfather's inside-leg

21

measurement and how many sugars his wife took in her tea; almost anything mentioned in a broadsheet over the last ten years will be there, as will stuff from US, European and Far Eastern newspapers, plus whole oceans of information from a zillion other sources.

The names posed it no problems. The five dead geezers all expired between six and four years ago and they were all connected with either the nuclear industry or the security services. Each death looked like suicide but all of them could have been murders; there was speculation in the press at the time that something murky was going on but nobody seemed to get anywhere. So far all Mr Archer's added to what I could find in the paper's library is some detail about exactly how the men died, and – tonight – that project name: Ares.

I sit in the car for a while, tinkering with the whisky article I've been working on for a while and wondering who or what Ares is. A few people use the phone box. I play some rather pathetic low-level games on the Tosh, wishing I had a decent colour machine with the speed and the RAM and the hard disk to run *Despot*. I roll a joint and smoke that, listening to the radio and then to my k.d. lang tape but it's too soporific and I turn the radio on but it's too inane so I scrabble in the glove-box until I find *Trompe le Monde* by the Pixies and that keeps me awake better than speed though the tape's stretched a bit because I've played it so much and so the sound comes and goes a bit but that's cool.

*

I'm running through the woods at Strathspeld, on a bright summer's day; I'm thirteen years old and while I'm running I'm also looking at myself from outside, as though I'm watching all this on a screen. I've been here many times before and I know how to turn away from this place, I know how to escape from it. I'm just about to do that when I hear a bell.

I wake up and the phone is ringing. It takes me a second to realise I've been asleep, and another second to remember where I am. I leap out of the car and into the box, just ahead of an old man walking his dog.

'Who is that?' says the voice.

'Cameron Colley again, Mr Archer. Look – '

'There is one other person who knows about the ones who died, Mr Colley: the go-between. I do not know his real name yet. When I find out I will tell you.'

'What –?'

'His code-name is Jemmel. I will spell that for you,' the Stephen Hawking voice says. It does so.

'Got that, Mr Archer, but who –?'

'Goodbye, Mr Colley. Take care.'

'Mr –!'

But Mr Archer rings off.

'Shit!' I shout. I forgot to record the call, too.

*

I sit in the car for a while, entering the name Jemmel into the Tosh. It means nothing to me.

I head back to the hotel for a piss and a last drink, another double: one for the road now that the first one's probably out of my system. I haven't eaten since this morning but I don't feel hungry. I force myself to eat some dried peanuts and have a half of Murphy's to wash them down and for the iron. (I used to drink Guinness but I've been boycotting the stuff since those bastards lied about moving their HQ to Scotland.)

In the car I suck a little speed (purely in the interests of road safety – it'll keep me awake), then smoke a joint as I drive away, just to keep things balanced. There's a Radio Scotland programme on at midnight which sometimes does a Tomorrow's Headlines bit right at the end; I listen to it and sure enough they mention our headline tomorrow, but we're leading with the manoeuvring in the Tory party on the run-up to the Maastricht vote. I feel let down, but then they mention that the photograph on our front page is of the Vanguard arriving at Faslane, so I know my story's there, and with any luck at all it'll be alongside the photo on the front page, rather than buried inside. I experience a modest thrill of news-fix; a dose of journo-buzz.

This is a kind of hit unique to the profession: near-instant in-print gratification. I suppose if you're a stand-up comic, a live musician or an actor the reward is similar and even quicker, but if what you're into is the printed word and the dubious authority of on-the-page black-and-white, then this is entirely the biz. The best fix of all comes from a front-page splash, but a page lead on an odd-numbered page provides a pretty sublime high, and only getting a basement piece on an even page produces any sensation of let-down.

I have another joint to celebrate but it makes me a little drowsy and it takes a definitely-last-of-the-night micro-lick of speed and another fix of *Trompe le Monde* to even things up again.

C H A P T E R

CHILL FILTER

I 'm very tempted to call in at the paper and pick up a copy fresh off the presses, which will be rumbling away now, shaking the whole building. The smell of ink and the greasy feel of the print always powerfully reinforce the news-fix buzz, plus I'd like to check my Vanguard story to see what violence the sub-editors have succeeded in inflicting on it; but as I drive down Nicolson Street suddenly the idea of subs cutting a story about a sub seems wildly amusing and I find myself giggling uncontrollably, making me sniff and sneeze and bringing tears to my eyes. I decide that I'm too wasted to be able to put on a sober face for the print-room boys, so I head home instead.

I get back to Cheyne Street about one o'clock and have the usual enforced tour of Stockbridge By Night looking for a parking place before finding one only a minute from the flat. I'm tired but not sleepy so I have a nightcap spliff and a two-fingers of Tesco's single malt.

During the next couple of hours I listen to the radio and watch all-night TV out of the corner of my eye and tinker with the whisky story on the PC and then deliberately do not play *Despot* because I know I'd only go and get involved and be up until dawn and sleep all day and not be up in time for tomorrow's job (I have an appointment with a distillery manager at noon), so instead I go back to *Xerium* and play that; recreational play in other words, not serious stuff; a game to wind down to, not get wound up by.

Xerium is an old favourite, almost like a pal, and even though there are still a few bits of it I haven't cracked I've never looked for hints or cheats in the magazines because I want to get there myself (which isn't like me) and anyway it's fun just flying around and adding to the map you gradually build up of the island continent the game's set on.

Finally I crash the good ship *Speculator* trying – as usual – to find a probably non-existent route between the peaks of the Mountains of Zound. I swear I've tried every gap in those damn hills – hell, I've even tried flying straight *through* the mountains, thinking one of them is supposed to be a hologram or something – but I crash every time; there just doesn't seem to be any way of getting through or of gaining enough height to fly over the damn things. There *is* supposed to be a way into the rectangular territory the mountains enclose somehow, but I'm fucked if I can work out what it is, not tonight, anyway.

I pass on another attempt and load the slower of my two *Asteroids* programs and obliterate a few zillion rocks in glorious wire-frame monochrome until my fingers ache and my eyes are smarting again and it's time for some decaff and bed.

*

I get up bright and fresh and – after a good five-minute cough and a shower – the only wake-me-up I have is some freshly ground Arabica. I munch some muesli and suck on a quartered orange while I look through the whisky story, which is due in today so this is really my final chance to work on it apart from any last-minute thoughts after seeing the distillery at lunch-time. I sneak a look at my current status in *Despot*, too, but resist firing the program up. I stare accusingly at the Tosh's NiCads, which I forgot to charge up last night, then transfer the tinkered-with whisky article to disk and search out some clean clothes from the pile on one side of the bed where I dumped them after last week's laundry run. Leaving the clothes on the bed can sometimes make you think there's somebody in there with you when there isn't, which can be comforting but is distinctly sad; you haven't had a fuck for well over a week, this pile of clean clothes on the duvet is telling me. Still, I'm seeing Y in a couple of days so even if nothing else turns up there's always that to look forward to.

There's some mail: junk and bills, mostly. Ignore for now.

Take the bleeper, mobile, Tosh, NiCads and slot-in radio down to the 205; the car has not been broken into or scratched (helps not to wash the Pug). Set the NiCads charging from the cigarette lighter. Take off into a cool blue-whiter; sunshine and clouds. Stop along the road for papers; scan headlines, make sure that no late-breaking story displaced the Vanguard piece and that it's intact (ninety-five per cent – a satisfyingly high score), check out Doonesbury in the *Grauniad*, then away.

Over the road-bridge and fast through Fife; once up to cruising speed – needle in that 85-to-90 region the jam-sandwich boys ignore unless they're particularly bored or in a *really* bad mood – steer with knees while rolling spliff, feeling good in a childish way and laughing at myself and thinking, *Don't try doing this at home, kids*. Leave number aside to smoke later; turn left at Perth.

The drive to the distillery takes me along part of the route to Strathspeld. I haven't been to see the Goulds for so long and I half wish I'd started out earlier so I could drop in, but I know it isn't really them I want to see, it's the place: Strathspeld itself, our long-lost paradise with all the aching, poison-sweet memories it holds. Though of course maybe it's Andy I really remember and miss; maybe I just want to see my old soul-mate, my surrogate brother, my other me; maybe I'd go straight there if he was at home, but he isn't, he's way far north and being reclusive and I must visit him too, someday.

I pass through Gilmerton, a wee village just outside Crieff, where I'd turn off for Strathspeld if I was heading that way. Used to be there was a collection of three identical little blue Fiat 126s sitting facing the road here outside one of the houses; they were there for years and years and I always meant to stop off here and find the owner and ask him, Why have you had these three little blue Fiat 126s sitting outside your house for the last decade? because I wanted to know and besides it might have made a decent story and over the years there must have been *millions* of people who've passed this way and wondered the same thing, but I never did get around to it; always in a hurry, rushing past, anxious to get to the tainted paradise that Strathspeld's always been to me . . . Anyway, the three little blue Fiat 126s disappeared recently so there's no point. Guy seems to be collecting transit vans these days. I felt hurt, almost grieved when I first saw that house without the three little cars outside; it was like a death in the family, like some distant but friendly uncle had copped it.

I play some old stuff from Uncle Warren for the same nostalgic reasons I came this way.

Deep in the glens at Lix Toll there's another automotive roadside attraction standing outside the garage there; a bright yellow Land Rover about ten foot tall facing the road, not on wheels but on four black triangular tracks like the bastard cross of a Landy and a Caterpillar earth-mover. Been there a few years now. Leave it another few and I might go in and ask them, Why have you –?

Sweep past, in a hurry.

*

The distillery is just outside Dorluinan, hidden in the trees off the Oban road, across the rail line and up a narrow lane through the forest. The manager is a Mr Baine; I go to his office and we do the usual distillery tour, through the damp, half-enticing smells and the kiln heat and past the gleaming stills, past the gushing glass cupboard of the spirit safe until we end up in the chill darkness

30

of one of the warehouses, standing looking out over the serried rows of broad-backed barrels, gloomily lit from above by a very few small, grimy armoured skylights. The roof is low, supported by thick, gnarled wooden struts resting on widely spaced iron columns. The floor is compacted earth, hard as concrete after a couple of centuries of use.

Mr Baine looks worried when I tell him about the article. He's a bulky, droopy-faced highlander in a dark suit with a Technicolor tie that makes me glad I'm facing him here in the soft darkness of the warehouse, not outside in the sunlight.

'Well, basically just the facts,' I'm saying, grinning at Mr Baine. 'That back in the 'twenties the Yanks objected to their whisky and brandy going cloudy when they added ice to it, so they told the distillers to fix what they regarded as a problem. The French, being the French, told them what to do with their ice cubes, while the Scots, being British, said, Certainly, here's what we'll do . . .'

Mr Baine's wounded-spaniel looks take on an extra tier of unhappiness as I tell him all this. I know I shouldn't have taken that micro-lick of powder while we were going through the tour earlier, but I couldn't resist it; there was an irresistibly appealing getting-away-with-it promissory glee about sticking my finger in my mouth, then my pocket, then my mouth again and nodding as Mr Baine talked and I looked interested while my tongue went numb and the chemical taste thickened in my throat and this firingly, chargingly addictive illegal drug did its business while we walked round this perfectly legal, government-financing drug factory.

So I'm gibbering but it's *good*.

'But, Mr Colley – '

'So the distillers brought in chill-filtering, lowering the temperature of the whisky until the oils that cause the cloudiness come out of solution and then straining the stuff through asbestos to remove the oil; only that removes a lot of the taste as well – which you can't put back – and the colour, which you can put back, using caramel. Isn't that right?'

31

Mr Baine has a hangdog look. 'Ah, well, broadly,' he says, clearing his throat and looking out over the ordered sea of barrel-backs disappearing into the gloom. 'But, ah, is this going to be, um, a what-do-you-call-it? An exposé, Mr Colley? I thought you just wanted –?'

'You thought I just wanted to do yet another article on what a grand, beautiful country we live in and how lucky we are to produce this world-renowned, dollar-earning drink and isn't it life-enhancing used in moderation and just generally great?'

'Well, well . . . it's up to you what you write, Mr Colley,' Mr Baine says (I have raised a smile). 'But, ah, I feel you might be misleading people by emphasising things like, well the asbestos, for example; people might think there's asbestos in the product.'

I look at Mr Baine. *Product*? Did I hear him say *product*?

'But I'm not going to be suggesting that at all, Mr Baine; this will be a straight, factual article.'

'Aye, aye, but facts can be misleading out of context.'

'Uh-huh.'

'You see, I'm not sure about the tone – '

'But, Mr Baine, I thought you were in sympathy with the tone of this article. That's why I'm here today; I was told you're thinking about producing a "real whisky", with no chill-filtering and no colouring; a premium brand, using the cloudiness and the oils that are left in as a selling point, basing the ads on it, even – '

'Well,' Mr Baine says, looking uncomfortable, 'the marketing people are still looking into that – '

'Mr Baine, come on, we both know the demand's there; the SMWS does a roaring trade, Caddenhead's shop in the Royal Mile – '

'Well, it's not that simple,' Mr Baine says, looking even more uncomfortable now. 'Look, Mr Colley, can we talk, you know, without you reporting it?'

'You want to talk off the record?'

'Aye; off the record.'

'All right.' I nod.

32

Mr Baine clasps his hands under his suit-clad belly and nods in a serious manner. 'Look, ah, Cameron,' he says, dropping his voice, 'I'll be honest with you: we have thought about test-marketing this premium brand you're talking about, and using the lack of chill-filtering as a Unique Selling Point, but . . . You see, Cameron, we couldn't survive on that alone, even if it did work, not for the foreseeable future at any rate; we've got other considerations to take into account. We'll probably always have to sell the vast majority of our product for blending; that's our business, that's our livelihood, and as such we rely on the goodwill of the firms we sell to; firms much, much larger than we are.'

'You're saying you've been told not to rock the boat.'

'No no no.' Mr Baine looks distressed at being imperfectly understood. 'But you have to realise that a great deal of the success of whisky has to do with its mystique, the . . . the *image* the customer has of it as a unique, high-value product. It's almost mythical, Cameron; it's the *uisgebeatha*, the water of life, as they say . . . It's a very strong image, and a very important one for the Scottish export drive and national economy. If we – as, frankly, a very junior player in all this – do anything that conflicts with that image – '

'Such as putting the idea into the public's head that all the other whiskies they can buy *are* chill-filtered and/or caramel-coloured – '

'Well, yes – '

'– then you'll rock the boat,' I say. 'So you've been told to shelve the new premium brand or forget about ever selling whisky for blending again, and so going out of business.'

'No no no,' Mr Baine says again, but as we stand there in the chilly gloom of the spirit-fragrant warehouse, surrounded by enough maturing hootch to float a Trident submarine, I can see that the real answer even off the record is yes yes yes, and I'm thinking, Yay! A conspiracy; a cover-up, arm-twisting, blackmail, corporate pressure on the little guy; this could be an even *better* story!

*

You enter through the back door using a crowbar; the door and the lock are both heavy, but the frame has rotted beneath its layers of paint over the years. As soon as you're in you take the Elvis Presley mask from your day-pack and slip it on, then pull the surgeon's gloves from your pocket and snap those on too. The house feels warm from the afternoon; it faces south and has an uninterrupted view out over the links of the golf course towards the estuary, so it catches a lot of sun.

You don't think there's anybody in yet but you aren't sure; there wasn't time to watch the place all day. It feels and somehow sounds empty. You slip from room to room, feeling sweaty beneath the slick latex of the mask. The late evening sun has turned the faint, high clouds over the sea pink and the light falls into every room, filling them with rose and shadows.

The stairs and a lot of the floorboards creak. The rooms look clean but the furniture is old-fashioned and mismatched; cast-off. You satisfy yourself there's nobody in, ending up in the main bedroom of the house.

You're not very happy with the bed; it's a divan. You inspect it, in that reddening gloaming, then heave the mattress off, leaving it propped against the wall. Still no good. You go through to the other front bedroom, which also looks out over the course and the sea; the room smells unlived-in, even slightly damp. This bed is better; this one has an iron frame. You pull the bedding off and start to tear the sheets into strips.

You look out of the window as you do this, watching a couple of military jets over the sea in the distance. To the right, beyond the railway line, you can see the curve of beach leading out to the wooded point, and catch a glimpse of the lighthouse there, rising above the trees.

Then you see Mrs Jamieson coming though the gate from the road and up the garden path and you duck down, walking quickly to the door and the top landing. You listen to the front door opening.

Mrs Jamieson comes in and goes through to the kitchen. You

remember the creaking stairs. You hesitate for a second, then walk normally to the stairs and go down them with a fairly quick, heavy tread, whistling. The steps creak.

'Murray?' Mrs Jamieson's voice calls from the kitchen. 'Murray, I didn't see the car – '

You reach the foot of the stairs. Mrs Jamieson's white-haired head appears beyond the banister rails to your right, her face turning to you.

You swing round, seeing her start to react, mouth dropping. You already know what you're going to do, how you're going to play this, so you punch her, knocking her down. She collapses to the floor, making little flustered, bird-like noises. You hope you didn't hit her too hard. You haul her up and keep your hand over her mouth as you drag her upstairs.

You pin her on the divan base and stuff a handkerchief in her mouth using the handle of the Stanley knife, then pull a pair of her tights over her head, tie them round her neck and mouth and put her inside the old, heavy wardrobe in the main bedroom, pulling out the few clothes hanging there and handcuffing her to the rail. She whimpers and cries but the gag muffles everything. You pull the tights she's wearing down and tie her ankles together above her sensible brown brogues, then you close the wardrobe doors.

You sit on the divan base, pull off the mask and sit there, breathing hard and sweating. You cool off, then put the mask back on and open the door again. Mrs Jamieson stands, trembling, her eyes through the dark grey mesh of the tights looking bright and wide. You shut the door, then close the curtains in that bedroom and the one with the iron-frame bed.

Her husband arrives half an hour later, parking the car in the drive. He comes in by the front door and you're waiting behind the kitchen door as he walks through; you make a noise, he turns and you punch him, sending him clattering back against the kitchen cabinet, producing an avalanche of willow-pattern plates. He tries to get up so you hit him again. He's very old and you're quite surprised it takes two punches to lay him out, though he's still a decent weight.

You stuff a pair of his wife's panties in his mouth and do the same trick with the tights, over the head and tied round the neck, then drag him upstairs to the second bedroom. You can smell he's been drinking recently; G & Ts, probably. Some cigarette-smoke smell, too. You're sweating again by the time you get him onto the bed with the iron frame.

You tie him to the bed, face down. He's starting to come round. When he's secured, you take out the Stanley knife. He was carrying a light windcheater which you left in the kitchen and he's wearing a blue Pringle sweater with a knickerbockered golfer depicted on the front, a Marks & Spencer's check shirt and a light string vest. You cut his clothes off, flinging them into one corner. His fawn slacks scatter golf tees when you throw them aside; his socks are bright red, his Y-fronts white. His golf shoes are brown and white, heavily spiked and with elaborate tongues and tasselled laces.

You take off your day-pack. You get the pillows from the main bedroom and stuff them and those from this bed under the old man's torso, raising his body from the bed. He's making spluttering, shouting noises now and moving weakly. You use a couple of rolled-up blankets to bring his rump up further, then go back to the day-pack and sort out the things you'll need. He struggles, as though wrestling with a pinned, invisible opponent. He's making a noise like he's choking but you don't do anything yet. You take the top off the cream.

There's a spitting, hacking noise and he must get at least some of the gag out of his mouth because he splutters, 'Stop this! Stop this, I say!' Not the gruff, home-counties voice you recall from the television; more high-pitched and strained, but that's hardly surprising in the circumstances. He sounds less frightened than you expected, though.

'Look,' he says, in something more like his normal voice; deep and no-nonsense. 'I don't know what you want, but just take it and get

36

out; there's no need for this; no need at all.' You squirt some of the cream onto the vibrator.

'I think you're making a mistake,' he says, trying to twist his head round to see you. 'Seriously. We don't live here; this is a holiday home. It's rented; there's nothing of value here at all.' He struggles some more. You kneel on the bed behind him, inside the inverted V of his scrawny, varicosed legs. There are broken veins on his back and upper arms. His shanks look grey and withered; his buttocks are very pale, almost yellowish, and the skin on his thighs, below the level shorts would come to, has a grainy, mottled appearance; his balls hang like old fruit, surrounded by wiry grey hair.

His cock looks slightly engorged. That's interesting.

He feels you get up onto the bed and shouts, 'Look! I don't think you know what you're doing. This is aggravated burglary, young man; you – ah!'

You've put the cream-smeared tip of the vibrator against his anus, grey-pink and pursed between his spread buttocks. The cream must feel cold. 'What?' he shouts, voice muffled by the gag. 'Stop! What d'you think you're doing?'

You start to work the creamy plastic dildo into him, twisting it from side to side and watching the skin round his anus stretch and whiten as the ivory-coloured plastic slides in; a thin collar of white cream builds up there.

'Ah! Ah! Stop! All right! I know what you're doing! I know what this is about! All right! So you know who I am; but this is no way to – ah! Ah! Stop! Stop! All right! You've made your point! Those women – look, all right, I may have said things I regretted later, but you weren't there! You didn't hear all the evidence! I did! You didn't hear the men who were accused! You couldn't form an opinion of their character! The same with the women! Ah! Ah! *Ah*! Stop! Please; you're hurting! You're hurting!'

You have the vibrator about a third of the way in, not quite up to its maximum girth. You press harder, pleased at how much grip the surgeon's gloves give you but half-wishing you could say something though you know you can't, which is a pity.

'Ah! Ah! Jesus Christ, for God's sake, man, are you trying to kill me? Look, I have money; I can – ah! Ah, you filthy bastard – ' He moans and farts at the same time. You have to turn your head away from the smell, but you push the vibrator in further. You can hear seagulls crying outside, beyond the closed curtains.

'Stop, just stop this!' he shouts. 'This isn't justice! You don't know all the facts about those cases! Some of them *were* dressed like whores, dammit! They'd let any man have them; they were no better than whores! Ah! Fuck, fuck, you filthy blackguard bastard! You filthy, fucking queer bastard! Ah!'

He pulls and bucks, rattling the bed and pulling the knotted sheet-strips tighter. 'You bastard!' he splutters. 'You'll pay for this! You won't get away with this! They'll catch you; they'll catch you and I'll make damn, fucking sure they give you a lesson in the cells you'll *never* forget! D'you hear me? Do you?'

You leave the vibrator in there and switch it on. He heaves and pulls again but it doesn't do any good. 'Oh, for God's sake, man,' he moans, 'I'm seventy-six; what sort of monster *are* you?' He starts sobbing. 'And my wife,' he says, coughing. 'What have you done with my *wife*?'

You get off the bed and take out the little wooden box from the zipped pocket of your shell-suit, carefully slide the lid off and tease apart the nest of toilet tissue inside. The wad of tissue holds a tiny vial of blood and a needle; it's a dirty disposable syringe needle, a little thing barely a centimetre long with a cone of ribbed orange plastic at the end that would fit onto the body of the syringe.

You listen to him as he curses you and threatens you, and you are still unsure. You couldn't decide when you were planning this whether to infect him with HIV-positive blood or not; you couldn't make up your mind whether he really deserved it, and so you've left it until now to make your decision.

Sweat runs into your eyes as you stand there.

'D'you get a thrill from this, do you? Is that it?' He spits. 'Closet queer, are you?' He coughs, then twists his head, trying to look back at you. 'Are you still there, are you? What are you doing now? Having a wank, eh? Are you?'

You smile behind the mask and fold the toilet tissue back over the vial and the needle, leaving them in the box. You slide the lid shut again and put it back in your jacket pocket. You take a couple of steps back towards the door, where he can see you.

'You filthy bastard!' he spits. 'You filthy, fucking bastard! I served the best I could for thirty years! You've no right to do this! This doesn't prove anything, d'you understand? It doesn't prove anything! I'd do it all just the same if I had my time again! All of it! I wouldn't change one sentence, you fucking little *cunt*!'

You rather admire the old fellow's attitude. You slip through to the other room to make sure his wife is all right. She's still trembling. You leave her hanging there in the mothball-scented darkness of the old wardrobe. You go downstairs, pack the Elvis mask back into the day-pack with the rest of the stuff and leave by the back door you arrived through.

It's still light and the evening is only just starting to turn chilly as you walk down the back path beneath a deep blue sky ridged with high, dark clouds. A cool wind comes in off the sea and you pull your jacket collar tight.

Your hands still smell of rubber, from the gloves.

*

I turn in the whisky story, with a teaser paragraph at the end promising further revelations concerning arm-twisting moves being made by the big corporate booze-barons to silence the brave little whisky wizards. Meanwhile I try to work out what's going on in the long-running mole story; the Ares story (Ares the god of massacre, according to the mythology dictionary in the paper's library). I throw

'Jemmel' at the databases but they draw a blank. Even Profile throws up its silicon hands in defeat.

*

'Cameron! It's yourself!' Frank informs me, indubitably. 'So you thought you'd put in an appearance; well, well. Hey; guess what the spell-check thinks Colonsay should be?'
    'No idea, Frank.'
    '"Colonic"!'
    'Hilarious.'
    'And Carnoustie?'
    'Hmm?'
    '"Carousing"!' He laughs. '"Carousing"!'
    'Even funnier.'
    'By the way, Eddie wants to see you.'
    'Oh.'

*

Eddie the Ed is a wee, wizened sandy-haired man of fifty-five or so who wears half-moon glasses on his pointy nose and always looks like he's just briefly tasted something extremely sour but is finding it actually quite amusing because he knows you're about to taste it too, soon, and for longer. Technically Eddie is only acting editor while our real Great Helmsman, Sir Andrew, is away for an indefinite period recovering from a heart attack (presumably brought on by that common editorial affliction of having too much heart).

Our resident cynic in the sports section pointed out that Sir Andrew's heart attack occurred only a short decent interval after the murder of Sir Toby Bissett back in August, and hazarded that it was a kind of pre-emptive strike to take him off the target list of what a few editors at the time half-suspected was some editor-offing loony whose next target was them personally. Well, blame a host of guilty consciences, and the confusion caused when the IRA apparently claimed responsibility for Tobe's murder, and then retracted it. No other editors were spiked (though at least that showed our assassin had a sense of humour), and anyway Eddie seems not to worry about such threats to his temporarily elevated position.

The editor's office of the *Caledonian* probably has one of the best views in all newspaperdom, looking out over Princes Street Gardens to the New Town, the river Forth and the fields and hills of Fife beyond, with a side-window view of the castle's best profile thrown in, just in case the occupant ever gets bored with the frontal aspect.

I have kind of a bad association with this room after an unsuccessful foreign trip last year which resulted in a visit here to see Sir Andrew. I left with my ears singed; if displaying editorial outrage was an Olympic sport, Sir Andrew would undoubtedly be on the British team and saddled with the crushing burden of being a Medal Hope. I'd have resigned there and then except I got the impression that was just what he wanted me to do.

'Cameron, come in, sit down,' Eddie says. Sir Andrew is into furniture politics; Eddie is sitting on – no; housed within – a throne of a chair, all black carved wood and buttoned red leather and looking like it's supported more than one royal rear. I'm perched on the class equivalent of an honest artisan, one fabric-covered step up from stackable plastic prole. Eddie did have the decency to look uncomfortable in this piece of power-seating when he first took over the job last month, but I get the impression he's grown to like it.

Eddie leafs through a print-out on his desk. The desk isn't quite as impressive as the chair – only single-bed size rather than the king-size I suspect Sir Andrew and maybe Eddie would prefer – but it still looks fairly impressive. There's a terminal on its surface but Eddie only uses that to spy on people, watching the system as we type notes, input a story, fax outside or e-mail insults to each other.

Eddie sits back in his chair, taking off the half-moon glasses and tapping them against the knuckles of one hand.

'I'm not sure about this whisky story, Cameron,' he says in the perpetually pained tones of Kelvinside/Morningside Refined.

'Oh? What's wrong with it?'

'The tone, Cameron, the tone,' Eddie says, frowning. 'It's a tad too combative, you know what I mean? Too critical.'

'Well, I'm just sticking to – '

'Aye, the facts,' Eddie says, smiling tolerantly and sharing what he thinks is a private joke. 'Including the fact that you obviously don't like some of the larger distilling concerns, by the sound of it.' He slips his glasses back on and peers at the print-out.

'Well, I wouldn't say that's how it comes across,' I say, hating myself for feeling defensive. 'You're bringing the fact that you know me to this, Eddie. I don't think somebody coming cold to – '

'I mean,' Eddie says, slicing through my waffle like a steak knife, 'all this about the Distillers Company and the Guinness take-over. Is that strictly necessary? It's old news, Cameron.'

'But it's still *relevant*,' I insist. 'It's in there to show the way big business works; they'll promise anything to get what they want and then renege on it without a second thought. They're professional liars; it's only the bottom line that matters, only the shareholders' profits; nothing else. Not tradition or the life of communities or the people who've worked all their lives in – '

Eddie sits back, laughing. 'There you go,' he says. 'You're writing an article about whisky – '

'The adulteration of whisky.'

'– and you've got stuff in here basically saying what a lying wee shite Ernest Saunders is.'

'Lying big shite; he's – '

'Cameron!' Eddie says, annoyed, taking off the half-moons again and tapping the print-out with them. 'The point is that even if this wasn't very possibly libellous – '

'But nobody recovers from senile dementia!'

'It doesn't *matter*, Cameron! It has no place in an article about whisky.'

'. . . adulteration,' I add, sullenly.

'There you go again!' Eddie says, standing and heading to the middle of the three big windows behind him. He half-sits on the window-ledge, hands on the wood. 'My God, laddie, you're a terrible one for getting bees in your bonnet, so you are.'

God, I hate it when Eddie calls me 'laddie'.

'Are you going to print it or not?' I ask him.

'Certainly not, as it stands. This is supposed to grace the front of the Saturday supplement, Cameron; it's for hungover people in their dressing-gowns to scatter their croissant crumbs across; the way it reads at the moment you'd be lucky to get it into the back of *Private Eye*.'

I glare.

'Cameron, Cameron,' Eddie says, looking pained at my expression and rubbing his chin with one hand. He looks tired. 'You're a good journalist; you write well, you meet deadlines and I know you've had offers to go down south with an even wider brief and extra money, and both Andrew and I give you more leeway than some people here think you deserve. But if you ask to do a Saturday special on whisky we do rather expect it to have something to do with the cratur itself, rather than read like a manifesto for Class War. It's as bad as that television piece you did last year.' (At least he hasn't mentioned the results of my little foreign trip.) He leans over and peers at the print-out. 'I mean, look at this: forcing Ernest Saunders to drink so much whisky his brain deteriorates to the "bovinely spongy state he claimed it was in at the end of the Guinness trial"; that's – '

'It was a joke!' I protest.

'It reads like incitement! What are you trying to –?'

'You'd let Muriel Gray away with it.'

'Not the way you've put it, I wouldn't.'

'Well, get it legalled, then; the lawyers – '

'I'm not *going* to get it legalled, Cameron, because I'm not going to run it.' Eddie shakes his head. 'Cameron,' he sighs, quitting the window to resume his throne again, 'you simply have to cultivate a sense of proportion.'

'What happens now?' I say, ignoring this and nodding at the print-out.

Eddie sighs. 'Rewrite, Cameron. Try to dilute the vitriol instead of harping on about this asbestos filtering.'

I sit and stare at the print-out. 'This means we'll lose the slot, doesn't it?'

'Yes,' Eddie says. 'I'm moving the National Trust series forward a week. The whisky piece will just have to wait.'

I purse my lips, then shrug. 'Okay, give me till – ' I look at my watch '– six. I can have it redone by then if I work right through. We can still make the – '

'No, Cameron,' Eddie says exasperatedly. 'I don't want a quick rehash with a few of the expletives deleted; I want you to rethink the whole thing. Approach it from a different angle. I mean, get your criticism on the moral corrosion of late capitalism in implicitly if you must, but *make* it implicit; keep it subtle. I know you . . . we both know you can do it, *and* that you're more effective when you're wielding the stiletto rather than the chainsaw. Take advantage of that, for goodness' sake.'

I'm not mollified but I make a half-smile and give a grudgingly confirmatory grunt.

'Agreed?' Eddie asks.

'Okay,' I say, nodding. 'Agreed.'

'Good,' Eddie says, sitting back. 'Anyway. How's everything else going? Liked that piece on the submarine, incidentally; nicely balanced; just hovering on the brink of editorialising, but never quite going over. Good stuff, good stuff . . . By the by, I hear rumours you might have something interesting coming up involving a government mole, that true?'

I fix Eddie with my best steely look. It seems to bounce off. 'What's Frank been saying?' I ask.

'I didn't say I heard it through Frank,' Eddie says, looking all innocent and open. *Too* innocent and open. 'A few people have mentioned you seem to have something on the go, something you're not telling anybody about. I'm not prying; I don't want to know anything about it yet. I just wondered if these rumours are true.'

'Well, they are,' I say, hating having to admit it.

'I – ' Eddie begins, then his phone rings. He looks annoyed as he answers it.

'Morag, I thought – ' he says, then his expression changes to one of sour resignation. 'Yes, all right. Just a second.'

He presses the mute button and looks apologetically at me. 'Cameron, sorry; this bloody Fettesgate thing. High-altitude leaning going on. Got to field all this stuff. Nice talking to you. See you later.'

I leave the office feeling like I've just been to see the headmaster. Retreat to toilets for nose-to-nose with Auntie Crystal. Thank fuck for drugs.

*

Andy and Clare and I walked through the Strathspeld estate, from the house across the lawn and the terrace and through the shrub garden and the forest, down into the glen and out again, up to the wooded hill beyond and the densely overgrown dip where the old air-shaft chimney was.

The chimney was one of two on the hill; the old railway line ran directly underneath. The line had been closed for thirty years and the tunnel entrances had been first boarded up and then filled in with rubble. The viaduct over the Speld a half-mile away had been demolished, so that only the piers were still visible in the rushing waters. The tracks themselves had been torn up, leaving a long, flat-floored canyon curving under the trees of the estate.

The two air-shaft chimneys – squat dark cylinders of undressed stone a couple of metres across and a little over half that high, each capped with an iron grating – had vented the steam and smoke from

45

the trains in the tunnel. You could climb up onto them and sit on the rusting iron grid – afraid it would give way but afraid to admit you were afraid – and look down into that utter blackness, and sometimes catch the cold, dead scent of the abandoned tunnel, rising up around you like some remorseless chilly breath. From there, too, you could let stones fall into the darkness, to land with a distant, hardly heard thud on the floor of the tunnel thirty or forty metres below. Once Andy and I had come here with old newspapers and a box of matches and dropped the lit, twisted papers into the hole and watched them slowly fall flaming, spiralling silently downwards into the blackness until they hit the tunnel floor.

Andy was eleven, Clare ten, and I was nine. We were there for a ceremony. Andy was slightly plump at the time, Clare agreeably normal. I was – everybody agreed – wiry, but I'd probably fill out, like my dad had.

'Blimey!' Clare said. 'Dark in here, isn't it?'

It was dark. In high summer the outrageously tangled bushes around the chimney grew fast and green and blocking, starving the hollow of light. We'd had to fight our way in here to the little oasis of calm clarity around the forgotten chimney itself. Now that we were here, in its little green cave, the light seemed dim and clotted.

Clare shivered and clung to Andy, face puckering in pretended terror. 'Argh, help!'

Andy grinned, putting an arm round her. 'Never fear, sis.'

'Do the dreadful deed!' she cried, making a face at me.

'You first,' Andy said, handing the packet to me.

I took the box, extracted a cigarette from it and put it in my mouth. Andy fumbled with the match, lit it, then quickly put it to the cigarette. I sucked hard, eyes narrowed.

I inhaled a smell of sulphur, coughed immediately, turned appropriately green and nearly threw up.

Andy and his sister laughed themselves hoarse while I kept on coughing.

46

They each tried smoking, too, and pronounced it utterly foul, quite disgusting, what did people see in it? Adults were mad.

Andy said, But it looked good; had we ever seen *Casablanca* with Humphrey Bogart? *There* was a film. And who could imagine Rick without a cigarette in his hand if not hanging from his mouth? (Clare and I could, as we mugged to each other. Hell, I'd seen that film a couple of Christmases ago, hadn't I? It was a Marx Brothers movie and there was nobody called Humphrey Bogart in it *I* could remember.)

We tried another cigarette, and by then I'd – maybe instinctively – sussed how to handle it.

I was getting a hit from the stuff! I really toked on that second fag. Andy and Clare just sipped at it, took it into their mouths but not their lungs, not their beings, didn't accept it into their own personal ecospheres; just giggled childishly, peripheral.

Not me. I sucked that smoke in and made it part of me, joined mystically with the universe right at that point, said Yes to drugs forever just by the unique hit I got from that one packet of fags Andy liberated from his dad. It was a revelation, an epiphany; a sudden realisation that it was possible for matter – something there in front of you, in your hand, in your lungs, in your pocket – to take your brain apart and reassemble it in ways you hadn't thought of previously.

This was better than religion, or this was what people always *meant* by religion! The whole point was that *this worked*! People said Believe In God or Be Good or Do Well At School or Buy This or Vote For Me or whatever, but nothing actually worked the way substances worked, nothing fucking well *delivered* like they did. They were truth. Everything else was falsehood.

I became a semi-junkie that day, that afternoon, that hour, that second-fag-length moment. In that first virginal rush of toxins to the brain I believe I started to become my later self; I finally had my internal eyes opened to my true being. Truth and revelation. What is *actually* going on? What is literally the case? What *really works*?

There you are, the Journo Catechism, the truth-teller's tale, written in any damn scrip or script you care to choose to denominate, elect to go for or designate. WHAT FUCKING WORKS?

I rest my case.

We threw the burned-out fag-butts down the chimney into the darkness without further ceremony. We walked back towards the house and while Andy was ahead of us he suddenly announced a race, so we yelled, protesting, and darted off after him over the last hundred metres, sprinting across the lawn and the gravel to the porch.

Breathless in the main hall, all pronounced the experiment at the old chimney a failure . . . but in my heart I knew different.

C H A P T E R

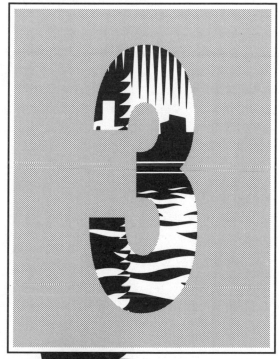

DESPOT

Despot is a world-builder game from the HeadCrash Brothers, the same team that brought us *Brits*, *Raj* and *Reich*. It's their latest, biggest and best, it's Byzantinely complicated, baroquely beautiful, spectacularly immoral and utterly, utterly addictive. It's only been out for two months and I've played it practically every day since the muggy Monday morning in late August when I first stepped out of the Virgin games shop on Castle Street clutching my shrink-wrapped copy and scuttled back to the office reading the outside of the pack like some 'sixties ten-year-old with the latest Airfix model.

I'm sat in the flat in Cheyne Street, playing the game when I should be working on a story. The trouble is that the game and the machine go together so well; the HeadCrash team designed *Despot* so that it takes advantage of whatever configuration of system it's being played on, with the maximum on a PC being a 386SX running at 25Mhz with at least 2Mb of RAM and 8Mb of hard-disk space free plus an S3-based graphics card fitted. The game will run on anything down to an Atari 520ST and still work (but it won't look remotely as good, run so fast or have all the interactive features) and obviously it'll look just as good and do everything on a better-than-maximum machine, but it just so happens that the above spec *is exactly what I've got on my machine.*

This is purely a coincidence, of course; it's not fate, not karma, not anything except a fortuitous accident, but dammit, it's just so *neat*! No waste! No fat! Just exactly the right, most elegantly eco-optimum system – as near to state-of-the-art as I could afford at the time, barely a year ago and I'm still paying the now quite superseded bastard off – to run this stunningly Machiavellian turbo-screamer of a game; an instant classic, easily a year ahead of its time and just possibly better than sex.

I'm playing *Despot* but I'm thinking about sex. I'm definitely seeing Y tomorrow and I can't *stop* thinking about sex. I've got an erection and I'm sitting here in front of the machine in the darkness, crouched here in the box room of the flat with the light off and the radio on and the computer screen awash with the seductive, gently scrolling graphics of *Despot* and the light from the screen – blue, ochre, red, green – throws the shadow of my cock onto my belly and the damn thing's getting in the way all the time so that I keep putting it under the desk where it rubs hard up against the metal strut at the front of the desk until that gets cold and uncomfortable and I have to push back in the chair and let the thick, bobbing weight of it rest against the edge of the chipboard, its big purple head and one little slit-mouth-eye staring dumbly, questioningly up at me like some mute, warm little puppy, distracting me, and I keep thinking I ought to have a wank but I don't want to because I want to save it all for Y, not because Y particularly desires that or it affects my performance but because it just seems important, part of the correct pre-coital ritual.

Maybe I should just put some pants on and control the thing but I kind of like sitting here in the nude and feeling the gentle breeze of warm air from the fan heater in the corner blowing over my skin.

So, the big wee man is throbbing, looking forward to a welcome in the hillsides, a homecoming in the glen (even if it's prepared to be palmed off with less), but meanwhile the game is there to be played, and threatens to play with itself if I do the same. Because *Despot* is interactive, *Despot* will go on building your world for you even if you leave it alone because it actually *watches* you; it learns your playing style, it *knows* you, it will actually try its little damnedest to *become* you. All world-builder games – emulating life or at least some aspect of it – develop and change according to their programmed rules if you leave them running alone, but *Despot* is the only one that with a bit of coaching will actually attempt to emulate *you*.

I light another Silk Cut and sip a little whisky. I'm staying off the speed for now but when I get to the next era-level in the game – and I'm hovering within a few GNP points of it at the moment – I'm going to roll a number. I draw hard on the Silk Cut, filling my lungs with the fumes. I've smoked a packet since six this evening when I started working and then turned to the game. Half a bottle of whisky's gone too, and the inside of my mouth's got that rough, granular feel it gets when I've been drinking the stuff.

I gag on the smoke.

This happens sometimes when I've been smoking too much. I grind the fag out in the ashtray and cough a bit and then look at the cigarette packet. I've been meaning to give up for a while. I keep thinking, What is the point of using this drug? The only cigarettes I ever get any actual hit from are the ones I have first thing in the morning (when I'm barely half-awake anyway and in no state to enjoy it and my chest's usually hurting from the morning cough), and sometimes the first one after I've had a few drinks. Oh, and the one I have after I've given up for a few days. Or hours.

I take the packet up in my hand. My fist almost closes. In fact it seems to me that I do actually see my hand close, see the packet crumple and contract, almost as though I've actually done it. But then I think, Shit, there's only five fags out of the box. I ought to smoke those first; it would be a waste not to.

I take out another cigarette, light it and draw deeply. I gag again, coughing and hacking and feeling the whisky and the can of Export I had earlier slosh around inside me, almost coming up. My eyes are watering. What a stupid drug, what a completely useless fucking drug; no real hit after the first drag, highly addictive and lethal in all sorts of ways, and even if the lung cancer or the heart disease doesn't get you you can look forward to gangrenous legs in your old age, bits of your body just rotting away still attached and dying in instalments for you, rotting and stinking while you're still alive and then they have to cut them off and you wake up after the operation wheezing and burning with pain and gasping for a fag. Meanwhile the tobacco companies sponsor sport and fight off advertising bans and look forward to all the new markets in the East and the Far East and more women taking up the weed to show that they can be brainless fucks too, and suits with worm-shit in their brains go on television and say, 'Well, nobody's actually proved how tobacco causes cancer you know,' and you sit there seething and then you find Thatcher is taking half a million from Philip Morris for a three-year consultancy and you swear never to buy any of *their* products ever again but at the end of the day you still light another cigarette and suck in the smoke like you enjoyed it and make more profits for those evil fucks.

Okay. I've worked myself up enough; I crush the packet. It doesn't crumple very satisfactorily because there are so many fags still inside it, but I persevere and use two hands and get it down to about half its earlier volume and then take it to the toilet and tear it open and empty the broken, folded cigarettes into the pan and pull the handle and watch most of them just float and swirl in the churning water and get so annoyed at them for not all just flushing away out of my life like I want them to that I get down on my knees and put my hands into the water and one by one push their broken bodies and the rest of the paper and tobacco debris down into the water and back round the U-bend so that they float up on the other side and I can't see them, then I wash my hands and dry them and by that time the cistern's full again and I flush it and this time the water's clear at the end and I can breathe at last.

I open the skylight in the toilet and the one in the box room to get a through draught and stand there shivering until I pull on my dressing-gown, feeling mightily pleased with myself. I sit down at the computer to find that my era-rating in *Despot* has slipped back a bit while all this has been going on, but I don't care; I feel righteous.

I suck the cold night air in and laugh, snapping the mouse around the desk surface like a wild thing while the little hand sprite on the screen flashes from control surface to display, grabbing icons and throwing them about my empire like thunderbolts, building roads, dredging ports, burning forests, digging mines and – using the very ironic Icon icon – opening more temples to myself.

A horde of barbarians from the unexplored steppes to the south tries to invade and I lose an hour fighting the bastards off and have to rebuild the Great Wall before I can get back to the Court display and continue my long-term strategy of weakening the power of the regional lords and the Church by making the palace so luxuriantly, sumptuously steeped in the ways of the flesh that the barons and the bishops become hopelessly decadent voluptuaries and hence ripe for the picking while my merchant classes prosper and I encourage cautious technological development.

I have another whisky and a bowl of Coco Pops with lots of milk. My hand keeps reaching for the place where the cigarette packet would normally be, but I'm coping with the cravings and surviving so far. I really want some speed but I know if I have any I'll want a cigarette afterwards, so I leave it alone.

I have a brainwave and get my secret police to go down to the bazaar and find some drug dealers; bingo! The dealers are introduced to the Court and soon most of the people I've been working on are thoroughly hooked. It occurs to me this might actually be a better way of controlling things than just bumping people off, which is what the secret police are usually best at. I call it a day at 4 a.m. and only feel slightly jittery as I head for bed. I can't get to sleep and I keep thinking about Y; after half an hour I give in and have a wank and fall gratefully asleep afterwards.

*

The building is warm and smells of dog. You pull him through the door and lock it. The hounds are already yelping and barking. You turn on the light.

The kennels block is about the size of a double garage; its breeze-block walls are bare. Strip-lights hang from the ceiling. There is a broad central corridor between two rows of pens, also made from breeze blocks. The internal walls extend to just over head height and are open at the top; the pens are floored with straw over concrete and the front of each pen is formed by a gate made from light angle-iron and chicken wire.

So far everything has gone well. You came across the fields and through the wood just after sunset, checking the place out with the night sight and finding the big house dark and empty. The alarm box high up on one gable wall glowed soft red; you had already decided not to attempt breaking in. You went down the drive. The gatehouse was dark, too; the gamekeeper would be back after the pub in the village closed. Far enough up the drive so that it wouldn't be seen from the main road, you felled a small tree with the handsaw, then sat down to wait. The Range Rover came growling up the drive two hours later. He was alone, still wearing his city suit; you coshed him while he was standing looking down at the tree; the car's idling motor covered any noise you made and he didn't even turn round. You just drove the Range Rover right over the tree.

His arms move weakly as you haul him across the concrete and prop him against the gate of one of two unoccupied pens. The dogs' barks change as they see their master. You put your day-pack down on the concrete, take out some plastic ties and hold them in your mouth as you try to haul him to his feet, but he's too heavy. His eyelids are flickering. You let him slump back again so that he's

56

sitting against the chicken-wire gate and when his eyes start to open you pull his head forward by the hair and cosh him again. He falls to the side. You put the plastic ties back in your pocket. You're thinking. The foxhounds continue barking and yelping.

You find a hose attached to a tap beside the doors; you remove the hose, throw one end over the breeze-block lintel of the empty pen, pull it through the chicken wire and tie it under his armpits. He makes a moaning noise as the hose tightens round his chest; you start to haul him upright, but the hose breaks and he falls back against the gate. 'Shit,' you say to yourself.

Eventually you have an idea. You lift the gate off its hinges and lay it down on the floor beside him. Then you roll him over onto it. He makes a noise somewhere between a moan and a snore.

You secure his wrists and ankles to the chicken wire with the plastic ties, using two at each point. You've tested the ties yourself; they look flimsy but you couldn't burst one when you tried, and you've seen US police on television use similar devices instead of handcuffs. Only you're not sure how strong the chicken wire is, so using two on each wrist and ankle and tying them round different hexagons in the wire seems a sensible precaution. The hounds are still barking intermittently, but they're making less fuss than they were. You use a length of the hose to tie his waist to the angle-iron strut that makes a Z-shape through the gate. You undo his belt and pull his trousers down; he has a deep tan from a holiday in Antigua last month, fading now. You haul and scrape the gate over to the wall of the empty pen, then you squat behind the top of the gate and heave it and him up, sucking in your breath and grunting and then pulling the gate up still further and then letting the top edge of the gate rest against the wall of the pen you took the gate from. The gate rests there at an angle of about sixty degrees.

He's starting to come round. You change your mind about letting him talk and take the electrical tape from your day-pack and bind it round his mouth and the back of his neck, through the wire, so that his head is held tight too. There is some blood leaking from under his long fair hair; it trickles down the nape of his neck and onto the collar of his shirt.

Then, while he's still making moaning noises through his nose, you take the two cut-out bits of newspaper and the little tube of glue from your day-pack and stick the articles onto the breeze-block wall straight across from him, one on either side of the gate. The dogs inside leap up and snarl at you as you do this, shaking the chicken wire.

The headline of the first article reads EX-MINISTER IN IRAN ARMS DEAL ROW, and in smaller writing underneath it says, 'It was my judgement that the interests of the West would best be served if the Iran-Iraq War went on for as long as possible.'

The headline of the second article reads PERSIMMON DEFENDS CLOSURE PLANS – 'PRIMARY CONCERN SHAREHOLDERS', and underneath are the words, '1000 jobs go after only five years as grant runs out.'

You wait for him to come round but he's taking a while. You were impressed by how far the house is from any others, and decide that rather than the silenced Browning you brought you will risk using the shotgun he was carrying in the back of the Range Rover. You go back out to the car and fetch the gun and a box of cartridges. You lock the door behind you again.

He's awake, though his eyes look glazed and uncoordinated. You nod to him as you walk up and stand in front of him, slotting a couple of the brown-red cartridges into the gun. His eyes move oddly as he tries to focus on you. You are wearing dark blue overalls and a skiing balaclava similar to the one you used in London. The gloves you're wearing are black ski-silks. The Rt Hon. Edwin Persimmon MP is mumbling behind the tape and still trying to focus on you. You wonder if you hit him too hard with the cosh, and whether you ought not just to do it with the gun here and now and forget about the rest because it will be quicker and less dangerous for you, but you decide to stick to the plan. It's important; it shows that you are not just some nutter, and the extra risk lifts you onto another plane of chance and luck.

You turn and go to the pen full of foxhounds; they start barking again. You work both barrels of the gun into one of the chicken-wire hexagons at about waist height, until the gun fits, then you angle it downwards, bend slightly so that your shoulder is firm behind the stock of the gun, and fire both barrels into the mass of snarling dogs.

The gun kicks against your shoulder. The noise is stupendous in the breeze-block space. Smoke rolls through the pen, where one dog lies blown in half, two more are lying prone and whimpering on the concrete and the rest are barking madly; several of them are running round furiously in tight circles, scattering straw. You break the gun; the cartridges pop out and one of them hits Mr Persimmon in the chest. His eyes are wide and he is shaking the chicken-wire gate he's tied to with all the might he can muster. You reload the gun without taking it out of the mesh, then aim more carefully and fire a barrel at a time, killing two more of the dogs outright and wounding three or four. The smoke is thick for a moment, and tastes acrid in your throat.

The dogs sound frenzied now, howling high and anguished. One of the animals is still running round all the time, but it keeps slipping on the blood. You reload and fire again, killing another two of the foxhounds, leaving maybe half a dozen of them still leaping up at the walls and barking. The one running round in a circle is bleeding from one back leg, but hasn't slowed down.

You turn to Mr Persimmon and pull the bottom of the balaclava up over your mouth, and above the squeals and the howls and the barks you shout, 'They enjoy it really, you know!' and wink at him. Then you reload the gun and blast another couple of them. You avoid the one running round in circles because you've decided you like that one.

The smoke makes you cough. You put the gun down and take the Marttiini out from the sheath in your right sock. You go over to Mr Persimmon, who is still shaking the gate he's tied to as best he can. It starts to slide down the wall with a scraping, grating noise, and you haul it upright again. His eyes are very wide. There is a lot of sweat on his face. You feel quite sweaty too. It's a warm evening.

You've left the bottom of the balaclava up so he can see your mouth. You go close to him so that he can watch you only through his left eye, and over the whimpers and whines and the few weak, hoarse barks from the pen opposite, you say,

'In Tehran, in the main cemetery, they had a red fountain; a fountain of blood, to the martyrs who died in the war.' You stare at him, and hear him trying to say or shout something, the noises coming down his nose sounding clogged and distant. You're not sure whether he's swearing at you or pleading with you. 'Those found guilty of capital offences during the later stages of the war weren't shot or hung,' you continue. 'They were made to contribute to the war effort too.'

You hold the knife up so he can see it. His eyes can't go any wider.

'They bled them to death,' you tell him.

You crouch down in front of him and make a deep downward incision into his left thigh, opening the artery to the air. The scream comes down his nose as he shakes the chicken-wire frame. The bright blood pumps out and up, spattering onto your gloved hand and jetting upwards in a pink spray that soaks his underpants and rises as high as his face, freckling it with red. You alter your grip on the knife to cut into the other leg. He's rattling the chicken-wire gate for all he's worth but everything holds and the gate can't slide forward because you're squatting there in front of it, blocking it with your boots. His blood spurts fiercely, shining in the overhead lights. It runs down both his legs, and drips off his underpants; it runs down to the trousers round his ankles and soaks into them.

You stand up, reach forward and take the neatly folded handkerchief out of the breast pocket of his jacket, flick it open and wipe the blade of the Marttiini on it until the knife is clean. The knife comes from Finland; that's why its name has such a strange spelling. It hasn't occurred to you before, but its nationality seems appropriate now and even funny in a grim sort of way; it's Finnish and you've used it to finish Mr Persimmon.

The blood is slowing now. His eyes are still wide but they look glazed again. He has stopped struggling; his body hangs limply, though he's breathing hard. You think he might be crying but maybe it's just sweat on his face, which is very pale now.

You actually feel rather sorry for him because he's become just another dying man, and so you shrug and say,

'Oh, come on; it could have been worse.'

You turn and pack your stuff away and leave him there, the blood only dribbling now, his skin very white beneath the tan.

Some of his blood has gathered on the concrete in front of him, and joins with the pool slowly spreading from the cage full of dead or whimpering dogs.

You put the lights out and hold the Browning up at your shoulder as you open the door and then check the grounds outside with the night sight.

*

I want to weep. I'm with Y but she's brought her husband along. They turned up together at the paper but when reception rang through they just said that she was there so I went skipping down the stairs like a kid on a promise and then I saw them together in reception standing looking at the display showing staff photographers' most recent efforts and my heart sank into my shoes. Yvonne; tall and lithe and sveltely muscular in a dark skirt and jacket. Silk shirt. Black hair short, trimmed to the nape in a new, even more severe haircut, but jutting peaked over her forehead. She turned to me just as my face was completing its fall. She smiled apologetically.

And William, turning too; broad, handsome face bursting into a grin when he sees me. William; blond as Yvonne is dark, built

like an Olympic oarsman, perfect teeth, and a handshake like a
gorilla.

'Cameron! Good to see you! Been too long. How are you?
Okay?'

'Fine, fine,' I said, smiling as sincerely as I could, nodding up at
him. William is high as well as broad; he towers over me and I'm
a shade over six foot. Yvonne put her hands on my shoulders and
kissed my cheek; she's almost my height in her heels. Heels; she
prefers flatties and only wears heels because they bring her ass
up to the right level when I'm taking her from behind. As she
brushed her lips across my cheek I smelled her perfume: *Cinnabar*;
my favourite. I exchanged pleasantries thinking, So much for taking
the afternoon off.

'Right.' William clapped his hands together and rubbed them
together. 'Where are we going to go?'

'Well, I was thinking of just popping down to Viva Mexico . . .'
I said (and almost added 'as usual'), looking plaintively at Yvonne's
bright red lips.

'Na,' William said, grimacing. 'I fancy some oysters. Let's go to
the Café Royal, what d'you say?'

I said, 'Umm . . .' I thought, Oysters . . .

'Our treat,' Yvonne said, taking her husband's arm and smiling.

*

I met Yvonne and William at university, back in the cusp of these
times, our years at Stirling neatly bracketing Thatcher's first and
second victories.

They were doing business-studies courses. He was from
Birmingham, though his parents were Scottish. She was from
Bearsden, outside Glasgow. They met in the first week and were
an item when I bumped into them in the sports pavilion a term
later, one Saturday afternoon when William was about to play
rugby and Yvonne was looking for a squash partner. I'd been

waiting for my opponent – a guy from my media-studies course – to show for half an hour and was about to give up and head for the bar when Yvonne suggested we played each other. She thrashed me. We must have played a couple of hundred games over the years since then and I've beaten her exactly seven times, usually when she's been about to go down with – or is just recovering from – a cold or some other ailment. I blame the drugs, and the fact that, apart from the occasional athletic sex session with Yvonne, a fortnightly game of squash is about the only exercise I get.

Yvonne and I were just pals until she and William moved to Edinburgh three years ago and one time when William was away she and I met to go and see – of all things – *Dangerous Liaisons*, but never made it to the film because we just got drunk in the pub instead and somehow started kissing, and then in the taxi on the way back to Cheyne Street had to be told to cool it by the driver because we were practically fucking on the back seat. We got half a metre inside the front door of the flat then it was knickers down, trousers down, and a knee trembler against the wall, her head forced forward by the gas meter and my backside getting cold from the draught coming in through the letter-box.

We usually make it to the bed these days but it's been an interesting and varied physical relationship and Yvonne swears she does things with me she'd never even mention to William, whose predilections seem to begin and end with quite liking his wife to wear a basque and stockings. Considering he looks like such a broth of a boy it's slightly disappointing to be told he's squeamish about blow jobs and quite horrified – however politely and apologetically – at the idea of going down on Yvonne. So that, plus wrestling covered in baby oil, eating ice-cream from her vulva, pretend rape and bondage sodomy are all treats reserved for me, apparently.

*

So we're sitting in the Café Royal after a breezy walk down North Bridge and William has slipped a dozen live oysters down his throat (Yvonne and I had chowder) and we're talking computers because I use them and I'm interested in them and William works for a company that makes them; their Scottish manufacturing base is in South Queensferry but the company's HQ is in Maryland in the States. He was due to fly out there today but just as he was about to kiss the lovely Yvonne goodbye this morning and leave their delightful, triple-garaged, split-level lounged, sauna'd, jacuzzi'd executive villa with ensuite facilities and satellite dish set in an exclusive walled prestige development amongst mature trees with a residents-only country clubhouse, restaurant, pool, Nautilus gym, squash and tennis courts, he got a phone call telling him the trip had been postponed for a few days.

We're sitting at a table in a corner of the restaurant; William and Yvonne sit side-by-side on a green leather bench seat opposite and I'm on an ordinary chair, directly across from Yvonne. She's playing footsie with me under the table, her shoe off, her black nylon foot stroking my right calf. I'm assuming the starched white tablecloth is long enough to hide this.

Meanwhile I'm talking about 486s and clock-doublers and the up-coming P5 chip and CD-ROM and there are at least three things going on in my head because part of my brain's busy handling my conversation with William, another part is revelling in the sensations being produced by his wife's foot sliding up to my knee, giving me a monstrous erection under my napkin, and a third part is sort of sitting back listening to me talk to this cheery, affable man I'm cuckolding and it's thinking what a cool bastard I am, and how chatty, informed and charming I'm being while suffering this delicious, hidden, public, prick-engorging distraction. We're talking about multi-tasking and I almost want to say to him, 'You want to know about multi-tasking? I'm doing it right now, pal.'

Yvonne is looking just a little bored with all this computer talk, which is probably why she started fondling my leg in the first place. She's not into computers; she's into bankruptcy management. Straight from university she joined a small firm specialising in easing the death throes of failing businesses. She's been all over Britain doing this stuff and last year they made her a director. It's not a small firm any more. Growth industry.

She delicately stifles a yawn and sits back in her seat, and I take a sudden breath which I have to disguise with a cough as her foot suddenly slides up between my legs. I foolishly lift my napkin to dab my lips after the pretend cough, and Christ, there's her foot resting on the front of my seat, her stockinged toes flexing forward to stroke my cock through the material of my trousers. I put my napkin down again quickly and return to the subject of full-motion video from CD-ROM, hoping nobody saw her foot. I don't think so. Could have been embarrassing if there'd been a waiter nearby. I surreptitiously pull the tablecloth over my lap and her foot as well. She's sitting back in her seat grinning slightly at me, toes curling and uncurling as they stroke me.

I lift my champagne flute, nodding wisely at something William has just said.

'Anyway, must dash for a slash,' he says, rising. Yvonne's foot tenses against my crotch, but she doesn't take it away.

Yvonne and I watch him go then we lean over the table towards each other at the same time.

'God, you look fuckable,' I tell her.

'Mm-hmm,' she says. She shrugs. 'Sorry about all this.'

'Never mind. God, you look fuckable.'

'Want to meet up the day he goes?'

'Yes,' I gulp. 'Yes yes yes.'

'Take off your shoe and get your foot up between my legs,' she says quietly. 'I'm not wearing any knickers.'

'Oh, Christ.'

*

An hour later and I'm standing in the gents toilet back at the paper with my right sock wrapped round my dick, masturbating. The smell of the sock clings to the skin around my nose; before I wrapped it round my cock I sat sniffing it, hauling its scent deep into my lungs. This is the second wank I've had; I really was about to come as I sat there eating my lobster with Yvonne's foot stroking my crotch and my foot up her skirt. I had to excuse myself, withdraw my foot, get my shoe back on and walk awkwardly down to the gents in the Café Royal to pull myself off before I disgraced myself at the table. Barely had to touch the thing. This is taking only a little longer. The sock reeks with a fiercely erotic woman-scent. Thank God we were eating seafood.

Yvonne . . . Ah, here we go . . .

*

'Cameron. You all right?'

'Fine, Frank.'

'You look a bit pale.'

'Feel all right.'

'Good. Carse of Gowrie.'

'Pardon?'

'Carse of Gowrie. You know; near Perth. Guess what the spell-check prefers?'

'I give in.'

'"Curse of Gorily"!'

'Stop it, you'll make me cry.'

'There's a better one – '

'Look, Frank, I've really got to do some research,' I tell him, grabbing a notebook and heading for the library. Hell, I have to work with the guy; better to stage a tactical retreat in the face of the utterly unamusing spell-check running-jape than lose the rag and tell Frank where to stick his software.

The *Caley* still has a library, where the cuttings are kept. When you start getting into a story the first step is usually getting the cuts up, and this is where they come from. I suppose in a few years absolutely everything will be stored in databases and you'll be able to do this sort of thing from anywhere in the world by modem, but for now there's a real place you have to come to if you want to look up the more obscure reference books, the paper's pre-computer files and back issues of the *Caledonian* itself (though even these are held on microfiche rather than actual newsprint). The *Caley*'s library is housed in a single cavernous room deep inside the building, two floors below the reception area; it has no windows, you can't hear any traffic or trains and it's actually pretty restful unless the presses are running. I exchange a few words with Joanie, our head librarian, then settle in and start exploring.

Apart from confirming that Ares is the god of massacre, which may or may not have any relevance to anything, I can't find much. There's no reference to anybody or anything called Jemmel. I find myself leafing through the stuff I've already discovered about Wood, Bennet, Harrison, Aramphahal and Isaacs.

Wood and Isaacs worked for British Nuclear Fuels Ltd, Bennet for the Nuclear Inspectorate, Aramphahal was a cryptography expert at GCHQ and Harrison was a DTI guy with rumoured links to MI6. Aramphahal went down to the railway track that ran at the bottom of his garden near Gloucester, tied a rope round his neck, secured the other end to a tree on one side of the track and himself to a trunk on the opposite side, and waited for an express. Wood lived in Egremont, a small village in Cumbria; he took a bath with an electric drill. Not the battery-powered type. Bennet was found drowned in a farm cesspit near Oxford. Isaacs tied an ancient and very heavy typewriter to his feet and threw himself into Derwent Water, and Harrison sat in a hotel room in Windermere and swallowed the two liquids which react together to make cavity-wall insulation foam: choked to death. They all seemed to know each other and they all had very hazy work records with long gaps in them when nobody seemed to know where they'd been, and none of them had any close colleagues – or at least none who'd admit to being close to them.

It all looked suspicious as hell and I know people on a couple of the London broadsheets who were trying to find out if this was more than a series of coincidences, but nobody ever got anywhere. There was a question asked in Parliament and a police investigation was launched but it promptly submerged and didn't discover anything either, or if it did it was kept very quiet.

According to Mr Archer the five dead men all had one thing in common: an injection mark on the arm and/or a contusion on the back of their skull where they'd been hit. The implication was that none of them had been conscious when they'd supposedly killed themselves. Mr Archer claimed to have seen copies of the original forensic records that proved this, but I – like other hacks – had checked with the relevant local cops and coroners and discovered nothing untoward, though admittedly the old guy in Cumbria who'd done the PMs on Isaacs, Wood and Harrison had died of a coronary shortly after the police investigation began, which was either a coincidence or not but unprovable either way, especially as he'd been cremated, like the other five had.

I'm shaking my head at all this conspiracy-theory stuff and just starting to wonder whether the sensation at the back of my eyes is the start of a headache or not when the library extension rings. Joanie calls me over; it's for me.

'Cameron?' It's Frank.

'Yes,' I say through my teeth. This had better not be another spell-checkism.

'Your Mr Archer's on the phone. Shall I put him through?'

Ah-ha. 'Oh, why not?'

There are a few clicks (while I think, Shit, I can't record this call either) and then the Stephen Hawking voice: 'Mr Colley?'

'Speaking. Mr Archer?'

'I have more.'

'What?'

'Jemmel's real name still eludes me. But I know the name of the agent, the sales representative for the end-user.'

'Uh-huh?'

'His name is Smout.' He spells it for me.

'Okay,' I say, thinking the name sounds familiar. 'And –?'

'He's the one they don't talk about, in Baghdad. But – '

But, the line goes dead. There are a couple of clicks, a sequence of faraway noises like touch-tones and a faint, barely audible echo: '. . . *they don't talk about, in Baghdad. But* – '

I put the phone down, feeling just a little dizzy; still somewhat tipsily drunk from lunch, cock-sore from two heavily frustrated wanks, and mind reeling with the implications of what Mr Archer's just told me, not to mention the heavy hint that – even if I wasn't able to – somebody somewhere was recording it all.

The thing is, I know who Smout is: I did an article on him. The forgotten hostage, the man who – like Mr Archer says – they don't talk about.

Daniel Smout is – or was – a medium-ranking arms dealer who's been in prison in Baghdad for the last five years, charged at first with spying and then convicted of drug smuggling; he was sentenced to death but that was commuted to life imprisonment. HMG has always shown a marked reluctance to have anything to do with him and the last time any diplomatic representative saw him was three years ago. But there's been a persistent rumour that he was an agent for the West, working on something so sensitive that nobody involved wanted the press or anybody else to know anything about it, and the reason he's been banged up is to stop him talking, after whatever deal he was working on finally fell through.

So we're talking about a project with the code-name of the god of massacre, involving Iraq, a very secret deal and five dead men including at least three who had access to nuclear intelligence and two to physical nuclear product – plutonium – in the place where they've managed to lose more weapon-grade material than your average nuke-ambitious third-world dictator has ever had wet dreams of acquiring.

British Nuclear Fuels Limited, General Communications Head-quarters, the Nuclear Inspectorate, the Department of Trade and Industry, and an agent – a sales rep for the end-user, Mr Archer called him – in Baghdad.

Dear holy shit.

I hit the news room to show my face and just as I get to my desk my phone goes and I jump and grab it and it's Mr Archer again. I get the Pearlcorder working this time.

'Mr Colley, I cannot talk now but if I can call you at home on Friday night I hope to give you something more then.'

'What?' I say, putting a hand through my hair. At home? This is a departure. 'All right; my number – '

'I have your home number. Goodbye.'

'. . . Goodbye,' I say to the silent receiver.

'Everything all right?' Frank asks, eyebrows arched in concern.

'Fine,' I say, grinning wildly and probably unconvincingly. 'Just fine.'

Retreat to toilets again claiming dodgy ingredient in lunch-time chowder and snort some speed, then take a walk out to Salisbury Crags and sit on rock looking out over the city, smoking a spliff and thinking, Oh, Mr Archer, whatever are we involved in?

C H A P T E R

INJECTION

'7970.'

'Uh . . . hi?'

'Andy, is that you?'

'Uh, yeah. Who is this?' The voice is slow, sleepy-sounding.

'What do you mean, "Who is this?" You rang me. It's Cameron. The man who left a message on your answering-machine all of ten minutes ago.'

'Cameron . . .'

'Andy! For Christ's sake. It's me: Cameron, childhood buddy; your best fucking friend. Remember me? Wake up!' I can't believe Andy sounds so sleepy. Okay, it is midnight but Andy never used to hit the hay much before two at the earliest.

'. . . Oh, yeah, Cameron. I thought I recognised that number. How you doing?'

'I'm all right. Yourself?'

'Oh, you know; yeah. Yeah, I'm all right. I'm fine.'

'You sound stoned.'

'Well, you know.'

'Look, if it's too late, I'll call some other time – '

'No, no, that's all right.'

I'm sitting in the box room of the flat, TV on, sound off, the machine on and the *Despot* status-screen showing. It's a Friday night and I should be out enjoying myself but I'm waiting for Mr Archer to call and besides I'm frightened if I do anything too enjoyable I'll want a fag, so that's another reason for staying in and watching TV and playing games but just then I started to think about Ares and those five dead guys and the lad in the clink in Baghdad and suddenly I thought, Cameron, you are definitely dealing with something from the desk of Pearl Frotwithe here, and got scared and wanted to hear another human voice so I rang Andy because I owe him a call and I've hardly spoken to him since he was here for a weekend during the summer but got his answer-machine, there in the dark hotel only a couple of hundred kilometres away though he still sounds faint and distant. I think I can hear his voice echoing in the spaces of that quiet, cold place.

'So, been doing anything exciting?' I ask him.

'Nothing much. Bit of fishing. Been up on the hill. You know. You?'

'Oh, the usual. Fucking about. Covering the story. Hey – I've given up fags.'

'Again?'

'No, finally.'

'Right. You still fucking that married piece?'

''Fraid so,' I say (and am glad that he can't see the grimace I make when I say this). This is awkward because Andy knows Yvonne and William from our Stirling days; he used to be really friendly with William and, though they seem to have gone their separate ways since, I don't want Andy to know about me and Yvonne. I always worry he'll guess it's her.

'Yeah . . . What was her name again?'

'I don't think I ever told you,' I tell him, laughing and sitting back in the chair.

'Frightened I'll tell somebody?' he says, sounding amused.

'Yeah. I live in perpetual fear our enormous circle of mutual friends will find out.'

'Huh. But you should find yourself your own lady.'

'Yeah,' I say, imitating a stoned-out drawl. 'Gotta find ma own chick, like, ma-an.'

'Well, you never did take my advice.'

'Keep trying. One day.'

'You ever go the other way these days?'

'Eh?'

'You know, with guys.'

'What? Good grief, no. I mean . . .' I look at the receiver in my hand. 'No,' I say.

'Hey, I just wondered.'

'Why, do *you*?' I ask, and then regret the tone because it sounds like I'm at least disapproving if not actually homophobic.

'Na,' Andy says. 'Na, I don't . . . I kind of . . . you know, I lost interest in all that stuff.' He chuckles, and I imagine again that I can hear the noise echoing in the dark hotel. 'It's just, you know; old habits die hard.'

'But they do die,' I tell him. 'Don't they?'

'I guess so. Usually.'

'Shit,' I say, leaning forwards and starting *Despot* running on the screen because I need to be doing something and normally at this point I'd be reaching for the cigarettes. 'I was thinking about coming up there sometime soon and dropping in on you. You're not going *weird* on me, are you, Gould?'

'Cabin fever, man. Highland angst.' He laughs again. 'No, you come on up. Let me know, like, first, but yeah; be great to see you. Look forward to it. Been too long.'

'Well, soon then.' I use the mouse to check the game's geo-update. 'You *done* anything with that fucking mansion?'

'Eh? Oh; the place.'

'Yeah, the place.'

'No, nothing. Nothing's changed.'

'Get any of the leaks fixed?'

'No . . . Oh.'

'What?'

'Tell a lie.'

'You have fixed the leaks.'

'No, I forgot; things have changed.'

'What?'

'Well, a couple of the ceilings fell down.'

'Ah-ha.'

'Well, it's wet up here.'

'Nobody hurt, though.'

'Hurt? How could anybody be hurt? There's only me here.'

'Of course. So there's plenty of room if I want to come and stay but I should bring a golf umbrella or a waterproof sleeping bag or a tent or something, right?'

'No, there are dry rooms here, too. Come on.'

'Okay. I don't know when I'll be coming up, but, well, before the end of the year.'

'Why not come up, like, next week or something?'

'Ah,' I say, thinking. Hell, I could. It all depends what's happening with the various stories I'm involved with, but theoretically I could. I need time off; I need a change of scene. 'Okay; why not? Just for a couple of days, probably, but yeah; pencil me in.'

'Great. When you going to arrive?'

'Um, say Thursday or Friday. I'll confirm.'

'Okay.'

We talk a bit more, reliving old times, before I sign off.

I put the phone down and sit there with *Despot* running but I'm not really paying attention, I'm thinking about my old friend, the ice-child, our wunderkind, archetypal 'eighties player and then victim.

I was always jealous of him, always somehow yearning for what he had even when I knew I didn't really want it.

And Andy always seemed to be elsewhere, and more involved. Two years before I went to Stirling he'd started at St Andrew's on an Army-sponsored course and by the time the Falklands War began he was a lieutenant in the Angus Rifles. He yomped from San Carlos to Tumbledown, was wounded in a botched attack on an Argentinian position and awarded a DSO. He sent the decoration back when the officer who'd been in charge of the attack was kicked upstairs instead of being court-martialled. Andy left the Army the following year, joined a big London advertising company, did well there (he dreamt up IBM's 'Insist On Perfection – We Do' campaign and Guinness's 'Pint Taken?' slogan) and then suddenly left to start The Gadget Shop in Covent Garden. Neither Andy nor his partner – another ex-ad-agency man – had any retail experience whatsoever, but they had lots of ideas and a degree of luck, plus they used their contacts in the media (me, for one) to produce a huge free advertising campaign in the shape of articles about themselves and the business. The shop and its mail-order catalogue were an immediate success. In less than five years Andy and his partner opened another twenty branches, made a modest fortune, and then sold out for an immodest one to a big retail chain a couple of months before the stock-market crash of '88.

Andy took six months off, went on a world trip – travelling first class – toured America on a Harley, and cruised round the Caribbean in a yacht. He was on a trans-Saharan trip when his sister Clare died. After the funeral he mooched around the family estate at Strathspeld for a few months, then spent some time in London doing nothing much except seeing old friends and clubbing. After that he seemed to lose it, somehow. He became quiet, then reclusive, and bought a big, old decaying hotel in the western Highlands and retired to live there alone, practically broke apparently and still not really doing anything apart from drinking too much, getting wrecked most nights, going a bit hippy – I mean, like, man – fishing from his dinghy, walking in the hills, and just lying in bed sleeping while the hotel – in a quiet, dark village that was busy once, before they built a new road and the ferry service stopped – crumbles quietly around him.

*

'Cameron! Kirkton of Bourtie.'
　'What's that, Frank?'
　'It's a wee village near Inverurie.'
　'Where?'
　'Never mind. Guess what –?'
　'Give in.'
　'"Kickoff of Blurted"! Ha ha ha!'
　'Stop, I can't breathe.'
I've taken the weekend off and spent it detoxing myself, laying off the powder and drinking nothing more deleterious to the system than strong tea. This regime has had the added advantage of helping to keep my tobacco cravings in check. I've played *Despot* a lot, ramping my era-level into something resembling the beginnings of an industrial revolution before my nobles revolted, the barbarians from the south and west struck together, and there was a major earthquake which resulted in a plague. By the time I've finished dealing with that lot I'd dropped back to an era-level comparable to Rome after the schism with the Eastern Empire and there was even a danger that the southern barbarians weren't so barbaric after all; maybe they were more civilised than my lot. This could be shaping up to a strategic defeat. My Empire licked its wounds and I took great delight in ordering the ceremonial execution of several generals. Meanwhile my cough's getting worse and I think I'm coming down with a cold and Mr bloody Archer never did call but on the other hand the credit-card company wrote to me being nice for a change and hiked my limit so I've got a bit more money to play with.
　'Think that nice Mr Major's going to get away with the Maastricht

78

vote?' Frank asks, his big ruddy face appearing round the side of my screen like the moon from behind a hill.

'Easily,' I tell him. 'His backbenchers are a bunch of spineless brown-noses and, even if there was any danger, those asshole Lib-Dems'll save the Tories' skins as usual.'

'Care to make a small wager?' Frank twinkles.

'On the result?'

'On the size of Uncle John's majority.'

'Twenty says the margin's into double figures.'

Frank thinks about this. He nods. 'You're on.'

I've been back on naval stuff again today, interviewing people at Rosyth dockyard, which may or may not be closed soon, putting another six thousand on the local dole queue. A lot depends on whether they get the contract to service the Trident subs or not.

I'm a few hundred words into the story when the phone goes.

'Hello. Cameron Colley.'

'Cameron, oh Cameron, oh thank goodness you're there. I was sure I'd got the time difference wrong again; convinced. I really was. Cameron, it's ridiculous; I mean it really is. I'm just at my wits' end, I really am. I just can't talk to him. He's impossible. I don't know why I married him, I really don't. He's mad. I mean literally mad. I wouldn't mind so much but I think he's driving me mad, too. I wish you'd talk to him; I wish you'd say something, I really do. I mean I'm sure he won't listen to you either but, but, but . . . well, at least he might *listen* to you.'

'Hello, Mum,' I say wearily, and reach for my jacket pocket where the cigarette packet ought to be.

'Cameron, *what* am I to do? Just tell me that. Just tell me what on earth anybody's supposed to do with such an impossible man. I swear he's getting worse, he really is. I wish it was just my imagination but it isn't, I swear it isn't. He's getting worse, he really is. It's not me. It's him; I mean, my friends agree. He'll be the – '

'What's the problem, Mum?' I lift a pencil from the desk and start gnawing the end.

'My stupid husband! Haven't you been listening?'

'Yes, but what –?'

'He wants to buy a farm! A farm! At his age!'

'What, is it a sheep farm?' I ask, because she's phoning from New Zealand and I understand they aren't short of a sheep or two out there.

'No! It's for . . . angoras. Angora . . . goats or rabbits or whatever it is they get the stuff from. Cameron, he's just getting impossible. I know he's not actually your father but you seem to get on all right and I think he listens to you. Look, sweetheart, could you come out and try and talk some sense into him, because –?'

'Come out there? Mum, for goodness' sake, it's – '

'Cameron! He's driving me up the wall!'

'Look, Mum, just calm down . . .'

And so begins another of my mother's marathon phone calls in which she complains at length, depth and breadth about some potential new business venture of my stepfather's she is certain is about to ruin them both. My stepfather Bill is a rotundly fit, quietly amusing Wellingtonian who retired from the used-car business; he met my mother on a Caribbean cruise three years ago and she moved out to New Zealand a year later. They live perfectly well off pensions and investments but Bill does occasionally express a hankering for getting involved in a business again. These schemes never come to anything, and usually turn out not even to be serious commercial propositions in the first place; as a rule Bill just says something quite innocent like 'Oh look, you can pick up a fast-food franchise in Auckland for fifty thousand,' and my mother instantly assumes he plans to do just that and then lose the lot.

She gibbers on while I browse the wires on the terminal, idly scrolling Reuters and PA to check on what's happening. This is pretty much an instinctive journo-reaction, and fully compatible with the equally programmed dutiful-son 'hmms' and 'mmms' I'm feeding my mum at intervals during her monologue.

I get her off the phone eventually, reassuring her that Bill is not about to sink all their savings into some decrepit hill farm and that – as ever – the answer is to talk to him about it. I promise to come and visit next year, probably. It takes a few attempts to say goodbye – Mother is one of those people who'll wish you well, say goodbye, thank you for calling or for being there when she called, say goodbye *again* and then suddenly tear into some whole new conversational seam – but I get the final 'Goodbye' in at last and connect handset with desk unit without actually cutting her off. I sit back.

'Take it that was the mater, was it?' Frank calls jovially from the far side of my screen.

Before I can reply, the phone rings again. I jump, grabbing the device and dreading it being her again, remembering something she forgot to say.

'Yes?' I squeak.

'Hello, civilisation calling,' says a slightly plummy English voice.

'What?'

'Cameron, it's Neil. You wanted to talk.'

'Oh, Neil, hi.' Neil is an ex-colleague who went to London to work in Fleet Street when Fleet Street wasn't full of Japanese banks. His father served in the Intelligence Corps during the Korean War, where he met Sir Andrew (Our Ed and recovering coronary patient). Neil is the coolest fogy I know; smokes opium and believes utterly in the Royal Family, despises socialism and Thatcher almost equally and votes Liberal because the family always has since Liberals were called Whigs. Shoots stags and hooks salmon. Hurtles down the Cresta Run each year. Drives a Bentley S2. They could have invented the word 'urbane' just for him. These days he freelances in Intelligence matters, occasionally for the broadsheets though mostly for corporate clients. 'How are you?' I say, frowning towards my screen. Just then, however, Frank stands up and saunters off, Biro between his teeth.

'Well, and busy,' Neil drawls. 'What can I do for you?'

'You can tell me what you found out about those five guys who popped their clogs in such suspicious circumstances between '86

81

and '88. You know; the guys who all have connections with Sellascale or Winfield or Dun-Nukin' or whatever they're calling it these days.'

There is a pause. 'Oh,' Neil says, and I can hear him lighting a cigarette. My mouth waters. *You lucky bastard.* '*That* old thing.'

'Yeah,' I say, putting my feet up on the desk. 'That old thing that reads like a spy novel and nobody ever came up with a decent explanation for.'

'No case to answer, boy wonder,' he sighs. 'An unfortunate sequence of coincidences.'

'Sounds like a Long Involved Explanation. No?'

Neil laughs, recalling our acronymic private code from the year we worked together. 'No; it's the Totally Reliable Utterly Trustworthy . . . damn, what was the last word?'

'Hint,' I tell him, grinning. 'We never did come up with a better alternative.'

'Indeed. Well, that's what it is; a Fucking Actualité, Cameron, Tovarisch.'

'You serious?' I say, trying not to laugh. 'All these guys who just happened to be connected with BNFL or GCHQ or Military Intelligence and just happened to croak violently within twenty months of each other? I mean, really?'

'Cameron, I do realise your Menshevik soul cries out for there to be a perfectly irrational fascist conspiracy behind all this, but the boring truth is that there isn't. Or, if there is, it's far, *far* too well run for it to be the work of any intelligence service *I've* ever encountered. There's never been any reliable hint it was anybody on our side; Mossad – arguably the only people capable of carrying out such a consistently successful campaign without leaving the scene scattered with their agency-issue trench-coats sporting name, rank and serial number sewn into the collars – had no discernible motive, and we can be even more sure of our friends in Moscow given that, since the unfortunate demise of the Workers' State, ex-KGB bods have been positively falling over each other in the

82

rush to beat the breast and confess their past sins, and not one of them has even mentioned those five deceased sons of Cumbria and environs.'

'Six, if you count the doc who did the PMs on the three Cumbrian stiffs.'

Neil sighs. 'Even so.'

I'm thinking. This could be a fairly important decision I'm making here. Do I tell Neil about Mr Archer and Daniel Smout? Or do I keep quiet about it? Christ, this story could just be the biggest fucking thing since Watergate; a plot – if I'm reading the hints right – involving the West, or just Her Majesty's Government, or at the very least a bunch of people who were in positions to pull it off, to arm our once-staunch-ally-against-the-fiendish-Mullahs – now number-one hate figure – Saddam Hussein with nukes, back when the Iran-Iraq war wasn't all going his way.

'You know,' Neil sighs again, 'I have the most terrible feeling I'm going to regret asking this question, but what leads you to make this enquiry, unless it's the simple explanation that news of these five sad deaths has only just arrived in Caledonia?'

'Well,' I say, playing with the telephone cord.

'What?' Neil says, in that why-are-you-wasting-my-valuable-time? voice.

'I've had a call from somebody who claims to know about this who's saying that there's another couple of names involved.'

'And who would they be?'

'I've only got one of the names so far.' I take a deep breath. I'll do a Mr Archer; I'll give him it a bit at a time. 'Smout,' I tell Neil. 'Daniel Smout. Our man in Baghdad.'

Neil is silent for a few seconds. Then I hear him exhale. 'Smout.' A pause. 'I see.' Another pause. 'So,' he says, slowly and thoughtfully, 'if Iraq was involved, it's not impossible Mossad *would* take an interest. Though of course one of our serial self-terminators was himself of the Semitic persuasion . . .'

'So was Vanunu.'

'Indeed. Hmm. Interesting. You do realise, though, that your informant is probably a crank.'

'Probably.'

'Have they been reliable before?'

'No; new source, as far as I can tell. And all they've come up with is a sequence of names. So it could easily be a crank. Very easily. In fact, probably. I mean, wouldn't you say? Don't you think it probably is?' I'm gibbering. I suddenly feel rather stupid and a little nervous.

'You said there was a sixth name,' Neil says calmly. 'Any hints there?'

'Well, I've got what my guy says is a code-name for him.'

'And that is?' Neil says patiently.

'Well, ah . . .'

'Cameron. I swear I shan't try to *scoop* you, if that's what you're worried about.'

'Of course not,' I say. 'I know that. It's just that . . . it could be nothing.'

'Very possibly, but – '

'Look, Neil, I'd like to talk to somebody.'

'How do you mean?'

'Somebody in the business; you know.'

'"Somebody in the business",' Neil says evenly.

Christ, I wish I had a cigarette. 'Yeah,' I say. 'Somebody in the business; somebody in the service. Somebody who'll look me in the eye and tell me MI6 or whoever had got nothing to do with all this; somebody I can give this to.'

'Hmm.'

I let him think for a bit. Eventually, Neil says, 'Well, there are always people one can talk to, certainly. Look, I'll suggest this to some contacts I have. See what their reaction is. But I know that, if I do suggest it, before they decide what to do they'll want to know who it is they're dealing with; they'll want to know your name.'

'I thought they might. That's okay; you can tell them.'

'Right you are, then. I'll report back what the reaction is, fair enough?'

'Fair enough.'

'Good. To tell the truth, I'll be fairly interested in seeing it myself. Assuming this isn't a crank we're dealing with.'

'Okay,' I say, looking over my screen and trying to peer over my bookcase, wondering who I can scrounge a fag off. 'Well, that's good of you, Neil. I appreciate this.'

'Not at all. Now, when are you next coming up to town, or do you Picts have to apply for a travel warrant or something?'

*

You arrive at Mr Oliver's home in Leyton at nine, as agreed when you saw him in his shop in Soho during the afternoon. He will have had time to get back from the shop, have his evening meal, watch one of his favourite soap operas and take a shower. The maisonette is part of a brick-built terrace over a row of shops, restaurants and offices. You press the entryphone button.

'Hello?'

'Mr Oliver? It's Mr Mellin here. Mr Mellin. From this afternoon?'

'Yeah. Right.' The door buzzes.

Inside, behind the sturdy, heavily secured door, the stairwell is richly carpeted and the walls are decorated with expensive Regency-style wallpaper. Ornately framed Victorian landscape paintings look down from the stairwell walls. Mr Oliver appears at the top of the stairs.

He is a plump little man with sallow skin and very black hair you suspect is dyed. He wears a cashmere cardigan over his waistcoat and trousers. His shirt is raw silk. Cravat. Slippers. He smells strongly of *Polo*.

'Good evening,' you say.

'Yeah, hello.' The second word actually sounds more like 'allow' but you know what he means. He stands back as you reach the top of the stairs, and puts out one pudgy hand while looking you up and down. You wish the light – from a miniature chandelier in the hall – was a little less bright. The moustache prickles under your nose. You shake hands. Mr Oliver's grip is damp, quite strong. His gaze drops to the fat briefcase you're holding. He waves one hand. 'Come in.'

The lounge is a little ostentatious; Mr Oliver favours thick white rugs, black leather furniture, chrome-and-glass tables, and a TV, video and hi-fi unit which takes up most of one wall.

'Sit down. Like a drink?' Mr Oliver says. It actually sounds like 'Sidahn, loy-a dring?', but again you understand.

You sit on the edge of a leather seat, hunched up and looking nervous, the briefcase on your knees. You're wearing a cheap suit and you still have your gloves on.

'Um, well, ah, yes, please,' you say, trying to sound nervous and unsure of yourself. Of course you are nervous, but not in the way you're implying.

Mr Oliver goes to a chrome-and-smoked-glass drinks cabinet. 'What would you like?'

'Um, do you have any orange juice?'

Mr Oliver looks at you. 'Orange juice,' he says, and bends to look in a small fridge set into the drinks cabinet.

He fixes himself a vodka and Coke and sits down on the couch to your left. You think he's looking at you slightly strangely and you worry that perhaps your disguise isn't fooling him. You cough nervously.

'So, Mr Mellin,' he says. 'What is it you've got for me?'

'Well,' you say, looking round. You watched the place all through the afternoon and you're fairly sure there's nobody else in here, but you're not absolutely certain. 'As I said, um, in the shop, it's something a bit . . . a bit special. Something I understand there is a demand for.'

'What sort of special we talking here?'

'W-w-w-well, well it's of a, shall we say, um, a violent nature.

86

Quite a violent nature, in fact. And involves, ah . . . and involves, ah, ch-ch-ch-children. I was told that you . . . you can, you can . . . that you deal in that sort of, um, item.'

Mr Oliver purses his lips. 'Well, you'd have to be a bit of an idiot to just tell people that, wouldn't you? I mean, you wouldn't want to confess to something like that to a stranger, know what I mean?'

'Oh,' you say, sounding crestfallen. 'You mean you don't – '

'Na, I'm not saying nothing, am I? I'm just saying you got to be careful, know what I mean?'

'Ah,' you say, nodding. 'Yes. Yes, of course. Of course one does have to be . . . careful. I see. I see what you mean.'

'Why don't you show me what you've brought, eh? We'll take a little look and then we'll see, eh?'

'Yes; yes, right. Of course. Ah, right; what I've brought, um, well, it's just part of it, to show you, but I think it amply demonstrates – '

'Video, yeah?'

'Yes, that's correct. On video.' You unclip the catches on the briefcase, take out a plain VHS60 cassette and put the briefcase on the floor to one side as you stand up, handing the video to him.

'Ta.' He takes it and goes to the video machine. You remain standing.

The cassette won't load properly; you can hear the VCR mechanism whining. Mr Oliver bends to look more closely at the machine. You come up behind him.

'Um, is there a problem?' you ask.

'Yeah; doesn't seem to be – '

The cassette will not load because you glued the hinged tape-cover down. Mr Oliver does not get to complete his sentence; you cosh him across the back of the head. However, he had started to move his head as you swung at him, and you only land a glancing blow.

He falls to one side, one hand trying to find purchase on the wall of hi-fi components, shifting the CD player and amp back on their shelves. 'What –?' he says. You smack the cosh hard into his face, breaking his nose, then stamp on his crotch as he falls back. He doubles up on the floor, lying on his side, snorting and gasping.

You're staring wildly round the room waiting for some burly minder to come charging in swinging a baseball bat, your other hand in the pocket of your suit where the Browning is, but nobody appears. You lean forward and cosh Mr Oliver across the back of the head. He goes limp.

You handcuff his arms behind his back and go to the briefcase to get the things you will need.

Once you have everything ready and the camcorder is set up you have to wait for him to wake up. You go down to the street door and lock and chain it, then pad round the maisonette making quite sure there is nobody else in.

Mr Oliver's bedroom is all wood, brass, furs and red velvet. A glass cabinet houses a militaria collection, specialising in the Waffen SS. A bookcase holds numerous books about Nazi Germany and Hitler. Mr Oliver's private videos are stored in a repro teak-and-walnut wardrobe. There is a large combination floor-safe under the Persian carpet.

You bring what looks like a representative selection of the videos down to the lounge where Mr Oliver is sitting, still unconscious and sagging slightly, handcuffed and tied in a chrome-and-leather chair you brought down from the second bedroom. You have gagged him with a sock and a silk scarf you brought from his bedroom. His right arm is firmly tied to the leather-padded arm of the chair. You have removed his cardigan and rolled his shirt sleeve up.

While you wait for Mr Oliver to regain consciousness you look at the videos you brought down from the bedroom.

Some feature the gang-buggerings of children; mostly male and mostly Asian or South American. Others show women being mounted by donkeys and other animals, in what looks like a prison. The men watching all have moustaches and wear military dress. These look like second- or third-generation recordings and the definition is not quite precise enough for you to be sure, but you think those might be Iraqi army uniforms. There are a couple of videos which may come from the same source and show people – men, women, children – being tortured with irons, hair-driers, curling tongs and so on. There is no actual snuff material here, but you wonder what the floor-safe you discovered contains.

Mr Oliver starts to moan behind his gag and you put on your gorilla mask. You wait for his eyes to open then start the little Sony camcorder running. You take the gas cylinder from the briefcase, turn the valve on and suck.

'Mr Oliver,' you say, in a high, absurdly babyish voice. 'Welcome back.'

He stares wide-eyed at you, then at the video camera, sitting on its miniature tripod on the coffee table.

You take another suck on the helium. 'You're going to star in your own video, isn't that funny?'

He shakes in the seat, roaring behind the gag. You go to the briefcase and bring out a wide-mouthed medicine bottle. Cling-film over the top of it is secured with elastic bands. You shake the bottle, then lift the syringe from the briefcase.

Mr Oliver screams when he sees these.

You suck on the helium again, then hold the dumpy medicine bottle up and show him the thick-looking off-white liquid inside. 'Can you guess what this is?' you ask him in the voice of a manic baby.

The syringe is a big mother; not like those dinky little disposable plastic things medics and junkies use. This device is made from stainless steel and glass; it has two hook-shaped finger-grips on either side of the barrel and it holds a fifth of a litre. You hold the medicine bottle sealed with cling-film upside down and slip the slanted tip of the big syringe needle into the clotted-cream-coloured liquid inside the bottle. Mr Oliver is still screaming behind the gag.

You suck on the gas again and tell him what you're going to do to him.

His muffled screams rise in pitch until they sound like he's been breathing helium too.

*

The next day I scrounge a Lambert & Butler off Rose in the Foreign News section, smoke it at my desk and get a real hit off it, then feel disgusted with myself and vow that's the last one I'm going to smoke. I really mean it this time and decide to reward myself by using my increased credit-card limit to buy myself something. The car needs a service, I could use a new suit and the carpet in the flat is getting threadbare, but as candidates for expenditure none of those has very high self-reward status; minimal feel-good factors there. My mouth goes a little dry as I sit staring at the whisky story – which I'm reworking very slowly – and think of what I could buy with the extra dosh. Dosh/Tosh. Hmm.

I pull open a drawer and dig out a computer magazine. Five hundred glossy full-colour pages plus a free software disk for less than two quid. It's the November issue but the prices might be out of date by now; usually with computers they go down but this time they might have gone up because, now we're out of the ERM and the pound's sinking against the dollar, the price of components bought abroad is sure to increase.

I leaf through, looking at the lap-top adverts.

Shit, I can afford one of these; I can afford a *colour* one at last, one that'll play *Despot*. Especially as I can write it off against tax; I'll use it for work, after all. And even more especially as I'm giving up smoking; that's twenty quid a week at least I'll save, even if I don't stop doing speed. The price of 386 lap-tops has fallen quickly recently, and colour screens are no longer luxuries in the portable market. Yo!

Before the more sensible bits of my brain can start coming up with convincing arguments for doing anything else with the money, I call up a manufacturer in Cumbernauld I've heard good things about and talk to one of the salespeople. I discuss what I want with him and we agree I might as well go for a 486. This means spending a little more money than I'd been thinking of, but it'll be worth it in the end. A decent-sized hard disk is a necessity too, and a spare battery, naturally. Plus I'll need cabling to transfer data between the PC at home and the lap-top. And of course for a little extra I can have a removable hard disk, which not only makes my data more secure but allows for easy up-grading of the disk unit if it ever proves too small. This is a quality machine after all and I won't need to change it for years. It's worth the little extra to future-proof it. They don't do part-exchange but the salesman can't imagine me having any problems selling a Toshiba, even an old one; they do have a good name, after all.

We settle on the exact specification. They have one in stock. I can pick it up today, tomorrow, whenever, or they can deliver within forty-eight hours for a tenner.

I decide I'll go and get it. I give them my credit-card number for the deposit and agree to show up at the factory within the next couple of hours. I'll have to buy the blighter on credit; the manufacturers have a deal with a financing company that sounds reasonable. (I'm close to the limit of my bank overdraft, even though it's nearly time for my salary to lift my bank account briefly into the black before it settles comfortably and familiarly back into the red for the rest of the month.) There are bills to pay but they can wait.

I'm so excited I finish the whisky story in half an hour.

'Right, Frank,' I tell him, pulling on my jacket. 'I'm off to Cumbernauld.'

'Ah, you mean Cumbered.'

'What?'

'Spell-check; "Cumbered". Ha ha.'

'Oh yeah; ha ha.'

'Will we be seeing you later?'

'Doubtful.'

91

*

I circle the room, breathing quick and deep. She swivels, following me, facing me, her body glistening. I'm breathing hard too; chest heaving, hands out in front of me, feet squeaking on the tiles. I'm conscious of my cock swinging between my legs. She gives a half-grunt, half laugh, and jumps towards the bath. I catch her ankle as her leap turns into a feint and she darts the other way, hauling the door open. Her oiled skin slides through my fingers as I stagger and almost fall into the jacuzzi, banging a knee on its tiled platform while she disappears through the doorway, slamming the door behind her. I quickly rub my knee where I banged it, then pull the door open and race through the dressing room to the dimly lit bedroom. No sign. I stand there, rubbing my knee, breathing through my mouth to make less noise so that I'll hear her. The bed is king-size, still rumpled, its mahogany foot- and headboards shining lustrously in the glow from the concealed lighting behind the bedside cabinets and shelving system. I pad over to the bedside, glance back to the dressing-room door, then squat slowly, feeling my prick slide caught between my calves with a delicious, anticipatory thrill. I pull up the covers fallen over the side of the bed and glance quickly underneath.

There's a hint of sudden noise behind me and I start to turn and rise (thinking, She *was* in the dressing-room wardrobe), but it's too late. She crashes into my back and side, knocking the wind out of me and bowling me over onto the bed, landing me on my face on the creased black satin sheets and trapping my dick painfully back between my thighs; before I can do much she's straddling me; slim, hard legs slipping oiled over my flanks while her taut little bum crunches down into the middle of my back, winding me further. She grabs my right arm, twists it until I shout – breathlessly – in pain and hauls it up my back towards my neck, pinning it there, about a centimetre below where it would hurt unbearably, and only a few more further down from where the humerus would break.

Serves me right for playing this sort of game with a woman who ran a self-defence course for female students, still regularly thrashes me at squash with technique or power depending on what sort of mood she's in, and does serious weights. I slap the slick black sheets with my other hand.

'All right. You win.'

She grunts, then pushes my arm that extra centimetre until I yelp in pain. 'I said all right!' I shout. 'I'll do anything!'

She lets go, rolls off me and lies there beside me, panting, laughing through each breath, her breasts rising and falling and jiggling all at once and her flat belly gently shaking. I lever myself up and throw myself on top of her but she's rolling away and I thump onto the sheets as she pulls one leg from beneath me and stands, arms on her hips at the side of the bed, looking down at me. Her feet are planted a metre apart and I stare at her black V of pubic hair, moaning softly.

'Patience,' she says, taking a deeper breath and sliding a hand through her short, slicked hair. She turns and moves off across the creamy pile of the carpet, balanced on the balls of her feet like a dancer. She reaches, stretching, up to a hinged cupboard above a built-in wardrobe, and I moan dramatically again, watching the muscles in her calves and buttocks clench and the dimples in the small of her back hollow and lengthen and the shadow of her breasts move across the polished ash of the wardrobe doors to one side while her reflection extends, naked and achingly beautiful in the mirrors on the other side. She's on her toes, feeling inside the cupboard. The fleshy mound of her sex shows dark between her legs, a glimpsed, precious, succulent fruit. I collapse back on the bed, unable to bear it.

Ten minutes later I'm kneeling on the bed, stretched backwards with my legs apart and my wrists tied to my ankles with silk scarves and my cock so hard it's sore, sticking way out in front of me, totally rampant but bizarrely vulnerable too and I'm breathing hard and my muscles are aching and I feel so close to coming if there's a *draught* across my cock that'll probably be enough and she pulls the last, unnecessary scarf tight and then slides round past me, in front of me, so leanly voluptuous, fit and hard and moist and soft together I'm past moaning any more and just have to laugh, casting my gaze to the ceiling and feeling the engorged weight of my cock waggle as I laugh and then she slips off the bed, grabs the remote control and announces she's going to watch *Eldorado* and I'm bellowing and she's laughing as the Trinitron clicks on and she turns the sound up to drown me out and I'm left here in what is starting to become some pain while she sits lotus-like, giggling now and again and pretending to be involved in this crap soap opera and I have to try and work my way back up the bed, waddling painfully on my knees and ankles until I finally make the metre or so back to the pillows and the headboard so at least I can support my aching shoulders and take some weight off, well, just about every other muscle in my body, it feels like.

Trapped there watching this shit and after five minutes even my cock is giving up, just starting to droop but then she turns and gives it a quick flicking lick with her tongue and I beg her to suck me off but she just turns away and watches the TV on the other side of the room again, and I struggle and strain but she's tied me too tight and my knees are really sore now and I try to reason with her, and say, 'Look, this really is starting to hurt,' but she ignores me apart from checking on the state of my erection every few minutes and giving me quick, incredibly hot and frustrating half-licks, half-sucks every now and again, or a single saliva-moistened finger-and-thumb flick and I'm roaring in frustration and desire and pain in about equal and immense amounts and finally, finally, thank fuck the Anglo-Spanish crap ends and the tune tinkles and the credits roll and she clicks the box to MTV and it's *still* not over! The teasing, tantalising bitch gets off the bed and goes out the door and I'm so stunned I can't speak; I'm left there with my mouth hanging open and my cock sticking out and I'm so fucking angry I'm looking from side to side at the bedside units to see what I can roll over and smash to produce an edge I can

94

cut the scarves on, and I'm just deciding on the crystal glass on her side that still holds some dark dregs of Rioja when she comes back again, carrying a glittering glass in one hand and a steaming mug in the other and smirking, and I know what she's going to do and I say, 'No, please; just let me go; my legs, my arms, my knees; I may never walk again, please, please, please,' but it doesn't do any good; she kneels in front of me and puts the glass to her lips and slips an ice cube into her mouth, looking at me and grinning and then lowering her mouth onto my cock.

Then it's the hot coffee from the mug but only briefly, it's not enough; then the ice again, then the coffee then the ice and I'm crying now, actually crying with pain and lust and the unbearable frustration of it, crying and begging; pleading with her to stop until finally she spits the last ice cube out and puts the glass and the mug down beside the wine glass and comes forward and straddles me, slipping me quickly, easily deep inside her and she feels hotter than the coffee, hot enough to scald, hot enough to burn and I give a small, shocked 'Ah!' as she moves up and down on me and puts her fingers to my neck and the other hand down behind her to my balls and suddenly I'm coming, still crying and sobbing now as the spasms shake me and she goes suddenly very still, whispering 'Baby, baby' to me as I jerk and pump and the motions make the pain in my legs and arms and joints worse and better at the same time.

The scarves have gone too tight to undo; she has to cut them with the gleaming weight of the hunting knife she keeps under her side of the mattress in case any rapist ever breaks in.

I lie cradled in her arms, panting, spent, exhausted, the agony in my muscles and bones and sockets gradually easing and the tears on my face drying and she says softly,

'How was that?' and I whisper,

'Fucking brilliant.'

*

Next morning I arrive at the paper bright and early, toting my new machine, all happy after my sprint through to Cumbernauld via the building society and back and then my evening with Y (she was disappointingly unimpressed with the super-sexy new machine, but I guess not everybody's into computers and fuck it, given the choice of it or her on my lap I'd take her) after which I returned to Cheyne Street – Y likes me to leave before it gets too late, worried that her neighbours in the exec development will talk. I was so tired that even though I was just dying to get the new lap-top going and make sure *Despot* runs all right (portable at last! The screaming orgasmic joy of it!) I fell asleep on the couch instead and somehow transferred myself to the bed at some point and so had a good night's sleep for a change. I get up with the dawn or not long after anyway, make it into the office slightly early for once and Frank's there in reception when I come in and I'm about to show off the new machine when he looks worriedly at me, draws me to one side away from the receptionists' desk and the small-ads and back-issues counter until we're standing in a corner and says, 'Cameron, Eddie wants to see you. He's got a couple of policemen in with him.'

'What's this?' I ask, grinning. 'Fettesgate again?' Fettesgate is a minor scandal involving the Lothian police force: a gay guy who felt he was being victimised broke into the cop HQ out at Fettes (with embarrassing ease) and found and copied lots of sensitive papers.

'No,' Frank says. 'Nothing to do with that, apparently. They're asking for you.'

'Me?'

'Yes; you, quite specifically.'

'Know their names?'

'No.'

'Hmm.' I know quite a few cops, some fairly high up, just like I know lawyers, advocates, doctors, politicians, civil servants and people in a variety of agencies. No big deal. 'Can't imagine why.' I shrug. 'What's it about, any idea?'

Frank looks uncomfortable. He glances at the commissionaire

behind his desk, nearby, and turns away from him. He leans his head close to mine and says quietly, 'Well, Morag overheard something of what they were saying on the intercom . . .'

I put my hand over my mouth and do a stage-snigger. I *thought* Eddie's secretary eavesdropped on him. I didn't know until now she confided in Frank.

'Cameron,' Frank says, dropping his voice still further. 'Apparently they're investigating some *murders*.'

C H A P T E R

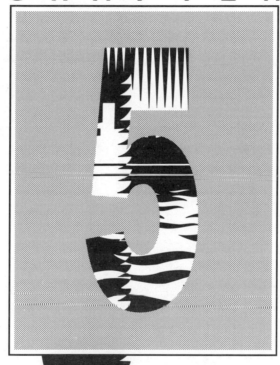

NAKED FLAME

The Mercedes estate comes grumbling down the drive, splashing in dark puddles under the dripping trees. The car draws up by the blank gable end of the dark cottage. As the headlights are switched off, you turn the night sight on. He gets out of the car carrying a large leather flight bag and walks to the front of the cottage. He is balding and of medium build, though with a paunch and rather a fat face. You watch him unlock the front door to the cottage. He enters, turning on the hall light and closing the door. You hear the alarm delay beep briefly before he turns it off. The rain patters down in front of you, and heavier drops from the overhanging trees plop all around. A light comes on at the back of the cottage, in the kitchen.

You give him a couple of minutes while you put the night sight away and take out a pair of thick, wire-rimmed glasses, then you go to the front porch, put the glasses on and bang urgently on the solid wooden door.

You take the bottle and the sanitary towel from your pocket, slip the towel's loops over your fingers, soak the towel with the liquid in the bottle, then put the bottle away again, holding the reeking towel closed in your fist.

You hammer on the door again.

'Sir Rufus!' you call when you hear noise behind the door. 'Sir Rufus! Ivor Owen here, from down the road!' You are modestly pleased with your gruff Welsh accent. 'Quick, Sir Rufus; it's your car!'

You hear an English voice saying, 'What!' and then a bolt slides. You let the door open. Mr Carter is holding a shotgun, but it is pointing downwards. You can't tell whether he has his finger inside the trigger guard or not but you have no choice; you dart forward, punching him hard in the stomach. He goes 'Oof!' and starts to fold at the waist and knees. The gun drops from his hand as you jump to one side and clamp the sanitary towel over his mouth, then get behind him and lock your other arm round his neck. He manages to fling you back against one wall and your glasses come off but you hold onto him. He is still winded, struggling for breath, and the ether works quickly. He sags and collapses. You go with him to the floor, keeping the towel tight over his face. He moves once more, weakly, then goes still.

The keys to the cottage are in his trouser pockets. You put him in the recovery position and go to the door. You put out the hall light, take the night sight from your day-pack and look around. It looks peaceful enough. You close the door and lock it but leave the alarm system off. You take off your moustache and wig, pick up the cracked glasses from the floor and stuff them all in the day-pack. From it you take your black ski balaclava and slip it on.

You have a look in the kitchen but it's a slate floor. You drag him into the living room, put more ether on the towel and leave it over his face, then you roll back the carpet. You take the nail gun out of the day-pack and use it to nail him to the floor through his clothes, pinning each leg of his trousers and arm of his jacket and shirt to the thick boards in five or six places. It's a noisy business. You take the sanitary towel off his face and pry his mouth open with the nail gun, to make sure he hasn't swallowed his tongue. You turn his face to the side.

Sir Rufus Caius St Leger Carter, to give him his full, wonderfully English title, dribbles saliva onto the dusty boards.

You take off one of his shoes and a sock, then shove the balled sock into his mouth and seal his lips with masking-tape. You hesitate, then you put the barrel of the nail gun onto the right cuff of his jacket, over the point where his upper wrist joins the bones of the arm; the place to put nails where they can't be torn out. You're not sure whether to do this or not; the nails through his clothes will hold him, trapped like an Armani-suited Gulliver; you don't need the nails through his arms, and it seems more elegant to use the nail gun and yet not do the obvious thing. You shake your head and put the nail gun aside.

He moans, then his eyes open slowly and he sees you and tries to move but can't. He screams down his nose. You are becoming familiar with men making this noise now.

You leave him shaking and screaming and go through to the store room off the kitchen, where there are a couple of calor-gas cylinders near the back door. One bottle is empty, waiting to be picked up after running the cottage's stove and central-heating system. The other cylinder feels full. You roll its chilly bulk through to where Sir Rufus is still making a racket on the living-room floor. He's sweating despite the chill. A corner of the tape over his mouth has come off. He's trying to shout something but you can't tell what it is.

You pull an easy chair over to where he can see it, near the cold, dark stone hearth. You roll the calor-gas bottle over to the chair, then haul the cylinder up and onto the chair until it rolls down the arms, resting against the back of the seat. The chair threatens to tip over backwards and you push it against the stones and slates of the fireplace so it can't move. Sir Rufus is still trying to work the gag off. You look in your day-pack and pull out the valve with the length of rubber pipe and the

103

brass nozzle attached. You secure it to the top of the calor-gas bottle.

There is a hacking, spitting noise from behind you. 'Look! For Christ's sake! What is this? Stop! I'm rich! I can – '

You go over to him, plant one foot on his head and soak the sanitary towel again.

'Ah! Look, I can get money! Christ! No –!'

You clamp the towel over his face again. He struggles for a while before he goes limp. You put another, bigger strip of tape across his mouth.

It takes a while to get the nozzle set just so on the seat of the easy chair. Then, as you are testing the gas-flow, you hear a whistling, retching noise, and turn in time to see twin streams of vomit spurting from Sir Rufus's nostrils and spattering over the floorboards.

'Shit,' you say, and go quickly over to him, tearing the tape off his mouth.

He gasps and splutters, almost choking. More of the vomit comes up, rolling out of his mouth and onto the floor. You smell garlic. He coughs some more, then breathes more easily.

When you are sure he isn't going to drown on his vomit and he's starting to make semi-comprehensible noises again, you hold the wispy hair at the back of his head and wind a length of tape right round his head a couple of times, sealing his mouth again.

You put your stuff away in the day-pack as he lies there, moving weakly then more powerfully, the noises coming down his nose faint, then strong; moans followed by what would be shouts if he could open his mouth.

You squat down by the side of the easy chair, where the rubber hose from the calor-gas bottle loops down and round and up before it ends in the brass nozzle. Sitting on the cushion of the easy chair, looking black and incongruous, is the iron grate from the living-room fire. You have tied the brass nozzle to the grate with wire, pointing it up at the scuffed red wall of the gas cylinder about fifteen centimetres above.

104

Sir Rufus's head is about a metre and a half from the easy chair. He has a good view of it.

'Well, Sir Rufus,' you say, tugging a pretend forelock and still imitating the sing-song of a Welsh accent. You tap the wall of the cylinder. 'I suppose you know what a blevey is, don't you?'

His eyes look like they're coming out of their sockets. His voice, coming down his nose, sounds strangled.

'Of course you do,' you say, smiling behind the mask and nodding. 'That ship; that LPG carrier of yours – well, your company's – did just that in the Bombay docks, didn't it?' You nod again; a sort of floating, bobbing nod you somehow associate with the Welsh. 'Thousand dead, wasn't it? Mind you, they're only Indians, eh? Still fighting it in the courts, are you? Shame these things always take so long really, isn't it? Of course, altering the corporate structure like that, making the ship the only asset of the company; that makes life a bit easier for you, doesn't it? Not nearly so much compensation to fork out, I suppose?'

He coughs down his nose, then sneezes and seems to be trying to shout something.

'Terrifying things, bleveys, they say,' you tell him, shaking your head. 'Ever wondered what one looks like close up, have you?' You nod again. 'I know I have. Well,' – you turn and pat the cold, fat shoulder of the gas cylinder – 'here's one I prepared earlier.'

You turn the knurled wheel on the valve. The gas hisses gently. You take a cigarette lighter from your pocket and hold it to the mouth of the little brass nozzle tied to the grate. You flick the lighter and the gas ignites, a small flickering yellow and blue flame blowing up towards the gas cylinder.

'Oh,' you say. 'That looks a bit tentative, wouldn't you say, Sir Rufus? You could be here all night!' You turn the valve wheel slowly until the jet is roaring and the fierce yellow-blue flame licks around the curved cylinder wall. 'That's better.' Sir Rufus is screaming quite hard now and his face is very red. You hope he doesn't have a heart attack before the blevey. That would be . . . well, just what you'd expect from a man like Sir Rufus: getting out of something through a loophole. Sadly, you can't hang around to make sure.

You take a quick look from the front door with the night sight, your hands shaking as you listen to the distant roaring sound coming from the living room (even though you know it will take a while yet), and the faint, almost childish screams.

It's still raining. You close the door and lock it and walk quickly off into the night.

Five minutes later, as you're about to start the bike and beginning to worry that it hasn't worked, that he's got free somehow, or the gas jet has blown itself out, or his mistress got here earlier than expected and had a key, or something else has gone wrong, the explosion bursts suddenly, fabulously into the night, lighting up the whole rain-swept valley and the clouds above and producing a small mushroom cloud of incandescent gas, climbing and rolling into the darkness. You start the engine with the noise still rumbling down between the Welsh hills.

*

'Right, Mr Colley, I'd better tell you what's happening here.'

'Suits me,' I say, with only slightly more bravado than I feel.

Detective Inspector McDunn and Detective Sergeant Flavell are sitting across the boardroom table from me. The *Caley*'s boardroom is directly above the editor's office, set into the slope of the building's castellated roof. It's an impressively raftered room containing a massive, venerable-looking table and seats that look like smaller versions of the one in the Ed's office. The walls are oak panels; they support dully formal paintings of former editors, stern faces glaring down to remind you this is one of the oldest newspapers in the world. Being a floor higher than the Ed's office, the view is even better but, despite the fact I haven't visited here before, I'm not spending too much time looking out the window.

The DI is a dark, heavy-set man with an accent that sounds

half Glaswegian and half English. He wears a dark suit and he's carrying a black coat. Young Sergeant Flavell, who's in charge of a cheap-looking briefcase, looks a little like Richard Gere with a thin moustache but spoils the effect by wearing a blue quilted anorak over his suit. Still, at least he's warm. I left my jacket hanging over the back of my seat in the news room and it's cold up here. Eddie suggested we used the boardroom after I went to his office, was introduced to the two cops and told they wanted a word with me.

The DI looks round the room. 'I suppose it's all right to smoke in here?' he asks me.

'I suppose so.'

Sergeant Flavell spots an ashtray on a window-ledge and goes to get it. The inspector lights a B&H. 'Smoke?' he asks me, seeing me watching him.

I shake my head. 'No, thanks.'

'Right, Mr Colley,' Inspector McDunn says in a getting-down-to-business sort of way. 'We're carrying out an investigation into a number of serious assaults and murders, plus related crimes. We think you might be able to help and we'd like to ask you a few questions, if you don't mind.'

'Not at all,' I say, breathing deeply as the cloud of smoke from McDunn's cigarette rolls over the table towards me. Smells good.

'Sergeant, could you . . .?' McDunn says.

The sergeant takes an A4 manila envelope from his briefcase and hands it to the inspector, who takes out a single sheet of paper. He hands it over to me. 'I assume you recognise this.'

It's a photocopy of a piece of TV criticism I did for the paper about fifteen months ago. Not exactly my speciality, but the regular guy had come down with an eye infection and I welcomed the opportunity to editorialise a bit. 'Yeah, I wrote this,' I say, grinning. Hell, my name's at the top of the piece, beside the headline RADICAL EQUALISER?

Inspector McDunn smiles thinly. I read the piece while the boys in blue – well, black and blue – look on.

As I read, and remember, I feel the hairs on the back of my neck prickle. This hasn't happened for twenty years or so.

I hand it back. 'So?' I ask.

The inspector looks at the A4 sheet for a moment.

'"Perhaps,"' he quotes from it, '"somebody should make one of these programmes for those of us who're fed up seeing the usual suspects get theirs (corrupt landlords, substance-abusing youths and of course the inevitable drug dealers; reprehensible villains all, no doubt, but too predictable, too *safe*) and introduce a Real Avenger, a Radical Equaliser who'll take on some alternative hate-figures. Somebody who'll give people like James Anderton, Judge Jamieson and Sir Toby Bissett a taste of their own medicine, somebody who'll attack the asset strippers and the arms smugglers (ministers of HMG included – listening, Mr Persimmon?); somebody who'll stand up against the tycoons who put their profits before others' safety, like Sir Rufus Carter; somebody who'll punish the captains of industry who parrot that time-honoured phrase about their shareholders' interests coming first as they close down *profitable* factories and throw thousands out of work, just so that their already comfortable investors in the Home Counties and Marbella can make that little bit extra that always comes in *so* handy darling when you're thinking about trading up to a 7-series Beamer or moving the gin-palace to a more expensive mooring."' The detective inspector smiles briefly, humourlessly at me. 'You did write that, Mr Colley?'

'Guilty,' I say, then give a small laugh. Neither man laughs uproariously, slaps his thigh or has to wipe tears from his eyes. I clear my throat. 'How *is* that nice Mr Anderton, anyway? Enjoying his retirement?' I sit back in my seat, feeling the carved wood against my back. I'm cold.

'Well, Mr Colley,' the detective inspector says, slipping the photocopy of the article into the envelope and handing it back to the sergeant, 'he's all right, I believe.' McDunn clasps his hands on the table. 'But Judge Jamieson and his wife were assaulted while on holiday in Carnoustie during the summer; Sir Toby Bissett was murdered outside his home in London in August, as I'm sure you're aware; and Mr Persimmon was murdered last month, at his house in Sussex.'

I'm aware my eyes are bulging. 'What? But I didn't know –! There's been nothing about Persimmon – he was supposed to have died peacefully at home!'

'There was a security aspect to Mr Persimmon's murder, as I'm sure you'll appreciate, Mr Colley.'

'But you kept it quiet for a *month*?'

'Needed a D-notice on one of the London papers,' the sergeant says, smirking. 'But they were cooperative.'

And it never got round the journo jungle-network. Shit. Must have been the *Telegraph*.

'And then on Friday night there, somebody blew up Sir Rufus Carter at his cottage in Wales. Burned to a cinder, he was; they only just identified the body.'

I don't react for a moment. Oh my God. 'Ah, sorry; what?'

He tells me again, then asks, 'Mind if we ask what you were doing on Friday night, Mr Colley?'

'What? . . . Ah, I stayed in.'

Sergeant Flavell looks significantly at the inspector, who doesn't return the look. He's watching me. He makes a strange sucking noise with his teeth, like he's straining something through them. I don't think he's aware he's doing it. 'All night?' he asks.

'Ah?' I'm a bit distracted. 'Yes, all night. I was . . . working.' I can see he spotted the hesitation. 'And playing computer games.' I look from the detective inspector to the detective sergeant. 'There's no law against playing computer games, is there?'

Christ, this is awful, I feel like I'm a child again, like I'm up before the headmaster, like I'm back being castigated by Sir Andrew for that botched Gulf trip. That was bad enough but this is ghastly. I can't believe they're actually asking me this sort of stuff. They can't really think I'm a murderer, can they? I'm a journalist; cynical and hard-bitten and all that shit and I do drugs and I drive too fast and

I hate the Tories and all their accomplices, but I'm not a fucking *murderer*, for Christ's sake. The sergeant takes out a notebook and starts making notes.

'You didn't see anybody else that evening?' McDunn asks.

'Look, I was here, in Edinburgh; I wasn't *in* Wales. How on earth am I supposed to get from here to Wales?'

'We're not accusing you of anything, Mr Colley,' The DI says, sounding mildly aggrieved. '*Did* you see anybody else that evening?'

'No; I stayed in.'

'You live alone, Mr Colley?'

'Yes. I did some work, then I played a game called *Despot*.'

'Nobody called round, nobody saw you?'

'No, they didn't.' I try to remember what happened that evening. 'I had a phone call.'

'About what time would that be?'

'Midnight.'

'And who was that from?'

I hesitate. 'Look,' I say. 'Am I being charged with anything? Because I mean if I am, this is just ludicrous but I want a lawyer – '

'You're not being charged with anything, Mr Colley,' the inspector says, sounding reasonable and slightly offended. 'These are enquiries, that's all. You're not under arrest, you don't *have* to tell us anything, and certainly you may have a lawyer present.'

Sure, and if I don't cooperate they might arrest me, or at least get a search warrant for the flat. (Gulp. There's a couple of quarters of dope, some speed and at least one ancient tab of acid in there.)

'Well, it's just, I'm a journalist, you know? I have to protect my sources, if – '

'Oh. Was this midnight phone call on a professional matter then, Mr Colley?' the inspector asks.

'Ah . . .' Shit. Decision time. Now what? What do I do? Fuck it; Andy won't mind. He'll back me up. 'No,' I tell the inspector. 'No, it was a friend.'

110

'A friend.'

'His name's Andy Gould.' I have to spell his surname for the sergeant, then give them the phone number for Andy's decrepit hotel.

'And he called you?' the inspector says.

'Yes. Well, no; I called him, left a message on his answer-machine and then he called me back a few minutes later.'

'I see,' the inspector says. 'And this was on your home phone, correct?'

'Yes.'

'The one that comes with your flat.'

'*Yes*. Not on my mobile, if that's what you're driving at.'

'Mm-hmm,' the inspector says. He folds the last three centimetres of his cigarette carefully into the ashtray and takes out a little notebook and flips it open to where the page is held by an elastic band. He looks from the notebook to me. 'And what about October the twenty-fifth, and September the fourth, and August the sixth, and July the fifteenth?'

I almost laugh. 'Are you serious? I mean, are you asking me do I have alibis?'

'We'd just like to know what you were doing on those dates.'

'Well, I was here. I mean, I haven't left Scotland, I haven't been anywhere near London, or . . . I haven't been down south for nearly a year.'

The inspector smiles thinly.

'Okay, look,' I say. 'I'd have to check in my diary.'

'Could you fetch your diary, Mr Colley?'

'Well, I say my diary; it's in my lap-top. My computer.'

'Ah, so you do have one of those. Is that in the building?'

'Yeah. It's downstairs. I just got a new one but all the files are transferred. I'll – '

I start to stand, but the inspector holds up one hand. 'Let Sergeant Flavell do that, eh?'

'All right.' I sit down again, and nod. 'It's on my desk,' I tell the sergeant as he goes to the door.

111

The inspector sits back in his seat and takes out his B&H packet. He sees me watching him again and waves the packet at me. 'Sure you won't –?' he asks.

'Um, yeah, I will, thanks,' I say, reaching out to take the cigarette and hating myself as I do it but thinking, Christ, these are exceptional circumstances here; I need all the help I can get; every prop counts.

The inspector lights my cigarette and then stands up and walks to the windows facing out towards Princes Street. I turn in my seat to watch him. It's a blustery day; cloud-shadows and patches of golden sunshine slide quickly over the face of the city, turning the buildings to dark then shining grey.

'Lovely view from here, isn't it?' the inspector says.

'Yeah, great,' I say. I'm getting a fairly decent hit from the cigarette. I should give up more often.

'Dare say they don't use this room much.'

'No. No, I don't think they do.'

'Shame, really.'

'Yes.'

'Funny thing, you know,' the inspector says, peering out over the city to the distant fields of Fife, grey-green under heavier clouds on the far side of the river. 'The night Sir Toby was killed, and the morning after Mr Persimmon was found, somebody rang up *The Times* and claimed they were IRA attacks.'

The inspector turns to look at me, face wreathed in smoke.

'Yes, well,' I say, 'I heard the IRA claimed they killed Sir Toby, but then retracted.'

'Yes,' the inspector says, looking, seemingly puzzled, at his cigarette. 'Whoever it was used the same IRA code-word both times.'

'Oh?'

'Yes; that's what's funny, you see, Mr Colley. You and me, we both know there are code-words the IRA use when they phone in a bomb warning or take responsibility for a murder or some other crime. You have to have these codes or otherwise any Tom, Dick or Paddy could call in and claim they were the IRA; close down

London, they could, first time. But our murderer . . . he knew one of the code-words. A recent one.'

'Uh-huh.' I'm feeling cold again. I can see where this is leading. Brazen it out. 'So, what?' I say, pulling on my fag, eyes narrowing. 'You suspect an ex-policeman, yeah?'

I am favoured with the inspector's thin smile again. He makes that funny sucking noise with his saliva and moves towards me and I have to lean to one side to make way for him. He reaches past me, flicking some ash into the ashtray, then steps back to the window. 'That's right, Mr Colley. We did think of a policeman, serving or not.' The DI looks like he is thinking. 'Or a telephone operator, I suppose,' he says, as though surprising himself.

'Or a journalist?' I suggest, raising my eyebrows.

'Or a journalist,' the inspector agrees blandly, leaning back against the window-frame, silhouetted by the bright gleam of rushing cloud outside. 'You wouldn't happen to know those codes, would you, Mr Colley?'

'Not off the top of my head, no,' I say. 'They're kept on the paper's computer system these days, protected by a password. But I do write on defence and security matters, amongst other things, and I do know the password, so I have got access to the codes. I can't prove I don't know what they are, if that's what you're getting at.'

'Not really getting at anything, Mr Colley. It's just . . . interesting.'

'Look, Detective Inspector,' I say, sighing and putting out my cigarette, 'I'm a single man, I live alone, I do a lot of work from home and from . . . all over Scotland; I phone it into the paper. I'll be honest with you; I really have no idea whether I've got alibis for all those dates or not. Quite possibly I do; I have a lot of professional lunches and dinners and just general meetings, keeping in contact with people; people whose word I think you'd take, like police top brass and lawyers and advocates.' It never does any harm to remind an inquisitive cop you know people like those. 'But, come on.' I laugh lightly, holding my arms out. 'I mean, anyway; do I *look* like a murderer?'

The detective inspector laughs too. 'No, you don't, Mr Colley.' He draws on the cigarette. 'No,' he says. He brings the cigarette carefully over to the table, leans past me to fold the stub into the ashtray and says, 'I helped interview Dennis Nilsen; remember him, Mr Colley? Guy that killed all those blokes?'

I nod as the DI returns to the window. I don't like the way we're going here.

'Young men, lots of young men; under his floorboards, buried in the garden . . . bloody football team of stiffs, he had.' He looks out the window again, away from me. He shakes his head. 'He didn't look like a murderer, either.'

The door opens and Sergeant Flavell comes in with my new lap-top. Suddenly I have a bad feeling about all this.

*

I'm in the bar of the Café Royal, through the wall from the restaurant where I had lunch with Y and William last week. Above the noise of the bar's chattering patrons I can hear the distant clanking and clattering of cutlery and crockery coming over the tall partition wall and echoing off the place's high, ornate ceiling. I'm staring at the gallery of the island bar while my pal Al is away having a pee and I'm experiencing an optical illusion or something because *things are not right*; I can see those bottles on the gallery ahead of me, and I can see their reflections behind them, but *I can't see me! I can't see my own reflection!*

Al comes back through the throng, politely elbows his way between a couple of people, lifts his coat off his bar stool and leans on the bar beside me, drinking his pint.

'Help me Al,' I say. 'I'm going crazy or I've become a fucking vampire or something.'

Al looks at me. He's older than me – forty-two, I think – mousy hair, teacup-sized bald patch, a couple of fetching parallel scars above his nose that make him look like he's frowning all the time but usually he's laughing, actually. Bit smaller than me. Engineering consultant; met him at one of these stupid paint-ball-guns-in-the-woods boys' games that management tend to think are such a team-spirit-building hoot.

'What are you talking about, you incredible cretin, Colley?'

I nod at the gallery ahead of me. I can see people there, behind the bottles, just as I can see people behind me. I swear they're the same people and I ought to be *between* them and the mirror behind the bottles but I still can't see myself. I nod again, hoping that the movement will show up in the mirror but it doesn't.

'Look!' I say. 'Look: in the mirror!'

It *is* a mirror, isn't it? I stare. Glass shelves. Brass supports. Bottle of Stoly Red facing me and its back visible in the mirror; likewise a bottle of blue Smirnoff, label facing me and the plain white back of the label visible through the bottle and the vodka inside. Same with the bottle of Bacardi alongside. I can see the little label on the back of the bottle in the mirror, and see it through the bottle from the front. Of *course* it's a mirror!

Al moves his head so that his chin is on my shoulder. He peers forwards. He takes a pair of glasses I know he's a little sensitive about from his jacket pocket and puts them on.

'What?' he says, sounding exasperated. A bar person gets in the way, pulling a pint and then turning to the optics above where I'm looking, and I have to move my head, trying to see, but I can't until she moves away.

'Cameron, *what* are you gibbering about?' Al says. He turns, looking at me. I look in the mirror again.

Christ! I can't see him either!

Maybe it's all those Southern Comforts we had earlier, drinking to Bush's defeat by Clinton. Thank fuck we didn't have Buds like Al suggested; how could he even *think* about polluting our bodies with a brewed-in-the-UK copy of a beer that's basically just fizzy piss even in its original incarnation (*and* they have the nerve to advertise it here as 'The Genuine Article'! Another one of those Great Lies In Advertising, aimed at the brain-dead of Essex, their grey matter irretrievably compromised by years of reading the *Sun* and drinking Skol, the bastards).

I point, getting a funny look from a bar person passing at the time as I almost poke her in the eye.

'I'm invisible!' I squawk.

'You're pissed,' Al says, going back to his pint.

One of the people in the mirror is looking at me. I realise I'm still pointing. I turn and look behind me but there's just a whole load of backs and bodies; nobody looking at me. I turn back and stare at the mirror, just as the bar person I almost assaulted reaches up and takes the bottle of Bacardi down from the shelf. I stare. Its reflection is still there! Even more amazing!

The man who was looking at me is still looking at me. Then it occurs to me I can see a bit of a tile mural on the wall above him. I turn round and look above the people behind me; there is still a fair bit of light coming in through the tall, engraved windows. No mural. I turn back again as the bar person puts the Bacardi bottle back on the shelf. It is not quite straight, and slightly out of position. One of the older male bar staff passes by, reaches up and sets the bottle in exactly the right position again to maintain the mirror illusion before going to a pump and filling a couple of pint glasses with 80-shilling. I glare at him as he comes towards me. The complete bastard. Then I pull back, afraid, as he comes right up and puts the glasses down in front of Al and me. I look down at my own glass and see it's empty just as the bar man takes it away and accepts the money from Al, who pours the last few millimetres from his old glass into his new one.

I shake my head. 'No, man,' I say, sighing and looking up at the ceiling. 'I can't handle all this.'

'What?' Al says, frowning.

'I can't handle this. Today's just been . . .'

'You look like shit, Cameron,' Al tells me. He nods past me. 'Look, there's a couple of proper seats. Let's sit down.'

'Okay. Let's get some fags, eh?'

'*No!* You're giving up, remember?'

'Yeah, but it's been a difficult day, Al . . .'

'Just head for those seats, okay?'

I forget my coat but Al remembers it. We sit at the end of one of the bar's ribbed green leather semicircular benches, pints on the oval table.

'Do I really look like shit?'

'Cam, you look shafted.'

'Fuck off, you uncivil bastard.'

'Just calling it the way I see it.'

'I've had a traumatic day,' I tell him, pulling my Drizabone about me. 'Grilled by the fuzz.'

'Sounds painful, certainly.'

'Thanks for coming for a drink, Al,' I tell him, looking into his eyes with drunken sincerity and punching him lightly on the forearm.

'Ouch! Will you stop that?' He rubs his arm. 'But anyway; think comparatively little of it.'

'Al, you got any fags on you at all, Al?'

'No, I still haven't.'

'Oh. Oh well. But I really appreciate you coming for this drink, really, Al. You're my only pal who isn't another fucking hack . . . Well, apart from Andy. And . . . well, anyway; I really appreciate being able to tell you all this shit.'

'And share it with the rest of the bar if I didn't keep telling you to shut up.'

'Yeah, but you wouldn't believe what they're getting at. I mean, you wouldn't believe what they're trying to fucking pin on me.'

'A badge that says Nil By Mouth, perhaps?'

I wave this away and bend closer to him. 'I'm serious. They think I've been murdering people!'

Al sighs deeply. 'What a gift for dramatic hyperbole you possess, Cameron.'

'It's true!'

'No . . .' Al says calmly. 'I think if it was true they wouldn't have let you go, Cameron. You'd be in a cell; you'd be looking at bars, not trying to drink one dry.'

'But I haven't got an alibi!' I whisper angrily. 'I haven't got *any* fucking alibis! Some cunt's trying to set me up! I'm not kidding; they're trying to set me up! They call me on the phone and get me to go to some lonely spot and wait for a phone call on a public box or get me to stay home all night, meanwhile they're offing some fucker! I mean, by the sound of it every one of the bastards deserved to die . . . though actually he hasn't killed them all, just seriously assaulted some of them, whatever the hell they mean by that, wouldn't tell me . . . but I *didn't do it*! And the police are fucking crazy, man! They think I had enough time to get to the fucking airport, get down south or wherever and kill these Tory fuckwits. Christ, they took my new computer! My lap-top! Heinous bastards! They've even told me to keep them informed of my movements; can you believe that? I've got to report in to the local police if I *go* anywhere! What a nerve! I tried ringing some of the cops I know, top-brass types, to find out what they knew about all this, but they were all out or at meetings. Suspicious as fuck.' I glance at my watch. 'I got to get home, Al; I have to flush all my stuff down the toilet, or eat it or something . . .' I drink some of my pint, spilling a little on my chin. 'But I'm being set up, I'm not kidding; some bastard rings up calling himself – '

'– Mr Archer,' Al sighs.

I stare at him. I can't believe this. 'How do *you* know?' I screech.

'Because this is about the fifth time you've told me this.'

'Shit.' I think about this. 'Do you think I might be getting drunk?'

'Oh, shut up and drink your beer.'

'Good idea . . . You got any fags on you at all, Al?'

*

An hour later and Al's made me return a packet of fags I bought and taken one slim panatella from my lips just as I was about to light it at the bar and taken me round to the Burger King and made me eat a cheeseburger and drink a large milk and I seem to have sobered up a bit except now my balance has gone and I'm having trouble standing. Al has to help me and insists we get a taxi and refuses to drive or let me drive and I accuse him of being scared because of his record.

'I'm heading for the hills, I'm telling you,' I tell him as we make it out through the door and into the open air.

'Sound thinking,' Al says. 'It's always worked for me.'

'Yeah.' I say, nodding emphatically and gazing up at the sky. It's sunset and the air is cold. We head west along Princes Street. 'I'm heading for the hills, getting out of town,' I tell him. 'I'm going to ditch all the gear in my flat first, but then that's me; I'm off. I think I'll tell the boys in blue exactly where I'm going so they can check up I'm not this fucking serial killer/assaulter or whatever, but I'm rattled, man, I'm telling you, I don't mind admitting it. I'm off to the Highlands, I'm off to Stromefirry-nofirry.'

'Where?' Al buttons his coat as we turn up Andrew Street and the wind gusts down from St Andrew Square.

'Stromefirry-nofirry.'

'Ha!' Al laughs. 'Aye, of course; Stromefirry-nofirry. I've seen that sign, too.'

Al leaves me propped against a wall while he pops into a shop and gets some flowers.

'Get us a packet of Rothmans, Al!' I shout but I don't think he hears me. I stand there sighing heavily and smiling bravely at passers-by.

Al reappears with a bunch of flowers.

I throw my arms wide. 'Al, you shouldn't have.'

119

'Good, because I haven't.' He takes me by the arm and we head to the kerb, looking for a taxi. He sniffs at the flowers. 'They're for Andi.'

'Andy?' I say, surprised. 'All right; I'll take them.' I reach for the flowers but miss.

Al nudges me in the ribs. 'Not *that* Andy,' he says, waving at a taxi with its light on. It clatters by. 'They're for my *wife*, you buffoon, not this dissolute 'eighties boom-victim moping in his gloomy mansion.'

'Hotel,' I correct him, and help him to wave at the next taxi. Somehow I stagger into the gutter and almost fall but Al saves me. The taxi – which was slowing down and turning towards us – steers away and picks up speed again. I glare after it. 'Bastard.'

'Idiot,' I hear Al agreeing. He takes my arm again and starts to lead me across the street. 'Come on, Mr Sobriety; we'll get one from the rank on Hanover Street.'

'But my car!'

'Forget it. Pick it up tomorrow.'

'Yeah, I will, and then I'm heading for the hills, I'm telling you.'

'Good idea.'

'Heading for the hills, I'm fucking telling you . . .'

'Yes, you are, aren't you?'

'. . . for the fucking hills, man . . .'

*

I get home and Al sees me to my door and I tell him I'm fine and he goes and I dump all my stuff down the toilet except for some speed which I snort, and the rest which I suck. Then I go to bed but I can't sleep and the phone rings and I answer it.

'Cameron; Neil.'

'Oh, wow, yeah; hi, Neil.'

'Yes . . . well, I'm just calling to say sorry, but I can't help you.'

'Yeah, right . . . *what*?'

120

'Do the words "chase", "goose" and "wild" mean anything to you?'

'Ah, pardon?'

'Never mind. As I said, I can't help you, old son. It's a dead end, understand? There's no link; nothing to find out. It's your story, but if I were you I'd drop it.'

'Ah, yeah, umm . . .'

'Are you all right?'

'Yeah! Yeah, I'm . . .'

'You sound stoned.'

'Yeah . . . No!'

'Well, I'm glad we've got that cleared up. I'll reiterate; I can't help you. You're on a wild-goose chase, so just let it drop.'

'Okay, okay . . .'

'Yes, well, I'll let you get back to whatever combination of substances it is you're currently abusing. Goodnight, Cameron.'

'Yeah; 'night.'

I put the phone down and sit on the edge of the bed, thinking, What the fuck was *that* about? So these guys all just died coincidentally? There's no connection with my Mr Archer or Daniel Smout? I really don't like the sound of all this.

I lie down again and try to sleep but I can't and I can't stop thinking about guys tied to trees with nooses round their necks waiting for a train, or jerking around in baths while a drill sparks and bubbles under the water, or drowning in farm cesspits; I try to stop thinking about that sort of gory, ghastly stuff and think about Y for a while instead and have a wank and *still* don't sleep and eventually after a lot more not-sleeping I'm dying for a cigarette and so I get up and go out but I must have slept after all because it's half two in the morning all of a sudden and there's nowhere open and by now my head's sore but I really need some tobacco so I hoof it uphill through Royal Circus and up Howe Street until finally a cab stops and I get him to take me through the quiet streets to the Cowgate where the Kasbar's still open, God bless the awful dive that it is,

121

and at last I can buy some fags – Regal because that's all they have behind the bar and the machine's not working but it doesn't matter; I've got a cigarette in my mouth and a pint in my hand (medicinal, and anyway I don't think they serve Perrier in the Kasbar and even if they did some seven-foot biker would probably push a glass in your face just on general principles and then drag you screaming into the gents and shove your head down an unflushed toilet but hey I'm not complaining that's part of the character of the place) and I'm happy now.

I leave at four, walking from the Cowgate up to Hunter Square where the waist-high glass-tiled roof of the underground toilets glows with hundreds of little blue marbles; one of the Lux Europae exhibits. I head down Fleshmarket Close, forgetting the station is still closed at this time in the morning, so detour up Waverley Bridge and stroll along Princes Street beneath more abstract light sculptures, watching a street-cleaning machine as it trundles growling along the road, brushing and sucking at the gutters.

I'm home by five and up again by eleven when there's a phone call that's more than ordinarily interesting that changes my plans and so I go into work and have to pay Frank ('Milltown of Towie? Give in? Molten of Toil!') his twenty quid because the Tories scraped through the Maastricht vote with less of a margin that I'd anticipated and I try to phone Neil to make sure I didn't dream that call last night, but he's out.

122

C H A P T E R

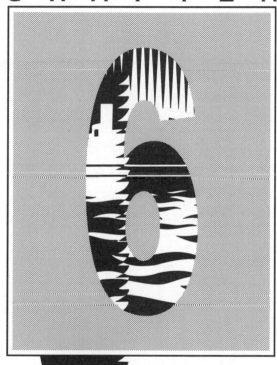

EXOCET DECK

I drive the car up the little single-track road leading towards the low hills; the headlights create a deep channel of illumination between the hedges. I'm dressed in black jeans, black boots and a dark blue polo-neck over a navy shirt and two vests. I've wearing thin black leather gloves. I find a track leading off the road into a stand of trees; I take the car up as far as it will go, then turn the lights out. The clock on the dash says it's 03:10. I wait a minute; no traffic passes, so I guess I haven't been seen. My heart is thudding already.

The night is cold when I get out of the car. There's a half-moon but it's obscured ninety per cent of the time by a lot of low, fast-moving cloud producing occasional freezing gusts of rain. The wind is loud in the leaf-bare branches overhead. I head down the track to the road, then look back to the car; it's almost fully hidden. I cross the tarmac and climb a fence, then take the ski-mask from my trouser pocket and pull it over my head. I follow the line of the hedge along the side of the road, ducking once as a car drives past on the road; its headlights sweep along the hedge above me. The car carries on into the night. I start breathing again.

I get to the fence leading downhill and follow it, stumbling now and again on the rocks and stones left at the side of the field; my eyes are still adjusting to the darkness. The ground underfoot is fairly firm, not too muddy.

At the hedge marking the foot of the field I have to look for a minute to find a way through. Finally I have to crawl through and underneath it, snagging my polo-neck. Trees heard but barely seen in the darkness make a great rushing, crackling sound above me.

I scramble down a muddy, leaf-littered bank and into a chilly stream at the bottom; it flows over one boot and I whisper, 'Shit,' and squelch up the far bank, holding onto the cold branches of bushes and the mud-slimy roots of trees. I force my way through some bushes at the top. I can see street lights ahead, and the geometric shapes of darkened houses. I keep crouched and make my way through the low bushes, heading diagonally through the wood towards the estate. I trip over a log and fall but don't hurt myself. I come to the two-metre-high brick wall which surrounds the estate and feel my way along it, stumbling over piles of earth and building debris until I get to the corner.

I measure sixty paces along the wall and then walk away from it to the nearest tree. A patch of moonlight means I have to wait nearly five minutes for the clouds to cover the moon again before I can climb the tree. I get far enough up to see the house and identify it by its position and the garden furniture, then I climb back down, go to the wall and jump up, catching hold of the concrete ridge tiles on top of the wall and pulling myself up. I rest on the top of the wall, my hands shaking, my heart pumping hard. I look at the dark house in front of me and the screens of tall shrubs and young trees on either side concealing the two neighbouring villas.

The moon threatens to come out from behind the clouds again and I have to jump down to the paving stones of the patio beneath.

126

There is a small wall beside the greenhouse which rises to within a metre of the top of the estate wall; that's my escape route. There are infrared-sensing security lights on the wall of the house and if they go on then the whole thing's off; I'm up and over the wall and back into the woods and away.

I walk quietly over the patio, onto the grass and towards the house, just waiting for the blaze of light from the security lamps. It doesn't happen. I reach the lower patio where the garden furniture stands by the side of the tarpaulin-covered pool and crouch down by the ghostly perforated shape of the cast-iron bench. I feel up inside the overhang where the back of the bench joins the arm, the leather of my gloves catching on rough splinters of metal. I can't feel enough. I take my glove off and try again, the metal cold and edges sharp against my skin. I feel the putty, then the embedded key and its short length of string. I take hold of the string and pull gently. The key comes out, clinking quietly once. I put my glove back on.

I walk carefully past the conservatory to the back door of the house, slide the key into the lock and turn it. The door opens silently. The house is warm inside and smells of washing powder. I lock the door; as I move away from it, a small, faint red light comes on with a tiny clinking noise, high up in one far corner of the room. The sensor doesn't set the alarm off; the system isn't armed.

I move very slowly through the utility room and into the kitchen (another little red light clicks on). My boots squelch and squeak on the tiles. I hesitate, then kneel and quickly take the boots off, leaving them by the dishwasher. When I stand up I see the wooden block full of knives on the work surface, just visible by moonlight next to the gently gleaming stainless steel of the sinks. I pull out the largest of the knives, then turn and leave the kitchen, heading down the corridor past the dining room and the study to the stairs. Beyond and to the side is the split-level lounge; a shaft of orange street light sifting through the trees round the front garden shows leather settees, chairs, bookcases full of videos, CDs and books, a couple of coffee tables and a big metal hood over a raised central

127

fireplace. Another sensor high in one corner glows red as I move towards the foot of the stairs.

The carpet on the stairs is thick and deep and I make no noise as I climb to the top, then pad along towards the master bedroom, tripping one more sensor. The bedroom door opens with only the softest of creaks.

At the head of the wide double bed there is a weak green glow. As I move round I see the numerals of a digital clock. The lime-coloured light spills faintly out onto white sheets and a single, sleeping face. I go closer, very slowly, the knife held in front of me. I watch her breathe. One of her arms lies outside the covers, hanging out pale and naked over the edge of the bed. She has short, dark hair and a slim, slightly boyish face; thin, dark brows, thin nose, pale lips with the hint of a pout, and a sharp triangular chin matching sharp, high cheekbones.

I creep closer. She stirs. I reach forward, the knife in one hand, the other glove touching then gathering and balling a fistful of duvet and then pulling it sharply, throwing it away behind me as I leap forward, seeing her pale nakedness in the same instant as I slap my hand over her mouth; her eyes open wide and she starts trying to push up; I force her back down into the bed, hand still over her mouth. I raise the knife so she can see it. She struggles, eyes widening further, but I pin her to the sheets with my weight and keep the glove firmly over her mouth even though she isn't making any noise. I rest the blade of the knife against her throat and she goes still.

'Make a noise and you're dead, understand?' I say. She seems not to hear, staring up at me. 'Understand?' I say again, and this time she nods quickly. 'Warning you,' I tell her as I slowly take my hand away from her mouth. She doesn't call out.

I push myself up, still keeping the knife near her throat. I undo the zip on my jeans. I'm not wearing any underpants and my cock falls out, already hard. She's staring into my eyes. I see her swallow. A pulse beats at the top of her long, white neck, under her chin. Her hand is creeping to the side of the bed. I look at it, and it stops. Her eyes look terrified now. I put the blade of the knife against her neck again and look down to the edge of the mattress. She's trembling. I feel under the edge of the mattress, above the wooden frame of the huge bed. I feel a wooden handle; I pull out a ten-inch hunting knife with a serrated blade. I whistle softly, then throw it across the carpets towards the windows. She's staring at me.

'On your front,' I tell her. 'On your knees, like a dog. Now.'

She starts to breathe raggedly, mouth open. Her whole body is trembling.

'Do it!' I hiss.

She rolls over, onto her front, then gets up onto her knees, taking the weight of her upper body on her hands.

'Face on the sheets,' I tell her. 'Hands up here.'

She rests her face on the sheet and puts her hands behind her. I take the handcuffs from my pocket and snap them over her wrists. I stop to put a condom on, then climb onto the bed behind her, put the knife onto the sheets just within reach, grip her hips with both hands and pull her onto my cock.

She shouts as I enter her. She's soaking wet and within a few thrusts I'm ready to come and she's panting, then grunting then calling out, 'Oh, fuck, *yes*!' and then it's all over and I collapse over her and then fall off her and almost cut my ear on the cool blade of the kitchen knife lying on the sheet.

She lies there on her side, facing me, watching me, still panting, hands still trapped behind her back, a strange, charged expression on her face, and after a bit she says, 'Is that it?'

I breathe deeply and say, 'No.'

I haul her roughly back up onto her knees with her face down on the sheets again and spread her buttocks and stick an index finger into her anus, sliding it quickly half into her. She gasps. I position my head above her backside and let some spit fall down onto where the knuckle is caught on the ring of muscle, then push my finger fully into her. She gasps again; I start to move the finger in and out, stroking her clitoris with my other hand. I use two fingers after a while, then I'm hard again; I pull the first condom off and put on another one, then I spit onto my rubber-sheathed prick and, guiding it with my fingers, ease it slowly into her rectum.

She comes screaming; I don't think I'm going to but then I do.

We collapse together onto the bed, breathing in time. I pull myself out of her. There is a faint smell of shit. I undo the handcuffs and lie there, holding her. She pulls the ski-mask from my head.

'Where are your shoes?' she whispers after a while.

'In the kitchen,' I tell her. 'They were muddy. Didn't want to make a mess.'

She laughs quietly in the darkness.

*

'But I was in control,' she says, over the noise of the streaming water as she soaps my shoulders and back. 'All I had to say was your name, and it was all over. That's what we agreed; I trust you.'

'But what's the difference?' I ask her, trying to see her over my shoulder. 'Anybody watching that would have said I was a rapist and you were being raped.'

'But we knew different.'

'But is that all it is? I mean just thinking that? What if it had been a real rapist?'

'What if it had been the wrong house?'

'I checked the furniture.'

'And you were just you; you moved like you, spoke like you; smelled like you.'

'But – '

'Look; I enjoyed it,' she says, soaping the small of my back and my buttocks. 'I don't think I want to do it again, but it was interesting to live it out. But what about you? How did you feel about it?'

'Nervous as fuck – I was certain I wouldn't be able to get it up, I mean just *certain*, especially as I'm still feeling the effects from getting pissed yesterday – and then, well . . . aroused, I suppose, when . . . when I realised you were.'

'Uh-huh. Not before.'

'No!'

'No.'

'I mean, I felt awful for long enough; I felt like a rapist.'

'But you weren't.' She slides her hand between the cheeks of my bum, then soaps my thighs and down my legs. 'You were doing something I'd always fantasised about.'

'Oh great, so that old fuck Jamieson was right and all women secretly want to be raped.'

Yvonne slaps my calves. 'Don't be stupid. Nobody wants to be raped, but some people have fantasies about it. The control isn't some detail, Cameron . . . knowing it's somebody you can trust isn't just by-the-way; it's everything.'

'Hmm,' I say, unconvinced.

'Men like Jamieson hate women, Cameron. Or maybe they just hate women who aren't totally in awe of men, women who aren't under their control.' She runs her hands up my legs to my buttocks again, sliding her fingers between my cheeks, touching my anus and making me go up on the balls of my feet, then her hand runs back down my legs. 'Maybe men like that should have it happen to them,' she says. 'Rape; assault. See how they like it.'

'Yeah,' I say, shivering suddenly despite the heat because we're getting into dodgy territory here. 'All those wigs and garters and funny gowns; fuckin askin for it, in't they? Know wot I mean?' The steam gets to my throat and I cough.

I'm wondering whether I should say anything to her about the police, and about the retired Judge Jamieson being 'assaulted', whatever that means. After my drunken afternoon with Al I don't feel the same need to offload as I did before, and I can't decide whether I ought to involve Yvonne or not.

She washes my feet. 'Or maybe,' she says, 'the Greers and the Dworkins are right, and the Pickleses and the Jamiesons are right too, and all men are rapists, and all women want to be raped.'

'Bullshit.'

'Mm-hmm.'

'But I still didn't like being made to feel like I was a rapist.'

'Well, we won't do that again.'

'And I still find the idea of you wanting me to do it . . . unsettling.'

She's silent for a while, then says, 'The other day' – she's soaping the front of my legs now, from behind – 'when you had to sit through *Eldorado* in that really uncomfortable position; you enjoyed that, didn't you?'

She's smoothing her sappled hands up and down my thighs.

'Well . . . eventually,' I concede.

'But if that had been somebody else doing that to you . . .' she says softly, so that I can hardly hear her over the quiet thunder of the shower. She's soaping my balls now, gently palping them, massaging them. '. . . Somebody you didn't know – male or female – tying you up, leaving you helpless, somewhere where shouting couldn't help you, and there was a big sharp knife under the bed . . . how would you have felt then?'

She stands up and rubs her body up against me, stroking my still mostly limp cock. I gaze out through the steam and the rivulets of water running down the glass of the shower cabinet. I'm looking out at the moodily lit bathroom and wondering what I would do if I suddenly saw William appear out there, flight bags in hand, a *Surprise, honey, I'm home!* look on his face.

'Petrified,' I admit. 'I'd be scared stiff. Well, scared soft.'

She's gently pulling on my prick. It doesn't really want to and I find it difficult to believe and I'm not sure *I* want to because I feel so fucking drained and sore, but the thing's actually responding, fattening and firming and rising in her kneading, soap-slick hands.

She puts her chin on my shoulder and a sharp fingernail against my jugular. 'Turn round, bitch-boy,' she hisses.

'Oh ha-bloody-ha.'

*

Yvonne wakes me up after an hour's sleep and tells me I have to leave. I turn over and pretend I'm still asleep but she pulls the duvet off me and switches the lights on. I have to dress in my sweaty, dirty clothes and go back down to the kitchen, grumbling while she makes me a coffee, and I complain about my wet boots and she gives me a fresh pair of William's socks to wear and I put them on and drink my coffee and whine about never being allowed to spend the night and tell her how *just once* I'd like to wake up here in the morning, and have a nice, civilised breakfast with her, sitting on the sunny balcony outside the bedroom windows, but she makes me sit down while she laces my boots up, then takes my coffee cup off me and sends me out the back door and says I've got two minutes before she arms the alarm and puts the infrared lights on stand-by so I have to go back the way I came, over the estate wall and through the wood and down into the stream where I get both feet wet and cold and I fall going up the bank and get all muddy and eventually drag myself up and through the hedge, scratching my cheek and tearing my polo-neck and then trudging across the field through heavy rain and more mud and finally getting to the car and panicking when I can't find the car keys before remembering I put them in the button-down back pocket of the jeans for safety instead of the side pocket like I usually do, and then having to put some dead branches under the front wheels because the fucking car's stuck and finally getting away and home and even in the street light I can see what a mess of the pale upholstery my muddy clothes have made.

*

I feel too tired to sleep so I play some *Despot* when I get home but my heart's not in it and the Empire is still in a tattered-looking state after all the earlier disasters and I'm almost wondering if I should start again but that would mean going back to the fucking dawn of civilisation and the temptation in *Despot* is always to swap PoV, which people who don't know the game always think sounds sort

133

of innocent, like some detail, but it isn't: you're not just swapping Point of View, you're swapping your current Despotic Power Level for something less, even if it's a regional lord or other king or a general or royal relation close to the throne, and it is not to be done lightly because as soon as you renounce the current Despot's PoV the computer takes over and it's a smart fucking piece of software. Try to swap too late, hold on too long and you get assassinated and that's it; that's you back to the cave with twenty other flea-bitten reduced-statures and the bright idea of *bringing some fire into the cave*! Swap too soon and the program takes over and performs some miracle that pulls the ass of the Despot you just abandoned *out* of the fire and next thing you know the secret police are banging down the doors and hauling you and your family off into the night and oblivion; the machine thereupon promptly declares itself the winner and it's back to that fucking cave again.

I give up after an hour of civilisational water-treading, hit Store and slope off to bed. I've smoked six fags without really meaning to.

*

I'm still heading for the hills. I get up bright and late. I phone Andy and confirm it's still all right to visit, then I ring Eddie and get the next three days off, tell the cops – they're based at Fettes, though the DI has gone back down to London, and no they're still not giving me back my new portable yet – and (after I've cleaned the car up a bit) head out of the city and across the grey bridge in a day of squally, buffeting rain that has the bridge's 40-limit signs on, high-sided vehicles banned and the 205 dancing its Dunlops sideways as the gusts hit.

Then it's up the M90, skirting Perth and heading northwards on the A9 with its frustrating mix of dual and single carriageways and its dire-warning signs about unmarked police cars before the fun begins at Dalwhinnie. Nirvana, Michelle Shocked, Crowded House and Carter USM provide the sound track. The rain eases as I head west; I catch the last of a wide, bloody-looking sunset over Skye and the Kyles and the floodlights turning Eilean Donan's grey stones green; I make it to Strome in four hours twenty minutes from home, arriving just as the stars are coming out above in the purple spaces between the dark, heavy clouds.

*

'You total bastard! You total utter and complete bastard! *That's* how you fucking do it! Bastard!'

Compensation and redemption; education, even. I'm in the dark hotel at the side of the black loch and it's close to midnight and I'm drunk but not stoned and so's Andy and his pal Howie and I'm sitting in the old ballroom on the lower ground floor, looking out over the waters to where grey ghostly moonlit mountains rise, tops glowing softly, capped with snow, and I'm *playing computer games*. In fact I'm playing *Xerium*, of all things, and blow me down, blow me up if I haven't just found out how to get over the Mountains of Zound at long, long last.

It's easy but sneaky; you ferry a dump of fuel, shielding, a nuke and a missile, load up on fuel and a nuke, fly out and up eight clicks, drop the nuke at the foot of the mountains, power-dive back down to base, load the shielding, fuel to the max with just one missile aboard (meanwhile the nuke explodes, shaking the ground; you don't want to be fueling at this point), then you climb like fuck, get to ceiling and then *hover in the air above the rising mushroom cloud*! The cloud comes up beneath you and carries you up with it over your normal ceiling. The shielding protects you – though you still need to do some fancy flying to stay stable within the radioactive thermals – then as the cloud dissipates you cut out and down, across the mountains – they look tiny! – swoop across the closed valley, loose the missile when the base's defence radar picks you up and use the last of

135

your fuel to escape over the far side while the missile takes out the base. Simple!

'Bastard,' I say, gliding the ship down to a fuel-dump and a gentle landing. I shake my head. 'Riding the fucking mushroom cloud; never even occurred to me.'

'You're not gung-ho enough,' Andy tells me, refilling my whisky glass.

'Aye; you've got to be a real man to play this game,' Howie says, winking and taking up his glass. He's a brawny Highland lad from one of the nearby villages, one of Andy's drinking partners. A bit rough and ready and with a highly incorrect attitude to women, but amusing, in a raw kind of way; a man's man.

'You have to be slightly crazy to play *Xerium*,' Andy says, sitting back in his seat. 'You have to be . . . just . . . crazy . . . enough.'

'Aye,' Howie says, draining his whisky glass. 'No, no, thanks, Drew,' he says as Andy goes to refill his dram too. 'I'd better be away,' he says, standing. 'Can't be late for my last day with the Forestry. Nice to meet you,' he says to me. 'Maybe see you later.' He shakes my hand; serious grip.

'Right,' Andy says, standing too. 'I'll see you out, Howie. Thanks for coming round.'

'Not at all, not at all. Good to see you again.'

'. . . wee going-away party tomorrow night?'

'Aye, why not?'

They wend off across the dully shining floor of the ballroom, heading approximately for the stairs.

I shake my head at the Amiga screen. 'Riding the fucking mushroom cloud,' I say to myself. Then I get up out of the creaking seat and stretch my legs, taking my glass over to the floor-to-ceiling windows which form one wall of the ballroom and look out over the gardens to the railway line and the shore of the loch. The clouds have shrunk to wisps and the moon stands somewhere overhead, filling the view with silver. A few lights burn further down the loch to the right, but the mass of mountains on the far side rises dark into the starry sky, grey becoming white at their snow-dusted summits.

The ballroom smells damp. It is illuminated only by the light shining from the stairwell and the desk lamp on the old trestle table which holds the computer. Torn, bleached-looking curtains hang at the sides of the six tall window bays. My breath smokes in front of me and mists on the cold glass. All the panes are dirty and some are cracked. A couple have been replaced with hardboard. In two of the window bays there are buckets to catch drips but one of them has overflowed and caused a puddle to form around it, discolouring and springing the parquet flooring, which looks burned in other places. Striped, faded wallpaper has unrolled down the walls in places to hang like giant shavings off a piece of planed wood.

The ballroom is scattered with cheap wooden chairs, tables, rolls of ancient, mouldy-smelling carpets, a couple of old motorbikes and lots of bits of motorbikes standing or lying on oil-stained sheets, and what looks and smells like an industrial-standard deep-fat frier with the associated hoods, filters, fan housing and ducting.

The hotel lies at the foot of a steep road which leads down through the trees from the main road. With the hill and the dark masses of the trees behind it to the south, the place doesn't get any sunlight in winter and not that much even in summer. The main road used to come here and the ferry took you over to the north side of the loch, but then they up-graded the way round the loch from a track to a road and the ferry stopped. The Inverness-Kyle railway still runs past and the train still halts if anyone requests it, but with the ferry gone and the road traffic diverted the place has gone to seed; there are a few houses, a craft shop, the railway platform, a wharf and an abandoned compound owned by Marconi, and the hotel.

That's it. There's a sign at the top of the road that's been there for years, ever since they opened the new road, and it says 'Strome Ferry – no ferry', and that just says it all.

A door closes in the distance, somewhere overhead. I drink my whisky and look out at the inky loch. I don't think Andy ever meant to do anything with this place. Like the rest of his friends, I assumed he was going to run it, put money into it; develop it. We all imagined he had some secret new money-spinning idea and soon we'd all be amazed at what he'd done to the place, and coming here to marvel at the crowds he'd managed to attract . . . but I don't think he was ever looking for a site for some viable business venture; I think he was just looking for somewhere suited to his burned-out, fed-up, pissed-off mood.

'Right,' Andy says in the background. He comes in from the stairwell and closes the double doors. 'Fancy some narcotics?'

'Oh! You have some?'

'Yeah, well,' Andy says, coming to stand near me and look out over the water. He's about my height but he's filled out a bit since he came here and he has a kind of stoop now which makes him look smaller and older than he is. He's wearing thick old cords worn smooth at the bum and knee but good-quality once, and what looks like a load of shirts and holey jumpers and cardigans. He's got a week's growth of beard which seems to be permanent, judging from the times I've seen him in the past. 'Howie's like a lot of them up here,' he says. 'They like a drink but they have a weird attitude to anything else.' He shrugs and takes a silver cigarette case from a pocket in one of his cardigans. 'There are a few travellers live in the area; they're cool.'

'Hey,' I say, remembering. 'Did the police call you?'

'Yeah,' he says, opening the cigarette case to reveal a dozen or so neatly rolled spliffs. 'Somebody called Flavell; asked about when I called you back the other night. I told him.'

'Right. I think I'm supposed to go and report to the local *polizei* tomorrow.'

'Yeah, yeah, it's a fucking police state,' he says tiredly, offering the spliff case to me. 'Anyway; fancy a blow, yeah?'

I shrug. 'Well, I don't normally, you understand.' I take one of the Js. 'Thanks.' I shiver. I'm wearing my jacket and my Drizabone but I still feel freezing. 'But can we go somewhere *warm*?'

Andy, the ice-boy, smiles.

138

*

We sit in the lounge off his bedroom, on the top floor of the hotel, smoking Js and drinking whisky. I know I'm going to suffer for this tomorrow – later today – but I don't care. I tell him about the whisky story and the chill-filtering and the colouring but he already seems to know it all. The lounge is moderately spacious and somewhere between shabby and cosy: scuffed velvet curtains, heavy old wooden furniture, lots of plump embroidered cushions, and – on a massive table in one corner – an ancient IBM PC; it has an external disk drive and a modem connected and the casing is sitting slightly askew. An Epson printer sits alongside.

We're sitting round a real fire burning logs, and a fan heater's whining away in the centre of the room's dark, threadbare carpet. I'm warm at last. Andy sits in an ancient bulging armchair, its fake brown leather rubbed through to the fabric net underneath in places and burnished to a deep black shine on the arms; he nurses his whisky and looks into the fire most of the time. His concession to the warmth of the room has been to take off his topmost cardigan.

'Yeah,' he's saying, 'we were the blank-cheque generation. I remember thinking in '79 that it was time to really go for something, to finally try something different; to be radical. It seemed like ever since the 'sixties there had been just one brand of government in two slightly different packages and nothing much ever changed; there was this feeling that after the burst of energy in the early-mid-'sixties everything had been going downhill; the whole country was constipated, bound up with rules and regulations and restrictive practices and just general, endemic, infectious ennui. I never could decide who was right, socialists – even revolutionaries – or the arch-capitalists, and it seemed we'd never find out in Britain because whatever way the popular vote went it never really brought any real change of direction. Heath wasn't particularly

139

good for business and Callaghan wasn't particularly good for the working class.'

'I didn't think you ever thought much of revolution,' I tell him, sipping my whisky. 'I thought you were always a devout capitalist.'

Andy shrugs. 'I just wanted change. It seemed like what was needed. It didn't really matter which direction it came from. I never said much because I wanted to keep my options open. I'd already decided I wanted to go into the Army and it wouldn't have been a good idea to have anything on my record about supporting some left-wing group. But it had occurred to me that if there was ever any . . . well, I don't know; armed revolt, popular uprising . . .' He laughs lightly. 'I can remember when that didn't seem so unlikely, and I thought, well, if anything like that does ever happen, and they're right and the establishment is wrong, then it wouldn't do any harm for there to be people like me in the Army who were basically in sympathy with the . . . movement, whatever.' He shakes his head, still staring at the fire. 'Though I guess that sounds pretty dumb now, doesn't it?'

I shrug. 'Don't ask me; you're talking to somebody who thought the way to make the world a better place was to become a journalist. Marks *me* down as a prime strategic thinker, and no mistake.'

'Nothing wrong with the idea,' Andy says. 'But if you're disillusioned now it's partly because of what I'm talking about; the radicalism of Thatcher that seemed so fresh. That promise, that lean, trimmed-down fitness we could all look forward to; here was the chance to follow one dynamic plan, pushed by somebody who wasn't going to chicken out halfway through. Stripping away all the inefficiencies, the cosy deals, the feather-bedding, the smothering worst of the nanny-state; it was a breath of clean new air, it was a crusade; something we could all take part in, all be a part of.'

'If you were rich to start with, or determined to be a bigger bastard than your mates.'

Andy shakes his head. 'You've always hated the Tories too much to see any of that clearly. But the point is it doesn't matter who was right, and even less who would have been right; all that matters is what people felt, because that's what produced the new ethos of the age; consensus had led to impasse, care to sterility, so: deliver a shock to the system, take the sort of radical risk with the country that you have to take with a business at least once in its history if it's to succeed; go for growth, take the monetarist shilling.' He sighs, takes out the cigarette case again and holds it out to me. I take a spliff.

'And I was one of those who did,' he says, lighting the J with his Zippo. 'I was a loyal trooper in the children's crusade to recover the lost citadel of British economic power.'

He watches the fire while I smoke the spliff.

'Though of course before that I'd already done my bit: I was one of Our Lads, I was an Expeditionary, part of the Task Force that recaptured Maggie's surrendered popularity.'

I don't know what to say, and, in a recently introduced policy initiative that has come with my advancing years, I don't say anything.

'Well, here we are,' Andy says, sitting forward and slapping his hands on his knees, then taking the J when I tap him on the elbow. 'Thanks.' He tokes on the spliff. 'Here we are and we've had our experiment; there's been one party, one dominant idea, one fully followed plan, one strong leader — and her grey shadow — and it's all turned to shit and ashes. Industrial base cut so close to the bone the marrow's leaking out, the old vaguely socialist inefficiencies replaced with more rabid capitalist ones, power centralised, corruption institutionalised, and a generation created which'll never have any skills beyond opening a car with a coat hanger and knowing which solvents give you the best buzz with a plastic bag over your head before you throw up or pass out.' He sucks hard on the number before holding it out to me.

'Yeah,' I say, taking it. 'But it's not like it was all your fault. You did your bit but . . . Islagiatt.'

141

'Yeah, it seemed like a good idea at the time . . .'

'Christ, man, I didn't think any of you guys should have been out there, but I don't think I could have done what you did, in the Falklands. I mean, even if there had been some war I did believe worth fighting, if I'd been called up or something, I'm a coward, I'm just not physically capable. You were. You did it; fuck the rights and wrongs of the war, once you're in there, under fire, and your mates are getting blown away around you, you have to be able to function. At least you did; I'm not sure I could.'

'So what?' he says, looking at me. 'So I'm more of a fucking man because I learned how to kill people, and did?'

'No, I just mean – '

'Anyway,' he says, looking away again. 'A lot of good any of that did when we had a captain who couldn't fucking hack it, didn't have the guts to admit it, and had to send good men into a fucking killing ground to prove how fucking brave he really was.' Andy lifts a log from the hearth and puts it on the fire, hitting the other logs with it and making them spark and blaze.

'Yeah,' I say. 'Well, I can't – '

'And you're wrong,' he says, getting out of his seat and going to the corner of the room. There's a half-open hatch there leading into what looks like a deep, oddly cube-shaped cupboard; it's a dumb waiter. He pulls the top part of the metal cover further up, and the lower half sinks at the same time; he reaches in and gathers an armful of logs, bringing them over to the hearth. 'We all have responsibility, Cameron. You can't escape it.'

'Chayzuz, Gould, you take a hard line, man, so ye dae,' I say, trying to lighten things up but sounding pretty pathetic even to myself.

Andy sits, takes the offered spliff and arranges the logs neatly round the edge of the hearth, to dry.

He glances at me. 'Yeah, and a long memory; I still haven't forgiven you for not trying to rescue me on the ice that time.' He takes a long draw on the J, while I sit there thinking, Oh shit, then he hands the number back to me again with a big grin on his face. 'Only kidding,' he says. 'I've been out-machoing men and bedding women with that story for twenty years.'

*

Andy shows me to my room, a floor down, at about four in the morning. It has a fan heater and an electric blanket on the single bed. Before I go to sleep I wonder about whether I should have said anything to him about Mr Archer and his phone calls and Ares. I came up here thinking I would; I assumed I'd need to offload on somebody, but somehow it never seemed to be the right time to introduce the subject.

Never mind. It feels good just to have had a talk.

As I drift off I have the start of the running-through-the-woods dream again but I get away from it and don't remember anything else.

*

The next day while Andy's still asleep I take (a) some painkillers and (b) the car into Kyle of Lochalsh to tell the local police I'm here.

Driving into the town I spot an Escort with a blue light on the roof and pull up behind it. A sergeant appears from what a plate beside the door indicates is the dentist's and I go up to him and tell him my name and that I've been told to report my movements by Detective Inspector McDunn. The gaunt, grey-haired sergeant fixes me with a studiously suspicious look and takes a note of my name and the time. I get the impression he thinks I'm a harmless crank. Anyway, he doesn't say much; maybe his mouth is still sore from his visit to the dentist's. I can't wait around to try and engage him in further conversation because my bowels suddenly decide they want to wake up too, and I have to make a dash for the nearest bar and the toilets.

God, I *hate* it when my shit smells of whisky.

*

Andy has a party that night, partly for me and partly because his pal Howie is leaving for a job on the rigs the following day. We go for a walk up into the hills in the afternoon; me puffing and panting and coughing after Andy as he strides quickly, easily up the rutted forest tracks. Back at the hotel, I help him clear up the lounge bar, which still bears the debris from Andy's last party a few months earlier. The bar is still stocked, though there is no draught beer, only cans. Andy seems to be assuming he'll be providing all the booze for the party, so I gather he's not quite as skint as I've heard.

Maybe a couple of dozen people show up for the party; about half locals – mostly men, though there's one married couple and a pair of single girls – and half travellers, New Age hippies from various scattered buses and vans parked in lay-bys and the highway equivalent of oxbows, where corners or short, twisty lengths of old roads have been replaced with more direct stretches.

In terms of people mixing, it's a party that at best emulsifies rather than combines; there's a hostility between some of the Highland lads (clean-shaven, short-haired) and the travellers (the opposite) that gets worse as everybody gets more drunk. I get the impression the indigenous locals know the travelling people keep disappearing to have some blow, and resent it. Andy seems not to notice, talking to everybody, regardless.

I do my best to mix as well. At first I get on best with the Highland laddies, matching them dram for dram and can for can, taking their cigarettes and suffering their remarks on the lines of 'No I still smoke' when I offer them my Silk Cuts but gradually as we get drunker I start

144

to feel uncomfortable with their attitude to the travellers and even more so to women, and Howie, the guy I met last night, talks about how he used to slap the wife around and now the bitch is in one of these fucking women's refuges and if he ever finds her he'll fucking kick seven kinds of shit out of her. The others suggest this isn't such a good idea but I get the impression they think this mainly because he'd only end up in prison.

I find myself gravitating towards the travellers.

At one point I see Andy standing staring out the windows of the lounge, towards the dark loch, his eyes wide.

'You all right?' I ask him.

He takes a moment to answer. 'We're ten metres above mean sea-level here,' he says, nodding out to the shore.

'You don't say.' I light a cigarette.

'The deck on the QE2 on that level we called the Exocet Deck, because that's the height the missile rides at.'

Ah, Falklands Lore. 'Well,' I say, peering out at the darkness and the far side of the loch, 'unless you have an irate neighbour with particularly good contacts in the arms trade – '

'The only thing I ever have nightmares about,' Andy says, his gaze still directed at the unseeable loch, his eyes still wide. 'Isn't that ridiculous? Nightmares about being blown to fuck by a missile, ten years ago. I wasn't even on that deck; we were billeted two up from there . . .' He shrugs, drinks and turns to me, smiling. 'You see your mum much?'

'Eh?' I say, confused at this sudden change in direction. 'No, not recently. She's still in New Zealand. How about you? Been back to Strathspeld?'

He shakes his head and I get a shiver, remembering just that gesture of his, repeated and repeated so that it became like a nervous tic after a while, back in Strathspeld, after Clare's funeral in '89; a gesture of disbelief, refusal, non-acceptance.

'You should go,' he tells me. 'You should go and see them. They'd appreciate that.'

145

'We'll see,' I say. A gust of wind throws rain against the window and shakes the frame; it's loud and surprising and I flinch but he just turns slowly and looks out into the darkness with what could almost be contempt before laughing and putting an arm round my shoulder and suggesting we have another drink.

Later a storm breaks over the hotel; lightning flares above the mountains across the loch, and the windows rattle as the thunder booms. There's a power cut; the lights go out and we light candles and gas lamps and end up – a hard core of seven of us; Andy, me, Howie, another two local lads and a couple of the traveller boys – down in the snooker room where there's a beat-up looking table and a leak in the ceiling that turns the whole of the stained, green-baize surface into a millimetre-shallow marsh, water dripping from each pocket and dribbling down the bulky legs to the sopping carpet, and we play snooker by the light of the hissing gas lamps, having to hit the white ball really hard even for delicate shots because of the extra rolling resistance the water causes, and the balls make a zizzing, ripping noise as they race across the table and sometimes you can see spray curving up behind them and I'm feeling really drunk and a bit stoned from a couple of strong Js smoked out in the garden earlier with the travellers but I think this dimly lit water-hazard snooker is just hilarious and I'm laughing maniacally at it all and I put an arm round Andy's neck at one point and say, You know I love you, old buddy, and isn't friendship and love what's it's really all about? and why can't people just see that and just be *nice* to each other? except there are just *so many* complete bastards in the world, but Andy just shakes his head and I try to kiss him and he gently fends me off and steadies me against one wall and props me up with a snooker cue against my chest and I think this is really funny for some reason and laugh so much I fall over and have distinct problems getting up again and get carried to my room by Andy and one of the travellers and dumped on the bed and fall instantly asleep.

*

I dream of Strathspeld, and the long summers of my childhood passed in a trance of lazy pleasure, ending with that day, running through the woods (but I turn away from that memory, the way I've learned to over the years); I wander again through the woods and the small, hidden glens, along the shores of the ornamental lochan and the river and its loch and I'm standing near the old boathouse in that defeatingly bright sunlight, light dancing on water, and I see two figures, naked and thin and white in the grass beyond the reed beds, and as I watch them the light turns from gold to silver and then to white, and the trees seem to shrink in on themselves, leaves disappearing in the chill coruscations of that enveloping white blaze while the view all around me becomes brighter and darker at once and all is reduced to black and white; trees are bare and black, the ground smother-smoothed in white and the two young figures are gone, while one even smaller one – booted, gloved, coat-tails flying behind – runs laughing across the white level of the frozen loch.

Someone calls out.

C H A P T E R

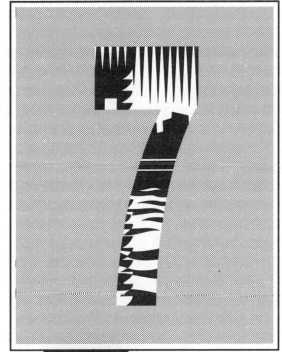

LUX EUROPAE

Twelve hours later I'm in the fucking Channel Islands still nursing a hangover and thinking, What in the fuck am I doing here?

*

'Eh? What?'

'Wake up, Cameron; there's a phone call.'

'Oh. Right.' I try to focus on Andy. I can't seem to get my left eye open. 'Is it important?'

'Don't know.'

So I get up and pull my dressing-gown on and head down to the cold, dusty lobby where the phone is.

'Cameron. Frank here.'

'Oh, hi.'

'So, are you enjoying your wee hol in the Highlands?'

'Oh, yeah,' I say, still trying to persuade my left eyelid to lift. 'What's the problem, Frank?'

'Well, your Mr Archer phoned.'

'Oh yeah?' I say warily.

'Yes. He said you might like to know' – I hear Frank rustling some paper – 'Mr Jemmel's real name is J. Azul. That's the initial J, then A-Z-U-L. And that Azul knew the full story but he was leaving on a foreign trip . . . well, this afternoon. That was all he'd say. I tried to ask him what he was talking about, but – '

'Wait a minute, wait a minute,' I say, pulling my left eyelid up and hurting my eye and starting that eye watering. I take a deep breath, trying to wake myself up. 'Say all that again.'

'Mis-ter,' Frank says slowly. 'Ar-ch-er . . . phon-ed . . .'

Frank repeats the message. Meanwhile I'm thinking. Leaving this afternoon . . . leaving from where?

'Okay,' I say, when Frank's finished talking to me as though I'm a *Sun* reader. 'Frank, could you do me a big favour and see if you can find who this guy Azul is?'

'Well, I'm quite busy you know, Cameron. We don't all treat deadlines with – '

'Frank, *please*. The name rings a bell; I think I've seen it . . . Christ, I can't remember, my brain's not working. But please, check it out, Frank, will you? Please? I'll owe you one. Please.'

'All right, all right.'

'Thanks; if you find anything call me right back, okay? Will you?'

'Yes, yes, all right.'

'Great. Brilliant. Thanks.'

'But if I'm ringing you I just hope you answer faster than you did yesterday.'

'What?'

'Your Mr Archer rang yesterday.'

'Yesterday?' I say, feeling my stomach churn.

'Yes; lunch-time. Ruby took the message. I was out but when I got

152

back I tried calling but there was no answer. I tried your mobile as well but I didn't think it would work up there in the mountains and sure enough all I got was the recording saying try again later.'

'Oh, Christ.'

'Anyway, another thing – '

He's going to come out with another of his ridiculous spell-check semi-jokes; I can't fucking believe it. Meanwhile my mind's racing, or at least trying to race; right now it feels like it's stuck at the side of the track trying to get its legs out of its tracksuit bottoms and hopping around and falling down while the race takes place elsewhere.

'. . . What if it's a common name?' Frank asks. 'What if half the people in Beirut or somewhere are called Azul? I mean it sounds like a sort of – '

'Frank, listen,' I say, suddenly inspired, and sounding a lot more sober and calm than I feel. 'I think I remember where I know the name from. I saw it in the back of *Private Eye*. Something to do with . . . I don't know; the sort of thing that gets into the back of the *Eye*. Please, Frank. He might be connected with defence, aerospace, intelligence or the arms trade. Try Profile; just type in "Get Azul" and – '

'I know, I know.'

'Thanks, Frank. I'm going to get dressed now. If I don't hear from you in about half an hour I'll ring anyway. Bye.'

Christ; those five murdered guys, not to mention all the others McDunn's investigating, and this guy leaving this afternoon. Rang yesterday. Christ, I hate deadlines! I'm panicking; I can feel it. My heart is racing. I'm trying to think but I don't know what to do. Decide!

I decide: When in doubt it's vitally important to *keep moving*. Velocity is important. Kinetic energy frees the brain and confuses the enemy.

*

153

I'm gulping hot coffee and pulling on my coat; my bag's sitting on the reception desk in the hotel lobby and Andy's standing, hunched and blinking and bleary-eyed, watching me stuff toast into my mouth and slurp coffee from a handle-free mug. Andy is looking at my bag. One of my socks is poking out from where the two zips meet, like a floppy white hernia. Andy pulls one of the zips open, pokes the sock back in and then recloses the bag.

'The phone often goes off,' he says apologetically. 'Probably the storm last night.'

'Never mind.' I glance at my watch. Past time to phone Frank.

'Listen,' Andy says, scratching under his chin and yawning. 'The police might want to talk to you – '

'I know; I'll let them know where I am, don't – '

'No, I mean the local cops.'

'*What*? Why?'

'Oh,' he sighs. 'There was a bit of a rumble last night when the boys left, outside. Looks like Howie and his pals jumped the two traveller guys on the road; landed one in hospital, apparently. Cops are looking for Howie. Anyway, you were asleep when it happened but they might want to have a word, so – '

'Jesus, I – ' I begin. The phone rings. I grab it and yell, 'What?'

'Cameron; Frank.'

'Oh, hi. Have you found anything?'

'I think so. Could be a Mr Jemayl Azul,' he says. He spells out the first name and I'm thinking Jemayl/Jemmel, uh-huh. 'British citizen,' Frank goes on. 'English mother, Turkish father. Born 17.3.49, educated Harrow, Oxford and Yale.'

'But is he in defence or –?'

'Has his own arms company. Connected with the Saudis but he's sold arms just about everywhere, including Libya, Iran and Iraq. He's bought up a lot of small UK firms in the past, mostly to close them down; been the subject of a question in the House. The Israelis accused him of selling nuclear information to the Iraqis in 1985.

154

You were right about him being mentioned in the *Eye*; appeared a few times and I got the cuts up . . .' More paper rustling. 'According to the report here, one of the aliases he used in share deals and bank accounts was Mr Jemmel. How's that?' Frank sounds pleased with himself.

'Brilliant, Frank, brilliant,' I tell him. 'So where is he?'

'Addresses in London and Geneva, an office in New York . . . but based on Jersey, in the Channel Islands.'

'Telephone number?'

'I checked: unlisted. And just an answering machine at his company address. But I called a pal of mine in St Helier who works on the local rag and he reckons your man's at home.'

'Right. Right . . .' I say. I'm thinking. 'What about an address?'

'Aspen, Hill Street, Gorey, Jersey.'

'Okay. Okay.' I'm still thinking. 'Frank, that's brilliant, an incredible help. Could you put me through to Eddie?'

*

'*What*?' Eddie says, when I tell him.

'Inverness to Jersey. Come on, Eddie; I'm onto something here. I'd pay for it myself but my card's up to the limit.'

'This had better be good, Cameron.'

'Eddie, this could be fucking enormous, I'm not kidding.'

'Well, so you say, Cameron, but your record overseas isn't terribly encouraging . . .'

'Come on, Eddie, that's cheap. And anyway, Jersey's barely overseas and I'm giving up a day's holiday here.'

'Oh, all right, but you're going economy.'

*

'Some life,' Andy says, putting my bag into the rear of the 205.

'Yeah,' I say, getting into the car. I can feel my headache

attempting to reassert itself. 'Looks exotic on occasion; doesn't feel it.'

I close the door and wind the window down. I'm not at all sure I'm fit to drive but I have to if I'm going to get to Inverness in time for the connecting flight.

Andy says, looking dubious, 'You sure you know what you're doing?'

'Covering the story,' I tell him, and grin. 'See you soon.'

*

I make Inverness Airport in ninety minutes, through showers of hail towed under tall, grey clouds. Sound track by Count Basie and Islam's answer to Pavarotti in the even more enormous shape of Nusrat Fateh Ali Khan; voice like a tripped-out angel in a dream even though I have no idea what he's singing about and always sneakingly suspect it's something on the lines of 'Hey, let's string up Salman Rushdie, yeah-yeah'.

The ticket's waiting for me at the desk. I'm still officially on holiday so I force myself not to read any newspapers. I think about buying some fags but the headache's still there behind my eyes and I have the feeling smoking a cigarette would make me want to throw up. Of course what I really need is something chemical and crystalline but I don't have any and wouldn't know where to start looking for it in Inverness. I feel the need to do something so I buy a dumb little hand-held game and sit playing it while I wait. The flight's delayed but only slightly; I change at Gatwick in breezy sunshine and the 146 touches down on Jersey in relatively balmy conditions. I even manage to hire a car with the credit card, which seems like a blessing.

The Nova comes with a map; I drive through the neat little lanes and some straighter, faster roads, feeling even in those few miles that the place is too damn clean and twee and crowded after the West Highlands. Gorey is easy to find, out on the east coast, looking out over the sands and round to the point where the castle I always thought was in St Helier actually is. Hill Street takes a little longer, but Aspen is conspicuous; a long white villa set just below the crest of a low, wooded ridge, surrounded by white walls with ornamental black railings and little ball-head shrubs standing in wooden tubs. Terracotta tiled roof. It looks cool. I imagine its value is probably pretty cool too.

There are tall black iron gates but they're hooked open so I just drive through and up a drive of pink bricks to the door.

I ring the bell and wait. There are no other cars in the drive but there's a garage block attached to the house with two double doors. The sun's dipping down over the trees and a breeze gets up, rustling the leaves on the ornamental shrubs and blowing some grit into my left eye, making it water again. I ring the bell once more. I look through the letter-box but I can't see anything; I reach in and feel a box on the far side of the thick door.

After a few minutes I take a look round the place, stepping under Moorish archways and over low white walls, past an astroturf tennis court and a swimming pool about the same size, uncovered and still. I kneel and test the water with one hand. Warm.

I try to look in the windows of the house but they're either covered with those plastic roll-down external shutters you usually see in France or closed off inside by Venetian blinds.

I go back to the car, thinking maybe Mr Azul's only out for a short while. Of course, maybe I've missed him entirely and he's already set off on whatever trip Mr Archer seemed to know about. I'll give it half an hour, maybe an hour or so, then I'll call the local paper and ask for Frank's contact. I consider playing the hand-held I bought in Inverness but I'm either not hooked on it yet or my jaded palate has produced game-boredom already.

I'm thinking there might be something wrong with my plan to wait as I close my eyes (only to rest them), but even as I yawn and put my hands into my armpits I think a spot of rest isn't such a bad idea so long as I don't fall asleep.

*

Andy runs out across the ice. I am five years old and he is seven. Strathspeld is everywhere white; the sky is still and shining, hiding the sun in a dazzling, brilliant haze, its light somehow distanced by the intervening layer of high cloud overlooking a chill wilderness of snow. The mountaintops are smothered, black crags violent spattered marks against that blankness; the hills and forests are blanketed too, the trees are frosted and the loch is hard and soft together, iced over then snowed upon. Here, beyond the gardens of the lodge and the woods and ornamental ponds, the loch narrows and becomes a river again, bending and funnelling and quickening as it heads towards the rocks and falls and the shallow gorge beyond. Usually from here you can hear the thunder of the falls in the distance but today there is only silence.

I watch Andy run out. I shout after him but I don't follow him. The bank on this side is low, only half a metre above the white plain of the snow-covered river. The grass and reeds around me are flattened under the sudden, overnight fall of snow. On the far side, where Andy is heading, the bank is tall and steep where the water has cut into the hill, removing sand and gravel and stones and leaving an overhang of earth and exposed, dangling tree-roots; the dark gravel space under that ragged overhang is the only place I can see where there is no snow.

Andy is yelling as he runs, coat-tails flapping out behind him, gloved hands outspread, his head thrown back, the ear flaps on his hat snapping and clapping like wings. He's almost halfway across and suddenly I go from being terrified and annoyed to being exhilarated, intoxicated; overjoyed. We were told not to do this, told not to come here, told to sledge and throw snowballs and

158

make snowmen all we wanted, but not even to come near the loch and the river, in case we fell through the ice; and yet Andy came here after we'd sledged for a while on the slope near the farm, walked down here through the woods despite my protests, and then when we got here to the river bank I said well, as long as we only looked, but then Andy just whooped and jumped down onto the boulder-lumped white slope of shore and sprinted out across the pure flat snow towards the far bank. At first I was angry at him, frightened for him, but now suddenly I get this rush of joy, watching him race out there into the cold level space of the stilled river, free and warm and vivacious in that smoothed and frozen silence.

I think he's done it, I think he's across the river and safe and there's a buzzy glow of vicarious accomplishment starting to well up within me, but then there's a cracking noise and he falls; I think he's tripped and fallen forward but he isn't lying flat on the snow, he's sunk up to his waist in it and there's a pool of darkness spreading on the whiteness around him as he struggles, trying to lever himself out and I can't believe this is happening, can't believe Andy isn't going to jump free; I'm yelling in fear now, shouting his name, screaming out to him.

He struggles, turning round as he sinks deeper, chunks and edges of ice rearing into the air and making little puffs and fountains of snow as he tries to find purchase and push himself out. He's calling out to me now but I can hardly hear him because I'm screaming so hard, wetting my pants as I squeeze the screams out. He's holding his hand out to me, yelling at me, but I'm stuck there, terrified, screaming, and I don't know what to do, can't think what to do, even while he's yelling at me to help him, come out to him, *get a branch*, but I'm petrified at the thought of setting foot on that white, treacherous surface and I can't imagine finding a branch, can't think what to do as I look one way towards the tall trees above the hidden gorge and the other along the shore of the loch towards the boat-house but there are no branches, there's only

159

snow everywhere, and then Andy stops struggling and slips under the whiteness.

I stand still, quietened and numbed. I wait for him to come back up but he doesn't. I step back, then turn and run, the clinging wetness round my thighs going from warm to cold as I race beneath the snow-shrouded trees towards the house.

I run into the arms of Andy's parents walking with the dogs near the ornamental ponds and it seems like an age before I can tell them what's happened because my voice won't work and I can see the fear in their eyes and they're asking, 'Where is Andrew? Where is Andrew?' and eventually I can tell them and Mrs Gould gives a strange little shuddering cry and Mr Gould tells her to get the people in the house and phone for an ambulance and runs away down the path towards the river with the four Golden Labradors barking excitedly behind him.

I run to the house with Mrs Gould and we get everybody – my mum and dad and the other guests – to come down to the river. My father carries me in his arms. At the riverside we can see Mr Gould on his stomach out on the ice, pushing himself back from the hole in the river; people are shouting and running around; we head down the river towards the narrows and the gorge and my father slips and almost drops me and his breath smells of whisky and food. Then somebody calls out and they find Andy, round the bend in the river, down where the water reappears from a crust of ice and snow and swirls, lowered and reduced, round the rocks and wedged tree-trunks before the lip of the falls, which sound muted and distant today, even this close.

Andy's there, caught between a snow-covered tree-trunk and an iced-over rock, his face blue-white and quite still. His father splashes deep into the water and pulls him out.

I start crying and bury my face in my father's shoulder.

The village doctor was one of the house guests; he and Andy's father hold the boy up, letting water drain from his mouth, then

160

lay him down on a coat on the snow. The doctor presses on Andy's chest while his wife breathes into the boy's mouth. They look more surprised than anybody when his heart restarts and then he makes a gurgling noise in his throat. Andy is wrapped in the coat and rushed to the house, submerged to the neck in a warm bath and given oxygen when the ambulance arrives.

*

He'd been under the ice, under the water, for ten minutes or more. The doctor had heard about children, usually younger than Andy, surviving without air in cold water, but never seen anything like it.

Andy recovered quickly, sucking on the oxygen, coughing and spluttering in the warm bath, then being dried and taken to a warmed bed and watched over by his parents. The doctor was worried about brain damage but Andy seemed just as bright and intelligent afterwards as he'd been before, remembering details from earlier in his childhood and performing above average in the memory tests the doctor gave him and even doing well in school when that started again after the winter break.

It was a miracle, his mother said, and the local newspaper agreed. Andy and I never did get properly told off for what happened, and he hardly ever mentioned that day to me unless he had to. His father didn't like talking about it much either and used to be slightly dismissive and jokey about it all. Mrs Gould gradually talked less about it.

Eventually it seemed it was only I who ever thought about that still, cold morning, recalling in my dreams that cry and that hand held out to me for help I could not, would not give, and the silence that followed Andy disappearing under the ice.

And sometimes I felt he was different, and had changed, even though I knew people changed all the time and people our age changed faster than most.

161

Even so, I thought on occasion there had been a loss; nothing necessarily to do with oxygen starvation but just as a result of the experience, the shock of his cold journey, slipping away beneath the grey lid of ice (and perhaps, I told myself in later years, it was only a loss of ignorance, a loss of folly, and so no bad thing). But I could never again imagine him doing something as spontaneously crazy, as aggressively, contemptuously fate-tempting and *unleashed* as running out across the frozen ice, arms out, laughing.

*

You're already wearing your moustache and wig and glasses and you have clip-on sunshades over the lenses because it is quite a bright day. You ring the doorbell, watching down the drive for any cars while you pull on your leather gloves. You're sweating and nervous and you know you're out on a limb here, you're in the process of taking some terrible risks and the luck, the *flow* that comes from being justified and in tune and not taking too much for granted, not being contemptuous or disrespectful of fate; all that's in danger here because you're pushing the envelope, you're maybe relying on one or two too many things going perfectly. Even getting it all set up to get you this far may have taxed your fortune to the limit already and there's still a long way to go. But if you're going to fail you'll do it full-face on, not flinching, not whining. You've done more than you thought you'd ever get away with and so in a sense it's all gain from here, in fact it's been all gain for some time and so you can't complain and you don't intend to if fate deserts you now.

He comes to the door just like that; no servants, no security phone, and that by itself gives you the green light; you haven't the time for any finessing so you just kick him in the balls and follow him inside as he collapses, foetal on the floor. You close the door, take off your glasses because your vision is so distorted, and kick him in the head; far too softly, then still not hard enough, as he scrabbles round on the floor, one hand at his crotch and the other at his head, making a spitting, wheezing noise. You kick him again.

This time he goes limp. You don't think you've killed him or severed his spine or anything but, if you have, that can't be helped. You make sure he can't be seen from the letter flap, which is covered by a sealed box, then you look round the hall. Golf umbrella. You take that. Still nobody coming. You walk quickly through, see the kitchen and go in there, pulling down the Venetian blinds. You find a breadknife but you keep the umbrella too. You find some tape in a kitchen drawer and go back to the front hall, turning him round so that you're between him and the door. You tie his hands and wrists together. He's wearing expensive-looking slacks and a silk shirt. Crocodile slip-ons and monogrammed socks. Manicure and a scent that you don't recognise. Hair looks slightly damp.

You take off both his shoes and stuff both socks into his mouth; they're silk, too, so they ball up very small. You tape his mouth closed, put the roll of tape in one pocket, then leave him there to search the rest of the house, pulling down the blinds in each room as you go. In the kitchen again, you find the door to the cellar. On the first floor you hear music and the sounds of water.

You creep along to an open doorway. Bedroom; probably the master bedroom. Brass bed; huge, maybe even gold-plated. Disturbed bedclothes, broad sunlit balcony beyond windows and pastel-pink vertical blinds. The sounds are coming from the en-suite bathroom. You go into the bedroom, checking the position of the mirrors; none of them ought to show you to anybody in the bathroom. You're listening as you approach the bathroom door. The music is loud. It's a Eurythmics song called *Sweet Dreams are Made of This*. A power cable stretches from a socket in the wall into the bathroom. That's interesting.

The voice sings along with the song, then turns into a hum. Your heart sinks. You were hoping he was alone in the house. You look

163

through the crack at the door hinge. The bathroom is big. In one corner there is a sunken jacuzzi with a young person in it, moving sinuously in the bubbling waters. Caucasian, with short black hair. You can't tell whether the person is male or female. The research you did on Mr Azul didn't cover his sexuality.

The ghetto-blaster lies less than a metre away from the lip of the jacuzzi. There is at least another couple of metres of flex coiled on the floor.

The young man or woman sings along with the song again again, putting their head back as they do so. Probably female; neck smooth, no real Adam's apple.

You look again at that power cable.

Your mouth is dry. What to do? It could be so quick, so easy and it would simplify things so much. It is almost as though fate is saying, Look, I've made it easy for you; just get on with it, do it. Whoever or whatever they are they're associating with this man and if they don't know what he does then they should.

But you're not sure. This violates the code, this goes against what you originally decided were your operational parameters. There have to be rules, laws, for everything; after all, there are even rules for war. Maybe this is fate testing you, offering you a litmus test, an apparently simple way round a problem that will prove you, find you out. If you take the easy way you will have failed, and nothing will save you then, not your skill, not your determination or righteousness, and not your luck because that will have turned against you.

The young person in the tub looks happy enough for now. You go to the bed, put down the umbrella and start looking in the drawers and cupboards built into the wall units surrounding the head of the bed. You keep glancing to the bathroom door. The drawers slide smoothly in and out without a sound; one of the perks of picking on the well-off rather than the chipboard classes.

You find a gun. Smith & Wesson .38. Loaded. Box of fifty

rounds. You permit yourself an almost inaudible sigh and grin to yourself.

You lay the knife beside the umbrella, heft the gun and put it under the duvet to click the safety off. Peek in the drawer again. No silencer; that would be too much to ask for.

But then in another drawer you find something maybe even more useful. You stare at the gear in the drawer, a glow in your belly spreading through you. You have made the right choice and you are being rewarded. You glance over the thick tubes that make up the emperor-size brass bedstead, and smile.

You take the bondage hood out of the drawer. It zips up the back and its only feature is a nose-shaped crease with a couple of little nostril slits at the base. You take out your penknife and cut a couple of eye-holes, continually glancing at the bathroom door.

You try the hood on, then take it off and slit some more leather off the eye-holes. You put it on again, zipping it up halfway at the back. It smells of sweat and that scent Mr Azul favours. You take one of the pairs of handcuffs from the drawer and go into the bathroom, pointing the gun at the figure in the tub.

'Jem,' she says, 'what are you –?'

You decide to use your Michael Caine voice. It doesn't sound very much like Michael Caine, but then it doesn't sound like your own voice either and that's all that matters.

'It's not fucking lover-boy, dear, now get out of the fucking bath and do as you're told and you won't get hurt.' It's not too bad; the mask helps disguise your voice too.

She stares at you, mouth open. It's a bad time for the doorbell to go, but that's what happens. She looks past you.

'Make a noise, darling,' you say quietly, 'and you're fucking history, understand?'

The doorbell goes again. The Eurythmics song finishes and you put a foot on the ghetto-blaster's power cable and drag it smartly across the bathroom tiles, pulling the lead from the back of the machine. You half expect the next song to start anyway because there are batteries in it, but, instead: silence.

The girl stares at you.

You watch her. It all feels strangely academic, as though you don't really care what happens next. If she does make a noise you probably won't shoot her, and anyway there's a chance she couldn't make enough of a noise to be heard outside the front door; it's a big house and although there are a lot of hard, sound-reflective surfaces in it, you're not convinced a scream would make it all the way to whoever's outside, either down the stairwell or through the double-glazed balcony windows. Plus, of course, you might have time to get over to her and hit her, knock her out before she could even gather a decent breath, but it's dangerous, edge-working stuff and you'd rather not have to think about that.

The doorbell doesn't go a third time.

You pull a towelling robe from the back of the door and throw it at her. She half catches it as it lands to one side of the jacuzzi. 'Right. Put that on now, come on.'

You expect her to crouch and try to put the robe on before she's fully out of the water, or to turn her back to you, but instead there's something like a sneer on her face as she stands up facing you and wraps the robe around herself with a kind of disdain. She has a good body, and that single vertical tuft of pubic hair you need if you're a model or the possessor of a high-cut swimsuit.

She puts her head back with a nervous, resigned sigh when you put the gun to her head but she doesn't try anything as you cuff her hands behind her back. You tape her mouth then you walk her down to the kitchen and down into the cellar. As you pass through the hall you notice that Mr Azul is just where you left him.

The cellar provides lots of rope. You tape her fingers together and then tie her – sitting on the floor – to a stout wooden workbench. You remove anything sharp from the workbench surface and check there's nothing within reach of her legs. You take some of the rope with you.

You go back up to Mr Azul, and he's gone.

You go stupid on yourself for a moment, as the luck wobbles, threatens to fly away and leave you; you stare at the place where he was, lying curled up, tied up in front of the door; you stare at the empty stretch of carpet, dumbly, as if staring will help.

Then you turn and run into the main lounge.

He's there, still curled up and still secured by the tape, but he must have wriggled his way through to here while you were down in the cellar; he's knocked over a table with the phone on it and he's just turning the phone the right way up as you enter the lounge and see him.

He wriggles, getting his face over the buttons on the base of the phone. He stabs at the buttons three times, then wriggles over to the handset and makes muffled shouts through the gag until you cock the gun and he hears it and looks round at where you stand, next to the wall, waving the telephone's wall-plug.

You haul him upstairs and throw him on the bed; he struggles and tries to shout. It's getting dark, so you turn the pink pastel vertical blinds closed and pull the curtains before putting on the lights. Mr Azul screams through his silk socks and masking-tape. You hit him. He's only groggy, not out, but you're able to secure him to the bed with the other set of handcuffs and the leather straps from the same drawer the hood came from. You're satisfied he's tightly held; the bed is sturdy and the straps are supple but quite thick. They fit perfectly. He struggles a little.

Then you take the rope you brought from the cellar and measure out four lengths, cutting them with your penknife.

You tie one length round Mr Azul's upper right arm, as close to his armpit as possible, over his silk shirt; you kneel on the bed and haul with all your might and the rope bites deep into the sheen of the pale silk shirt; Mr Azul cries out behind his gag; a strangled, anguished shriek.

You do the same to his other arm.

You tie his legs too, fitting the rope up to his crotch and tying it tight, bunching the fabric of the slacks. Mr Azul bucks up and down on the bed in a bizarre parody of sexual energy. His eyes are popping and sweat stands out on his skin. His face is going red as his heart struggles to pump blood down arteries blocked off by the ropes.

Then you take out the little plastic box from your jacket and show him the syringe needle. He's still bucking up and down and he's shaking his head too now and you're not sure he understands, but it doesn't matter all that much. You prick him once on each arm and leg. This is a refinement you thought of only recently and are quietly proud of. It means that even if he is discovered in time, before necrosis sets in, he will be HIV-positive.

You leave him there and go down to check the woman is all right. Mr Azul's screams sound harsh and hoarse and far away.

It's sunset when you leave, locking the quiet house securely behind you. The sun flames orange and pink behind the trees above the house, the breeze is cool rather than cold, scented with flowers and the sea, and you think what a pleasant if rather bland place this would be to settle down.

*

I jolt awake with a bad taste in my mouth and my left eyelid stuck down again. It's almost dark. I look at my watch. Where the fuck *is* this guy? I take another look round the house; no lights. Back in the car, I try to use the mobile but the batteries are flat and the Nova doesn't seem to have a cigarette lighter. I head for St Helier.

*

'Shit.' I've just tried the local newspaper but Frank's pal has gone out and they won't give me a contact number.

I'm standing in a phone box near the harbour. I watch a white Lamborghini Countach trundle past on the street outside and shake my head in disbelief. A Lambo. More than two metres broad and barely one high. Just the car to have on an island full of lots of narrow, high-hedged twisty roads and a 60-miles-per-hour speed limit. I wonder if he ever gets the beast out of second gear.

Maybe I should phone the police: hello hello I've just spotted a cretin recklessly in charge of an obscene amount of money is there a reward? (Tempting.)

*

Every bastard's out. Frank isn't at home, Azul's unlisted, I try the local paper here but they can't or won't help and the airlines refuse to give out information on passengers. I put the phone down. 'Shit!' I shout. It sounds very loud in the phone box. I phone Yvonne and William's house but there's only William's voice on the answer-machine. I remember Yvonne saying something about being away on a job for the next few days. I think about phoning her mobile but she hates me doing that so I don't.

Oh, bugger this. If I was some fucking private eye or something I'd head back out to Mr Azul's big house and break in somehow and find something really interesting or a body or a beautiful woman (or just get slugged on the back of the head and wake up wise-cracking). But I'm tired, I've still got a headache, I feel beat and out of ideas and I feel *embarrassed* dammit. What in the fuck am I doing here? What was I thinking of? Hell, this seemed like such a good idea this morning.

I can still make a flight back to Blighty which will connect with the last plane to Inverness. Forget covering the story. Sometimes a tactical retreat is the only course to follow. Even Saint Hunter would agree. If I feel the need to *do something* I can always exercise my creative abilities trying to think of a story that'll appease Eddie. Fat chance. I take the Nova back to the airport.

An hour to kill. Time to hit the bar. I start off with a Bloody Mary as this is breakfast in a sense, then cleanse the palate with a bottle of Pils. I buy a packet of Silk Cut and carefully smoke a cigarette – making sure that I'm actually enjoying it, not just doing it out of habit – while managing to fit in a couple of large and very refreshing G&Ts before the flight's called and there's just time for a single knocked-back whisky to provide a bit of nominal support for the Scottish export drive.

I board the plane feeling no pain, eat the evening meal and continue with the G&T theme, land in Gatwick and make the connection via the smoking area of the bar and another gulped Gordon's, then pass on the second offered dinner but not the accompanying booze and quietly pass out somewhere over the West Midlands, to be woken by a dishy blonde with an impudent, dimpled smile and we're here we've landed we've arrived, we're on the stand at the airport and I'd ask her what she's doing later because I'm drunk enough to not care when she says 'No' as she probably will, but I know I'm too tired and besides my left eyelid's stuck again and I suspect it makes me look a bit like Quasimodo, so I don't say anything except, 'Uh, thanks,' which is cool or sad, I'm not sure which.

I walk into the terminal thinking, Well, at least there isn't that smell of sewage around you sometimes get when you arrive in dear old Embra; I'm not sure I could handle that right now. I walk through the lounge thinking something looks wrong somehow, then stop and stand still where the lounge opens out into the main terminal building, suddenly filled with horror and confusion; it's all too small and not shaped right! This isn't Edinburgh! Those amiable but blatantly incompetent buffoons have brought me to the wrong fucking airport! Dickheads! Can't they even *navigate*, for fuck's sake? Christ, I bet there isn't even a flight back from . . . Where the hell am I?

I see the sign saying Welcome to Inverness just as I remember where I left the car and where I left from this morning and just before I turn and stamp to the nearest desk and demand in my highest dudgeon to be taken to Edinburgh on a charted Lear if

170

necessary or limoed immediately to the highest-starred hotel within a reasonable radius for a free overnight dinner, bed and breakfast and unlimited bar tab.

Narrow escape from Terminal Embarrassment.

People are walking past looking at me oddly. I shake my head and set a course for the car park.

It's kind of late now and I'm in no condition to drive so when I get the 205 I only take it as far as the outskirts of Inverness where I stop at the first lit Bed and Breakfast sign I see and talk politely and slowly to the pleasant middle-aged couple from Glasgow who run the place and then say goodnight, close the door of my room and fall fast asleep on the bed without even taking off my jacket.

C H A P T E R

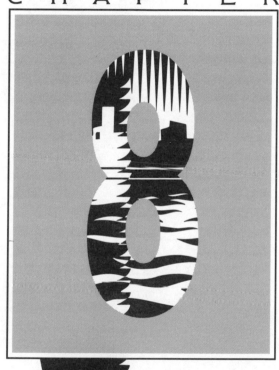

FRIENDLY FIRE

I head south after what I think's called a hearty breakfast and
an even heartier cough. I fuel up at a wee petrol station just
before the A9 and phone Fettes while the tank's filling.

Sergeant Flavell sounds a little odd when I talk to him and
tell him I've been to Jersey for the day but I'm on my way back to
Edinburgh. I ask him if I can have my new lap-top back and he says
he isn't sure. He suggests I come straight to Fettes; they want to talk
to me. I say okay.

South on the A9, sound track Michelle Shocked, The Pixies, Carter
and Shakespear's Sister. I catch a bit of radio while I'm changing
cassettes just north of Perth and hear something called *I'll Sleep
When I'm Dead* by Bon Jovi which isn't a patch on Uncle Warren's
song of the same name and makes me more than reasonably annoyed.
Into Edinburgh by late lunch-time, past the signs trumpeting the
up-coming Euro-summit. I don't know how they've done it but the
typography on the signs makes *me* want to pronounce the word
Edin-burg, and I *live* in the place, for God's sake.

Christ in a bucket: independent bastarding deterrent, The Genuine Shit Article, cold fucking filtering, Edin-burg, Edin-borow, Sleep when I'm a de-rigueurly long-haired white-skinned head-banging high-pitched middle-aged sub-grunge light-metal Zep-clone. What a pile of shit everything is!

On Ferry Road, within sight of Fettes School's preposterous spire and only minutes from the police HQ, I have the first cigarette of the day, not because I really want it, just to feel bad. (Uncle Warren knows a thing or two.)

This turns out to be smart thinking in a way because when I get to Cop Central they promptly arrest me.

*

The hotel is dark and very quiet. The cellars are full of junk, most of which might have been useful once but all of which is now covered in water or mud or fungus. Some of the timbers under the floor are white with fuzzy rot. On the lower ground floor you pass through the snooker room, the ballroom and a store room. The table in the snooker room is waterlogged, its baize stained and its wooden sides cracked. The old motorbikes, tables, chairs and carpets in the ballroom look like forlorn toys in some long-neglected doll's house. Rain beats softly against the windows: the only sound. Outside, it is black dark.

The stairs from here to the top floor stretch upwards around the dilapidated grandeur of the stairwell. On the next floor up the reception area is dusty and bare, the bar smells of sour booze and stale cigarette smoke and the empty dining room is redolent of dampness and decay. The kitchen is cold and hollow and echoing. There is one old domestic stove, powered by bottled gas, and one sink. There's an apron hanging on a nail.

You take the apron and put it on.

The next two floors hold bedrooms. There is dampness here too, and in some of the rooms the ceiling has fallen in, the plaster and

176

lath lying draped over the heavy, old-fashioned furniture like some clumsy travesty of a dust-sheet. The rain is hitting the windows harder now, and the wind is getting up, whistling through cracks in the panes and the window-frames.

The top floor feels a little less damp, a little more warm, though the wind and rain still sound loud outside and above.

At one end of the dark corridor, past the wedged-open fire door, a door lies ajar. The living room inside is lit by the remains of a log fire, collapsing now into ashes. A couple of logs lie on the hearth, drying, and the air smells of their pine scent and cigarette smoke. An old coal scuttle to the side of the fireplace holds a can of paraffin, almost full.

In the corner of the room the dumb waiter contains a selection of logs of various sizes, most of them still damp. You take the biggest of the logs, which is about the size of a man's arm, and walk softly across the room to the bedroom door. You go through and stand listening to the rain and the wind, and – just audible – the noise of a man breathing slowly and rhythmically in the bed. You hold the log out in front of you as you walk towards the bed.

He moves in the darkness, something you hear more than see. You stop and stand still. Then the man in the bed starts to snore.

Rain drums on the window. You smell whisky and old tobacco smoke.

You get to the bedside and raise the log over your head.

You hold it there.

This is different, somehow. This is somebody you know. But you can't think about that because that isn't the point; although you know it does matter, you can't allow it to matter, you can't let something like that stop you. You bring the log down with all your might. It hits his head and you don't hear the noise it makes because you cry out at the same time, as though it's you in the bed, you being attacked, you being killed. There's a terrible, sucking, bubbling noise from the figure in the bed. You raise the log and bring it down again, calling out once more.

The man in the bed doesn't move or make a sound.

You turn on the torch. There is a lot of blood; it looks red where it seeps into the white sheets, black where it quietly pools. You take the apron off and cover his shoulders and head with it. Then you go downstairs to get the gas bottle out of the old stove in the kitchen.

The twice-soaked bed linen lights quickly, paraffin overcoming blood. You leave the gas bottle on the floor at the foot of the bed and walk quickly away along the shorter length of corridor and step through the emergency exit out into the loud darkness of the night. You run down the metal fire escape on the gable end of the building.

You stop at the top of the road and look back, to see the flames just starting to become visible over the edge of the hotel roof, dancing orange into the night.

Maybe you hear the gas bottle explode a couple of minutes and a couple of miles later, when you're on the loch-side road heading away, but it's blowing quite hard by then and you're not sure.

*

It's been three days now I'm not sure though I could be wrong because I haven't slept very well I have nightmares of a man and they think it's me but it isn't, is it? *Is* it? I'm starting to wonder. He has a gorilla mask on and he talks with the voice of a baby and he has a huge syringe and I'm *tied to the seat screaming*. I can't take it. They keep questioning me, always asking where I was what I did why I did it, did all of them where I was who I was with who am I trying to kid why don't I just admit I did it well if I didn't do all these things, who did? I'm in London I'm in the nick I'm in fucking Paddington Green for Christ's sake, the high-security station they use for the Provos and they think I'm so dangerous so much a security risk they've got me here and even holding me under the Prevention of Terrorism Act Jesus God because some of them still aren't convinced they aren't dealing with some unholy alliance

178

of the IRA, Welsh Nationalists and uppity jocks. They brought me down that day from Edinburgh, bundled me into a transit van with seats but no windows, handcuffed to a big quiet London lad who wouldn't talk to me at all and didn't even say much to the other two cops in the back of the transit just sat staring ahead and we seemed to drive all night just stopping once at some service station on the M1, took a while to arrange everything, then they came in with a selection of cans of soft drinks and sandwiches and pasties and pork pies and chocolate and we all sat there munching then they asked me did I need the toilet and I said yes and they opened the door and it was straight over the grass into the gents' toilets, two cops guarding the door and some men, looked like truckers, standing watching me, waiting for their turn after I'd had my private visit; only wanted a pee but I couldn't do it even though the big lad wasn't actually watching just having him standing there handcuffed to me was enough so they checked the stalls and then took the cuffs off me and I had to leave the door open a crack while I went, then back out and I see the other cop cars Christ a Range Rover and a Senator too I'm a fucking VIP, then it's into the van and on with the journey to London where the questioning starts; they're concentrating on Sir Rufus's murder, for now, because they found a card a fucking business card in the woods near the burned cottage; not mine that would have been too obvious but a card from a guy I know on *Jane's Defence Weekly* with some scribbled notes on the back:

> *Ctrl + Alt 0 = PoV chnge*
> *Shft + Alt = Chn of Cmnd zoom (bounces)*
> *Milk Cheez Bred Shavng Foam*

They ask me, Is that your writing? and it is of course it is those are *Despot* control codes from when the computer's mouse was misbehaving and that's the way I always spell when I do a shopping list. I vaguely recall writing down the codes months ago and losing whatever it was I wrote them on. I stare at the muddied, warped little card sealed in a deal-sized plastic bag, recognising my own writing and feeling my mouth go even drier than it already is and I can only gibber something about, Well, it *looks* like my writing but, I mean, and anyway, somebody, anybody could have taken that, I mean . . . but they just look quietly pleased and the questions go on.

And all I can think is *Don't confess, don't confess, don't confess*. There are detectives and DCIs and Chief Supers and Commanders every fucking where; more tecs and CID guys and Anti-Terrorism Squad chaps and regional guys than you can shake a nightstick at, all asking questions, all asking the same fucking questions and me trying to give the same fucking answers; seeing DI McDunn, sucking saliva through his teeth and letting me share his B&Hs, is like meeting an old pal even though he's got all his questions too. It's a relief when the Terrorist Squad boys seem to lose interest but that still leaves all the rest and I can't think I can't think straight I can't sleep.

It's bad enough at first but then it gets worse even as they keep me because they found *more*, they found two more and that was while I was *here* for Christ's sake while they held me while things were still happening more stuff came in while they were questioning me and they looked at me with disbelief horror disgust and I was going What? What is it? Now what? What am I supposed to have done now? And they told me about Azul, in Jersey, and before that I think it was before that they showed me the forensic photographs of all of them: Bissett skewered on the railings, grotesque and spread and limp; the blood-smeared vibrator used on the retired judge, Jamieson; the drained shapeless white body of Persimmon, tied to his grid above a pool of blood, then nothing when there should have been something; then what was left of Sir Rufus Carter, blackened bones, distorted and bent, the black skull's jaw hinged down in a blind scream but the flesh all gone very much a dental-records job and it was all black, the nails, the wood and the bones too but it's their mouths their jaws I remember, their silent screams, hanging slack or jammed open and it gets worse because they show me the fucking video they show me the video they think I made or that I think they think I made but I didn't; they make me watch it and it's horrific; there's a man and he's dressed in black or dark blue and he has a gorilla mask on and he keeps sucking on this little bottle he's carrying which must be helium because it gives him that baby voice disguising his own voice and he has this fat little guy strapped to a chrome seat, his mouth taped, one arm tied down onto the arm of the chair, shirt rolled up and the little guy's shrieking as hard as he can but it sounds quiet because the noise is having to come down his nose while the man in the gorilla mask looks from the camera to the guy in the seat and holds up this huge fucking syringe like something from a nightmare from an old movie from a horror film and I can feel my heart beating wildly because *that's what this is.* This is a horror movie a fucking horror movie this lunatic is making his own horror film and you can't even tell yourself Hell it's only a story aren't the special effects good it isn't real because that's exactly what it is and the gorilla man is explaining in that hideous high-pitched baby's voice what he has in this bottle and in this syringe and I throw up halfway through but they pause the video for me.

After it's over we cut to another scene and there's somebody who might be the little guy again and he's *still* strapped to a chair but this time it's a tall hospital chair with wheels and a little fold-away table in front of him and the straps holding his torso would be easy to undo but his hands are limp. There's some sort of board behind his head and a towel or something round his forehead holding his head upright but the eyes Christ the eyes there's nothing there and McDunn says Persistent Vegetative State they call it apparently; Persistent Vegetative State and it looks it man it looks it.

And then of course there are the other two. First it's Azul and his girlfriend. She's traumatised and dehydrated but otherwise unharmed but he's got soul brother's limbs where his own ought to be; necrosis like frostbite, blood-death at the extremities but the extremities start at shoulder and groin; he's alive but if you were him you'd rather not be. Arms salesman; okay the Avenger the Equaliser the Total Fucking Nutter went for the legs too but still, and the editor spiked, and the rapist-lenient judge raped and the pornographer poisoned and *stroked* and the man who was so callous about the bloodshed in the Iran/Iraq war forced to watch his penned animals die like cattle like soldiers like cattle and then bled to death in his own private fountains of blood and the businessman who put profits before safety and not only helped kill a thousand people but then tried to get out of paying the survivors and dependants any compensation gets his own gas explosion – blevey is the technical term apparently – and fuck me whoever he is (assuming he *is* a he), he's got a sense of humour or at least irony why he's produced what's almost a snuff video effectively a snuff video if you mean brain-death anyway it's the closest anyone will admit to ever having seen or found one even the Obscene Pubs Squad who've been looking for years but although everybody assumes they exist nobody's ever seen one until old gorilla man comes along and just makes his own, specifically to warn off any other porn merchants thinking of dealing in snuff! It's hilarious, it's really ironic and you explain all this to McDunn and you laugh because it actually isn't the fault of the police you're not sleeping it's the nightmares where you're stalked by a gorilla with the voice of a baby and a huge syringe and he wants to fuck you with it, isn't that hilarious? You can't sleep you're actually providing your own sleep deprivation and you say hey, next thing you know I really will be falling down the stairs! but he doesn't seem to get the joke and then it's back to the cell and then the interview room with the barred, opaqued windows so you can't see out and they switch on the tape-machine recording everything as usual and it's getting more bizarre; they get me to do a Michael Caine voice! They ask me to impersonate Michael fucking Caine, can you believe that? And then there's this technician or something here and they ask me to breathe in helium from a mask and make me repeat some of the things gorilla man said on the video so I feel like I'm becoming him they're trying to make me him; I don't think I sound the same as the guy on the brain-snuff video but fuck knows what they think there are too many to know *what* the fuck they think; loads of them, officers from all over the fucking place with different accents, London, Midlands, Welsh, Scottish, elsewhere, God knows, it's not just Flavell and McDunn though I still see them now and again especially McDunn who looks at me kind of weird most of the time like he can't really believe it was me did all these things and I get this bizarre feeling that he thinks I'm kind of pathetic I mean that in a grudging, still-determined-to-bust-the-fucker way he actually has more respect for gorilla man than he does for me because I've just gone to pieces under the questions and the things they put in my head with those photographs and that video (ha which means gorilla man has already put stuff into my head, already has fucked my brains, filling my head with the *idea* of that, the vision, the *meme* of that) and I thought I was some tough cookie but I was wrong I'm just a dunked digestive baby I'm soft I'm flopping I'm disintegrating and that's why unless I'm the best fucking actor he's ever seen McDunn can't accept I was capable of the things gorilla man did, yet so much of the evidence, especially the dates and times that sort of stuff, points at me not to mention that piece of TV-crit I did that reads like a hit-list now.

And it just goes on keeps going on another night another nightmare and then back to the interview room again and the tape machine again and more questions about Stromefirry-nofirry and Jersey and flights and that's when they tell me about the other one that's when they say oh by the way your best friend Andy is dead blown up in the hotel when it burned down; probably beaten to death first head stoved in but of course you probably know all that because you did that too, didn't you?

*

I lied about something. Earlier. I told it the way it felt, not as it actually was. Or the way it feels and actually is. Whatever.

'Andy; Yvonne.'

'Hi,' she says, shaking his hand.

'And that's William out there,' I tell Andy. 'With the big sword.'

Andy turns and watches William. William; masked, clad in white, grasping his sabre and suddenly lunging forward, one leg darting ahead. His opponent jumps back and tries to fend off the blows with his own sabre but he's off-balance and William presses forward, swinging the sabre in a hacking, sweeping motion, whacking the edge of the heavy curved blade into the side of his opponent's torso.

'Aw, rats,' the other guy says, as William stands back, relaxing. They take off their masks and William comes over to us, mask under his arm, sabre hanging from his hand, his face red and sheened with sweat, glistening in the sports hall's brilliant lights. I introduce him and Andy.

Andy with his short hair and his blazer and neatly creased jeans, face handsome but a little spotty, expression slightly disdainful and wary. He's twenty-one; two years older than us, but William looks the more confident and assured.

'Hi,' William says, tossing back some blond hair fallen over his forehead. 'So you're Cam's soldier boy.'

Andy smiles thinly. 'You must be . . . Willy, is it?'

I sigh. I'd hoped these two would get on.

Yvonne taps William on the shoulder with her mask. She's been fencing too, her long black hair tied back from her face, her face bright with sweat. I think she looks like some Italian princess, daughter of an ancient minor house with no real pretensions but still casually opulent; huge faded villas in Rome and on the Grand Canal and in the Tuscan hills. 'Shower,' she tells him. 'We have to get stuff ready for tonight.' She smiles at me. 'Quick drink in the bar, ten minutes?'

'Great,' I say. Andy is silent; Yvonne turns to him.

'Coming to the party?'

'Yes,' he says. 'If that's all right.'

'Of course.' She smiles.

*

184

'Ah! Hot hot hot!'

'What?'

'Took the hot chilli . . . crunched on a whole fucking green chilli . . . ha . . .' Yvonne says, fanning her mouth and hanging onto my arm. 'Woof; thanks.' She reaches into my vodka and lemonade and hoiks out an ice cube. 'Here,' she says thickly, handing me a joint while she rolls the ice cube round in her mouth and tries to breathe through it at the same time. I'm grinning widely at her; she's frowning hurtfully at me. Andy is at my side but then ducks away into the throng. The music is loud, the campus flat packed with people. It's a warm May evening, the exams are over and everybody's partying. The windows are open to the night, spilling the sound of the Pretenders' first album out over the slope of grass towards the small loch and the lights of the library and Admin buildings on the far side.

'Ah, my mouth!' Yvonne says. She slaps me on the shoulder. 'Look more sympathetic, you pig,' she tells me. Her eyes are watering.

'Sorry.'

Andy comes back with a glass of milk. 'Here,' he says, offering it to Yvonne. She looks at him. He nods at her mouth. 'Ice won't work,' he tells her. 'The . . . the stuff that causes the heat in chillis' and I smile, because I just *know* from the way he phrased that that he knows the technical term but doesn't want to appear too smart-alec 'isn't soluble in water, but it is soluble in fat. Try it; it'll work.'

Yvonne looks round. I offer my hand and she slips the remains of the ice cube delicately into my palm, then sips the milk. I shrug and put the lozenge of ice back into my drink.

Yvonne finishes the milk. She nods. 'That *is* better. Thanks.'

Andy gives a small smile, takes the empty glass from her and heads back through the crowds to the kitchen.

'Hoo,' Yvonne says, dabbing at her cheeks with a tissue. She glances after Andy. 'So boy scouts have their uses after all.'

'Ask him to show you his Swiss Army knife later,' I laugh, feeling a little treacherous. Yvonne's wearing a black scoop-necked T-shirt and a simple, black ankle-length wrap skirt. Her hair is tied back from her face and held by a long white lacy ribbon, but tumbles down loose behind. Her arms look firm and muscled and her tanned breasts are full and high, nipples producing little bumps on the black cotton of the T-shirt. The final effect is perversely exotic and I feel my usual pang of jealousy.

I glance into my glass and hand her back the J; her eyes close as she draws on it and I put my lips to my glass, slipping that sucked-on sliver of ice into my own mouth and rolling it around there, pretending it's her tongue.

*

'But it was true, Labour *wasn't* working.'

'Wasn't producing the profits the capitalists want to see, you mean. The implication of the ad was that Labour had produced mass unemployment and the Tories would cure it. Not only have they made it worse, they *knew* they would; even if they genuinely thought their policies were somehow better for Britain as a whole, they knew damn well they'd put hundreds of thousands of people out of work, and Saatchi & Saatchi must have known that, too, if they'd bothered to think. It was a lie.'

'It was an election,' William says, looking tired.

'What's that got to do with it?' I exclaim. 'It was still a lie!'

'It doesn't matter, and anyway it's just a short-term thing; they *will* produce more jobs eventually. They're just getting rid of the dead wood at the moment; there'll be new jobs in new growth industries.'

'Bull*shit*! Even *you* don't believe that!'

William laughs. 'You don't know what I believe. But if that ad helped win the election for Maggie, that's fine by me. Ah, come on; all's fair in love and war, Cameron. You should stop whingeing and start trying to make things work.'

'All is *not* fair in love and war! Haven't you heard of the Geneva

Convention? If Yvonne fell in love with somebody else, would you kill both of them?'

'Fucking right,' William says matter-of-factly as Andy appears at our sides holding a can of lager. Somebody passes him a J but he just hands it on to me. William shakes his head. 'You get this all the time, too?' he asks Andy.

'What?'

'Oh, this continual ear-bending about the Tories and what beastly cheats they are.'

'All the time,' Andy smiles.

'They lied to get in,' I say. 'They'll lie to try and stay in. How can you trust them?'

'I trust them to try and sort out the unions,' William says.

'It was time for a change,' Andy says.

'Country needs a kick up the fucking bum,' William agrees, defiantly.

I'm horrified. 'I am surrounded by selfish bastards I thought were my friends,' I say, slapping my forehead with the hand holding the J and almost setting my hair alight. 'This is awful.'

Andy nods. He drinks from his can and looks at me over the top of it. 'I voted Tory,' he says quietly.

'*Andy*!' I say, appalled, almost despairing.

'Shock therapy.' He grins, more at William than me.

'How *could* you?' I shake my head and pass the number to William.

Andy looks exaggeratedly thoughtful. 'It was that advert that did it, I think. Don't know if you know the one: "Labour Isn't Working," it said. Great political advert; succinct, memorable, effective, even mildly witty. I've got a poster copy of that in my room back at St Andy's. Did you ever see that advert at all, William?'

William nods, watching me and grinning. I am trying not to over-react but it's difficult.

'Very fucking funny, Andy,' I say.

Andy looks at me. 'Oh, Cameron, come on.' His voice pitched

somewhere between sympathy and exasperation. 'It happened. Accept it. It might all end up better than you hoped.'

'Tell that to the fucking unemployed,' I say, moving away towards the kitchen. I hesitate. 'Either of you two Tory bastards need a drink?'

*

I'm lying awake in my room in the flat I share a floor down from William and Yvonne's. Took some speed a friend turned up with so I can't get to sleep. Stomach a bit churny too; too many voddies and lemonades probably, and the punch at the party was evil. The flat I share looks in the opposite direction to theirs, across the access road and the lawns to the old estate wall and the tall old trees rising on the ridge beyond. The window is open and I can hear the sound of the wind in the branches. It will be dawn soon. I hear the front door of the flat open and close, then a few seconds later the door to my room opens. My heart beats hard. A dark figure kneels at my bedside and I can smell perfume.

'Cameron?' she says quietly.

'Yvonne?' I whisper.

She puts her hand behind my head, then her lips to mine. I'm in the middle of the kiss before it occurs to me I might be dreaming, but I know immediately I'm not. I put one hand to the back of her neck, then to her shoulder. She shrugs off her dressing-gown and slips into the little single bed beside me, warm and naked and already wet.

She makes love quickly, strongly, almost silently. I try to keep quiet too, and – because I had a quick, quiet wank earlier – don't come too quickly. She gives a brief, cut-off little cry like a chirp as she comes, and sinks her teeth into my shoulder. It is quite sore. She lies on top of me, breathing hard, head on my shoulder for a few minutes, then she stirs, pulls herself up so that I flop out of her and her hard little nipples stroke my chest. She puts her lips to my ear.

'Taking advantage of you, Cameron,' she purrs, barely audible.

188

'Hey,' I whisper, 'I'm a man of easy virtue.'

'William drank too much; fell asleep at a really frustrating point.'

'Ah-hah, Well; any time.'

'Mm-hmm. This never happened, all right?'

'Between these four walls.'

She kisses me, then she's out, slipping on the dressing-gown and padding away and clicking the door closed behind her.

I can hear gentle snoring coming from the room next to mine; one of my flat-mates. The only extra sound-proofing on the breeze blocks between his room and mine is a couple of layers of paint, which is probably why Yvonne was being quiet.

I lift my head up and look down to the floor at the foot of the bed, where Andy is lying curled up in his sleeping bag, unseen in the shadows, which is why *I* was being quiet.

'Andy?' I whisper very quietly, thinking that maybe he slept through it all.

'Lucky fucking bastard,' he says in a normal voice.

I lie back, laughing silently.

I can feel blood on my shoulder, where her teeth broke the skin.

*

Another morning, another interview, interrogation, little chat . . .

I sit down in the grey plastic chair in the featureless room with McDunn and a man from the Welsh squad; a big blond brindle guy in a tight grey suit; he has a rugby player's neck and steely eyes and huge hands that are clasped on the table, lying there like a mace of flesh and bone.

McDunn's eyes narrow. He makes that sucking noise through his teeth. 'What you been doing to your eyes, Cameron?'

I swallow, take a long sigh and look at him. 'Crying,' I tell him. He looks surprised. The Welsh boyo looks to one side.

'Crying, Cameron?' McDunn says, his dark, heavy-looking face creasing into a frown.

I take a deep breath, trying to control things. 'You said Andy was dead. Andy Gould. He was my best friend. He was my best friend and I didn't . . . fucking . . . kill him, all right?'

McDunn looks at me, as though slightly puzzled. The Welsh lad's got this steady gaze on me like he wants to use my head as a rugby ball.

Another deep breath. 'So I've been grieving for him.' And another. 'Is that all right?'

McDunn nods slowly, slightly, a distant look in his eyes like he's not really nodding at what I've just told him; hasn't been listening to a word I've said, in fact.

The Welsh guy clears his throat and picks up his briefcase. He takes out some papers and another tape recorder. He passes an A4 sheet over to me. 'Just read out the words on this sheet of paper, all right, Colley?'

I read the words through first; looks like it's the statement our man phoned in after Sir Rufus was flame-grilled; Welsh Nationalist extremists apparently claiming responsibility.

'Any particular voice?' I ask. 'Michael Caine, John Wayne, Tom Jones?'

'Let's try your own voice first, eh?' steely-eyes says. 'Then we'll try you with a Welsh accent.' He smiles, the way I imagine a prop forward smiles just before he bites your ear off.

*

'Cigarette?'

'Ta.'

Afternoon session. McDunn again; McDunn seems to be settling out as the Colley specialist. He lights a cigarette for me, holding it in his mouth. My hands aren't shaking so bad right now so maybe this isn't strictly necessary but I don't care. He hands the fag to me. I take it and it tastes good. I cough a bit but it still tastes good. McDunn looks on sympathetically. I actually find that I appreciate this. I know how they're supposed to work, I know all about the importance attached to establishing a rapport and initiating trust and building confidence and all that shit (and I'm almost flattered they haven't done the old good-cop bad-cop routine, though maybe they just don't do that at all any more because everybody knows about it from the TV), but I really do feel something for McDunn: he's like my lifeline back to reality, my ray of sanity in the nightmare. I'm trying not to get too dependent on him but it's hard not to.

'So?' I say, sitting back in the grey plastic seat. I'm wearing a blue prison-issue shirt – open-neck, of course – and the jeans I was wearing when they arrested me. They don't hug so well without the belt; bum's a little saggy, to tell the truth, but fashion isn't my top priority these days.

'Well,' McDunn says, looking at his notebook, 'we've found people who think they remember seeing you in the Broughton Arms Hotel on the night of Sunday the twenty-fifth of October, when Sir Rufus was murdered.'

'Good, good,' I nod.

'And the times for you getting down to London for the attack on Oliver, if you include the times you – or whoever – were seen in the toilets at Tottenham Court Road, are looking very tight; there was a delay on all the flights from Edinburgh into Heathrow that day . . . makes it impossible, really.'

'Great,' I say, rocking back and forward in my seat. 'Brilliant.'

'Unless,' he says, 'you had a double in Edinburgh or a lot of people are lying, it means you'd have to have an accomplice in London; somebody you'd hired to . . . ah, make the collection.' McDunn looks at me levelly. I still can't read him; I'm not able to tell whether he thinks this is likely or not, whether he thinks this is evidence I'm not his man or he still thinks I am but I had help.

'Well, look,' I say, 'put me on an identity parade – '

'Now, now, Cameron,' McDunn says tolerantly. This is something I've suggested before, something I keep on suggesting because it's all I can think of. Will the limbless Mr Azul think I'm the guy he saw at the front door? What about rent boys from the toilets at TCR? The cops think I'm the right build and they suspect gorilla man wears a wig and false moustache sometimes and maybe false teeth too. They've taken some very carefully set-up photographs with a big fucking camera and I suspect – from an aside or two they probably didn't expect me to understand – that these snaps will be the basis for some computer manipulation to see how well I fit the bill. Anyway, the upshot is McDunn doesn't think it's time for a parade yet. He looks wise and fatherly and says, 'I don't think we want to be bothered with that, do you?'

'Come on, McDunn, give me a shot; I'll try anything. I want out of here.'

McDunn taps the fag packet round and round on the table a couple of times. 'Well, that's up to you, isn't it, Cameron?'

'Eh? What do you mean?'

Oh, he's got me now; I'm interested, I'm leaning forward, elbows on table, face forward. Hooked, in other words. Whatever he's going to try and sell me, I'm buying.

'Cameron,' he says, like he's just come to some big decision, and sucks air through his teeth, 'you know I don't think it's you.'

'Oh, great!' I say, and laugh, sitting back and looking round the room at the bare paint walls and the constable sitting by the door. 'Then what the fuck am I –?'

'It's not just me, Cameron,' he says tolerantly. 'You know that.'

'Then what –?'

'Let me be frank with you, Cameron.'

'Oh, be as frank as you like, Detective Inspector.'

'I don't think it's you, Cameron, but I think you know who it is.'

I put my hand to my brow, looking down and shaking my head, then sigh theatrically and look at him, letting my shoulders slump. 'Well, I don't know who it is, McDunn; if I did I'd tell you.'

'No, you can't tell me yet,' McDunn says quietly and reasonably. 'You know who it is, but . . . you don't know that you know.'

I stare at him. McDunn's going metaphysical on me. Oh, shit. 'You're saying it's somebody I know.'

McDunn splays one hand, smiling smally. He chooses to tap his fag packet round and round on the tabletop again rather than speak to me, so I say, 'Well, I'm not sure about that, but it's certainly somebody who knows *me*; I mean, I think that card with my writing on it proves that. Or, it's something to do with those guys in the – '

'– Lake District,' McDunn sighs. 'Yes . . .' The DI thinks my theory it's the security forces trying to fit me up is pure paranoia. 'No.' He shakes his head. 'I think it is somebody you know, Cameron; I think it's somebody you know well. You see, I think you know them as well . . . well, nearly as well . . . as they know you. I think you can tell me who it is, I really do. You only have to think about it.' He smiles. 'That's all you have to do for me. Just think.'

'Just think,' I repeat. I nod at the DI. He nods back. 'Just think,' I say again. McDunn nods.

*

Summer in Strathspeld: the first really hot day that year, air warm and thick with the coconut smell of gorse – swathed richly yellow on the hills – and the sweet sharpness of pine resin, lying dropleted on the rough trunks in thick translucent bubbles. Insects buzzed and butterflies filled the glades with silent flashes of colour; in the fields the corncrake stooped and zoomed, its strange, percussive call stuttering through the scent-laden air.

Andy and I went down by the river and the loch, clambering up the rocks upstream then back down, watching fish jump lazily out on the calm loch, or strike at the insects speckling those flat waters, jaws snapping underneath; dispatching, swallowing, leaving ripples. We climbed some trees looking for nests but didn't find any.

We took off our shoes and socks and waded among the rushes surrounding the hidden, scalloped bay where the stream draining the ornamental pond near the house splashed down to the loch,

193

a hundred metres up the shore from the old boat-house. We were allowed to take the boat out ourselves by then as long as we wore life-jackets and we thought we might do that, later; get in some fishing or just some pottering around.

We climbed the low hills northwest of the loch and lay in the long grass under the pines and the birch, looking out over the small glen to the forested hill on the far side where the old railway tunnel was. Beyond that, over another wooded ridge, unseen and heard only on occasion when the breeze veered from that direction, was the main road north. Further beyond that, the Grampians' southernmost summits rose green and golden-brown into the blue sky.

Later that evening we were all going into Pitlochry, to the theatre. I wasn't too impressed with this – I'd rather have seen a film – but Andy thought it was all right, so I did too.

Andy was fourteen, I'd just turned thirteen and was proud of my new status as a teenager (and, as usual, of the fact that for the next couple of months I was only a year younger than Andy). We lay in the grass looking up at the sky and the fluttering leaves on the silver birch trees, sucking on our reed stalks and talking about girls.

We were at different schools; Andy was a boarder at an all-boys school in Edinburgh and came back only at weekends. I was at the local high school. I'd asked my mum and dad if I could go to a boarding school – the one in Edinburgh Andy was at, for example – but they'd said I wouldn't like it and besides it would cost a lot of money. Plus, there wouldn't be any girls there, didn't that worry me? I was a bit embarrassed about that.

The comment about the cost confused me; I was used to thinking of us as being well-off. Dad ran a garage and petrol station on the main road through Strathspeld village and Mum had a wee gift and coffee shop; Dad had been worried after the Six-Day War when they'd introduced the fifty-miles-an-hour speed limit and even issued fuel-rationing books, but that hadn't lasted very long and, even though petrol cost more nowadays, people were still travelling and using cars.

I knew our modern bungalow on the village outskirts overlooking the Carse wasn't as grand as Andy's mum and dad's house, which was practically a castle and stood in its own estate: ponds, streams, statues, lochs, rivers, hills, forests, even the old railway line passing through one corner of it; one big garden in effect and vast compared to our single acre laid to lawn and shrub. But I'd never thought of us as really having to worry about money that much; certainly I was used to getting more or less what I wanted and had come to think of this virtually as a right, the way only children are apt to if their parents are anything other than actively hostile to them.

It never occurred to me that other children weren't spoiled as a matter of course, the way I was, and it would be years – and my father would be dead – before I understood that the expense of sending me to a boarding school was just an excuse, and the simple, sentimental truth was that they knew they would have missed me.

*

'You have not.'
   'Bet you I have.'
   'You're kidding.'
   'I'm not.'
   'Who was it?'
   'None of your business.'
   'Ah, you're making it up, you little tramp; you never did.'
   'It was Jean McDuhrie.'
   'What? You're kidding.'
   'We were in the old station. She'd seen her brother's and she wanted to see if they all looked like that and she asked me so I showed her mine, but it was only if she'd show me hers and she did as well.'
   'Dirty wee rascal. Did she let you touch it?'
   '*Touch* it?' I said, surprised. 'No!'
   'Ah! Well, then!'

'What?'

'You're supposed to touch it.'

'No, you're not, not if you just want to *look*.'

'Of course you are.'

'Rubbish!'

'Anyway, what did it look like; was there any hair on it?'

'Hair? Ugh. No.'

'No? When was this?'

'Not long ago. Last summer maybe. Maybe before. Not that long. I'm not making it up, honest.'

'Huh.'

I was pleased we were talking about girls because I felt this was a subject where Andy's two extra years didn't really count; I was effectively the same age as him, and maybe I even knew more than he did because I mixed with girls every day and he only really knew his sister Clare. She was away shopping in Perth with her mother that day.

'Have you ever seen Clare's?'

'Don't be disgusting.'

'What's disgusting? She's your sister!'

'Exactly.'

'What do you mean?'

'You don't know anything, do you?'

'Bet I know more than you do.'

'Crap.'

I sucked on my hollow reed for a while, staring up at the sky.

'Have you got hairs on yours, then?' I said.

'Yeah.'

'You haven't!'

'Want to see?'

'Eh?'

'I'll show you it. It's pretty big too because we've been talking about women. That's what's supposed to happen.'

'Oh, yeah; look at your trousers! I can see it! What a bulge!'

196

'Look . . .'

'Ah! Ugh! Wow!'

'That's called an Erection.'

'Wow! God, mine never gets *that* big.'

'Well, it's not supposed to. You're still young.'

'Charming! I'm a teenager, do you mind?'

I watched Andy's cock, huge and golden and purple and sticking out of his fly like a gently curved plant, some sweet exotic fruit growing into the sunlight. I looked around, hoping there wasn't anybody nearby, watching. We were only visible from the top of the hill where the railway tunnel was, and usually nobody went there.

'You can touch it if you like.'

'I don't know . . .'

'Some of the guys in the school touch each other's. It's not the same as being with a girl, of course, but people do it. Better than nothing.'

Andy licked his fingers and started to stroke them up and down over the purple bulge of his cock. 'This feels good. Do you do this yet?'

I shook my head, watching the saliva on that full, taut hood glisten in the sunlight. There was a thickness in my throat and a tight feeling in my stomach; I could feel my own cock throbbing.

'Come on; don't just lie there,' Andy said matter-of-factly, leaving his cock alone and lying back in the grass, putting his arm behind his head and staring up at the sky. 'Do something.'

'Oh, God, all right,' I said, tutting and sighing, but really my hand was shaking. I pulled up and down on his cock.

'Gently!'

'All right!'

'Use some spit.'

'Good grief, I don't know . . .' I spat into my fingers and used them, then found his foreskin was loose enough to be rolled back and forth over the head, and did that for a while. Andy breathed hard and his free hand went to my head, stroking my hair.

197

'You could use your mouth,' he said, voice shaky. 'I mean, if you want.'

'Hmm. Well, I don't know. What's wrong with – ah!'

'Oh, oh, oh . . .'

'Yuk. What a mess.'

Andy took a deep breath and patted my head, chuckling. 'Not bad,' he told me. 'For a beginner.'

I wiped my hand on his trousers.

'Hey!'

I put my face up to his. '*I've* seen Clare's,' I told him.

'What! You –!'

I jumped up and ran laughing down through the grass and the bushes, down into the glen. He jumped up too, then cursed and hopped about, struggling to get his fly shut before he could chase me.

C H A P T E R

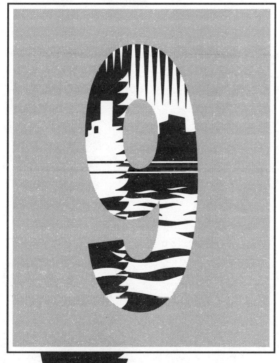

GROWTH

I remember that, remember the feeling of his warm, cooling, sunlit juice on my hand, slippy becoming sticky, but I can't think about it any more without thinking of gorilla man and the little guy tied to the chair. I think they were surprised when I threw up; I hope they were, I hope they were surprised and very interested and thought, 'Ullo 'ullo 'ullo it wasn't 'im then after all; he ain't the villain, he's been fitted up so help me . . . Oh God, I hope my belly spoke for me better than my fucking brain, in other words.

Not guilty, didn't do it that's why what gorilla man did sickened me; no blood well hardly any blood literally a drop, a drip, a fucking pixel on the screen and the only thing slicing into flesh was a needle, tiny and delicate not a chainsaw or an axe or a knife or anything, but it's that image that idea that old devil *meme*, I keep dreaming about it, keep having nightmares about it, and I'm the trapped one, I'm the man in the leather-and-chrome chair and he's there with his gorilla face and his squeaky baby voice, explaining to the camera that what he has in this bottle and in this syringe is sperm; the crazy fucker's loaded it up with jism man looks like half a fucking milk bottle of the stuff and he's going to inject it into the little guy's veins and he ties something round the naked upper arm of the little guy strapped to the chair and pulls it tight and waits for the vein to show while the little guy howls and screams like a child and tries to shake the chair to bits or rip it apart but he's too well strapped in there no purchase no leverage and then the man in the gorilla mask just does it; sinks the needle into the little guy's skin with a bit of blood and empties the whole syringe into him. I throw up onto the floor and they pause the video for me and somebody goes to get a mop.

After I've stopped chucking and coughing they restart the video and we cut to the other scene and the tall hospital chair and the little guy again with empty eyes and McDunn says his bit about Persistent Vegetative State.

Well, indeed. They did a DNA-fingerprint test and found he had a bus-load of people in him, linked it to some guy who was in the toilets under Centre Point the day before hiring rent boys but he didn't want the full business just wanted them to wank into this bottle thank you for your contribution young man every little bit helps going to a good home thank you mind how you go . . .

*

I'm thinking.

*

'This is the trickle-down effect in action, is it?'

'No, this is the show-off effect in action,' Clare tells me, having to shout over the din. Everybody else seems to be cheering. Andy and William are standing on a seat; Andy leans out over a table laden with glasses, a champagne bottle in one hand and his other arm held by William, who leans out the opposite way to balance him.

The table Andy is perched over is stacked with several hundred champagne glasses, forming a glittering pyramid rising a couple of metres from the table's surface. Andy is filling the single champagne glass at the apex of the pyramid with champagne; it is overflowing, filling the three glasses beneath it; they in turn are overflowing, filling the glasses on the level beneath them, which are also full and so spilling over to the level underneath, and so on and so on down almost to the bottom; Andy is on his eighth magnum. He glances down at the final layer of glasses.

'How we doing?' he roars.

'More! More!' everybody shouts.

'William!' somebody yells from the crowd. 'Fifty quid if you just let him go!'

'Don't you fucking dare, Sorrell!' Andy shouts, laughing, up-ending the magnum over the topmost glass as the bottle emp-ties.

'Not for a measly fifty,' William laughs, as he and Andy pull together and draw together, tottering on the seat while Andy throws the emptied bottle to someone in the crowd and is handed another full magnum by his partner in The Gadget Shop, a fellow ex-ad-man who's a few years older than Andy. It strikes me the symbolism of this whole venture would be better were it he and Andy balancing together on the seat, but I get the impression Andy's partner isn't fully into such flamboyance.

'Winch me out there, Will!' Andy bellows.

'God, though, it's tempting,' William says, leaning back and letting Andy crane out over the pyramid of glasses again.

'This is infantile,' Clare says, shaking her head.

'What's what?' Yvonne asks, making her way through the crowd. She clutches a bottle of champagne.

'This; infantile,' Clare says, nodding at the pyramid of glasses. She sees the bottle in Yvonne's hand. 'Oh, I say, well done that woman.' She holds out her flute. Yvonne fills the glass.

'Cameron?'

'Ta.'

She fills her own glass and stands beside Clare and me, watching Andy pouring the champagne onto the top of the pyramid. Yvonne's wearing a little black number that to my untutored eye looks like it could have cost ten quid or a thousand; Clare is rather more ostentatious in a short, sparkling, crimson creation that looks like it wants to be a ball-gown when it grows up. Andy and William are in monochrome; black and white, DJs removed for the bubbly-waterfall operation.

Yvonne grins. 'Boys,' she says, sounding long-sufferingly affectionate.

I look around. When Andy invited me to the launch of the The Gadget Shop I naively assumed it would be in the shop itself, in Covent Garden. But that didn't measure up to Andy's sense of showmanship; it wasn't glitzy enough, dramatic enough, or even big enough. Instead, he hired the Science Museum. Part of it, anyway. That got people interested. A shop is just a shop, and even a shop selling expensive executive toys is still just a shop, but a museum is, well, glamorous. People reckon the Natural History Museum is the most glamorous — partying in the shadow of all those dinosaurs in that huge space is just the business — but for The Gadget Shop the Science Museum along the road was the obvious venue, as well as being cheaper. Besides, everyone who matters has already been to some sort of bash at the Natural History Museum; this is new.

There's a full-size hovercraft held tipped on wires directly above us; a virtually circular thing with a tiny cabin and a huge fluted central air-intake. I vaguely recall making an Airfix kit of that thing when I was a kid. It floats above us, gleaming in the darkness as if supported on a cloud of talk and booze while the people below swarm and chat and roar Andy on; the champagne — already dripping down off the edges of the table onto the temporary matting beneath from spillages – is almost overflowing the second-last level of glasses.

'More! More!' people yell.

'Oh, less, less,' Clare mutters, sniffing.

'Nearly there yet?' Andy shouts.

'More! More!' everybody roars.

I look at them all. These are people like me. Christ. Media people, people from the advertising company Andy has just left, a few politicians – mostly Tory or Social Democrats though there are a couple of Labour guys – bankers, lawyers, business advisers, investment experts, actors, TV people – at least one film crew, though their lights are switched off for now – various other city types, a scattering of people who are, well, just professionally famous, and the remainder seemingly either part of some enormous floating meta-party or hired from some agency to impersonate people having a whale of a time: Rent-a-Hoot or something similar. I'm mildly surprised we haven't had a kiss-o-gram, but maybe that's a little lo-rent for Andy. Clare told me he'd taken *rather* a lot of convincing – once he'd determined to do the slightly naff champagne-pyramid stunt in the first place – not to try doing it with proper champagne flutes but to use the perry glasses like everybody else did; too tall, too unstable otherwise.

'You're very quiet, Cameron,' Yvonne says, smiling at me.

'Yeah,' I say helpfully.

'I think Cameron,' Clare says, sniffing, 'disapproves.' She draws out the 'oo' sound in the word.

Clare is a tall, auburn girl with striking angular looks she shares with her brother, but whereas Andy is – at the moment – bulkily fit-looking and tanned, Clare is just thin, and luminously pale. I reckon she's overly keen on coke and spends too much time in clubs, but maybe I'm just jealous; my cub-reporter status on the *Caley* and the triumph-of-miniaturisation salary that goes with it make habits that expensive out of the question. Clare has always had rather more in the way of aristocratic pretensions than Andy, who has that aura of classless broth-of-a-boyhood that usually only the congenitally rich can carry off convincingly.

Clare works for an estate agent so far up-market it's mostly estates they deal in, not humble houses, no matter how extensive; if it doesn't boast a couple of salmon rivers, a few square miles of trees and a brace of hills, lochs or lakes, then they just aren't interested.

'Cameron,' Clare continues, 'is content to lurk here on the sidelines radiating self-righteous socialist disapproval and imagining how after the revolution we'll all have to pull ploughs, eat raw turnips and take part in interminable self-criticism sessions long into the candle-lit night on the collective farm, aren't you, Cameron?'

'You don't pull ploughs,' I reply. 'You push them.'

'I know, dear – there is a farm next door to us back on the dear old homestead and Daddy does usually describe himself as a farmer – but I meant that we capitalist parasites would be taking the place of the oxen, not the horny-handed salt-of-the-earth types cracking the whip over them.'

'Well, I'm sorry to disappoint you,' I tell her, 'but I'm afraid you're assuming a rather more lenient revolution than the one I had in mind. I had you down as bone-meal actually, come the day. Sorry.' I shrug, watching Andy start to pour what everybody nearby seems to agree will be the last magnum required before the glass pyramid is finally full of champagne.

Clare looks at Yvonne. 'Cameron always did take a hard line on these things,' she tells her. 'Oh well, might as well enjoy ourselves while we can before the commissars take their gloating revenge. I'm off to powder my nose; would you like to come?'

Yvonne shakes her head. 'No, thanks.'

'I'll leave you with young Hot-to-Trotsky here, then,' Clare says, patting Yvonne on the shoulder and winking at me as she sidles off through the cheering crowd. The pyramid is still not quite full.

'One more bottle! One more bottle!' everybody is shouting.

I turn to Yvonne. 'So, how's the venture-capital business these days?'

'Venturesome,' Yvonne says, flicking back her shoulder-length black hair. 'How's the newspaper business?'

'Folding.'

'Oh; ha ha.'

I shrug. 'No, I'm enjoying it. Money's not brilliant but sometimes I see my name on the front page and I feel almost successful for a while, until I come to something like this.' I nod at Andy, taking yet another opened magnum and leaning out over the glass-stacked table. His task is almost finished; the pyramid is nearly full.

Yvonne glances at the pyramid with what might be contempt. 'Oh, don't let your head get turned by all this shit,' she says.

The tone of her voice surprises me. 'I thought you'd love all this,' I tell her.

She looks slowly around, at the people and the place. 'Hmm,' she says, and packs a disconcerting amount of cold equivocation into that single sound. She fixes her gaze on me. 'But don't you just long for a neutron bomb sometimes?'

'Constantly,' I tell her, after a pause.

She nods, eyes narrowed, for a moment, then she shrugs, turning to me and grinning. '"Hot-to-Trotsky"?' she asks, looking after Clare, still heading, thinly majestic in the thick of the crowd, for the ladies.

'I made the mistake of trying to get Clare into bed once,' I confess.

'Cameron! *Really?*' Yvonne looks delighted. 'What happened?'

'She just laughed.'

Yvonne tuts. She glances round. 'I'd have given you a reference, Cameron,' she says quietly.

I smile and drink my champagne, remembering when Andy came to Stirling for Yvonne and William's party, five years ago. It seems like a lot longer.

'Did you ever tell William about that?' I ask her.

207

Yvonne shakes her head. 'No,' she says. She shrugs. 'Maybe when we're older.'

I think about telling her that Andy was there, in his sleeping bag, listening the whole time, but while I'm thinking about it something goes wrong; there must have been a flaw in one of the glasses, or the weight is just too much, because there's a cracking sound and one side of the pyramid starts to collapse, sending an avalanche of falling glass and frothing champagne spilling crashing down off the table and smashing, bouncing and splashing onto the mats and the floor below.

Andy goes, 'Aww . . .' and holds his arms straight out.

People cheer.

*

Still thinking.

*

Four years later Clare and her latest fiancé were spending a weekend at Strathspeld when she died of a heart attack. I heard the news from a guy I knew who still lived in the village. I couldn't believe it. A heart attack. Overweight male execs squeezing themselves behind the wheel of their Mercs; they died of heart attacks. Arthritic working-class guys raised on a diet of fish and chips and fags; *they* died of heart attacks. Not young women in their mid-twenties. Christ, Clare was even *fit* at the time; she'd given up doing coke and taken up healthy shit like running and swimming. It *couldn't* be a heart attack.

And that was exactly what the doctor thought; that was precisely what helped kill her. The local doc – the guy who'd helped save Andy after he almost died under the ice all those years earlier – was on holiday at the time and there was a locum, a deputising doctor in charge of the practice, except from what the locals muttered later it

208

seemed he'd treated his stay in Strathspeld as a holiday, too, and spent more time on river banks with a rod in his hands than at bedsides toting a stethoscope. The family called him when Clare started to complain of chest pains in the late afternoon but he didn't come out; told them she'd just strained something; rest and painkillers. They called him twice again, and eventually he appeared that evening once it was explained the family wasn't used to this sort of treatment (and once he realised the best salmon stream in the area ran through the estate). He still couldn't find anything wrong, and left again.

They called an ambulance when Clare became unconscious and her lips turned blue, but by then it was too late.

Andy and his partner had sold The Gadget Shop chain the previous year; Andy was still thinking about what he wanted to do next – now he was rich – and was deep in the desert on a trans-Saharan expedition when Clare died. The funeral was private, family only; Andy got back just in time. I rang the house a week later and talked to Mrs Gould, who said Andy was still there. She thought he would like to see me.

*

A grey day in a cold April, one of those winter's-end days when the land looks exhausted and worn and it seems like all the colour is gone from the world. The cloud was thick and low and moving slowly on a damp, chilling wind, a lidding expanse hiding the sky and the snow on the distant hills. The trees, bushes and fields were all the same dun shade, as though a thin layer of dirt had been sprayed everywhere, and wherever you looked there seemed to be mud or rotting leaves or bare, dead-looking branches. I thought that, if I'd just come from the Sahara to here, I'd head back as soon as possible, family duties or not.

I stopped at the house to give my condolences to Mr and Mrs Gould. Mrs Gould was covered in flour and smelled faintly of gin. She was a tall, nervous woman who'd gone grey early; she always wore large bifocals and usually dressed in tweeds. I'd never seen her without a single string of pearls, which she fingered constantly. She apologised for the mess, wiping her hands on her apron and then shaking my hand while I said how sorry I'd been to hear. She looked around the hall distractedly, as if wondering what to do next, then the door to the library opened and Mr Gould peeked out.

He was about the same height as his wife but he looked stooped now, and he was wearing a dressing-gown; normally he was the epitome of tweedy country-squiredom, an archetypal laird in three-piece suit, clumpy shoes, checked shirt and cap; he resorted to a beaten-up, much reproofed Barbour when the weather turned particularly foul. I'd never seen him in anything as soft-looking, as *human* as the pair of scruffy trousers, open-necked shirt and dressing-gown he wore then. His strong, square face looked drawn and his thinning brown hair hadn't been combed. He came out of the library when he saw it was me, shook my hand and said 'Terrible thing, terrible thing' a few times, while Beethoven sounded loudly from the opened library door and his wife tutted and tried to smooth his errant hair. His eyes kept looking away over one of my shoulders or the other, never meeting my gaze, and I got the impression that like his wife he was constantly waiting for something important to happen, expecting someone to arrive at any moment, as though they both couldn't believe what had happened and it was all a dream or a ghastly joke and they were just waiting for Clare to come gangling through the front door, kicking off muddy green wellies and loudly demanding tea.

*

Andy was out shooting. I could hear the shotgun barking as I walked through the dim, dripping woods from the house, staying off the muddy path as much as possible and walking on the

210

flattened, exhausted-looking grass at its side to keep my shoes from clogging up.

The field was surrounded by trees and looked out towards the river upstream from the loch. The river wasn't visible, but there had been a lot of rain over that week and one corner of the field had flooded, leaving a shallow temporary loch reflecting the tarnished dark silver of the clouds; its waters were still and flat.

There was a stretch of curved gravel, edged with planks, near this end of the field; six posts stood along the front edge of the gravel stand, and on top of each post there was a little flat piece of wood like a tray. Twenty yards in front of the gravel pathway was a low mound where the launcher mechanism for the clays sat. There were two other mounds about the same distance away to either side. I could hear the little generator puttering away inside the central mound as I got closer, clearing the trees and looking across and down at where Andy stood. I watched for a moment.

Andy wore cords, shirt and jumper and body-warmer; a cap hung from the top of one of the nearby posts. He was very tanned. A big box of shells sat opened on top of the post in front of him; a foot switch at the end of a long, snaking flex operated the catapult in the pit. He slotted six cartridges into the long-barrelled pump-action gun and turned to aim.

His foot tapped once, and the clay shot out of the hide, spinning away into the greyness in a day-glo orange blur. The gun roared and the clay disintegrated somewhere out over the field. When I looked carefully I could see lots of orange fragments scattered over the sodden grass and glistening brown earth of the field.

The generator revved up and down, providing power to the automatic launcher; it had some sort of randomly set variation built into where it was aiming because the clays came out at a different angle and heading each time. Andy got them all with his first shot except for the last one. He even tried to reload fast enough to have another crack at it, but it thumped into the wet heather near the river before he could get the shell into the gun.

211

He shrugged, put the cartridge back into the box, checked the gun and turned to look at me. 'Hi, Cameron,' he said, and I knew then he'd been aware of me all the time. He put the pump-action down carefully on an oiled gun bag lying on the gravel.

'Hi,' I said, walking up to him. He looked tired. We shook hands a little awkwardly, then hugged. He smelled of smoke.

*

'Fucking squaddie culture, yeah; adoration of the fucking Maggie and pit bulls and getting some scoff down your neck and let's get pissed on lager and all moon together from the bus and camouflage jackets in the high street and yeah-well-I'm-inarestid-in-martial-arts-in't-I? I'm not a fucking Nazi I just collect militaria I'm not a fucking racist I just hate blacks and gun magazines instead of magazines for guns wanking over the glossy photos of chromed Lugers I'll bet; half of them think Elvis is still alive, buncha fucking stupid little *cunts*! The dip-shit little bastards deserve the fucking Micks turning them into mince; saw the inside of an armoured car once; been blown to buggery; thrown a hundred feet into the air and then rolled all the way down a hill; we took turns looking inside just to prove we were real men; looked like the inside of a fucking slaughter-house . . .'

I sat with Andy while he ranted on. We were drinking whisky. He had a big room on the second floor of the house at Strathspeld; we'd played here as kids, making models, fighting wars with toy soldiers and the train set and Airfix tanks and forts made from Lego; we'd conducted experiments with our chemistry sets, raced our Scalextric cars, flown gliders out the window down to the lawn and shot at targets in the gardens with our air rifles and killed a couple of birds and smoked a few packets of illicit fags from the same window. We'd smoked untold spliffs here, too, listening to records with pals from the village, and with Clare.

'Why are people so fucking *incompetent*?' Andy screamed

suddenly, and threw his whisky glass across the room. It hit the wall near the window and smashed. I remembered the disintegrating pile of champagne glasses in the Science Museum, only four years earlier. The whisky left in the glass he'd thrown made a pale brown stain on the wall. I focused on the liquid as it slowly dribbled down.

'Sorry,' Andy muttered, not sounding sorry at all, getting unsteadily out of his seat and going to where the bits of glass lay broken on the carpet. He squatted and started to pick them up, then let them drop back to the floor and just crouched there and put his hands over his face and started to cry.

I let him cry for a bit and then went over to him and squatted down beside him and put my hand over his shoulders.

'Why are people so fucking *useless*?' he sobbed. 'Fucking let you down, fucking can't do their fucking *job*! Fucking Halziel; Captain fucking Michael fucking Lingary DSO – cunts!'

He pushed away from me and stood up and stumbled over to a wooden chest, tearing one of its drawers right out so that it crashed to the carpeted floor and a load of jumpers fell out. He got down on his knees behind the drawer and I heard tape rip.

He stood up holding an automatic pistol and started trying to slot a magazine into the grip. 'Fucking brain-ectomy coming up, Doctor fucking Halziel,' he said, still crying and still trying to get the magazine to fit into the gun.

Halziel, I thought. Halziel. I recognised Lingary's name from the times Andy had talked about the Falklands; he'd been Andy's CO, the one Andy blamed for the deaths of some of his men. But Halziel . . . Oh yeah, of course: the name of the locum who'd let Clare die. The guy the locals thought was more interested in fishing than doctoring.

'Fucking load, cunt!' Andy screamed at the gun.

I got up, suddenly feeling cold. I hadn't felt like this when I'd seen him firing the shotgun. It hadn't occurred to me to feel frightened of him then. Now it did. I wasn't at all sure I was doing the right

213

thing but I got up and started towards him as he finally got the clip to slide into the gun and snick home.

'Hey, Andy,' I said. 'Man, come on . . .'

He glared up at me as though seeing me for the first time. His face was red and blotchy and streaked with tears. 'Don't you fucking start, Colley, you little cunt; you let me down too, remember?'

'Hey, hey,' I said, putting my hands out, and retreating.

Andy crashed into the door, opened it and almost fell out into the landing. I followed him down the stairs, listening to him curse and shout; in the front hall he tried to get a jacket on over his clothes but couldn't get it to fit over his hand holding the gun. He hauled the front door open so hard that when it hit the stop the stained-glass panel shattered. I looked woozily around for Mr and Mrs Gould but there was no sign of them. Andy slammed the heel of his hand off the half of the storm door that was still closed, then fell out into the night.

I went after him; he was trying to get into the Land Rover. I stood beside him while he cursed at the keys and thumped the side window. He put the gun sideways in his mouth to give him two free hands and I thought about trying to grab it off him but I thought I'd probably kill one of us and even if I didn't I was no match for him and he'd just take it off me again.

'Andy, man,' I said, trying to sound calm, 'come on; this is crazy. Come on. Don't be insane, man. Killing this dickhead Halziel isn't going to bring Clare back – '

'Shut up!' Andy yelled, throwing the keys down and grabbing me by the collar and slamming me back against the side of the Landie. 'Shut the fuck up, you stupid little shit! I fucking *know* nothing'll bring her back! I know that!' He banged my head against the Land Rover's side window. 'I just want to be sure that there'll be one stupid incompetent fuck *less* in the world!'

'But – ' I said.

'Ah, fuck off!'

He hit me in the face with the gun; an inefficient, glancing blow with more chaotic anger than directed malice behind it; I fell down, correspondingly, more because I felt I ought to than because I was actually knocked out. Still hurt, though. I lay on the gravel, face up. It was only then I realised it was raining.

I worried distantly about being shot and killed. Then Andy slammed the gun side-on against the Land Rover and kicked the door.

'Christ!' he bellowed. He kicked the door again. 'Christ!'

I was getting wet. I could feel water seeping through my jumper and making my back damp.

Andy bent down and looked at me. His eyes screwed up.

'You all right?'

'Yeah,' I said wearily.

He flicked something on the gun and stuffed it down the back of his cords, then held a hand out to me. I put my hand up to his. I remembered William and Andy, balanced on the chair under the old hovercraft.

He pulled me up. 'Sorry I hit you,' he said.

'Sorry I was a prat.'

'Oh, man, Christ . . .' He put his head on my shoulder, breathing hard but not crying. I patted his head.

*

Still thinking.

*

Yvonne and I at South Queensferry a couple of summers ago, across the road from the Hawes Inn at the slipway underneath the tall stone piers of the rail-bridge, the mile-wide river bright before us, people promenading along pavements and down the pier, an occasional smell of frying onions from the snack bar beside the Inshore Lifeboat shed. We were there to witness William getting to grips with his brand-new Jet Ski; this process seemed to consist largely of getting on, powering away, trying to turn too fast and falling off in an extravagant splash. His big blond head kept coming up, shaking once and then bobbing through the water as he struck out for the machine. There were another three Jet Skis buzzing around on that part of the river and a few water-skiers with their big-engined speedboats, all creating a fair old racket, but we could still hear William laughing; the guy thought buying a frighteningly expensive piece of machinery and spending most of your time falling off it into the water was just the most enormous wheeze.

'What do you actually use these things for?' I asked.

'What, Jet Skis?' Yvonne said, leaning on the sea wall and clinking ice around in her fruit juice. 'Fun.' She watched William bank into a turn, narrowly miss another Jet Ski and plough into the wash of a water-ski boat, sending William – in a new variation on his repertoire of falls – somersaulting over the handlebars of the Jet Ski and flopping on his back into the water in a cloud of spray. His laughter whooped above the revving motors. He waved to show he was all right, then swam back to the floating machine, still laughing. Yvonne put her sunglasses on. 'They're for fun; that's what they're for.'

'Fun,' I said, nodding. William was still laughing. I watched Yvonne watching him. He waved again as he got onto the Jet Ski. She waved back. Listlessly, I thought.

Yvonne was slim and muscled in shorts and T-shirt. Her breasts were pushed up by the wall she was leaning against. We had been lovers for a year or so. She shook her head gently as William gunned the machine's engine again. I leant on the wall beside her.

'Do you ever think about leaving him?' I asked her quietly.

She paused, turned to me, put her sunglasses down her nose and looked at me over them. 'No?' she said.

And there was a question in her voice; it was asking me why I'd asked such a thing.

I shrugged. 'I just wondered.'

She waited for a family to pass by, eating ice-creams, then she said, 'Cameron, I've no intention of leaving William.'

I shrugged again, sorry I'd asked now. 'Like I say, it just occurred to me.'

'Well, un-occur it.' She glanced at where William was bumping enthusiastically across the waves, miraculously still upright. She put a hand out and briefly touched my arm. 'Cameron,' she said, and her voice was tender, 'you're the excitement in my life; you do things for me William couldn't even imagine. But he's my husband, and even if we do stray now and again, we'll always be an item.' She narrowed her eyes then added. '. . . probably.' She looked at him again as he executed a slower turn, wobbling but upright. 'I mean, if he ever gave me AIDS I'd give him a Colombian necktie – '

'Eugh,' I said. I'd seen a photograph of one of those; they cut your throat and pull your tongue out through the slit. Surprisingly big, the human tongue. 'You told him that?'

She laughed once. 'Yeah. He said if I left him he'd demand custody of the Merc.'

I turned and looked at the subtly tarted, much breathed-upon 300 sitting at the kerb, then made a show of sizing up Yvonne.

I shrugged. 'Fair enough,' I said, turning to look out across the water and drinking my pint. She kicked me on the knee.

Later, when we were helping William take the Jet Ski out of the water, some very loud people – all wearing black leather jackets with BMW logos – arrived with a gleaming black Range Rover and a big black ski boat. They demanded that everybody get out of their way so they could launch their boat, while people who'd been there for the best of the tide were already bringing their craft out. Their triple-engined ski boat had blocked the exit to the road and when people asked them to move it the BMW people started arguing. I even heard one of them claiming to have booked the slipway.

There was impasse for about ten minutes. We got the Jet Ski

onto its trailer but William's Merc was one of the cars trapped on the slip; he tried to reason with the BMW people, then sat in the car and sulked. Yvonne seemed silently furious, then announced she was going up to the lifeboat shed to buy some souvenir crap or whatever.

'When in doubt, shop,' she told us, slamming the car door.

William sat tight-lipped, looking in his rear-view mirror at the argument continuing further up the slip. 'Bastards,' he said. 'People are so fucking inconsiderate.'

'Shoot the lot of them,' I said, thinking about getting out and having a cigarette (no smoking on the champagne-hued leather of the Merc).

'Yeah,' William said, hands kneading the steering wheel. 'People might be a bit more polite if everybody carried guns.'

I looked at him.

It was all sorted out after some confusion and a lot of ill-feeling; the BMW people moved their boat forward so cars and trailers could get past it to the road. We picked Yvonne up at the top of the slip by the RNLI shed where they sold stuff to help pay for the lifeboat.

She didn't seem to have bought much; she tossed me a box of matches as she got into the car. 'Here,' she said.

I studied the matchbox. 'Wo. Hey, you sure about this?'

I looked back as we powered away up the hill through the trees, heading for Edinburgh. There was another commotion going on down on the slip; the BMW people were gesticulating wildly and pointing at the tyres on one side of the trailer holding the big ski boat, which appeared to be listing slightly in that direction now. It looked like it was all getting rather heated again down there; then the leaves got in the way and we couldn't see any more. I was sure I'd seen a punch thrown.

I turned back to find Yvonne's grinning face looking past me in the same direction. She looked suddenly innocent and sat back in her seat, humming.

I remembered the time Andy and I had let down all the wheels of his dad's car, folding matches in half and sticking them into the tyre valves. I opened the box of matches Yvonne had given me, but you couldn't have told whether there were a couple of them missing or not.

'Looks like they had some sort of problem with their trailer there,' I said.

'Good,' William said.

'Probably a puncture,' Yvonne sighed. She glanced at William. 'We do have *lockable* tyre valves on this thing, don't we?'

*

William in the woods, outskirts of Edinburgh, almost within sight of the estate where his and Yvonne's new house is, toting a paint gun on another of these stupid but grudgingly-sometimes-fun-in-a-terribly-boyish-sort-of-way paint-ball games (his computer-company boys and girls versus the crack troops of the *Caledonian* news room). My gun jammed and William recognised me and came forward laughing and firing shot after shot at me while I waved and tried to duck and these yellow paint balls went splat, splat, thunking into my hired camouflage trousers and combat jacket and smacking into my visored helmet while I waved at him and tried to get the damn gun to work and he just walked forward slowly shooting me; bastard had his own paint gun and he'd probably had it souped up; knowing William, that was almost inevitable. Splat! Splat! Splat! He was getting closer and I was thinking, Christ does he know about me and Yvonne? Has he guessed, has somebody told him, is that what all this is about?

It was pretty fucking annoying even if it wasn't; I really wanted to get the bastard because we'd been having this stupid argument before we'd started about how greed really *was* good and how William had been so disappointed at how poorly the argument was put across by the Gekko character in *Wall Street*.

219

'But it *is* good,' William protested, waving his gun around. 'That's how we measure fitness to survive these days.' We were being shown round the paint-ball site, having flagpoles and log barricades and that sort of stuff pointed out to us. 'It's *natural*,' William insisted. 'It's evolution; when we still lived in caves we used to go out and hunt and whoever brought back the mammoth or whatever ate the best meat and got to fuck the women, and all that was *good* for the human race. Now it's got a bit more abstract and we use money instead of animals but the principle's the same.'

'But it *wasn't* just individuals who hunted animals; that's exactly the point,' I told him. 'It was all about cooperation; people worked together and got results and shared the spoils.'

'I agree,' William agreed. 'Cooperation is *great*. If people didn't cooperate you couldn't *lead* them so easily.'

'But – '

'And you'll always need leaders.'

'But greed and selfishness – '

'– have produced everything you see around you,' William said, waving the paint-ball gun around again.

'Exactly!' I exclaimed, throwing my arms out wide. 'Capitalism!'

'Yes! Exactly!' William echoed, also gesturing with his hands. And we stood there, me with a great big frown on my face, quite mystified that William couldn't see what I was getting at . . . and William smiling but looking equally puzzled that I appeared to be incapable of understanding what *he* meant.

I shook my head, exasperated, and brandished my paint-ball gun. 'Let's fight,' I said.

William grinned. 'I rest my case.'

So I really wanted to nail the bastard – preferably with the cooperation of my team-mates just to prove the point – but the fucking technology let me down and the gun jammed and he had me pinned, firing shot after shot at me, and finally I gave up trying to un-jam the gun and made to throw it at him though I could hardly see because there was yellow paint all over my visor, but he ducked and tripped and sat down on a trunk, holding his stomach, and the bastard was laughing his socks off because I looked like a giant dripping banana, only I'd just realised the gun wasn't jammed after all, the safety catch was on. I must have knocked it or something and I'd a couple of shots left and I ought to have shot the swine but I couldn't, not while he was sitting there killing himself laughing.

'Bastard!' I yelled at him.

He twirled his paint gun around one gloved finger. 'Evolution!' he shouted. 'You learn a lot when you live with a liquidator!' He started laughing again.

Later at the buffet lunch in the marquee he barged to the front of the queue saying, 'Oh, I don't believe in queuing!' and when somebody behind him objected, convinced her with a sort of apologetic bashfulness that actually he has diabetes, you see, and so needs to eat *right now*. I cringed, blushed, and looked away.

*

Still thinking; thinking about all the times I've seen people I know do something for revenge, or do anything vindictive or sneaky or smart or even threaten to. Hell, everybody I know's done something like that at some time or another but that doesn't make them a murderer; I think McDunn's crazy but I can't tell him that because, if he's wrong about that and I'm wrong about it being something to do with those guys who died in the Lake District a few years ago, then there's only one suspect left and that's me. The trouble is my theory's looking shakier all the time because McDunn's convinced me it really was all just a smoke-screen: there is no Ares project, never was any Ares project, and Smout in his prison in Baghdad isn't connected to the guys that died; it was just somebody coming up with a clever conspiracy theory, just a way of getting me to go to remote places and wait for phone calls and deprive me of an alibi while gorilla man did something horrible to somebody else somewhere else. Of course McDunn points out that I could still be the murderer; this could all be a story I've made up. I could have recorded the mysterious Mr Archer's phone calls and had them directed to the office while I was there. They found most of the equipment to do just that in my flat when they searched it: an answer-machine, my PC and its modem; another lead or two and it would have been easy to set it up if you knew what you were doing, or just used trial and error and were patient.

McDunn really wants to help, I can see that, but he's under pressure, too; the circumstantial evidence against me is so strong people who don't know the details of the case are getting impatient over the lack of progress. Apart from that fucking business card they have no forensic evidence; no weapons, bloodstained clothes or even minutiae like hairs or fibres to link me with any of the attacks. I suspect they don't think I'd be identified by any of the witnesses or I'd have been on an identity parade by now, but it just all looks so obvious: it must be me. Lefty journalist goes loco, wastes right-wingers. Apparently I've missed some good headlines while I've been in here. Actually, I missed some good ones in the couple of days' holiday I took; if I'd just bothered to look at a single fucking news-stand after I left Stromeferry I'd have seen this story starting to break about this guy – 'The Red Panther' the tabloids decided on eventually – murdering these right-leaning pillars of the community.

McDunn doesn't want to charge me with any of the other murders but they're going to have to make a decision before too long because my initial time under the PTA is nearly up and the Home Secretary isn't going to grant an extension; I'll have to appear in court soon. Hell, I might even get a lawyer.

I'm still terrified, even though McDunn's on my side, because I can see he's not so hopeful any more and if they take him off this I might get the bad cops, the ones that just want a confession and Christ I'm in England, not Scotland, and despite the McGuire Seven and the Guildford Four they still haven't changed the law: down

222

here you can still be convicted on an uncorroborated confession even if you try to retract it later.

I'm getting paranoid about that, determined not to sign anything, worried that maybe I already have when they first brought me here and said it was just a receipt for personal effects or a legal-aid application or whatever, and I worry about them getting me to sign something when I'm tired and they've been interviewing me in shifts and all I want to do is go to bed and sleep and they say oh do us all a favour and sign this and you can sleep, come on now; it's just a formality you can always deny it later, change your mind, but you can't you can't of course, they're lying and you can't; I even worry about signing something in my sleep, or them hypnotising me and getting me to do it that way; hell, I don't know what they get up to.

*

'Cameron,' McDunn says. It's day five; the morning. 'They want to charge you with all the murders and assaults and take you to court, day after tomorrow.'

'Oh, Jesus.' I accept a fag; McDunn lights it for me.

'You sure you can't think of anything?' McDunn asks. 'Anything at all?' He makes that sucking noise with his teeth again. It's starting to annoy me.

I shake my head, rubbing my face in my hands, not caring that the smoke from the fag goes in my eyes and my hair. I cough a bit. 'Sorry. No. No, I can't. I mean, I've thought of lots of stuff, but nothing – '

'But you're not telling me about it, are you, Cameron?' the DI says, sounding regretful. 'You're keeping it all locked up inside you; you won't share it with me.' He shakes his head. 'Cameron, for God's sake, I'm the only one who can help you. If you have any suspicions, any doubts, you have to let me know about them; you have to name names.'

223

I cough again, looking down at the tile floor of the room.

'This might be your last chance, Cameron,' McDunn tells me softly.

I take a deep breath.

'If there's anybody you can think of, Cameron, just give me their name,' McDunn says. 'It'll probably be easy to eliminate them from the enquiry; we aren't going to frame anybody or hassle anybody or pull anything heavy.'

I stare at him, still uncertain. My hands are still splayed over my lower face. I take another drag on the fag. Fingers shaking again. McDunn continues. 'There are, or were, people on this case who are very good, dedicated, and enthusiastic officers, but the only thing they're enthusiastic about nowadays is getting you charged with the rest of the attacks and getting you into the dock. I've persuaded the people who matter that I'm the best man to work with you to help us clear this up, but I'm like a football manager, Cameron; I can be replaced at a moment's notice and I'm only as good as the results I get. At the moment I'm not getting any results, and I could go at any time. And believe me, Cameron, I'm the only friend you've got in here.'

I shake my head, frightened to speak in case I break down.

'Names; a name; anything that might save you, Cameron,' McDunn says patiently. 'Is there anyone you've thought of?'

I feel like a worker in Stalinist Russia denouncing his comrades but I say, 'Well, I thought of a couple of friends of mine . . .' I look at McDunn to see how I'm doing. There's a concerned-looking frown on his dark, heavy face.

'Yes?'

'William Sorrell, and . . . well, it sounds daft, but . . . his wife, umm, Yvo – '

'Yvonne,' McDunn says, nodding slowly and sitting back. He lights a fag. He looks sad. He taps the cigarette packet round and round on the table surface.

I don't know what to think or feel. Yes, I do: I feel sick.

'Are you having an affair with Yvonne Sorrell?' McDunn asks.

I stare at him. I really *don't* know what to say now.

He waves his hand. 'Well, maybe it doesn't matter. But we've looked into Mr and Mrs Sorrell's movements. Discreetly, once we knew they were friends of yours.' He smiles. 'Always have to be alive to the possibility it's more than one person, Cameron, especially with a group of crimes spread out over so much territory, and fairly complicated ones at that.'

I nod. Looked into. Movements looked into. I wonder how discreet is discreet. I want to cry very much now because I think I'm admitting to myself that, no matter what happens, life is never going to be the same again.

'As it turns out,' McDunn says, while the fag packet goes *tap*, *tap*, 'although they are both away from home a lot, their movements are very well documented; we know pretty well what they were doing during all the attacks.'

I nod again, feeling like my guts have been ripped out. So I've denounced them and there wasn't even any point to it.

'I thought of Andy,' I tell the floor, looking down there, avoiding McDunn's eyes. 'Andy Gould,' I say, because – apart from everything else – Andy stayed with me during the summer, round about the time the card with my writing on it went missing. 'I thought it might be him, but he's dead.'

'Funeral's tomorrow,' McDunn says, flicking ash and then inspecting the glowing end of his cigarette. He scrapes it round the edge of the light metal ashtray until the tip of the fag is a perfect cone, then smokes it carefully. My ash falls on the floor. I sweep it to nothing with my foot, guiltily.

God, I could use some dope; I need to mellow out, I need to calm down. I'm almost looking forward to prison; plenty of dope in there, if I'm allowed to mix with other inmates. Christ, it's going to happen. I'm accepting it, I'm coming to terms with it. Christ.

'Tomorrow?' I say, swallowing. I'm trying not to cry and I'm trying not to cough, either, because that might make me cry.

'Yes,' McDunn says, tapping ash carefully off his cigarette again. 'Burying him tomorrow, at the family estate. What's it called again?'

'Strathspeld,' I tell him. I look at him but can't tell if he really forgot the name or not.

'Strathspeld.' He nods. 'Strathspeld.' He rolls the word around his mouth, as if savouring a good malt. 'Strathspeld on the Carse of Speld.' He sucks air through his teeth again. I wish he'd get his teeth seen to; do they have special police dentists or do they have to go to the ones everybody else goes to and hope the dentist doesn't have some . . . have some grudge . . . some grudge against . . .?

Wait a minute.

Wait a fucking minute here . . .

And I know.

It's like a speck of dust drifts down and goes into my eye and I look up to see where it came from and I'm hit by this tonne of bricks; it hits me that hard. I sit there for a second thinking, No, it can't be . . . But it is; it won't go away, and I do know, and I know that I know.

I know and I feel sick but it's something just to feel this certain about anything again. I can't prove anything and I still don't understand it all, but I *know*, and I know that I have to be there, have to get to Strathspeld. I could just tell them to get there, be there, keep watch there, because he's bound to be there, has to be there, there of all places. But I can't let it happen like that, and whether they get him or not – and I doubt they will – I have to be there.

So I clear my throat and look McDunn in the eyes and say, 'All right. Two more names.' Pause. Swallow, something sticking in my throat. Jesus, am I really going to say this? Yes, yes I am: 'And I've got something else for you.'

McDunn tips his head to one side. His brows say, 'Oh yes?'

I take a deep breath. 'I want something from you, though.'

McDunn frowns. 'What would that be, Cameron?'

'I want to be there tomorrow, at the funeral.'

McDunn frowns more deeply. He looks down at the fag packet and taps it round another couple of revolutions on the table. He shakes his head. 'I don't think I can do that, Cameron.'

'Yes, you can,' I tell him. 'You can because of what I've got for you.' I pause, take another breath, the air catching in my throat. '*It's* there, too.'

McDunn looks puzzled. 'And what would that be, Cameron?'

My heart is hammering, my hands are balled into fists. I swallow, throat dry, tears finally coming into my eyes and eventually I squeeze the words out:

'A body.'

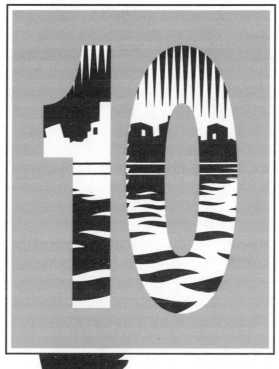

CARSE OF SPELD

I run down the hill, into the sunlit glen and then up the far side, with Andy crashing through the bushes, heather and ferns behind me. I shake my hand free of most of his semen and deliberately let my hand brush across the leaves and blades as I dash past, wiping the rest off. I'm laughing. Andy's laughing too, but shouting threats and insults as well.

I run up the hill, seeing movement ahead and assuming it's a bird or a rabbit or something, and almost run straight into a man.

I stop. I can still hear Andy pumping up the hill behind me, tearing through the bushes and yelling curses.

The man is dressed in walking boots, brown cords and a shirt and green hiking jacket. He wears a brown rucksack on his back. He has red hair and he looks furious.

'What do you boys think you were doing?'

'What? Eh? Ah . . .?' I say, looking back to see Andy coming up the hill behind me, suddenly slowing and looking wary as he sees the man.

'You!' the man shouts at Andy. His voice makes me jump. I hide

231

my sticky hand behind me, as if it's brightly stained. 'What were you doing there with this boy, eh? What were you doing?' he shouts, looking around. He puts his thumbs between the shoulder straps of his rucksack and his jacket and sticks his chest and chin out. 'Come on! What d'you think you were doing, eh? Answer me, boy!'

'None of your business,' Andy says, but his voice is shaky. I can smell something funny. I worry that it's coming from my sticky hand and I'm frightened that the man will smell it.

'Don't you talk to me like that, boy!' the man yells, glancing round again. He spits as he shouts.

'You've got no right being here,' Andy says, sounding frightened. 'This is private property.'

'Oh, is it?' the man says. 'Private property, is it? And that gives you the right to do dirty, perverted things, does it?'

'We – '

'Shut it, laddie.' The man takes a step forward, looking over my head at Andy. The man's so close I could touch him. I get that smell even stronger. Oh God, he's bound to smell it now. I feel myself trying to shrink, cowering. The man thumps himself in the chest with one finger. 'Well, let me tell you something, sonny,' he tells Andy. 'I'm a *policeman*.' He nods, drawing back and upright again. 'Aye,' he says, eyes narrowing. 'You may well look frightened, boy, because you're in deep bloody trouble.'

He looks down at me. 'Right; this way, come on!'

He takes a step away. I'm trembling, rooted to the spot. I glance back to see Andy looking uncertain. The man grabs my arm and pulls me. 'I said come *on*, boy!'

He drags me after him through the woods. I start crying and try to break away, struggling weakly.

'Please, mister, we weren't doing anything!' I wail. 'We weren't doing anything! Honest! We weren't doing anything, honest we weren't! Please! Please let us go, please; please let us go, we won't do it again, honest; please, please, please . . .'

I look back through my tears at Andy, who's following, looking desperate and uncertain, biting on one knuckle as he follows us through the bushes.

We're near the summit of the hill, deep in the bushes under the thin cover of trees; the smell is very strong and my knees feel like the bones are gone. If I wasn't being held up by the man's gripping hand hauling me through the ferns I feel like I'd fall down.

'Leave him!' Andy shouts, and I think he's going to burst into tears like me. He seemed so old a few minutes ago and now he's like a little kid again.

The man stops, whirls me round and holds me against his chest. He feels very warm behind me and the smell is even stronger.

Andy comes to within a couple of yards.

'Come here!' the man shouts. I can see spittle arc out from above me as he shouts. Andy looks from him down to me; I can see his jaw trembling.

'Come *here*!' the man screeches. Andy comes forward a couple of feet. 'Take off those trousers!' he hisses at Andy. 'Go on; I saw you! I saw what you were doing! Take off those trousers!'

Andy shakes his head, backing off.

I start to sob.

The man shakes me. 'Right!' he says. He leans over me, puts his big fingers to the zip of my jeans and starts trying to pull the zip down. I'm struggling and howling but I can't get free. The smell is all around me; it's him; it's his sweat, his smell.

'Leave him, you bastard!' Andy shouts. 'You're not a policeman!' I can't see what Andy's doing because the man's body is in the way, but then Andy hits into him, bowling him backwards and he shouts and I wriggle away from them; I scramble off through the ferns on all fours and then stop and look back and the man's got Andy, he's struggling with him, leaning over him, folding him, pressing him down, and Andy's breathing hard, grunting, trying to break free. 'Bastard! Leave me *alone*! You're not a policeman! You're not a policeman!'

The man doesn't say anything; he pushes Andy down into the ferns, and gets a hand free and punches Andy in the face. Andy goes limp but then moves weakly; the man is breathing very hard and when he looks at me his eyes are wide and staring. 'You!' he gasps. 'You; just stay there! Stay there, d'you hear?'

I'm shaking so hard I can hardly see straight. Tears fill my eyes.

The man pulls Andy's trousers down; I can see Andy looking round groggily. His gaze fastens on me.

'Help,' he croaks. 'Cameron . . . help . . .'

'Cameron, is it?' the man says, glancing at me and pulling down his own trousers. 'Well, you just stay there, Cameron; you just stay there, right?'

I shake my head and back off.

'Cameron!' Andy wails; the man is struggling with his underpants as Andy tries to get out from under him. I'm stumbling backwards, almost falling; I have to turn to stop myself tripping and the turn becomes a run and I can't stop myself, I just have to escape; I race away through the woods, tears burning on my face, sobbing hysterically, the breath whistling and whooping in and out of me, hot and desperate and livid in my throat; ferns whip at my legs and branches lash at my face.

*

I gave McDunn the two names last night and told him the respective professions of their owners, then clammed up, just refused to say any more about them or about the body. There was a lot of tooth-sucking for a while as he tried to get me to say more and that was almost funny, given that it was the tooth-sucking that made me think of it in the first place, suddenly thinking. The dentist! Recalling going into Kyle, while I was at Stromefirry-nofirry, and remembering that nightmare vision of the burned-black man after the blevey – Sir Rufus with his black bones, black nails, black wood and his black jaw hinged back and very much a dental-records job – and thinking, *How did they identify Andy?*

The names worked even better than I expected. I can see a way out now. I feel like Judas, but there's a way out; not with any honour, perhaps, but I've looked at myself pretty closely over the last few days and I've had to admit to myself that I'm not quite as wonderful a guy as I liked to think I was.

I've imagined myself in situations like this, made up speeches in my head, speeches about truth and freedom and protection of sources, speeches I imagined delivering from the witness box just before the judge sentenced me to ninety days or six months or whatever for contempt of court, but I was kidding myself. Even if it's true that I would have gone to prison to protect somebody else or make some dubious point about the freedom of the press, I know I'd only have been doing it to make myself look good. I'm just like everybody else: selfish. I can see a way out and I'm taking it, and the fact it's a kind of betrayal doesn't really matter.

Besides, I'm paying for the betrayal by telling them about the body. By itself it doesn't prove a thing, but it's my way of getting them to take me to Strathspeld for the funeral; I can look McDunn in the eye and tell him the truth and he knows it's the truth and he'll take me. I think.

And, perhaps, with this act of treachery I can finally buy my freedom from the burden of buried horror that bound me to Andy twenty years ago, so that – dispossessed of that trespass – I'm left free to betray him again, now.

*

McDunn's in very early this morning; we're here in the same old interview room. The place is familiar, becoming home, taking on a tinge of spurious cosiness. McDunn's standing behind the table, smoking. He waves me to sit in the chair and I do, yawning. I actually slept fairly well last night, for the first time since I got here.

'They've both disappeared,' McDunn says. He's staring at the table. He draws on the B&H. I'd quite like a cigarette, too, even

235

though it's still early and I've barely got over the morning cough but McDunn seems to have forgotten his manners.

'Halziel and Lingary,' he says, staring at me, and he looks really concerned, worried and harried and tired for the first time; yes, it's all change here in Paddington Green. 'They've both disappeared,' the DI tells me, sounding shaken. 'Lingary just yesterday, Doctor Halziel three days ago.'

He pulls the seat back and sits in it. 'Cameron,' he says. '*What body?*'

I shake my head. 'Take me there.'

McDunn sucks his teeth and looks away.

I just sit there. I feel in control at last. I suppose in theory I could be lying through my teeth and have some other reason for wanting to go to Strathspeld – maybe I'm just getting homesick for Scotland – but I'm certain he knows that I'm not lying and that there is a body; I think he can see it in my eyes.

McDunn breathes hard, then glares at me. 'You do know, don't you? You know who it is.' He sucks on his teeth. 'Is it who I think it is?'

I nod. 'Yes, it's Andy.'

McDunn nods grimly. He frowns. 'So who was it in the hotel? There's been nobody reported missing up there.'

'There will be,' I tell him. 'Guy called Howie . . . I can't remember his second name; begins with a G. He was supposed to leave for Aberdeen the day I left, to start some job on the rigs. Anyway, a few of us had a drink in the hotel that night, and apparently there was a fight; this was after I got drunk and got put to bed. Andy told me Howie and another two locals jumped a couple of travellers who'd been at the party as well. The local cop was called and he was looking for Howie.' I hold my hands out. 'I mean, this is all stuff that Andy told me, so it could be just a story, but I'd bet that up to that point it's all true. I think Andy offered to let Howie hole up in the hotel while the cops were looking for him, and everybody else up there just assumes Howie's offshore at the moment.' I tap my fingers on the table and look at McDunn's cigarette packet, hoping he'll get the hint. 'Grissom,' I tell McDunn, suddenly remembering. Couldn't think of it all night but now I have, just by talking about it. 'That's who it was. Howie Grissom; his second name was Grissom.'

There's a terrible sick, empty feeling in my guts. My hands are shaking again and I put them between my legs. I give a small laugh. 'I even saw the local cop outside the dentist's, day of the party. I just assumed he was there to get a tooth filled or something, but Andy must have broken in and switched the records then.'

'We're checking the dental records of the body from the hotel with the Army's records,' McDunn says, nodding. He glances at his watch. 'Should have something this morning.' He shakes his head. 'And why those two? Why Lingary and Doctor Halziel?'

I tell the DI why; I tell him about two more betrayals; about the commanding officer who had let men die to cover up his own inadequacy (or at least Andy believed he had, which was all that mattered), and I tell him about the locum doctor who couldn't be bothered to attend a patient and then, when he eventually did pay a visit, just assumed her pain was something trivial.

McDunn finally offers me a cigarette. Oh, joy. I take it and suck hard, coughing a bit. 'I guess,' I tell him, 'he's getting personal now because his usual targets have become more wary.' I shrug. 'And maybe he's guessed I'll put you onto him, or that you'll just work it out for yourselves, so he's settling old scores while he can, before they're warned, too.'

McDunn is staring at the floor and turning the gold B&H packet over and over on the table. He shakes his head. I get the impression he agrees with what I'm saying and he's just shaking his head at the sheer extent of human deviousness and spite. I think in a strange sort of way I feel sorry for McDunn.

There's a pause while a young constable comes in with some tea; the man at the door gets his cup, and McDunn and I sip ours.

237

'So, Detective Inspector,' I say, sitting back in my chair. Hell, I'm almost enjoying this, sick feeling or not. 'Are we going there or not?'

McDunn sucks his lips in and looks pained. He nods.

*

I trip on something in the ferns, twisting in mid-air as my ankle gives underneath me and I slam backwards into the ground, winding myself. I lie there, gulping for air, terrified of the man coming to get me while I lie there helpless; then I hear a scream.

I get to my feet.

I look down at what I tripped over; a fallen branch, about the size of a man's arm. I stare at it, thinking down the depth of years to that frozen day by the river.

Get a branch.

The scream again.

Get a branch.

I'm still staring at the branch; it's like my brain's screaming at me inside my own head and I don't know what else it is that's listening, except it *isn't* listening; my brain's screaming *Run! Run!* at me but the message isn't getting through, there's something else in the way, something else pulling me back, back to Andy and back to that frozen river bank; I hear Andy crying out and I can still see him reaching towards me and he's about to slip away from me again and I can't do anything . . . but I can, this time I can; I can do something and I will.

I take hold of the branch and pull it ripping out of the grass and ferns. I start to run again, back the way I've just come, the branch held out in front of me in both hands. I can hear Andy's muffled shouting; for a moment I think I've lost them and run past them somehow; then I see them, almost straight ahead. The man is moving up and down over Andy, his backside looks large and white against the green of the ferns; he still has the rucksack on and it looks weird, frightening and comical at the same time. He has one hand over Andy's face, clamped tight; his head is turned away from me, red hair fallen down over one ear. I put the branch two-handed over my right shoulder as I run up to them, jump over a small bush and then as I land at their side bring the branch swinging down. It whacks into the man's head with a dull, hollow sound, jerking his head to one side; he grunts and starts to get up, then goes limp. I stand over him.

Andy is wheezing, struggling for breath; he pulls himself out from underneath the man; there is blood round his backside. He pushes the man away; the man flops onto his side, then rolls forward onto his face again, groaning.

Andy sucks breath, staring at me; he pulls his trousers up, then he puts out his hand and takes the branch from me. He raises it over his head and brings it crashing down on the back of the man's head; once, twice, three times.

'Andy!' I shout. He raises the branch again, then drops it. He stands there, shaking, then hugs himself, chin on his chest, staring down at the man, his head and whole body trembling.

There is blood leaking from the back of the man's head, beneath the red hair.

'Andy?' I ask him. I put my hand out to him but he flinches.

We both stand and stare at the man, and at the blood spreading amongst the red hair.

'I think he's dead,' Andy whispers.

I put one shaking hand out and roll the man over. His eyes are half-open. He doesn't seem to be breathing. I hold one of his wrists for a while, trying to find a pulse.

'What are we going to do?' I ask, letting the man roll forward onto his face again. Sunlight dapples the grass and ferns around us. Birds call from the trees above and I can hear the distant sound of traffic on the main road, through the forest.

Andy is silent.

'We'd better tell somebody, don't you think? Andy? We'd better tell somebody, eh? We'd better tell . . . tell, tell, tell your mum and dad. We'll have to tell the police; even if he is . . . even if he was . . .

239

I mean, this was self-defence, they call it, it was self-defence. He, he, he, he was trying to kill us, kill you; it was self-defence, we can say that, people'll believe us, it was self-defence; self-defence – Andy turns to me, face set and pale. 'Fucking shut up.'

I shut up. I can't stop shaking.

'Then what are we going to *do*?' I wail.

'I know,' Andy says.

*

A civvy Granada to Heathrow. London on a bright November morning. People and cars and buildings and shops. I watch the real life go by outside like it's something from an SF movie; I can't believe how alien it all looks, how strange and foreign. I feel a bizarre sense of loss and yearning. I watch the men and women as they crowd along the streets or sit in their cars and vans and buses and trucks, and their freedom seems inestimably precious, exotic and vicariously intoxicating. To be able just to walk, or drive, wherever you want; Christ, I've been away from all this for less than a week and I feel like somebody coming out after thirty years.

And I know these people don't feel free, I know they're all hurrying along or sitting there worrying about their jobs or their mortgages or being late or an IRA bomb in the nearest litter-bin, but I look at them and feel a terrible sense of loss, because I think I've surrendered all this; the ordinariness of life, the ability just to be part of it and take part in it. I want to hope that I'm being melodramatic and everything will settle back to the way it used to be, before all this ghastliness, but I doubt it. In my guts I feel that, even if everything goes the best it possibly can for me, my life has changed completely and forever.

But fuck it; at least I'm back in the real world, and with a modicum of control.

I'm discreetly handcuffed to Detective Sergeant Flavell – McDunn has the key – and we have a couple of burly plain-clothes men with us I strongly suspect are tooled up, but the pressure seems to be off me a bit. I don't think I'm suspect numero uno any more; I think McDunn at least believes me and that's enough for now. The unfortunate Captain – later Major – Lingary (retired) and Doctor Halziel have done me a lot of good by disappearing so mysteriously. I try not to think what Andy might be doing to them. I try even harder not to think about what he might do to me if he ever got the chance.

We're on the dear old elevated section of the M4 where lorries are so apt to break down when there's a call for McDunn; he takes the handset, listens and sucks his teeth for a bit, then says, 'Thank you.' He puts the phone down and looks back at me. 'Army records,' he says. He turns back to face the front as we head through the late-morning traffic. 'The body in the hotel was not Andrew Gould's.'

'Did they check the records against the ones in Howie's file?' I ask.

McDunn nods. 'They match Gould's. Not perfectly; he's had work done since, but they say they're ninety-nine per cent sure. They were switched.'

I sit back, smiling; for a while there's a glow in my belly which displaces the sickness. For a while.

McDunn gets on the phone to somebody from Tayside police and tells them to contact the Goulds and stop the funeral.

Lunch for five at 35,000 feet, then Edinburgh from the air: greyly grand and a tad misty. We land just after one o'clock and get straight into a Jag jam-sandwich (so a Ford at both ends – ha!). The XJ speeds north over the road-bridge, no lights or siren on but we clip along and it's the smoothest fucking motorway journey I've ever had; just a total hassle-free zone creaming along around the ton with no worries about unmarked police cars and *hoo-wee* the traffic in front of us just fucking evaporates; man, just brakes (and wobbles sometimes as the guy probably gets the cold sweats and the wo-where'd-my-stomach-go? feeling), swings meekly left and brakes again; you've never seen a beefy BMW 5-series duck in so fast in your life; might as well all be driving 2CVs. It's beautiful.

*

241

We take a leg each and drag the man face-down through the ferns towards the northeast end of the hill. His cord trousers are still rolled down round his ankles and get in the way and we have to stop and turn him over and pull the trousers back up, fastening them by one button. His cock is small now and there is dried blood crusted on it. We pull him away beneath the trees; in his other hand, Andy is still holding the branch we hit him with.

We come to a thicket under the trees; a cluster of rhododendron and bramble bushes. Andy clears a way through the undergrowth and we drag the man beneath the thorns and soft fruit of the brambles and the glossy leaves of the rhodies, into the green darkness; his rucksack catches on the branches above and Andy takes it off him, pushing it ahead of us.

We come to a stubby cylinder of undressed stone; the second of the two chimneys from the old railway tunnel under the hill.

*

We make good time on the road from the motorway; people actually *help you overtake* when you're in a cop car. Unbelievable. I almost wish I'd become a cop-car driver instead of a journalist now; this is such *sweet* driving. Still, maybe it kind of takes some of the sport out of it.

At Gilmerton, where the three wee blue Fiat 126s used to live, there's a Sapphire Cosworth orange-and-white squatting just off the road by the junction; it flashes its lights at us as we pass. There's another patrol car at the turn-off to Strathspeld.

'Kind of high-profile here, aren't we?' I ask McDunn.

'Mm-hmm,' is all he'll say.

We come to the village. I look up at our old house; bushes and trees are taller. Satellite dish. Conservatory on one side. I watch the familiar shops and houses go by; Mum's old gift shop (now a video shop); the Arms, where I had my first pint; Dad's old garage, still doing business. Another police car, parked on the village green.

242

'Will the Goulds be at the house?' I ask.

McDunn shakes his head. 'They're in that hotel we just passed.'

I'm relieved. I don't think I'd know what to say to them. Hi; the good news is I didn't kill your son, in fact he isn't dead at all, but the bad news is he's a multiple murderer.

Five minutes later we're at the house.

The gravel circle outside the house looks like the car park at a cop convention. I hear a clattering in the air as McDunn gets out of the Jag and I look up over the trees into high, bright overcast. Fuck me, they've even brought a chopper.

McDunn stands talking to some heavily brassed uniformed cops on the steps of the front door. I look round the old place; the window surrounds have been painted, the flower-beds look a bit unkempt. Nothing else has changed; I haven't been here since that day a week after Clare died, and it had the same muddily washed-out look about it then.

McDunn comes back towards the car, catches Flavell's eye and beckons him. We get out and follow McDunn into the house.

Nothing much different inside, either; still looks and smells the same: polished parquet flooring, sumptuous but fading old rugs, assorted mostly very old furniture, lots of big houseplants on the floor and time-dulled landscapes and portraits on the wood-panelled walls. We walk under the angle of the main staircase, into the dining room. The place is full of cops; there's a map of the estate on the table, almost covering it. McDunn introduces me to the other officers. I have never had so many hard, suspicious looks in my life.

'So, where's this body?' one of the uniformed guys from Strathclyde asks. He's here because they've loaned the helicopter.

'Still here,' I tell him. 'Unlike . . . unlike the man you're looking for.' I look at McDunn, the one friendly-ish face in here and the only one I can look at without feeling like a five-year-old who's just wet his pants. 'I thought the idea was to let the funeral go ahead, or at least make it look like it was; he was bound to be here. You might have caught him then.'

McDunn's face gives a good impression of being stone-clad. 'That was not felt to be the most suitable way of proceeding in this matter,' he says, sounding like a police spokesman for the first time.

There's a sensation of well tailored black uniforms rustling in the room and I get the impression from the general atmosphere and a few exchanged looks that this is a contentious point.

'We're still waiting for this body,' says the man with the braid from Tayside, the boys officially in charge. 'Mr Colley,' he adds.

I look down at the map of the estate. 'I'll show you,' I tell them. 'You'll need a . . . crowbar or something, about fifty metres of rope and a torch. A hacksaw might be handy, too.'

*

Andy reaches up to the iron grating and pulls at it.

'This one comes away,' he grunts; his voice is still shaky.

I help him; we lift the rusting grating up at one end but the far side is still secured by an iron pin and we can't shift it any further.

Andy takes the branch we hit the man with and wedges it under the grating; part of it sticks through but there's a stump where a smaller branch has broken off and the grating rests on that, held a half-metre or so off the stone rim.

Andy throws the man's rucksack into the shaft, then bends and takes the man under one armpit, trying to heave him up.

'Come on!' he hisses.

We haul the man up, his back against the stone of the vent, his head flopping down onto his chest. There's a little blood on the stones of the chimney. Andy takes the man's calves under his armpits and lifts; I get underneath and force the man's shoulders up; his head goes over onto the stone rim of the vent, beneath the grating. We both push and heave and the man's shoulders scrape over the rim; his arms drag up and over as Andy pushes, grunting, feet slipping on the old leaves and soil. I push the man's behind up, lifting with all my might. The man's trousers snag on the stone and start to come down again, then the branch holding the grating shifts and the iron grid falls down, thumping into the man's chest.

'Shit,' Andy breathes. We struggle to lift the grating up and wedge the branch underneath again. The man's head is poised over the shaft, drooping down into it. We push his legs but they buckle at the knees, so we have to hold them up above our heads as we push to make them stay straight, then as we shove and his trousers are rolled down by the rim of stone, his arms flop over the far side of the shaft rim and it suddenly gets easier to push him. He slides out of our grasp, slipping into the shaft with a scraping noise. His trousers bunch round his ankles again, then catch round his boots and disappear over the edge of the chimney, kicking up at the last moment and hitting the grating; the branch slips and the grating slams down. The branch falls through it into the shaft and drops after the man.

We stand there for a second or two. Then there is – unless we each imagine it – a very faint thump. Andy suddenly jerks into motion and scrambles up onto the rim of the chimney. He stares through the grating, down into the darkness.

'Can you see him?' I ask.

Andy shakes his head. 'But let's get some branches anyway,' he says.

We prop the grating open with another branch and spend the next half-hour pulling fallen branches and logs from all over that part of the hill, dragging them into the clump of bushes and throwing them into the shaft; we snap dead branches off trees and bushes and haul and peel living ones off; we scrape together armfuls of dry leaf litter and throw those over the edge of the chimney, too; everything goes under the grating and down into the shaft. We still can't see anything down there.

Eventually a large branch with lots of other branches on it and lots of leaves – half a bush, practically – snags only a few metres down the shaft and we stop, breathless, sweating, trembling from exertion and delayed shock. We let the grating fall back and throw the last branch down into the darkness; it catches on the branches stuck near the top of the shaft. We sit on the dead leaves at the foot of the vent, backs against the stone.

'Are you all right?' I ask Andy after a while.

He nods. I put a hand out to him but he flinches again.

We sit there for some time but I keep glancing up, and gradually become terrified that the man is somehow not dead or has become a zombie and is climbing back up the shaft towards us, to push the grating up and put his already rotting hands down and grab us both by the hair. I stand up and face Andy. My legs are still shaky and my mouth has gone very dry.

Andy stands too. 'A swim,' he says.

'What?'

'Let's – ' Andy swallows. 'Let's go for a swim. Down to the loch, the river.' He glances back at the stones of the air shaft.

'Yeah,' I say, trying to sound cheerful and unconcerned. 'A swim.' I look at my hands, all scraped and dirty. There's some blood on them. They're still shaking. 'Good idea.'

We crawl out of the undergrowth into the bright day.

*

There are a few minutes, perhaps not more than three or four, when I exist in a bewildering storm of hope, joy, incomprehension and dread, when they don't find the body at the bottom of the shaft.

We walked here through the gardens and the woods, past the hill where Andy and I lay in the sunlight all those summers ago, into the little glen, then up through the bushes and the dead auburn wreckage of the ferns, to the trees at the summit of the small hill. A damp wind blew from the west, shaking drips off the high, bare trees and taking the sound of the main road away.

There are about twenty of us altogether, including half a dozen constables carrying the gear. I'm still very much attached to Sergeant Flavell. I'd naively thought they could mount some low-profile operation to catch Andy watching his own funeral; I'd imagined cops slinking through the undergrowth, whispering into radios, gradually closing in. Instead we're here mob-handed, crashing through the undergrowth towards a dead body.

Except it isn't there. I tell them it is; I tell them there's a man's body at the bottom of the air shaft and they believe me. It takes them long enough to cut a way through to the chimney of the air shaft, sawing through the rhodie branches and tearing away the brambles and other undergrowth; then they lever off the iron grating over the shaft without any difficulty, and one of the younger cops, in an overall and a hard hat, wraps the rope around himself – proper climbing rope they had in the back of one of the Range Rovers – and abseils down into the darkness.

McDunn's listening on a little radio handset.

It crackles. 'Lot of branches,' the cop on the end of the rope says. Then: 'Down, on the bottom.'

The helicopter clatters overhead. I'm wondering where Andy is by now when I hear the guy in the shaft say, 'Nothing here.'

What?

'Just a load of branches and stuff,' the cop says.

McDunn doesn't react. I do; I stare at the radio. What's he talking about? I feel dizzy. It did happen. I remember it. I've lived with it ever since, had it at the back of my head ever since. I know it happened. I feel like the woods are revolving around me; maybe if I wasn't still handcuffed to the sergeant, I'd fall over. (And I remember the man saying, can remember his voice perfectly, hear him again as he says, 'I'm a *police-man!*')

Some of the other cops gathered round the air shaft are wearing knowing looks.

'Wait a minute,' the cop in the tunnel says.

247

My heart thuds. What has he found? I don't know if I want him to find him – it – or not.

'There's a rucksack here,' the voice on the radio says. 'Large day-pack size, brown . . . looks full. Fairly old.'

'Nothing else?' McDunn asks.

'Just the branches . . . can't see to the end of the tunnel in either direction. Patch of light in the distance . . . eastwards.'

'That's the other air shaft,' I tell McDunn. 'Back that way.' I point.

'Want me to have a look round, sir?'

McDunn looks at the Tayside chief, who nods. 'Yes,' McDunn says. 'If you're sure it's safe.'

'Safe enough, I think, sir. Untying.'

McDunn looks at me. He sucks his teeth. I avoid the eyes of the other cops. McDunn's eyebrows rise a little.

'He was there,' I tell him. 'It was Andy and I. This guy attacked us; abused Andy. We hit him with a log. I swear.'

McDunn looks unconvinced. He peers over the edge of the stonework, down into the shaft.

I'm still feeling dizzy. I put a hand out to the stones of the air-shaft chimney, to steady myself. At least the rucksack's there. It did *happen*, for Christ's sake; it wasn't an hallucination. The guy was probably dead when we tipped him into the shaft – we just assumed he was at the time though the older I got the less sure of that I was – but even if wasn't, he *must* have been killed when he hit the bottom; it's thirty metres at least.

Could Andy have decided since that the body wasn't well enough concealed, and come back and removed it; hauled it up, taken it away and buried it? We'd never talked about that day, and we never again came near this old air shaft; I don't know what he might have done since but I'd always assumed he was like me and just tried to forget about it, pretend it never happened.

Denial. Hell, sometimes it's best.

'– ear me yet?' the radio crackles.

248

'Yes?' McDunn says.
'Found him.'

*

It will take a while to get the body out; they have to get more guys down there, take photographs; the usual shit. Most of us return to the house. I don't know what the hell to feel. It's finally over, it's out, people know, other people know; the police know, it's no longer just between me and Andy, it's public. I do feel some relief, no matter what happens now, but I still feel I have betrayed Andy, regardless of what he's done.

The man's body was under the other air shaft. The poor fuck must have crawled all that way, a hundred metres or more to that second patch of light; our bright idea of putting the branches down after him to cover him up was pointless; for all these years it would only have needed some more kids to have come along with torches or bits of burning paper to discover the body. They reckon there was a load of fallen branches lying under the air shaft before we pushed the guy down it; according to the young cop who first went down it looked like he'd crawled out from the middle of the pile. Even so, I don't know how he survived that fall; God knows what he broke, how he suffered, how long he took to crawl there to the other slightly brighter patch of light; how long he took to die.

Part of me feels sorry for him, despite what he tried to do, what he did do. God knows, maybe he'd have ended up killing Andy, killing both of us, but nobody deserves to die like that.

On the other hand there's a part of me that rejoices, that is glad he paid the way he did, that for once the world worked the way it's supposed to, punishing the wrongdoer . . . and that saddens and sickens me too, because I think that this must be the way Andy feels all the time.

*

249

It's strange to be in Strathspeld, to be in the house and not have seen Mr and Mrs Gould. Some of the cops have gone; there are only ten cars and vans on the gravel drive now. The chopper went to refuel, came back and buzzed around some more and then returned to Glasgow. Apparently they had road blocks and patrols on roads all over the area, and they searched the grounds of the house. Fat chance.

Back at the house, in the library, I tell a DI from Tayside all that happened that day, twenty years ago. McDunn sits in, too. It isn't as painful as I thought it would be. I tell it just as it happened, from where we ran up the hill almost straight into the man; I leave out what Andy and I were doing just before, and the man's line about dirty, perverted things. I can't tell that with McDunn sitting there; it would be like telling my father. Actually, I guess I wouldn't want to tell it to anybody, not so much because I'm ashamed (I tell myself) as because it's private; one last thing I can hide that's between me and Andy only, so letting me feel that there is one thing at least in which I've not betrayed him utterly.

Sergeant Flavell has been released from me to take notes; I'm attached to myself now, wrists cuffed together. The aged, respectable leather-bound tomes of the Gould family library look down upon the nasty tale I have to tell with musty distaste. Outside, it's dark.

'Think I'll be charged?' I ask the two DIs. I already know there's no time limit between committing a murder and being charged with it.

'Not for me to say, Mr Colley,' the Tayside guy says, gathering up his notebook and tape recorder.

McDunn's mouth twists down at the edges; he sucks through his teeth, and for some reason I feel encouraged.

They've ordered food from the Strathspeld Arms; the same food the funeral guests would have eaten. A bunch of us eat in the dining room. I'm handcuffed to one of the London burlies now and we both have to eat with one hand. I'd kind of been hoping they'd take the cuffs off me altogether by now but I suppose they're thinking that the body in the shaft doesn't prove anything by itself, and that

Andy could still be dead, or he could be alive and he – or somebody else – could have kidnapped Halziel and Lingary to provide cover for me.

McDunn comes in as I'm chasing bits of quiche around my plate with my fork.

He comes up to me, nods to the burly and unlocks the cuffs.

'Come here,' he tells me, putting the handcuffs in his pocket. I wipe my lips and follow him to the door.

'What is it?' I ask him.

'It's for you,' he says, striding across the hall towards the phone, where the handset's lying on the table and an officer is attaching a little device like a sucker to the phone; a wire leads from the sucker to a Pro Walkman. The officer starts the machine recording. McDunn glances back at me before stopping at the phone and nodding down at it. 'It's Andy.'

He hands me the phone.

C H A P T E R

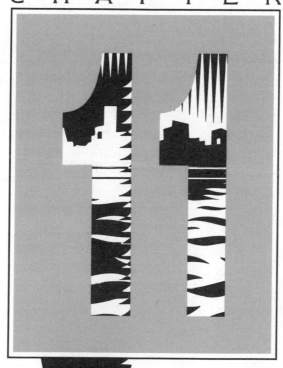

SLAB

'Andy?'

'Hello, Cameron.'

It is his voice, urbane and controlled; until this moment some tiny part of me still believed he was dead. I get the shivers, and the hair on the nape of my neck prickles. I lean back against the wall, looking at McDunn, who's standing with his arms crossed a metre away. The young officer who turned on the Walkman hands McDunn a pair of earphones plugged into the machine. McDunn listens in.

I clear my throat. 'What's going on, Andy?'

'Sorry to drop you in it, old son,' he says in a conversational sort of way, as though apologising for some thoughtless remark or landing me with a mismatched blind date.

'Yeah? Are you?'

McDunn makes a circular waving motion with one hand; keep going. Oh, Christ, here we go again. They want me to keep him talking so they can trace him. One more betrayal.

255

'Well, yes,' Andy says, sounding as though he's a little surprised to find he actually is sorry, albeit only slightly. 'I feel a bit bad about that, but at the same time I felt you deserved it. Not that I thought you'd go to prison for it; wouldn't inflict that on you, but . . . well, I wanted you to suffer for a while. I take it they found that card I left in the woods near Sir Rufus's place.'

'Yes, they did. Thanks, Andy. Yeah; great. I thought we were *friends*.'

'We were, Cameron,' he says, reasonably. 'But you did run away, twice.'

I give a small, despairing laugh, glancing at McDunn again. 'I came back the second time.'

'Yes, Cameron,' he says, and his voice is smooth. 'That's why you're still alive.'

'Oh, thanks very much.'

'But anyway, Cameron, you're still part of it. You've still played your part in it. Like me; like all of us. We're all guilty, don't you think?'

'What is this?' I ask, frowning. 'Original sin? You becoming a Catholic or something?'

'Oh, no, Cameron; I believe we're born free of sin and free of guilt. It's just that we all catch it, eventually. There are no clean rooms for morality, Cameron, no boys in bubbles kept in a guilt-free sterile zone. There are monasteries and nunneries, and people become recluses, but even that's just an elegant way of giving up. Washing one's hands didn't work two thousand years ago, and it doesn't work today. Involvement, Cameron, connection.'

I shake my head, staring at the little window in the Walkman where the tape spindles are patiently revolving. The strange thing is, it *is* like talking to a dead man, because he sounds like the Andy I used to know. Andy the mover and shaper, the Andy from before Clare's death, before he gave it all up and became a recluse; it's that voice, calm and untroubled, that I'm hearing now, not that of the man I knew from that dark, decaying hotel, flat with resignation or audibly sneering with a kind of cynical despair.

McDunn's looking impatient. He's writing something on his notebook.

'Listen, Andy,' I say, swallowing, mouth dry. 'I told them about the guy in the woods; they've been down the air shaft. They found him.'

'I know,' he says. 'I saw.' He sounds almost regretful. I close my eyes. 'They almost caught me, actually,' he says conversationally. 'That'll teach me to break my own rules and attend the funeral of one of my victims. But then it was supposed to be my own, after all. Anyway, you told them, did you? Kind of thought you might, one day. That a weight off your mind, is it, Cameron?'

I open my eyes as McDunn nudges me and shows me the two names he's written on his notebook.

'Yes,' I tell Andy. 'Yes, it is a weight off my mind. Listen, Andy, they want to know what's happened to Halziel and Lingary.'

'Oh, yes.' He sounds amused. 'That's why I called.'

McDunn and I exchange looks. 'Look, Andy,' I say. I laugh nervously. 'I kind of think you've made your point, you know? You've scared a lot of people – '

'Cameron, I've *murdered* a lot of people.'

'Yeah, yeah, I know, and a lot more are terrified to open their doors, but the point is you've *done* it, man; I mean you might as well let these guys go, you know? Just . . . just let them go, and, and, and you know; I'm sure if we can just talk about this, you know, talk about – '

'*Talk* about this?' Andy says, laughing. 'Oh, stop gibbering, Cameron.' He sounds so relaxed. I can't believe he's talking this long. He must know they can trace calls really quickly these days. 'What next?' he asks, sounding amused. 'Are you going to suggest I give myself up and I'll get a fair trial?' He laughs again.

'Andy, all I'm saying is let those guys go and just fucking stop all this.'

'All right.'

'I mean . . . what?'

'I said all right.'

'You'll let them go?' I look at McDunn. He's raised his eyebrows. A uniformed cop comes in the front door and whispers something to McDunn, who takes one of the earphones out to listen. He looks annoyed.

'Yeah,' Andy says. 'They're a boring couple of farts and I guess they've suffered enough.'

'Andy, are you being serious?'

'Of course!' he says. 'You'll get them back unharmed. Can't vouch for their mental state, of course; with any luck the bastards'll have nightmares for the rest of their lives, but . . .'

McDunn looks pained. He makes the waving keep-going signal again.

'Listen, Andy; I mean, I guessed you were Mr Archer – '

'Yes, I used a voice synthesiser,' Andy says patiently.

'But all that Ares stuff; was it all . . .?'

'A diversion, Cameron, that's all. Hey,' he laughs, 'maybe there *was* some heinous plot linking those five dead guys, but if so I've no idea what it was, and as far as I know there's no link between them and Smout and Azul. Pretty neat conspiracy theory, though, don't you think? I know you hacks just love that sort of thing.'

'Oh, yeah, had me fooled.' I smile weakly at McDunn, who motions me to keep talking.

'But how did you . . .?' I have to swallow again, fighting my nausea. I feel like I've got a coughing fit coming on, too. 'How did you know those IRA code-words? I never told you.'

'Your computer, Cameron; your PC. You had them in a file on your hard disk. Made everything a lot easier when you got that modem. Don't think I ever told you I'd become a bit of a hacker in my spare time, did I?'

Christ.

'And that time I rang the hotel and you phoned back, when you must have been in Wales . . .?'

'Yes, Cameron,' he says, sounding indulgently amused. 'Answer-machine at the hotel, linked to a pager; called up the machine, heard your message, rang you back. Easy-peasy.'

'And you were on the same plane as me to Jersey?'

'Four rows back; in a wig, glasses and 'tache. Got a taxi while you were still looking for the hire-car desk. Anyway,' he says, and I imagine I can hear him sighing and stretching, 'must dash; this technical stuff's all very fascinating but I do have a faint suspicion they're getting you to keep me talking. I'm on a mobile, which is why they haven't traced it yet; this is a biggish cell I'm in. Hey, that's a coincidence, isn't it, Cameron? You in a cell last week, me in one now . . . Well, maybe not. Anyway, as I say, it's a biggish cell but if I keep talking I'm sure they can find me here too, eventually, so – '

'Andy – '

'No, Cameron, just listen; I'll return Halziel and Lingary tonight, in Edinburgh. There's a double call box in the Grassmarket outside The Last Drop pub; I want you to be in the coin-operated box at seven o'clock. You personally, nineteen hundred hours tonight, coin-op box outside The Last Drop public house, in the Grassmarket, Edinburgh. Bye now!'

The line goes dead. I look at McDunn, who nods. I put the phone down.

*

Edinburgh on a cold November evening; the Grassmarket, light-bright under a smir of rain below the castle, a rotund floodlit presence in the orange darkness above.

The Grassmarket is a kind of long square in the hollow southeast of the castle, surrounded by mostly old buildings; I can remember when it was a seedy, run-down old place full of winos but it's moved gradually up-market over the years and it's a fairly cool area to hang out now; chic eateries, good bars, fashion outlets and shops specialising in things like kites, or minerals and fossils, though there's a still a homeless hostel round the corner, so it hasn't been irredeemably gentrified.

The Last Drop is at the east end of the Grassmarket, near the split-level curve of Victoria Street, home of yet more specialist shops including one that mystifyingly seems to provide a living selling only brushes, brooms and very large balls of string.

The pub's name is less jolly and more witty than it sounds at first; the city gallows used to be right outside.

No obvious cop cars around. I'm sitting – handcuffed to Sergeant Flavell – in an unmarked Senator with McDunn and two plain-clothes guys from Lothian. There's another unmarked car at the far end of the Grassmarket, several others nearby, and a couple of vans full of uniform guys parked in side streets, plus various cruising patrol cars in the vicinity. They say they've checked the box itself and all likely vantage points, but I'm still worried that Andy's not finished with me yet, that he's lying through his teeth and if I step into that telephone box I'll get a rifle bullet through the head. A plain-clothes guy is in the box, pretending to use it, so it'll be free when Andy calls. It's already wired up so they can record everything. I look at the façade of The Last Drop. There's a new up-market Indian restaurant within sniffing distance, too, near where the old Traverse Theatre used to be.

A pint and a curry. Jesus. My mouth waters. We're spitting distance from the Cowgate and the Kasbar, too.

McDunn looks at his watch. 'Seven o'clock,' he says. 'I wonder –' He breaks off as the cop in the phone box waves at us.

McDunn grunts. 'Military precision,' he says, then nods to Flavell; we get out of the car as the driver switches something on the radio, producing a ringing tone in time with the one I can hear coming from the box.

Flavell squeezes into the box with me while the other cop waits outside.

'Hello?' I say.

'Cameron?'

'Yeah, it's me.'

'Change of plans. Be in the same place at three o'clock this morning; you'll get them back then.' Click. The line goes dead. I look at Flavell.

'Three o'clock, did he say?' Flavell says, looking peeved.

'Think of the overtime,' I tell him.

They take me to a cop shop in Chambers Street, about a minute's drive away. I get fed and watered and put into a cell that looks damp and smells of disinfectant. The food they give me is crap; gristly stew, mushed potatoes and brussels sprouts.

But there is one wonderful thing.

They've given me back my lap-top. McDunn's idea. I try not to feel too pathetically grateful.

I check the files first; nothing missing. I give half a thought to going into *Xerion* to try the mushroom-cloud-riding trick Andy showed me, but it's only half a thought; instead I go straight into *Despot*.

I can't believe it's the same game. I feel my mouth open.

It's a wasteland. My kingdom is gone. The land is still there, some of the people are, and the capital city, designed in the shape of two giant crescents of buildings around two lakes, so that from the air it says 'CC' . . . but something terrible seems to have happened. The city is crumbling, largely abandoned; aqueducts fallen, reservoirs cracked and dry, districts flooded, others burned down; the activity taking place within the city is about what you'd expect from a small town. The countryside has either become desert or marsh or returned to forest; huge areas are barren, and where there is any agriculture it's in the shape of tiny strip-fields around little villages deep in the woods or on the fringe of the waste. The ports are drowned or silted up, the roads and canals have fallen into disrepair or just disappeared altogether, the mines have caved in or been flooded, all the cities and towns have shrunk back, and all the temples – all *my* temples – are ruined, dark, abandoned. Bandits roam the land, foreign tribes raid

261

the provinces, plagues are rife and the population is much smaller, less productive and individually shorter-lived.

The civilisation to the south that I had so many problems with seems to have retreated or relapsed as well, but that is the extent of the good news. The worst of it is there's no head man, no Despot, no me. I can look at all this but I can't *do* anything about it, not on this scale. To start playing again I'd have to trade this omniscient but omni-impotent view for that of . . . God knows, some tribal warrior, village elder, a mayor or a bandit chief.

I range over it all for a while, looking down, appalled. Somebody must have started it up just to look, then left it running while they checked out the other stuff, or maybe they tried to meddle, played with the game but couldn't control it . . . Unless this is what they wanted, what they designed; I guess a radical Green or Deep Ecologist would think it's a pretty cool result.

The battery alarm beeps. Might have known they wouldn't have charged the damn thing up properly.

I watch the unfolding of my once great realm until the machine senses too little power to work with, and closes itself down. The screen fades out on the overhead view of my capital; I watch my vainglorious 'CC'-shaped city just dissolve quietly into darkness. They put the cell lights out a few minutes later.

I sleep on the narrow little metal cot with the lap-top cradled in my arms.

*

Three in the morning; dry, now, but cold. The police driver leaves the engine running and our exhaust smoke drifts into the air to one side on a chilly breeze. The Grassmarket is silent. The car isn't; the radio chirps now and again and I can't stop coughing.

The cop in the phone box waves, bang on three.

'Corner of West Port and Bread Street, soon,' Andy says, then hangs up.

It's walking distance, but we take the car anyway, pulling up outside the Cas Rock Café bar. Nothing much here; office buildings, shops across the street. Another unmarked car is parked on Bread Street itself. The vans with the uniformed police are parked on Fountainbridge and the Grassmarket, and the various patrol vehicles are still cruising in the neighbourhood.

McDunn takes a walk around, then comes back to the car.

We have some coffee from a big thermos, sipping it black. It helps my cough a bit.

'Soon,' McDunn says, contemplatively, looking into his plastic cup as if searching for coffee grounds to read.

'That's what he said,' I tell him, clearing my throat.

'Hmm.' McDunn leans forward to the two guys in the front. 'Don't smoke, do you, lads?'

'No, sir.'

'I'll go outside to be unhealthy, then.'

'That's all right, sir.'

'No; I want to stretch my legs anyway.' He looks at me. 'Colley; smoke?'

I cough again. 'Can't make me any worse.'

Handcuffed to the DI: I guess it's a kind of promotion. We light our fags and have a stroll, down past the pub, across the road to look in the window of a second-hand bookshop, then walk up past a video shop, a butcher's and a sandwich shop, all of them dark and quiet. A taxi rattles past, for-hire light on, heading into the Grassmarket. We stand leaning over the pedestrian barrier at the kerb. The tenement buildings behind look run-down and from here I can see the Victorian pile of the old Co-op building which closed just this year, and the 'sixties-modern Goldberg's department store, shut down the year before.

Doesn't even smell too good right here; there's a wet-fish shop just behind us and a chip shop down the road but upwind; even the pavement looks greasy. Can't imagine they'll be bringing the Euro-heads of state down this neck of the woods for a black-pudding supper and a dirty video. Christ; that beano's only three weeks away now. Bet the Lothian police boys are enjoying this little outing when they've got all that to look forward to. I expected to be busy doing lots of Euro-articles for the paper in the run-up, right about now. Ah well.

'He had a good Army record, your friend,' McDunn says after a while.

'So did Lieutenant Calley,' I suggest.

The DI ruminates upon this. He studies the cone of his cigarette, smoked down almost to the filter now. 'Do you think he's politically inspired, your friend? Looks it, up till now.'

I stare up High Riggs as another taxi comes bumping down towards us. McDunn folds his cigarette neatly against the railing of the barrier we're leaning on.

'I don't think it's political,' I tell McDunn. 'I think it's moral.'

The DI looks at me. 'Moral, Cameron?' He sucks through his teeth.

'He's disillusioned,' I say. 'He used to have lots of illusions, and now he's got only one: that what he's doing will make any difference.'

'Hmm.'

We turn to go; I drop my fag to the greasy pavement and grind the butt out with my shoe, then look up. The lights of the cab turning out of High Riggs and rattling down West Port swing across behind us.

I stare. McDunn's saying something but I can't hear what it is. Funny noise in my ears. McDunn's tugging at my wrist with the handcuffs. 'Cameron,' I hear him say, somewhere in the distance. He says something else after that but I can't hear what it is; there's this weird roaring noise in my ears; high-pitched but roaring. 'Cameron?' McDunn's saying, but it's still no good. I open my mouth. He taps me on the shoulder, then holds my elbow. Finally he brings his head round in front of me, putting his face between me and the fish shop. 'Cameron?' he says. 'You all right?'

I nod, then shake my head. I nod again, pointing forward, but when he looks he can't see anything; the shop is dark and the street lights don't light up the interior.

'Ha . . .' I begin. I try again. 'Have you got a torch?' I ask him.

'A torch?' he says. 'No; got my lighter. What is it?'

I nod my head at the fish-shop window again.

McDunn flicks his lighter. He peers in, face close to the glass. He shields his eyes with his other hand, taking my hand with it.

'Can't see anything,' he says. 'Fish shop, isn't it?' He glances up at the shop's sign.

I nod back towards the unmarked car. 'Tell them to reverse up Lauriston Street and put full beam on. On here,' I say.

McDunn looks narrow-eyed at me, then seems to see something in my face. He waves to the car. They put the window down and he tells them.

The car whines backward up Lauriston Street, lights on.

Full beam; we turn away from the glare and stand just to one side of the shop front.

The fish shop has a pull-up front window. Inside there is a single slab of what looks like green granite, sloped a little off the horizontal, where the fish are displayed when the shop's open. It has stubby, rounded walls at each side and a little gutter at the bottom, near the window.

On the slab there are bits of meat, not fish. I recognise liver – ruddy chocolate-brown and silky-looking – kidneys like dark, grotesque mushrooms, what is probably a heart and various other cuts of meat, in steaks, cubes and strips. At top centre of the slab there is a large brain, creamy-grey-looking.

'Good Christ,' McDunn whispers. Funny, it's that that brings the shivers, not the sight, not after that first glimpse and realisation in the taxi's headlights.

I look back at the neat, almost bloodless display. I suspect even a *Sun* reader would know none of this came from a fish; I'm *fairly* sure it's human, but just to leave us in no doubt, at bottom centre of the slab there is a man's genitalia; uncircumcised penis small and shrivelled and grey-yellow, scrotum crumpled and brown-pink, and the two testes pulled out, one to each side, little egg-shaped grey things like tiny smooth brains, connected by slender convoluted pearly tubes to the scrotal sac, so that the final effect is oddly like a diagram of ovaries connected to a womb.

'Halziel or Lingary, I wonder?' McDunn says, sounding a little croaky.

I look up at the sign. Fish.

I sigh. 'The locum,' I tell him. 'The doctor; Halziel.' I start coughing.

The lights behind us flash, just as I'm about to ask him for another fag. The car comes quickly across the street to us, turns to face down West Port, and the passenger's window opens again.

'Found one of them, sir,' Flavell says. 'North Bridge.'

'Oh, my God,' McDunn says, putting his free hand up to the back of his head. He nods down the street to the other car. 'Get those lads here; the other one's lying in this fish shop, dissected.' He looks at me. 'Come on,' he says, rather unnecessarily as we're still handcuffed together.

In the car, he unlocks the cuffs and pockets them without comment.

*

And so to North Bridge; slanting over the platforms and glass roofs of Waverley Station, newly painted, floodlit, the link between the old and the new towns, and barely a cobble's throw from the *Caley* building.

There are two cop cars there already when we arrive. They're pulled up near the high end of the bridge, on the west side where the view looks across the station and Princes Street Gardens to the Castle.

The decorated parapet of the bridge here holds a couple of large plinths, one on either side. On the east, where during the day you can see Salisbury Crags, the countryside of Lothian and the scoop of the Forth coast at Musselburgh and Prestonpans, the plinth supports a memorial to the King's Own Scottish Borderers; a group-sculpture of four giant stone soldiers. There is a similar plinth on the west side, where the cop cars are, blue lights strobing along the painted panels of the parapet and the grubby blond stonework of the plinth. Until now that plinth has been empty, sitting there unoccupied and unused except to provide temporary parking for the odd wittily removed road cone or possibly a platform for an adventurous rugby fan to demonstrate high-altitude pissing from.

Tonight, though, it has another role to play; tonight it is the stage for Andy's tableau of Major Lingary (retired), in full-dress major's uniform, but with the insignia torn off, and with his sword lying, broken, beside him.

He has been shot twice in the back of the head.

McDunn and I stand looking at him for a while.

*

In the morning, at Chambers Street, they feed me a fairly decent breakfast and give me back my own clothes. I was back in the same cell for the rest of the night, but this time the door wasn't locked. They're letting me go, after a few statements.

The interview room at Chambers Street is smaller and older than the one at Paddington Green; green painted walls, lino floor. I'm becoming something of a connoisseur of interview rooms and this one definitely wouldn't rate a star.

First there's a CID guy from Tayside wanting to be told the whole story about the man in the woods who became the body in the tunnel. Gerald Rudd, the man's name was; been on the Missing Persons list for twenty years, assumed to have walked into the Grampians and disappeared, and (ironically) he really was a policeman, if only part-time. A special constable and scoutmaster from Glasgow, he was already under investigation for interfering with one of the boy scouts.

Coffee at eleven – they even send somebody out to get me fags – then another statement, punctuated by my coughs, to a couple of Lothian CID lads covering what I know about Halziel and Lingary.

They haven't got much from last night. Inside the fish shop the display got even more bizarre – Andy had used the doc's fingers to spell out I LIED on the counter (only the 'E' gave him any problems) – and somebody saw a white Escort driving away from the plinth on North Bridge shortly before Lingary's body was discovered. The car was later found abandoned on Leith Walk. They're dusting the fish shop and the car but I don't expect they'll find anything.

McDunn comes in with another plain-clothes guy about half twelve. He introduces the other cop as Detective Inspector Burall, from Lothian. They're holding on to my passport and they still want me to keep them informed of my whereabouts, in case the Procurator Fiscal decides to prosecute on the Rudd case. I have to sign for the passport. I'm coughing a lot.

'I'd get to a doctor about that cough,' McDunn says, sounding concerned. I nod, tears in my eyes from the coughing.

'Yeah,' I wheeze. 'Good idea.' After I've had a walk and a few pints, maybe, I'm thinking.

'Mr Colley,' the Lothian cop says. He's a serious-looking guy, a bit older than me with very pale skin and thinning black hair. 'I'm sure you'll understand we're concerned about Andrew Gould possibly still being in the city, especially with the European Summit coming up. Detective Inspector McDunn believes there is a chance Andrew Gould will attempt to contact you, and even that he might try to attack or kidnap you.'

I look at McDunn, who's nodding, mouth compressed. I have to admit the idea of Andy paying a visit had occurred to me as well, after that I LIED. Burall continues: 'We'd like your permission to station a couple of officers at your flat for a while, Mr Colley; we'll put you up in a hotel if this is agreeable to you.'

268

McDunn sucks through his teeth, and I almost want to laugh at the sound now. I don't; I cough instead.

'I would advise you to say yes, Cameron,' McDunn says, frowning at me. 'Of course, you'll want to pick up some clothes and things first, but – '

The door swings opens and a uniform guy rushes in, glances at me and whispers into McDunn's ear. McDunn looks at me.

'What sort of present for you would he leave at Torphin Dale?'

'Torphin Dale?' I say. The sickness comes back. Oh Christ oh Christ oh Christ. It's like I've been kicked in the balls. I have to struggle to make my mouth work. 'That's where William and Yvonne live; the Sorrells.'

McDunn stares at me for a moment. 'Address?' he says.

'Four Baberton Drive,' I tell him.

He glances up at the uniformed guy. 'Got that?'

'Sir.'

'Get some cars out there, and get one for us.' Then he's up out of his chair, nodding at Burall and me. 'Come on.'

I stand up but my legs don't work too well as we walk quickly out of the station into a bright, cold afternoon. A uniformed driver runs out ahead of us, pulling on a jacket and blipping the doors on an unmarked Cavalier.

A present for me, at Torphin Dale. Oh, sweet Jesus, no.

*

'Come *on*! Get out the *way*!'

'Now, Cameron,' McDunn says.

Burall puts the radio handset down. McDunn asked me for the telephone number of William and Yvonne's house; Chambers Street is ringing there now and they'll call us if they get through.

'*Come on!*' I mutter under my breath, willing the road to clear for us.

The driver's doing his best; we've a siren going and blue lights flashing behind the grille, we're darting in and out of the traffic and taking a few risks, but there's just *too much traffic*. What are all these people *doing* on the road? Why aren't they at work or at home or on public transport? Can't the bastards *walk*?

We go wailing across the red lights at Tollcross, snarling traffic up in all directions, take the right-turn lane heading up Howe Street, dodge a little old lady on the pedestrian crossing at Bruntsfield and scream down Colinton Road through thinning traffic. The radio gibbers away at us; I lean forward, trying to listen. A patrol car's there at the house; no sign of anybody. My hands are hurting; I look down and see they're clenched tight, tendons standing out on my wrist. I sit back, thrown to one side as we swerve for a car coming suddenly out of a side street. The radio tells us the garage doors are open at the house. The beat cops can't get any answer at the front door.

We sweep across the by-pass. I'm sitting back in the seat, staring at the headlining of the car's roof, coughing now and again, tears in my eyes. Oh Christ, Andy, please, no.

We enter the executive development of Torphin Dale between the tall sandstone gateposts of the old estate; on Baberton Drive, everything looks the way I remember it apart from the orange-and-white parked in the short driveway from the bottom of the cul-de-sac to the house. The three garage doors are all tipped open. I don't know why but this gives me a bad feeling.

William's Merc is there; Yvonne's 325 isn't.

We pull into the drive. It takes a second for me to remember that I'm not handcuffed to anybody. The driver stays in the Cavalier, talking into the radio.

A uniformed cop comes down the drive from the front door, nodding to Burall and McDunn.

'No answer, sir. We haven't looked inside yet; my mate's round the back, looking in the garden.'

'There a door from the garage to the rest of the house?' McDunn asks.

'Looks like it, sir.'

McDunn looks at me. 'You know these people, Cameron; they in the habit of leaving the place unattended like this?'

I shake my head. 'Pretty security-conscious,' I tell him.

McDunn sucks on his teeth.

We walk into the garage under the tip-up doors. The usual garage stuff, if you're filthy nouveau riche; packing cases, golfing gear, the Jet Ski on its trailer, a work bench, a grid on the wall holding neatly arrayed car and garden tools, most of them gleaming and unused, pairs of ski-boot bags and ski bags hanging from the wall, a steam-cleaning outfit, a little mini-tractor lawn mower, a big grey-black wheelie bin and a couple of mountain bikes. The triple garage is huge but still cluttered; if Yvonne's car was here it would be positively crowded.

McDunn knocks at the door into the rest of the house. He frowns, looks back at Burall. 'We got any disposable gloves with us at all?'

'In the car,' Burall says, and jogs back to the Cavalier.

'You've been here before, have you, Cameron?' McDunn asks.

'Yes,' I say, coughing.

'Right; let us know about any nooks and crannies, will you?'

I nod. Burall comes back with a handful of the sort of gloves you can buy at service stations for working on the car. We all get a pair, even me. McDunn opens the door and we go into the utility room. Nothing in the cupboards in the utility room; nothing in the kitchen.

The four of us spread through the house; I stay with McDunn. We walk through the main lounge, looking behind the curtains, the couches, under the tables, even up inside the hood of the central fireplace. We head upstairs. We check one of the back bedrooms. The officer in the rear garden, walking back towards the house, sees us; he waves and makes a hands-out shrugging motion, shaking his head.

McDunn inspects the drawers built into the divan bed. I look in the built-in wardrobe, sliding my mirrored image out of the way, my heart in my mouth.

271

Clothes. Just clothes, hats and a few boxes.

We go to the main bedroom. I try not to think about what we were doing here the last time I was in this room. I have that roaring noise in my ears again and I've got a cold sweat and I feel like I could just collapse at any second. I have a weird, invasive feeling, being here with the detective inspector, clumbering around the expensively delicate domesticity of this house with no William or Yvonne here.

I look in the dressing room while McDunn checks under the bed, then looks out onto the balcony. I open the dressing-room wardrobes. Lots of clothes. I pull them back, hands shaking.

Nothing. I put the mirror doors back. I walk towards the bathroom. I put my hand on the door; a pale, pastel light shines from the room as the door starts to open.

'Cameron?' McDunn says, from the bedroom. I retreat, padding through, leaving the door half-open. He's looking out the window towards the drive. He glances at me, nods. 'Car.'

I go to the window; a red BMW325. Yvonne's car.

It's as if the car's hesitating, just in front of the drive, put off by the patrol car and the unmarked Cavalier parked in front of the garage.

Then it parks across the bottom of the drive, blocking our way out but leaving an escape route for itself. McDunn looks suspicious but I feel relieved. If Andy was here, he's long gone; that's an Yvonne move.

And it's her. Sweet Jesus, it's her, it's her, it's her. She gets out of the car holding a big black torch about two foot long, her face set in a frown. She's wearing jeans and a leather jacket over a sweatshirt. She's had her hair cut again. Her sharp, lean-featured face is un-made-up and looks aggressively distrustful. She looks wonderful.

'That Mrs Sorrell?' McDunn says quietly.

'Yes,' I say, on an outrush of breath, something in me easing. I want to cry. Yvonne looks away up the drive as another patrol car swings in. She puts the torch away as the car pulls to a stop and two

272

uniformed officers get out. She walks up to them, nodding back to the house.

'Let's get down there and see what she's got to say, shall we?' McDunn says.

We go past the dressing-room door. 'Just a minute,' I say. McDunn waits as I go through the dressing room. I press the door to the bathroom open. The pale light spills out onto me.

Nothing. I look in the shower, the Jacuzzi, the bath. Nothing. I take a swallow and a deep breath and join McDunn to head downstairs.

'Cameron!' Yvonne says as we get to the bottom of the stairs. She's putting a newspaper and a couple of pints of milk down on the telephone table. The two cops from the second car are behind her. She glances at McDunn then comes up to me, hugs me, holding me tight. 'Are you all right?'

'Fine. Are you?'

'Yes,' she says. 'What is all this? Somebody from the paper said you were the man they were holding for all those murders.' She pulls away, still with one arm round my waist. 'Why the police?' She looks at McDunn.

'Detective Inspector McDunn,' he says, nodding. 'Good afternoon, Mrs Sorrell.'

'Hello.' She looks at me, stepping back but still holding my hand, searching my face. 'Cameron, you look . . .' She shakes her head, sucking on her lips. She looks around and says, 'Where's William?'

McDunn and I exchange looks. Detective Inspector Burall comes downstairs, saying, 'Nothing up there . . .' as he sees Yvonne.

She lets go of my hand, taking a step back and looking around at all of us, as the cop from the first patrol car comes into the hall from the study, and I see her gaze falling on my transparently gloved hands, and on the hands of the other men.

There's an instant when I suddenly see her as a young woman in her own home, surrounded by all these men who've invaded it, just turned up uninvited; all bigger than her, all strangers except for one she's been told might be a serial killer. She looks wary, angry, defiant, all at once. My heart feels fit to melt.

'Was your husband here when you left, Mrs Sorrell?' McDunn asks, in a comfortingly natural voice.

'Yes,' she says, still looking round us all, settling on me, evaluating, enquiring, before looking back to McDunn. 'He was here; I only left about half an hour ago.'

'I see,' McDunn says. 'Well, he's probably popped out for a moment, but we had a message that there might be some problem here. We took the lib – '

'He's not in the garden?' she asks.

'Apparently not, no.'

'Well, you don't just "pop out" from this estate, Detective Inspector,' Yvonne says. 'The nearest shops are ten minutes' drive away, and his car's still there.' She looks at the cop who was upstairs. 'You've been searching for him, searching the house?'

McDunn is all charm. 'Yes, Mrs Sorrell, we have, and I apologise for this invasion of privacy; it's entirely my responsibility. The investigation we're involved in is a very serious one, and the tip-off we had was from a source that has been reliable in the past. As the house was open but apparently unoccupied, and we had reason to believe there might have been a crime committed I thought it right to enter, but – '

'So you haven't found him,' Yvonne says. 'You haven't found anything?' She looks, suddenly, small and frightened. I can see her fighting it, and I love her for it, and want to hold her, shush her, comfort her, but another part of me is full of a terrible jealous despair that the person she's so concerned about is William, not me.

'Not yet, Mrs Sorrell,' McDunn says. 'What was he doing when you last saw him?'

I see her swallowing, see the tendons on her neck stand out as she tries to control herself. 'He was in the garage,' she says. 'He was going to take the Honda out – the wee tractor – and sweep up leaves in the back garden.'

274

McDunn nods. 'Well, we'll just have a look, shall we?' He looks at the two cops who've just arrived and holds up one hand, flexing it. 'Gloves, lads.'

The two cops nod and head back for the front door.

The rest of us troop towards the garage, through the hall and the kitchen. My feet feel like they're wading through treacle and that roaring noise is coming back. I try not to start coughing.

McDunn stops at the utility room. He looks slightly embarrassed. 'Mrs Sorrell,' he says, smiling. 'I couldn't ask you to put a kettle on, could I?'

Yvonne stands looking at him. She looks hard and suspicious. She swivels on her heel and marches towards the work surface where the kettle is.

McDunn opens the door into the garage and I see the Mercedes and I'm thinking, The car; the boot of the car. I see the packing cases; Christ, there too.

I don't feel so good. I start coughing. McDunn and the officers look in the packing cases and the car, and it's like they're not seeing the big black wheelie bin. I stand to one side and lean against the wall, listening to them talk, watching them open and lift and peer, and that big black bin is just standing there, ignored, bulking dark against the light of the day outside where a breeze stirs, swirling dust and leaves into the air, pushing a few of the leaves onto the white-painted garage floor. McDunn looks under the car. Burall and the other cop are removing some of the packing cases and tea chests against the wall to look in the ones beneath. The two cops from the second patrol car are walking up the drive, pulling on plastic gloves.

I push myself away from the wall when I can't take it any longer, just as Yvonne comes into the garage from the house; I stagger across to the fat, chest-high bin. I can feel the others looking at me and sense Yvonne behind me. I'm coughing as I put my hand on the bin's smooth plastic handle. I lift it.

A rotting, fishy smell comes out, faint and tinged with other scents. The bin is empty.

275

I stare into it, perversely shocked, reeling back. I let the lid fall.

I bump into Yvonne and she holds me. The breeze eddies in through the open garage doors again; one of the poised garage doors creaks. Then something snaps, overhead, and the middle door swings suddenly down in the faces of the two policemen coming up the drive, making me flinch and step back, and as that middle section of the light closes off and the door slams clanging down in a cloud of dust and Yvonne gives a quick, cut-off scream, I see William; William, strapped to the internal bracing of the door with tape and twine round his wrists and ankles, his head covered with a black rubbish bag, tied tight round his throat with more black tape, his body limp.

I turn away, doubling up and coughing and coughing; blood comes suddenly from my mouth, splattering red on the white of the garage floor as, in that particular instant of loneliness, through my tears I see McDunn come forward and put a hand on Yvonne's shoulder.

She turns away from him and from William and from me and puts her hands up over her face.

C H A P T E R

BASRA ROAD

The little speedboat swings round the low island. The island is covered in whin and bramble and a few small trees, mostly ash and silver birch. Grey-black walls and roofless ruins and a few slanted headstones and memorials are visible through the bushes and trees, surrounded by ferns turning fawn, and yellowing grass covered by brown, fallen leaves. A gun-metal sky looks down.

Loch Bruc constricts here – amongst the low, bare hills near the sea – until it is only a hundred metres in breadth; the little funeral isle fills most of this bend in the narrows.

William guns the engine once, sending the speedboat surging ahead towards the little jetty which slants into the calm, dark water. The jetty's stones look old. They're unevenly sized, mostly very large, and on the top surface of smooth, dressed stone there are time-worn iron rings, set into circular depressions. On the shore behind us there is an identical slipway, angling out from the end of a track through the trees and the reed-clumped grass.

'Eilean Dubh; the dark isle,' William announces, letting the boat

279

drift in towards the island jetty. 'Old family burial ground . . . on my mother's side.' He looks around at the gently sloped hills and the higher, steeper mountains to the north. 'A lot of this used to belong to them.'

'Was that before or after the Clearances, William?' I ask.

'Both,' he grins.

Andy sips whisky from his hip-flask. He offers me some and I accept. Andy smacks his lips and looks around, giving the impression he's drinking in the silence. 'Nice place.'

'For a cemetery,' Yvonne says. She's frowning, looking cold even though she has her ski gear on: down-plump jacket and big Gore-tex mitts.

'Yeah,' I say in an approximation of a down-home American accent. 'Kinda morbid for a graveyard, isn't it, Bill, old buddy? Couldn't ya kinda liven it up a bit, know what I mean? A few neon gravestones, talking holograms of the departed, and – hey – let's not forget a flower concession stand featuring tasteful plastic blooms. A ghost-train ride for the youngsters; necro-burgers made with *real dead meat* in coffin-shaped polystyrene packs; high-speedboat trips in the funeral barge used in *Don't Look Now*, the movie.'

'Funny you should say that, actually,' William says, tossing his blond hair back and leaning out to fend the stone jetty off with his hand. 'I used to run boat trips out here from the hotel.' He puts a couple of white plastic fenders over the gunwales to protect the boat, then steps up onto the slip, holding the painter.

'Locals take to that all right?' Andy asks, standing up and pulling the stern of the boat closer in to the pier.

William scratches his head. 'Not really.' He secures the painter to one of the iron rings. 'Funeral party turned up one day while one lot were having a barbie; bit of a fracas.'

'You mean this place is still *used*?' Yvonne says, accepting William's hand and being pulled up onto the slipway. She tuts and looks away, shaking her head.

'Oh, hell, yeah,' William says as Andy and I get out too; a little unsteadily, it has to be said, as we weren't totally sober when we woke up – around noon – in William's parents' house at the top of the loch, and we've been getting stuck into the whisky in first my hip-flask then his on the twenty-kilometre journey down the loch. 'I mean,' William says, flapping his arms. 'That's why I wanted you guys to see this place; this is where I want to be buried.' He smiles beatifically at his wife. 'You too, blue-eyes, if you want.'

Yvonne stares at him.

'We could be buried together,' William says, sounding happy.

Yvonne frowns severely and walks past us, heading towards the island. 'You'd only want to go on top as usual.'

William laughs uproariously, then looks briefly crestfallen as we follow Yvonne onto the grass and head up to the ruined chapel. 'I meant side-by-side,' he says plaintively.

Andy chuckles and screws down the cap of the hip-flask. He looks thin and kind of hunched. This visit to the west coast was my idea. I invited myself and Andy here for a long weekend with William and Yvonne at William's parents' place on the shores of the loch, not so much for my own enjoyment – I get jealous around William and Yvonne when they're in their weekend-horseplay mode – but because it was the first idea I'd had for a break that Andy didn't reject immediately. Clare died six months ago and, apart from a month of night-clubbing in London which seemed to leave him more depressed than ever and certainly less wealthy and healthy, Andy hasn't left Strathspeld since; I've tried a dozen different ways of getting him away from the estate for a while but this was the only one that sparked any interest.

I think Andy just plain likes Yvonne and is sort of morbidly fascinated with William, who spent a large part of the journey down the loch telling us about his non-ethical investment policy: deliberately putting money into arms businesses, tobacco companies, exploitative mining industries, rain-forest timber concerns; that sort of thing. His theory is that if the smart but ethical money is getting out, the dividends have to get bigger for the smart but unscrupulous

281

money that takes its place. I assumed he was joking, Yvonne pretended not to listen, but Andy was taking him quite seriously, and from William's appreciative reaction I suspect the guy wasn't kidding at all.

We walk up between gravestones of various ages; some are only a year or two old, many date back to the last century, and some are dated in the seventeen and sixteen hundreds; others have been worn smooth by the elements, their text levelled and obliterated back into the grainy nap of the rock. Some of the stones are just flat, irregular slabs, and you get the impression that if the poor people who erected these – and could not afford a stonemason – could write, and did carve the names and dates of their loved ones on such slabs, the letters and numerals must only have been scratched onto the surface of the stone.

I stand looking at some long, flat gravestones set into the ground with crude depictions of skeletons chiselled into them; other carvings are of skulls and scythes and hourglasses and crossed bones. Most of the horizontal stones are covered in grey, black and light green lichens and mosses.

There are a couple of family plots, where more affluent locals have walled off bits of the little island, and grander gravestones of marble and granite stand proud, if they're not covered by brambles. Some of the more recent graves still have wee cellophane parcels of flowers lying on them; many have small granite flowerpots, covered by perforated metal caps that make them look like giant pepperpots, and a couple of these have dead, faded flowers in them.

The walls of the ruined chapel barely come up to shoulder-height. At one end, beneath a gable wall with an aperture like a small window at the apex where a bell might have hung once, there is a stone altar; just three heavy slabs. On the altar there's a metal bell, green-black with age and chained to the wall behind. It looks rather like a very old Swiss cow-bell.

*

'Apparently some people nicked the old bell, back in the 'sixties,' William told us last night, in the drawing room of his parents' house, while we were playing cards and drinking whisky and talking about heading down the loch in the speedboat to the dark isle. 'Oxford students, or something; anyway, according to the locals the guys couldn't sleep at night because they kept hearing the sound of bells, and eventually they couldn't stand it and came back and replaced the bell in the chapel and they were all right again.'

'What a load of old nonsense,' Yvonne said. 'Two.'

'Two,' William said. 'Yes, probably.'

'Oh, I don't know,' Andy said, shaking his head. 'Sounds pretty spooky to me. One, please. Thanks.'

'Sounds like fucking tinnitus to me,' I said. 'Three. Ta.'

'Dealer takes two,' William said. He whistled. 'Oh, baby; *look* at these cards . . .'

*

I take the old bell up and let it ring once; a flat, hollow, appropriately funereal sound. I set it carefully back down on the stone altar and look round the walled oblong of hill, mountain, loch and cloud.

Silence: no birds, no wind in the trees, nobody talking. I turn slowly, right round, watching the clouds. I think this is the most peaceful place I have ever been.

I walk out, among the cold, carved little stones, to find Yvonne standing glaring at a tall gravestone. Euphemia McTeish, born 1803, died 1822, and her five children. Died in childbirth. Her husband died twenty years later.

Andy strolls up, drinking from his flask, grinning and shaking his head. He nods up to where William is standing on the wall of the chapel, looking down the loch with a pair of small binoculars. 'Wanted to build a house here,' Andy says. He shakes his head.

283

'*What*?' Yvonne says.

'Here?' I say. 'On a *graveyard*? Is he mad? Hasn't he *read* Stephen King?'

Yvonne looks coldly at her distant husband. 'He was talking about building a house up here, but I didn't know it was . . . *here*.' She looks away.

'Tried to persuade the local authority with a *really good deal* on a bunch of computers,' Andy says, chuckling. 'But they wouldn't play. For the moment he's had to settle for being allowed to get buried here.'

Yvonne draws herself up. 'Which might happen sooner than he's expecting,' she says, and marches off towards the chapel, where William is staring down into the building's interior and shaking his head.

*

Hard rain on a soft day; it falls from the leaden overcast, continual and drenching, creating a huge rustling in all the grass, bushes and trees around us.

William's body is laid to rest in the thick peaty soil of the dark isle. According to the pathologist's report, he was clubbed unconscious and then suffocated.

Yvonne, beautiful and pale in slim black, her face veiled, nods to the mourners and their few soft words, and murmurs something of her own. The rain drums on my umbrella. She glances at me, catching my gaze for the first time since I got here. I barely made it in time; I had a hospital appointment for this morning – yet more tests – and had to drive hard across country, towards Rannoch and the west. But I got here, got to the Sorrells' home, met William's father and brother, and saw Yvonne briefly but did not get a chance to talk to her before it was time for us all to set off for the circuitous drive round the mountains and down to the far end of the loch, and the hotel there, and the drive up the track to the slipway facing Eilean

Dubh and the two little boats that shuttled us across, the last one bringing the coffin.

The minister keeps the service short because of the rain, and then it's over and we're queuing at the slip while the little rowing boats ferry us four at a time back to the mainland, and Yvonne's standing on those old, smooth stones of the slanted pier, receiving the condolences of the other guests. I just stand there, watching her. We all look slightly ridiculous because as well as our formal black clothes all of us sport Wellington boots – some black, most green – to deal with the mud-slicked grass of the island. Somehow Yvonne looks dignified and attractive even in those. Though of course maybe that's just me.

It's been a funny few days; getting back to work, trying to pick up the threads there, having a long soul-to-soul with a very sympathetic Eddie, getting embarrassing slaps on the back and we-were-rooting-for-yous from colleagues and finding that Frank had run out of amusing Scottish place-name spell-checks for me. I've been staying with Al and his wife in Leith while the police stake out my flat, but there's been no sign of Andy.

Meanwhile I've been to the doc, and been sent for various tests at the Royal Infirmary. Nobody's mentioned the C-word yet but I feel suddenly vulnerable and mortal and even *old*. I've given up smoking. (Well, Al and I had a pipe or two of dope the other night, just for old time's sake, but there was no tobacco involved.)

Anyway, I'm still coughing a lot and I get a sick feeling now and again, but there's been no more blood since that afternoon we found William.

I shake Yvonne's hand as I wait for my return trip in the wee rowing boat. The fine black tracery of her veil, scattered with tiny black gathered specks, makes her look at once mysteriously distant and rawly seductive, rain or no rain, wellies or no wellies.

Through the trees on the mainland, I can see and hear the cars reversing and manoeuvring and bumping away back down the track to the village and the hotel. The tradition is that Yvonne, as the widow, is last onto the last boat; sort of like a captain and a sinking ship, I guess.

'You all right?' she asks me, eyes narrowed, her sharp, evaluating gaze flitting over my face.

'Surviving. And you?'

'The same,' she says. She looks cold again, and small. I want so much to take her in my arms and hug her. I feel tears prick behind my eyes. 'I'm selling the house,' she tells me, looking briefly down, long black lashes flickering. 'The company's opening a Euro office in Frankfurt; I'm going to be part of the team.'

'Ah.' I nod, not sure what to say.

'I'll drop you a line with my new address, once I'm settled.'

'Right; good, okay.' I nod. There's a splashing, swirling sound behind me, and a soft, hollow bumping noise. 'Well,' I say, 'any time you're in Edinburgh . . .'

She shakes her head and looks away, then smiles gallantly for me and tips her head, indicating. 'That's your boat, Cameron.'

I just stand there, nodding like an idiot, wanting to say the one right thing that must exist for me to change all of this, make it good, make it all better, make it eventually happen happily for us, but knowing that that thing just doesn't exist and there's no point looking for it, and so just stand there nodding dumbly with my lips trapped compressed between my teeth, looking down, not able to look her in the eyes and knowing that's it, the end, goodbye . . . until after those moments she puts me out of my misery and puts out her hand and gently says, 'Goodbye, Cameron.'

And I nod and shake her hand and after a while I get my mouth to work and it says, 'Goodbye.'

I hold her hand one last time, just for a moment.

*

The hotel at that end of the loch is full of dead stuffed fish in glass cages and mangy-looking taxidermised otters, wild cats and eagles.

I don't know many people and I think Yvonne's avoiding mc, so I have a single whisky and a few sandwiches, then I leave.

The rain is still torrential; I have my wipers on quick-time but even so they're hardly coping. The moisture coming off my brolly and coat lying puddling on the back seat is fighting a pretty equal battle with the heater and blower to mist up the glass on the inside.

I get about fifteen miles on the single-track road round the mountains when the engine starts to misfire. I glance at the instruments; half a tank of fuel, no warning lights.

'Oh, no,' I groan. 'Come on, baby, come on, don't let me down; come on, come on.' I tap the car's dashboard gently, encouragingly. 'Come on now, come on . . .'

I'm heading up a slight hill into a stretch of road through a Forestry Commission plantation when the engine does a passable impression of me in the morning, coughing and spluttering and not quite firing on all cylinders. Then it dies completely.

I coast quickly to a stop in a passing place. 'Oh, Christ . . . Shit!' I yell, slamming the dashboard, then feeling stupid.

The rain makes machine-gun noises on the roof.

I try starting the engine but there's just another bout of coughing from under the bonnet.

I release the bonnet-catch, put my coat back on, take up the sopping umbrella and get out.

The engine makes little metallic, creaking, tinking noises. Steam wisps up as raindrops hit the exhaust manifold. I test the plug leads and look for something obvious like a loose wire. It doesn't appear to be anything obvious. (I don't think I've heard of anybody in a situation like this *ever* finding it was something obvious.) I hear an engine and look round the side of the raised bonnet to see a car heading in the same direction as me. I don't know whether to try and wave them down or not. I settle for just looking pleadingly at the approaching car; it's one guy in a beaten-up Micra.

He flashes his lights and pulls in ahead of me.

'Hi,' I say as he opens the door and gets out, pulling on an anorak and shoving a deerstalker hat on. He's red-haired, bearded. 'It just stopped.' I tell him. 'I've got fuel but it just cut out. Could be the rain, I suppose . . .' My voice trails off as I suddenly think, Christ, it might be him. It might be Andy; this could be him, disguised, come for me.

What am I doing? Why didn't I get round to the boot and get out the fucking tyre-iron the instant the car stopped? Why aren't I carrying a baseball bat, a can of mace, anything? I stare at the guy, thinking, Is it him, is it? He's the right height, the right build. I stare at his cheek and his red beard, trying to see a join, trying to see glue.

'Aye,' he says, stuffing his hands in his anorak pockets and glancing down the road. 'Ye goat any WD40, pal?' He nods at the engine. 'Looks like yon bit there could do with some.'

I'm staring at him, my heart pounding. There's a weird roaring noise in my head and I can hardly hear him over it. His voice sounds different but he was always good at accents. My belly feels like a solid chunk of ice and my legs like they're about to buckle and give way. I'm still staring at the guy. Oh Christ, oh Christ, oh Christ. I'd run but my legs won't work and he was always faster than me anyway.

He frowns at me and I feel like I've got tunnel vision; all I can see is his face, his eyes, his eyes, just the right colour, just the right look . . . Then he changes somehow, seems to straighten and relax, and in a voice I recognise says, 'Ah. Very perceptive, Cameron.'

I don't see what he hits me with; just his arm swinging round at me, quick and blurring as a striking snake. The blow lands above my right ear and fells me, sends me folding down in a galaxy of flickering stars and a huge growling swell of noise as if I'm falling through the air towards a great waterfall. I twist as I fall and hit the engine, but it doesn't hurt, and I slide off it and down and fall towards the puddles and the road and I hit the road but I don't feel that either.

*

288

Oh God help me here on the island of the dead with the cries of the tormented, here with the angel of death and the acrid stench of excrement and carrion taking me back in the darkness and the pale fawn light to the place I never wanted to go back to, the man-made earthly black hell and the human scrapyard kilometres long. Here down amongst the dead men, midst-ways with the torn-souled and their wild, inhuman screams; here with the ferryman, the boatman, my eyes covered and my brains scrambled, here with this prince of death, this prophet of reprisal, this jealous, vengeful, unforgiving son of our bastard commonwealth of greed; help me help me help me . . .

*

My head hurts like buggery; my hearing feels . . . blurred. That's not the right word but it is. Eyes shut. They were shut with something earlier, shut *by* something, but not any more, at least I don't think so; I sense light beyond my eyelids. I'm lying on my side on something hard and cold and gritty. I'm cold, and my hands and feet are tied, or taped. I shiver uncontrollably, scraping my cheek across the chill, granular floor. Bad taste in mouth. The air smells sharp and I can hear . . .

I can hear the dead men, hear their flayed souls, wailing on the wind to no ear save mine and no understanding at all. The view behind my eyelids goes from pink to red then purple into black, and is suffused with a rumbling shift into a terrible, tearing roaring noise, shaking the ground, filling the air, pounding my bones, dark going dark, black stinking hell o mum o dad o no no please don't take me back there

*

And I'm there, in the one place I've hidden from myself; not that cold day by the hole in the ice or the other day in the sunlit woods

289

near the hole in the hill – days deniable because I was then not yet the me I have become – but just eighteen months ago; the time of my failure and my simple, shaming incapacity to reap and work the obvious power of what I was observing; the place that exposed my incompetence, my hopeless inability to witness.

Because I was there, I was part of it, just a year and a half ago, after months and months of badgering, cajoling and entreating Sir Andrew he finally let me go when the deadline was up and the trucks and tracks and tanks were about to roll I got my wish, I got to go, I was given the chance to do my stuff and show what I was made of, to be a genuine front-line journalist, a rootin-tootin-tokin-tipplin God-bijayzuz gonzo war correspondent, bringing the blessed Saint Hunter's manic subjectivity to the ultimate in scarifying human edge-work: modern warfare.

And forgetting the fact the drinks were few and far between and that the whole media-managed event was so unsportingly one-sided and mostly happened far away from any journos, *tendance* gonzoid or not, when it came to it – and it did come to it, I did have my chance, it was put right there in front of me practically screaming at me to *fucking write something* – I couldn't do it; couldn't hack it as a hack; I just stood there, awestruck, horrorstruck, absorbing the ghastly force of it with my inadequate and unprepared *private* humanity, not my public professional persona, not my skill, not the face I had laboured to prepare to face the sea of faces that is the world.

And so I was humbled, scaled, down-sized.

I stood on the sunless desert, beneath a sky black from horizon to horizon, a rolling, heavy sulphurous sky made solid and soiled, packed with the thick, stinking effluence squeezed erupting from the earth's invaded bowels, and in that darkness at noon, that planned, deliberated disaster, with the bale-fire light of the burning wells flickering in the distance with a dirty, guttering flame, I was reduced to a numb, dumb realisation of our unboundedly resourceful talent for bloody hatred and mad waste, but stripped of the means to describe and present that knowledge.

I crouched on the tar-black grainy stickiness of the plundered sands, within scorching distance of one of the wrecked wells, watching the way the fractured black metal stub in the centre of the crater gouted a compressed froth of oil and gas in quick, shuddering, instantly dispersing bursts and bubbles of brown-black spray into the furious, screaming tower of flame above; a filthy hundred-metre Cypress of fire, shaking the ground like a never-ending earthquake and bellowing madly in a strident jet-engine shriek, shuddering my bones and jarring my teeth and making my eyes tremble in their sockets.

My body shook, my ears rang, my eyes burned, my throat was raw with the acid-bitter stench of the evaporating crude, but it was as though the very ferocity of the experience unmanned me, unmade me and rendered me incapable of telling it.

Later, on the Basra road, by that vast linearity of carnage, a single strip of junk-yard destruction stretching – again – from horizon to horizon on the flat dun face of that dusty land, I wandered the scorched, perforated wreckage of the cars and vans and trucks and buses left after the A10s and the Cobras and the TOWs and the miniguns and the thirty-mill cannons and the cluster munitions had had their unrestrained way with their unarmoured prey, and saw the brown-burned metal, the few bubbled patches of sooty paint, the torn chassis and ripped-open cabs of those Hondas and Nissans and Leylands and Macks, their tyres slack and flattened or quite gone, burned to the steel cording inside; I surveyed the spattered shrapnel of that communal ruin rayed out across the sands, and I tried to imagine what it must have been like to be caught here, beaten, retreating, running desperately away in those thin-skinned civilian vehicles while the missiles and shells rained in like supersonic sleet and the belching fire burst billowing everywhere around. I tried, too, to imagine how many people had died here, how many shredded, cindered bodies and bits of bodies had been bagged and removed and buried by the clean-up squads before we were allowed to see this icon of that long day's slaughter.

291

I sat on a low dune for a while, maybe fifty metres away from the devastation on the strip of ripped, bubbled road, and tried to take it all in. The lap-top sat on my knee, screen reflecting the grey overcast, the cursor winking slowly at the top-left edge of the blank display.

I gave it half an hour and still couldn't think of anything that would describe how it looked and how I felt. I shook my head and stood up, twisting back to dust my pants.

The black, charred boot was a couple of metres away, half-buried in the sand. When I picked it up it was surprisingly heavy because it still had the foot inside it.

I wrinkled my nose at the stink and let it drop, but it still didn't help, didn't break the log-jam, didn't (ha) kick-start the process.

Nothing did.

I filed a minimum of uninspired war-is-hell-and-frankly-so-is-peace-if-you're-female-out-here stories from the hotel and smoked some mind-bendingly powerful dope I got from an affable Palestinian helper who – as soon the journos left – was picked up by the Kuwaiti authorities, tortured and deported to Lebanon.

When I got back Sir Andrew told me he wasn't at all impressed with the stuff I'd filed; they could have run AP stories for a lot less money and just as much impact. I didn't have an argument against this, and so had to sit there and take the old man's verbal battering for half an hour. And, even though at the time I knew it was wrong, unjustifiable and a feeble, contemptible piece of self-important self-pity, for a while, under that withering deluge of professional contempt, I felt like something trapped and pulverised amongst the dust and greasy ashes on the Basra road.

*

I'm hearing the cries of the dead men above the roar of the screeching, broken well-heads, and I smell the thick, cloying brown-black oil and the sweet gagging odour of corruption; then the cries turn to the calls of seagulls, and the smell to that of the sea, with an acrid overtone of bird-shit.

I'm still tied up. I open my eyes.

Andy is sitting across from me, his back against a rough concrete wall. The floor underneath us is concrete, as is the roof. There is a doorway to Andy's left; no door, just a pitted aperture to the sunlight outside. I can see more concrete buildings, all derelict, and a skinny concrete tower spattered with seagull droppings. Beyond there are chopping waves rolling white at their tops, and a glimpse of distant land. The wind sighs through the doorway over little stones and shards of glass; I can hear waves hitting rocks. I blink, looking at Andy.

He smiles.

My hands are tied behind my back; my ankles are taped together. I work back to the wall behind me and lever myself up until I'm sitting, too. I can see more of the water outside now, and more land; a faraway scatter of houses, a couple of buoys bobbing in the wind-patterned water, and a small coastal freighter heading away.

I work my mouth; it tastes foul. I blink, start to shake my head to try and clear some of the fuzziness, but then think the better of it. My head aches and throbs.

'How are you feeling?' Andy asks me.

'Fucking awful, what do you expect?'

'Could be worse.'

'Oh, I'm sure,' I say, and feel very cold. I close my eyes and put my head carefully back against the chilly concrete of the wall. My heart feels like it's beating air; too fast and faint to be propelling anything as thick as blood. Air, I think; Christ, he's injected me with air I'm going to die, heart thrashing on foam on froth on air, brain dying, starved of oxygen, sweet Jesus no . . . But a minute or so passes and, while I still don't feel too good, I don't die either. I open my eyes again.

Andy is still sitting there; he's wearing brown cord trousers, a combat jacket and hiking boots. There's a big camouflaged rucksack

293

against the wall a metre to his left and a half-full bottle of mineral water in front of him. By his right hand there's a cellphone; by his left, a gun. I don't know very much about handguns beyond the difference between a revolver and an automatic, but I think I recognise that grey pistol; I think it's the one he had that night a week or two after Clare died, when he was all set to take vengeance right then on Doctor Halziel. Maybe – I'm thinking now – I should have let him.

I'm still wearing what I was when he kidnapped me: black suit, dirty and stained now, and a white shirt. He's removed my tie. My Drizabone is lying, neatly folded but looking scruffy, a metre to my right.

He stretches out one leg, and his hiking boot touches the water bottle. He taps it. 'Water?' he says.

I nod. He gets up, takes the top off the bottle and holds it to my lips. I glug down a few mouthfuls, then nod, and he takes it away. He sits back where he was.

He takes a bullet out of his combat jacket and starts turning it over and over in his fingers. He takes a deep, sighing breath and says, 'So, Cameron.'

I try to get comfortable. My heart's still beating like hell and making my head pound, my bowels are threatening terrible things and I feel kitten-weak, but I'm fucked if I'm going to plead with him. Actually, I'm probably fucked no matter what I do, and – being realistic – when it comes to it I'll probably plead like a little kid, but for now I might as well tough it out.

'You tell me, Andy.' I keep my voice neutral. 'What happens now? What have you got in store for me?'

He grimaces and shakes his head, frowning down at the bullet in his hand. 'Oh, I'm not going to kill you, Cameron.'

I can't help it; I laugh. It's not much of a laugh; more of a gasp with pretensions, but it raises my spirits. 'Oh yeah?' I say. 'Like you were going to give back Halziel and Lingary unharmed.'

He shrugs. 'Cameron, that was just tactics,' he says reasonably.

'They were always going to die.' He smiles, shaking his head at my naivety.

I inspect him. He's clean-shaven and fit-looking. He looks younger than he did; a lot younger; younger than he was when Clare died.

'So if you're not going to kill me, Andy, what?' I ask him. 'Hmm? Give me AIDS? Chop off my fingers so I can't type?' I take a breath. 'I hope you've taken into account the advances in computer voice-recognition which are making keyboard-free word processing a realistic possibility in the near future.'

Andy grins, but there's something cold in it. 'I'm not going to hurt you, Cameron,' he says, 'and I'm not going to kill you, but I need something from you.'

I stare meaningfully at my taped-together ankles. 'Uh-huh. What?'

He looks down at the bullet again. 'I want you to listen to me,' he says quietly. It's as though he's embarrassed. He shrugs and looks me in the eye. 'That's all, really.'

'Okay,' I say. I flex my shoulders, grimacing. 'Could I listen with my hands untied?'

Andy purses his lips, then nods. He takes a long knife out of his boot. It looks like a thin bowie knife; the blade is very shiny. He squats while I turn round and the knife slices slickly through the tape. I tear the rest off, taking some hairs with it. My hands tingle. I look at my watch.

'Jesus, how hard did you hit me?'

It's half nine in the morning, the day after the funeral.

'Not that hard,' Andy tells me. 'I kept you under with ether for a while, then you just seemed to sleep.'

He sits back where he was, sliding the knife back into his boot. I put one hand out and lean to the side, looking out the doorway. I squint into the distance.

'Christ; that's the fucking Forth Bridge!' Somehow it's a relief that I can see the bridges and know home's only a few miles away.

'We're on Inchmickery,' Andy says. 'Off Cramond.' He looks around. 'Place was a gun battery during both wars; these are old Army buildings.' He smiles again. 'You get the occasional adventurous yachtsman trying to make a landing, but there are a couple of bolt-holes they can't find.' He pats the wall behind him. 'Makes a good base, now the hotel's gone. Mind you, it's under the flight path for the airport and I suspect the security boys'll want to give it the once-over before the Euro-summit, so I'm bailing out today, one way or the other.'

I nod, trying to think back. I don't like the sound of that 'one way or the other'. 'Do I remember you bringing me here in a boat?' I ask.

He laughs. 'Well, I don't have access to a helicopter.' He grins. 'Yes. An inflatable.'

'Hmm.'

He looks to each side, as if checking the gun and the phone are still there. 'So; sitting comfortably?' he asks me.

'Well, no, but don't let it put you off.'

He gives a small smile that disappears quickly. 'I'm going to give you a choice later, Cameron,' he says, sounding calm and serious. 'But first I want to tell you why I did all those things.'

'Uh-huh?' I want to say, It's perfectly fucking obvious why you did them, but I keep my mouth shut.

'It was Lingary, of course, first,' Andy says, looking younger still now, and staring down at his hand and the bullet. 'I mean, I'd met people I despised in the past, people I had no respect for and who I thought, Well, the world would be a better place without *them*. But I don't know, maybe I was being naive and expected that in a war, especially in a professional army, it would somehow be better; people would rise above themselves; stretch their own moral envelope, you know?'

I nod cautiously. I'm thinking, Moral envelope? Coast-speak.

'But of course it's not true,' Andy says, rubbing the little copper and brass shape of the bullet between his fingers. 'War is a magnifier, a multiplier. Decent people act more decently; bastards get to be even bigger bastards.' He waves one hand. 'I'm not talking about all that banality-of-evil stuff – organised genocide is different – I mean just ordinary warfare, where the rules are obeyed. And the truth is that some people do rise above themselves, but others sink beneath themselves. They don't gain, they don't shine the way some people do in combat and they don't even muddle through the way most people do, scared to death but doing their job because they've been well trained and because their mates are depending on them; they just have their faults and weaknesses exposed, and in certain circumstances, if that person is an officer and his flaws are of a particular type and he's risen to a certain level without ever encountering a real battlefield, those faults can lead to the deaths of a lot of men.'

'We all have moral responsibility, whether we like it or not, but people in power – in the military, in politics, in professions, whatever – have an imperative to care, or at least to exhibit an officially acceptable analogue of care; duty, I suppose. It was people I knew had abused that responsibility that I attacked; that's what I was taking as my . . . authority.'

He shrugs, frowns. 'The situation was a little different with Oliver, the porn merchant; that was partly to throw them off the scent and partly because I just despised what he was doing.

'And the judge, well, he wasn't quite so culpable as the others; I was comparatively lenient with him.

'The rest . . . they were all powerful men, all rich – several of them very rich indeed. All of them had all they could ask for in life, but they all wanted more – which is okay, I suppose, it's just a failing, you can't kill people for that alone – but they all treated people like shit, literally like shit; something unpleasant to be disposed of. It was like they'd forgotten their humanity and could never find it again, and there was only one way to remind them of it, and remind all the others like them, and make them feel frightened and vulnerable and *powerless*, the way they made other people feel all the time.'

He holds the bullet up in front of his face, peering at it. 'There wasn't one of those men who hadn't killed people; indirectly, the way the Nuremberg Nazis mostly did, but definitely, unarguably, beyond any reasonable doubt.

'And Halziel,' he says, taking a deep breath. 'Well, you know about him.'

'Jesus, Andy,' I say. I know I should shut up and let him talk on as much as he likes but I can't help it. 'The guy was a selfish bastard and a lousy doctor; but he was incompetent, not malicious. He didn't hate Clare or anything or wish her – '

'But that's just it,' Andy says, holding his hands out. 'If a certain level of skill – of competence – translates into the gift of life or death it *becomes* malice when you don't bother to exercise that skill, because people are relying on you to do just that. But,' he holds up one hand to me, forestalling, and nods, 'I'll admit to a level of personal vengeance there. Once I'd done all the others and I reckoned I didn't have much longer to operate overground, as it were, well, it just seemed the right thing to do.'

He looks up at me, a strange, wide-eyed open smile on his face. 'I'm shocking you, aren't I, Cameron?'

I gaze into his eyes for a while, then look away out the doorway towards the water and the small white shapes of the circling, crying birds. 'No,' I tell him. 'Not as much as when I realised it was you who'd spiked Bissett like that and it was you behind that gorilla mask and you who burned Howie – '

'Howie didn't suffer,' Andy says matter-of-factly. 'I stoved his head in with a log first.' He grins. 'Probably saved him from a terrible hangover.'

I stare at him, feeling sick and close to tears at the off-handed way the man I've always thought of as my best friend is talking about murder, and also feeling pretty vulnerable and at risk myself right now, too, no matter what he's said and even though he has untied my hands.

Andy reads my expression. 'He was a cunt, Cameron.' He pauses, looks at the ceiling. 'No that's not fair, and that's what he usually called women, as well; so let's say he was a prick, a dickhead; and a violent prick, a vindictive bullying dickhead, at that. Over the years he broke his wife's jaw, both her arms and her collarbone; he fractured her skull and he kicked her when she was pregnant. He was just an unmitigated pig-fuck of a man. He was probably battered as a kid himself – he never talked about it – but fuck him. That's what we're human for, so we can choose to alter our behaviour; he wouldn't do it himself, so I did it for him.'

'Andy,' I say. 'For Christ's sake; there are laws, there are courts; I know they're not perfect, but – '

'Oh, *laws*,' Andy says, voice saturated with scorn. 'Laws based on what? With what authority?'

'Well, how about democracy, for example?'

'Democracy? A two-way choice between tough shit and not-quite-so-tough shit every four or five years if you're lucky?'

'That's not what democracy is! It's not just that; it's a free press – '

'And we have that, don't we?' Andy laughs. 'Except the bits that are free aren't read very much and the bits that are most read aren't free. Let me quote you: "They're not newspapers, they're comics for the semi-literate; propaganda sheets controlled by foreign billionaires who just want to make as much money as technically possible and maintain a political environment conducive to that single aim."'

'All right, I stand by that, but it's still better than nothing.'

'Oh, I know it is, Cameron,' he says, sitting back and looking slightly shocked at being so misunderstood. 'I know it is; and I know that what powerful people *can* get away with, they *will* get away with, and if the people they exploit let them, well, in a sense that serves them right. But don't you see?' He jabs himself in the chest. 'That includes me!' He laughs. 'I'm part of it, too; I'm a product of the system. I'm just another human being, a bit better off than most, a bit smarter than most, maybe a bit luckier than most, but just another part of the equation, another variable that society's thrown up. So I come along and I do what I can get away with, because it seems fit to me to do it, because I'm like a businessman, you see? I'm *still* a businessman; I'm addressing a need. I've seen a niche in the market unfilled and I'm filling it.'

'Wait, wait; hold on,' I say. 'I'm not buying this crap about fulfilling a need anyway, but the point about the difference between your authority and everybody else's is that you're just *you*; you've made up all this . . . this rationale by yourself. The rest of us have had to come to some sort of agreement, a consensus; we're all trying to get along because that's the only way for people to exist together at all.'

Andy smiles slowly. 'Numbers make the difference, do they, Cameron? So when the two greatest nations on Earth – over half a billion people – were so scared of each other they were quite seriously prepared to blow up the world, they were *right*?' He shakes his head. 'Cameron, I'd be prepared to bet that more people believe Elvis is still alive than subscribe to whatever flavour of secular humanism you currently think represents the One True Way for humanity. And besides, where has this consensus of yours brought us?'

He frowns and looks genuinely mystified.

'Come on, Cameron,' he chides. 'You know the evidence: the world already produces . . . *we* already produce enough food to feed every starving child on earth, but still a third of them go to bed hungry. And it *is* our fault; that starvation's caused by debtor countries having to abandon their indigenous foods to grow cash crops to keep the World Bank or the IMF or Barclays happy, or to service debts run up by murdering thugs who slaughtered their way into power and slaughtered their way through it, usually with the connivance and help of one part of the developed world or another.

'We *could* have something perfectly decent right now – not Utopia, but a fairly equitable world state where there was no malnutrition and no terminal diarrhoea and nobody died of silly wee diseases like measles – if we all really wanted it, if we weren't so greedy, so racist, so bigoted, so basically self-centred. Fucking hell, even that

300

self-centredness is farcically *stupid*; we know smoking kills people but we still let the drug barons of BAT and Philip Morris and Imperial Tobacco kill their millions and make their billions; smart, educated people like us know smoking kills but we still smoke *ourselves*!'

'I've given up,' I tell him defensively, though it's true I'm dying for a cigarette.

'Cameron,' he says, laughing with a kind of desperation. 'Don't you see? I'm agreeing with you; I listened to all your arguments over the years, and you're right: the twentieth century *is* our greatest work of art and we *are* what we've done . . . and *look at it*.' He puts a hand through his hair, and sucks breath through his teeth. 'The point is, there is no feasible excuse for what we are, for what we have made of ourselves. We have chosen to put profits before people, money before morality, dividends before decency, fanaticism before fairness, and our own trivial comforts before the unspeakable agonies of others.'

He stares pointedly at me and his brows flex. I nod, reluctantly recognising something I wrote once.

'So,' he says, 'in that climate of culpability, that perversion of moral values, nothing, *nothing* I have done has been out of place or out of order or wrong.'

I open my mouth to speak but he waves his hand, and with a faint sneer says, 'I mean, what am I supposed to do, Cameron? Wait for the workers' revolution to make everything right? That's like Judgement Day; it never fucking comes. And I want justice *now*; I don't want these bastards dying a natural death.' He takes a deep breath and looks at me quizzically. 'So, how am I doing so far, Cameron? Do you think I'm mad, or what?'

I shake my head. 'No, I don't think you're mad, Andy,' I tell him. 'You're just wrong.'

He nods slowly at this, looking at the bullet he's turning over and over in his fingers.

'You're right about one thing,' I tell him. 'You are one of them. Maybe this spotting-a-niche-in-the-market stuff isn't so fatuous after all. But is a sick response to a sick system really the best we can do? You think you're fighting it but you're just joining in. They've poisoned you, man. They've taken the hope out of your soul and put some of their own greedy hate in its place.'

'"Soul", did you say, Cameron?' He smiles at me. 'You getting religion?'

'No, I just mean the core of you, the essence of who you are; they've infected it with despair, and I'm sorry you can't see any better response than to kill people.'

'Not even when they deserve it?'

'No; I still don't believe in capital punishment, Andy.'

'Well, *they* do,' he sighs. 'And I suppose I do.'

'And what about hope, do you believe in that?'

He looks disparaging. 'What are you, Bill Clinton?' He shakes his head. 'Oh, I know there's goodness in the world, too, Cameron, and compassion and a few fair laws; but they exist against a background of global barbarism, they float on an ocean of bloody horror that can tear apart any petty social construction of ours in an instant. *That's* the bottom line, that's the real framework we all operate within, even though most of us can't or won't recognise it, and so perpetuate it.

'We're all guilty, Cameron; some more than others, some a *lot* more than others, but don't tell me we aren't all guilty.'

I resist the urge to say, Who's sounding religious now?

Instead I ask, 'And what was William guilty of?'

Andy frowns and looks away. 'Being everything he claimed to be,' he says, sounding bitter for the first time. 'William wasn't a personal score, like Halziel or Lingary: he was one of *them*, Cameron; he meant everything he ever said. I knew him better than you did, when it mattered, and he was quite serious about his ambitions. Buying a knighthood, for example; he'd been giving money to the Conservative party for the past ten years – he gave money to Labour, too, last year and this because he thought they were going to win the election – but he'd been putting respectable amounts into Tory coffers for a decade, as well as keeping an eye on how much the average successful businessman has to donate to ensure a knighthood. He once asked me which charity he'd be best advised to join, to provide the usual excuse; wanted one that didn't encourage scroungers.

'This was all long-term, but that was the way William thought. He was *still* determined to build a house on Eilean Dubh, and he even had a complicated scheme involving a front company and a threatened underground toxic-chemicals store in the area which, if it had worked, would have had grateful locals practically begging him to take the island. And a few times when he was drunk he talked about trading in Yvonne for a more up-market, user-friendly model, preferably one with her own title and a daddy in serious big business or the government. His non-ethical investment programme wasn't a joke, either; he pursued it, vigorously.'

Andy shrugs. 'It was just a coincidence that I knew him, but I don't think there was any doubt William was going to turn into a man like the others I killed.'

He rolls the bullet around in his palm, eyes lowered. 'However, for what it's worth, if killing him screwed up things between you and Yvonne, I'm sorry.'

'Oh,' I say, 'that makes it all right, then.' It's meant to sound sarcastic, but it just sounds dumb.

He nods, not looking at me. 'He was a very charming but actually quite an evil man, Cameron.'

I stare at him for a while; he rubs the bullet between his fingers. Finally I say, 'Yes, but you're not God, Andy.'

'No, I'm not,' he agrees. 'Nobody is.' He grins. 'So what?'

I close my eyes, unable to bear the relaxed, merely mischievous expression on his face. I open them again and look out through the empty doorway, at the water and the land and the ceaseless, wheeling birds. 'Yeah. I see. Well,' I say, 'I don't think there's any point in trying to argue with you, is there, Andy?'

'No, you're probably right,' Andy says, suddenly all cheery decisiveness. He slaps both knees and jumps up. He lifts the gun and sticks it down the back of his cords. He hoists the rucksack up and puts it over one shoulder. He nods down at the cellphone lying on the concrete floor.

'Here's your choice,' he tells me. 'Phone and turn me in, or not.'

He waits for a reaction from me, so I raise my eyebrows.

He shrugs. 'I'm heading down to the boat now; put the kit bag aboard.' He grins down at me. 'Take your time. I'll be back in ten, fifteen minutes.'

I stare at the phone on the littered floor.

'It's working,' he reassures me. 'Your choice.' He laughs. 'I'll be all right, whatever. Leave me be, and . . . I don't know; I might retire now, while I'm ahead. But on the other hand there are still a lot of bastards out there. Mrs T, for one, if that piques your interest, Cameron.' He smiles. 'Or there's always America; land of opportunities. On the other hand, if I end up in jail . . . Well, there are people in there I'd really like to meet, too; the Yorkshire Ripper, for example, if it's possible to get to him. I'd need just a small blade, and about five minutes.' He shrugs again. 'Whatever. See you in a bit.'

He skips out into the sunlight and the swirling wind, taking the steps two at a time down to a walkway between two concrete blockhouses. I lean back as he disappears, whistling.

I squat on my taped-together feet and lift the cellphone. It looks charged and connected. I dial the number of my mum and dad's old house in Strathspeld village; I get an answer-machine; a man's voice, gruff and curt.

I switch the phone off.

It takes a minute to get the tape off my ankles. I lift my Drizabone from the floor and dust it down, then put it on.

The coat-tails flap round my legs as I stand in the doorway, Fife to my right, the trees of Dalmeny Park and Mons Hill to my left and the two bridges ahead upstream; one tensed, webbed-red and the other straight-curved, battleship grey.

The firth is ruffled blue-grey, the waves marching away, wind blowing from behind, out of the east. Two minesweepers are heading upstream under the bridge towards Rosyth; a huge tanker sits tall and unladen at the Hound Point oil terminal, attended by a pair of tugs; two huge crane-barges float nearby, where they've been most of this year, installing a second terminal pier. A small tanker is almost level with the island, heading out to sea, low in the water with some product from the Grangemouth refinery. North, beyond Inchcolm, a red-hulled LPG tanker sits at Braefoot Bay, loading from the pipelines connected to the Mossmorran plant a few kilometres inland, position marked by white plumes of steam. I watch all this maritime activity, surprised at how industrial, how continuingly mercantile the old river is.

Above and around, the seagulls bank and ride, hanging in the air, bills open, crying to the wind. The concrete blockhouses, towers, barracks and gun emplacements on the small island are all covered in seagull-shit; white and black, yellow and green.

I rub the back of my head, wincing as I touch the bump. I look at the phone in my hand, breathe in the sharp, sea air, and cough.

The cough goes on for a while, then it goes away.

So, what to do? One more betrayal, even if it is one that Andy seems half to want? Or become, in effect, his accomplice and leave him free to murder and maim God knows who else, a free radical in our systemic corruption?

What *is* to be done?

Shake head, Colley; look round this concrete dereliction and survey this breezily industrious river, and try to find an inspiration, a hint, a sign. Or just something to take your mind off a decision you're sure to regret, one way or another.

I punch the number into the phone.

Various tones and beeps sound in my ear as I watch the clouds all moving away overhead. Then the connection's made.

'Yes, hello,' I say. 'Doctor Girson please. Cameron Colley.' I look around, trying to see Andy, but there's no sign of him. 'Yes. Cameron. That's right. I was just wondering if you have the results through yet . . . So you have . . . Well, if you could just give me them

305

now, that'd be . . . Well, over the phone, why not? . . . Well, I do. I think it is. Well, it's my body, isn't it, doctor? . . . I want to know now . . . Look, let me ask you a direct question, doctor: have I got lung cancer? Doctor . . . Doctor . . . No, Doctor . . . Look, I'd really like a straight answer, if you don't mind. No, I don't think . . . Please, doctor; have I got cancer? No, I'm not trying to . . . No, I'm just . . . I'm just . . . Look; have I got cancer? . . . Have I got cancer? Have I got cancer? Have I got cancer?'

The doctor loses his temper eventually and does the smart thing and hangs up.

'See you tomorrow, Doc,' I sigh.

I switch the phone off and sit down on the step, looking out to the water and the two long bridges under a blue and cloud-strewn sky. A seal pops its head out of the water about fifty metres out into the waves. It bobs there for a while, looking at the island and maybe at me, then it disappears back into the rolling grey water.

I look at the key pad of the cellphone and put my finger on the 9 button.

For all I know Andy is going to come back, cheerfully say, 'Hi,' and then blow my brains out, just on general principles.

I don't know.

My finger hovers over the button, then retreats.

No, I don't know.

I sit there for a while, in the wind and the sunlight, coughing now and again and looking out and holding the phone tightly in both hands.

C H A P T E R

SLEEP WHEN I'M DEAD

At the heart of the grand grey elegance of this festive city there is a literal darkness, an old void of disease, despair and death. Beneath the eighteenth-century high-rise of the City Chambers, slotted into the steep hillside between the banked S of Cockburn Street and the cobbled width of High Street opposite the Cathedral of St Giles, there is a section of the old city which was walled up four hundred years ago.

Mary King's Close was abandoned and covered over in the sixteenth century, left just as it was, untouched, because so many people had died of the plague in that part of the old town's swarming tenement-warrens. The bodies consigned to the shared grave that their homes had become were simply left to rot, and the bones only removed much later.

So, in the glacier-scoured debris east of the castle-crag's volcanic plug, deep underneath the civic core of this dormant capital, that old, cold utter darkness sits to this day.

And you have been there.

You went there five years ago with Andy and the girls you were going out with at the time. Andy knew people in the council and arranged a visit while he was in the city for the opening of The Gadget Shop's Edinburgh branch; just for a laugh, he said.

The place was smaller than you expected and dark and it smelled of damp and the black roof and black walls ran with glistening water. The girl you were with couldn't handle it and just had to go back up the steps to the corridor above where the old caretaker who'd shown you in had gone, and when the lights went out suddenly a few minutes later there was a darkness more complete and final than anything you had ever known before.

The girl with Andy gave a small scream, but Andy just chuckled and produced a torch. He'd set it all up with the caretaker: a joke.

But in those moments of blackness you stood there, as though you yourself were made of stone like the stunted, buried buildings around you, and for all your educated cynicism, for all your late-twentieth-century materialist Western maleness and your fierce despisal of all things superstitious, you felt a touch of true and absolute terror, a consummately feral dread of the dark; a fear rooted back somewhere before your species had truly become human and came to know itself, and in that primaeval mirror of the soul, that shaft of self-conscious understanding which sounded both the depths of your collective history and your own individual being, you glimpsed – during that extended, petrified moment – something that was you and was not you, was a threat and not a threat, an enemy and not an enemy, but possessed of a final, expediently functional indifference more horrifying than evil.

*

And so you sit on Salisbury Crags, remembering that still-present darkness and looking out over the city, feeling sorry for yourself and cursing your own stupidity and the institutionalised thoughtlessness, the sanctioned legal, lethal greed of the companies, the governments, the shareholders; all of them.

A tennis ball.

They say it's about the size of a tennis ball. You slide your hand inside your coat and jacket and press up under the floating rib on your left side. Pain. You're not sure whether you can feel it, the thing, the growth itself or not; you cough a bit as you press, and the pain gets worse. You stop pressing and the pain eases.

An operation, injections; chemotherapy. Sickness and premature baldness, probably temporary.

You hunch up, rocking back and forward and looking out across the spires and roofs and turrets and chimneys and trees of the city and the parks and lands beyond, towards the two bridges. Looking right, you can see Cramond Isle, Inchcolm, Inchmickery and Inchkeith. Inchmickery looks small and building-cluttered, two towers prominent.

*

Andy came back up the steps after quarter of an hour, whistling. He asked you what you'd done; you told him you'd rung your doctor. He smiled, told you to keep the phone and asked you to give him an hour's start. Then he put his hand out to you.

You shook your head, not his hand, and looked down. He grinned and shrugged and seemed to understand. He said, 'Goodbye,' and that was it; he skipped down the steps and away.

Five minutes later, from a circular concrete gun emplacement on the island's east side, surrounded by shit-stains and mobbed by raucous, screeching gulls, you watched the little black inflatable go scudding across the waves, heading for Granton. The city and the hills to the south rose sharp and bright beyond.

You gave him the hour. Twenty minutes after you dialled 999, a couple of police launches came slapping and bouncing across the waves towards the island; more cops arrived later, after one of the

311

boats put back to port to collect them.

They discovered the remainder of Doctor Halziel in one of the ammunition magazines sunk deep into the rock of the island.

You had one last interview with McDunn, telling and retelling everything that happened both on Inchmickery and the day before, on the road back from the funeral – the cops checked your car; Andy had put a little semi-permeable plastic bag full of sugar into your fuel tank while you were all out at the funeral isle.

You told McDunn Andy hid the cellphone in the buildings on the island and it took you an hour to find it. You don't know if he believed you or not. You told him that Andy let you call your doctor – with a gun to your head – to prove the phone was working before he hid it. McDunn nodded wisely, as though it was all fitting into place.

The cops are remaining in your flat for another few days, still vainly hoping Andy will appear there. Meanwhile, Al and his wife seem happy to let you stay with them in Leith.

You tried to rescue *Despot* a couple of times, but not very hard, and not with any noticeable result. You tried the trick Andy showed you in *Xerium* and it worked. But you can't be bothered with games just now. This morning a redirected letter arrived from the finance company saying they're going to repossess the lap-top unless you make your payments. You think you'll let them take it.

At the paper they know you're not well, and everybody's been very sympathetic and supportive. They aren't asking too much of you, but Sir Andrew rang Eddie from Antigua and suggested you might like to do a series of articles on your experiences: the definitive word on the whole story. Other papers are interested too; there's no shortage of offers, ways to make money out of the deal.

*

You can see rain in the air, sweeping abundantly over the city towards you on the turned, westerly wind, obscuring the view of the bridges now and dragging huge curved veils slowly over the islands in the firth. Could be sleet, not rain.

You went down to the Cowgate last night and scored a little coke to cheer yourself up for a while.

You make sure there's nobody else around, then turn and hunch over, back to the wind. You gather your coat around you, take the little tin box out of your jacket pocket and open it. The stuff inside's been razored already, and you lift some out with your car key and sniff it, two tiny white heaps for each nostril, then three and then four when your throat doesn't go quite as numb as it should. That's better.

You put the tin away, sniffing. You tap the other packet in your jacket, then shrug, take it out and open it. You bought these last night, too. What the fuck. Screw the world, bugger reality. Saint Hunter would understand; Uncle Warren wrote a song about it.

You light a cigarette, shake your head as you look out over the grey-enthroned city, and laugh.